Forbidden Relics

A Matthew Paine Mystery

Forbidden Relics

A Matthew Paine Mystery

Lee Clark

Cypress
River
Media
LLC

Burlington, NC

Cypress River Media, LLC
Burlington, NC 27215
CypressRiverMedia.com

First Edition: April 2024

The publisher is not responsible for websites (or their content) that are not owned by the publisher.

Clark, Lee.
    Forbidden Relics / Lee Clark.—First edition.
        Pages ; cm.—(A Matthew Paine mystery)
    ISBN 979-8-9864074-9-4 (hardcover)—ISBN 979-8-9864074-8-7 (paperback)—ISBN 979-8-9864074-7-0 (e-book) 1. Paine, Matthew (Fictitious character)

Matthew Paine Classic Mystery Series (in order)

Pre Kill (prequel short story)

Dead Spots

Prefer Death

MIA

Christmas Punch

Iced

Forbidden Relics

Killer Convergence (coming soon)

Dedication

It is so often the case that our heroes are those who do the things that we ourselves cannot do. I admit that this is the case for me. I admire Matthew Paine for the patients he treats and the people he's able to help with his medical abilities. In real life, I admire my dear friend—who has stood by me through the good, the bad, the ugly, and the lovely—since we were four years old. She's been a nurse for more years than either of us care to admit. (OK, I'm the one who doesn't want to admit how long that's been; she, quite practically, says it's only a number.) She's not just been a nurse through the COVID pandemic, but she's been an emergency department nurse through it all!

Tera McWhorter, and all healthcare workers on the front line, day in and day out, have my undying admiration and appreciation!

Forbidden Relics, therefore, is dedicated to Tera Rea McWhorter, my life-longest dear friend, and all of the other healthcare workers who put us back together and keep us going through it all!

CONTENTS

1 ~ CONFIDENTIAL PROPOSITION

"Thanks for agreeing to meet with me," said Mark Kushner, concern showing clearly in his eyes as he took in both Matthew and Danbury with a sweeping glance. "I have a serious situation that I hope you can help with."

"Sure," said Matthew, wondering what Pastor Mark could possibly want to talk to both him and homicide detective Warren Danbury about. What could be so urgent that he'd call them to his office on a Monday evening to discuss?

"Here's the deal," said Mark. "You know that we, as a church, support missionaries all over the world."

Young family physician Matthew Paine had been attending the church in north Raleigh, North Carolina with his family most weekends his entire life. Over the years, he'd heard and met many of the missionaries the church supported. He nodded.

"If you were here two weeks ago, you heard the Ukrainian missionary team speak."

"I was, and I did," Matthew responded as he ran his fingers through his soft, wavy brown hair, one eyebrow raised as his big brown eyes stared curiously.

"We help them bring teams to the US to give updates on their ministry and to raise awareness. They speak at the churches that are supporting them and visit prospective ones while they're here. Usually, they're here for a couple of weeks each year. This year, a team of four was visiting: Grygoriy Starkovich—who we call Greg—and his wife

Darya brought two young pastors they're training with them. Rostyslav Pavelko—who we call Ross—and Ivan Domitrovich."

"OK," said Matthew, confused as to how this could be in any way relevant to him or to Danbury—who Pastor Mark had specifically asked to talk to. Casting a sidelong glance at the big Nordic-looking detective, Matthew saw that his expression, as usual, was unreadable.

Was his pastor about to ask him to travel with a mission group to Ukraine, Matthew wondered. His foot began tapping and his knee jumping in concentration as he pondered that thought. If that was it, why the urgency? Why now? Why him? And how could Danbury— who didn't attend this church and hadn't attended any others in many years—possibly be involved?

Before he could voice any of those questions, Mark Kushner—who had been the senior pastor of the church Matthew's entire life— continued. "The mission team you met here was due to travel back to Ukraine yesterday."

"Did they?" asked Matthew.

"No," said Mark, shaking his graying head in concern. There was one spot above the left side of his face that was graying faster than the rest of his hair, and it looked a bit like a skunk stripe, though Matthew would never have said so.

Instead, Matthew asked, "Where are they now?"

"I wish I knew. That's what I hope you can help me find out. Discreetly. If you're willing," added Mark, looking between Matthew and Danbury—who were seated across a large, highly polished mahogany desk from him. "We don't know where they are. Nobody has heard from them since Friday morning. And that's very concerning."

Danbury—who had been intently listening but characteristically quiet until he had something meaningful to say—spoke up in his usual staccato but direct manner, "Would they have defected? Or sought asylum here for some reason?"

"No. That's not possible," said Mark definitively and without hesitation.

"How can you be certain?" Danbury persisted, albeit far more softly and gently than his usual brusque manner.

"I've known Greg for many years, and I've worked alongside him both here and in Ukraine. He's passionate about his ministry and mission there. He's had obstacles to overcome in his country, but he works tirelessly. As does Darya. I haven't known her as long as Greg—since they got married about ten years ago—but he's known her his entire life. Their work in ministry is how they got together. So, I am certain that they would have returned home to continue their work if they were able to."

Mark swallowed before he added, "I'm very concerned." His brows knit above bright blue eyes that were tearing up as he spoke. "For their well-being. I have no idea what could have happened to them, but it can't be good, or they'd be back home by now. Or we'd at least have heard from them. They'd have contacted us for help if..." He swallowed, harder this time. "If they were able to."

"Where were they last? Can you trace them backward?" asked Matthew earnestly, wanting to be helpful.

"They spoke here at our church first," said Mark, clearing his throat. "Two weeks ago, yesterday."

Matthew nodded, remembering having enjoyed their presentation that Sunday morning. Greg exhibited the perfect balance of compassion, enthusiasm, and humor to keep audiences spellbound as he described their work in Ukraine. Darya and the two young pastors, Ivan and Ross, had filled in with specific parts of the presentation, but Greg carried it.

"The four of them flew in the Friday before and had a couple of days with us to rest and recover from jet lag. After that, they had a full itinerary," said Mark, handing a copy of it to each of them. The printed pages contained a long list of churches, complete with addresses, primary contact information, and phone numbers for all but the last one. The last entry had been handwritten on the bottom of the third sheet.

"They left here early Monday morning for a church in the tidewater area of Virginia and spoke at a luncheon there. Then they wound northwest through Virginia into West Virginia, then into Ohio and Illinois before heading south again to Kentucky and Tennessee,

Georgia, and into north Florida. As you see, they stopped at numerous churches along the way."

"All of that in two weeks?" asked Matthew incredulously, realizing that his eyes had glazed over halfway through the recitation of locations as he scanned the list. "They weren't coming back here?"

"They were until they added that last church. They were supposed to return here for one last night before they flew home to Ukraine. Greg called me Wednesday morning to tell me about their change in plans—that they were flying home from Fort Lauderdale, Florida, instead. He left a box here for safe keeping, and he asked if I would ship it back to Ukraine for him. I jotted the information he gave me for the church they added at the end of their itinerary."

"Did you? Ship the box back?" asked Danbury.

"Not yet. Of course, I agreed to ship it for him. Sea mail is less expensive, but it sounded urgent. He seemed upset about leaving the box behind, so I was trying to get a feel for when he needed the package back in Ukraine."

"Why do you think he was upset about leaving it?" asked Matthew.

"I think he and his wife Darya might have been disagreeing about it when they brought it to me. They were speaking Ukrainian outside of my office, so I couldn't understand what they were saying. Their voices weren't raised, but I got the impression that they weren't in agreement about something. Maybe it was unrelated to the box, I don't know. Darya looked very concerned as Greg handed it over to me. With the aggressive itinerary they had planned, I assumed they were discussing the trip. It was a tight schedule, as you saw."

"What did he tell you about the box when he gave it to you?" Matthew prodded.

"He asked me to lock it up somewhere safely until they returned for it. It sounded like he didn't want it out in my office, that he didn't want it to be in my way. Perhaps that wasn't what he was concerned about. When he and Darya went with me to put it in a storage closet, Greg checked the door handle on the storage room. I didn't think much of it then, but now I think he was probably making sure it locked securely."

"You didn't ask more about it?"

"It didn't occur to me to ask at the time. Thinking back on it now, though, he did seem tense. But like he was trying not to be."

"And now you can't reach him?" asked Matthew.

"Not after last Friday. I texted Friday morning and told him I had a question for him when he had a moment to talk. He responded that their cell service was spotty and he'd call me later. When I didn't hear from him, I called him Friday evening. I got his voicemail, and I left a message. He's usually responsive, even in Ukraine. When I still hadn't heard from him by Saturday, I tried again. This time, I got nothing. Just a message that the voice mailbox was full. I kept trying all day Saturday."

"Are you sure it was Greg? Friday morning. It was a texted response?" asked Danbury.

"Yes, he replied to my text with a text. The response came from Greg's number."

"We could have traced a call," said Danbury. "To see where he was. From cell towers. You didn't talk to him? After Wednesday?"

"Right," said Mark. "I have numbers for Darya, Ross, and Ivan too. I tried calling all of them individually yesterday. When I didn't get a response from any of them, I called the last church that's printed there on the list in north Florida—Aurora Springs Chapel. Greg and his team were supposed to have been there Friday around lunch time to speak at a dinner Friday evening."

"But they weren't?" asked Matthew.

"No. The pastor there said they never arrived. He said he couldn't reach them when he called Friday to see if they were still coming. I've contacted all the pastors on this itinerary today. Greg and his team were at all the churches on their schedule before Friday. They left the Christ Walk Church in Macon, Georgia Thursday evening. They weren't staying with church members overnight on that one part of the trip, and nobody can account for them after that. None of the pastors noticed anything unusual or heard Greg mention anything about changing plans. None of them have any idea where they could be. I specifically asked those questions."

"They were due in north Florida at Aurora Springs Chapel on

Friday and then St. Athanasius Orthodox Church on Sunday," summarized Matthew, staring at the last entry that was handwritten on the bottom of the page.

"Right. They were supposed to be driving down to that last church—a Greek Orthodox church north of Miami—sometime on Saturday," said Mark.

"St. Athanasius Orthodox Church. In Miami," Matthew repeated—deep in thought—one eyebrow raised and foot tapping. Cringing slightly, he remembered the heat and humidity on a trip to Miami the summer before.

"That's the one that was added late. They were to present to the church leadership there in Sunny Isles Sunday afternoon. Then fly out of the Fort Lauderdale airport Sunday— yesterday—evening. The pastor from the church in Sunny Isles says they never arrived and he hasn't heard from them. They didn't make their flight home, and they haven't contacted anyone I've spoken to—not since responding to my text message on Friday."

"Have you contacted the police?" asked Matthew. "They've been missing for three days, at least."

"One of our pastors did, yes. Evelyn Rawlins contacted both Georgia and Florida state police this afternoon while I was calling the pastors. She gave them the names and descriptions of all four of them and information about the rental car they were driving." Taking a deep breath, Mark added, "I know what I'm asking is huge. We need to find this team of missionaries and get them home safely, if that's possible."

Mark swallowed hard before adding, "Or at least find out what happened to them—if that's not possible." He frowned, and worry lines between his eyebrows creased deeply as he spoke.

"I'm not sure I can be of much help," said Matthew.

"You two found the missing young woman down in Miami last June, didn't you?"

"We did, yes," admitted Matthew, glancing over at Danbury.

"You already know your way around down there. I don't want to put you in danger, Matthew. If you agree to go search for them and it starts to feel dangerous at all, get on the next plane home. Your safety comes first. The church will buy the plane tickets and pay for your accommodations and expenses, of course. The elders discussed the proposition this morning. We unanimously agreed that it is a top priority to find Greg and his team. We sponsored them coming, and we are responsible for getting them home safely."

"You know I have a day job and this isn't it?" Matthew asked jovially.

"I know it's a big ask. And I wouldn't if I felt like I had a choice. You know we support lots of missionaries here, but I've connected more closely with Greg than others. He is like a son in so many ways."

Traveling to Miami wasn't Matthew's favorite thing to do the first time, and he wasn't excited at the prospect of doing it again. But then it would be a nicer place to be the end of January than it had been in late June. The heat and humidity wouldn't be as oppressive. And there were missing missionaries involved, one of whom was like family to his pastor.

"You know I'm not a detective, right?" he asked, still hedging even after Mark's impassioned plea.

"I do, but that's also why you might be better able to find them. You can likely go places and do things that law enforcement can't. Or so I've heard," Mark answered.

Fleetingly, Matthew wondered where his pastor had gotten that information. Then he remembered that his mother was a church elder and would have been involved in the morning discussion. He didn't have time to ponder how she would have felt about this trip but he knew she'd be praying about it—and specifically for him.

"I've done what I could from here. One of our church members is a US Senator, as I'm sure you know," Mark said to Matthew. "At my request, he asked the US agencies to help find the Ukrainian team this morning. He's getting stonewalled. You might have heard about it, but tensions are high between Ukraine and Russia right now."

Tensions had been high for several years, thought Matthew. That wasn't new. The thing that was new to him now in late January of 2020, was a growing concern about travel. As a physician, he'd been monitoring updates from the World Health Organization about a virus that resembled SARS.

The original severe acute respiratory syndrome virus had originated in China in 2003 and spread around the world. The new virus—also reported first in China, in Wuhan City—was spreading rapidly and claiming lives ferociously. This version of the virus looked much more menacing. Cases on the west coast of the United States had been confirmed a week prior. Matthew weighed that new development into the equation that was forming in his mind for successfully tracking the missionaries—and the cost involved.

Instead of mentioning his travel concerns, Matthew asked instead, "How does that tension between the countries affect finding this group from Ukraine here in the US?"

"That last church—the one written in on the bottom of the list—is the problem. I don't understand why, because Greg and his team didn't disappear from there. They never made it that far. From what our local senator tells me, there's a population of over twenty-two thousand people living in Sunny Isles."

"OK," said Matthew nodding.

"Of those, over a thousand are Russian-born residents," continued Mark. "He says that concentration is higher than in any other country, including Europe and Asia. It's an uphill battle to get US agencies to acknowledge that four Ukrainian citizens are missing anywhere near that area."

"Ah," said Matthew, understanding. "It isn't any wonder the US is reticent to get involved in potential Russian interests, at least overtly. But this is different," replied Matthew indignantly. "The Ukrainians are on US soil. *Our* territory. *Our* country. They're not in Russia. The missionaries aren't US citizens, so I guess there's less willingness to help. But neither are they Russian. Politically, it sounds like it could be explosive. I'm surprised there isn't a stronger governmental interest in locating them."

"I agree. Politically, it's a powder keg," said Mark, nodding.

Startled, Matthew jumped and turned to the doorway behind him as Evelyn Rawlins—one of the pastors on staff—burst in, breathless and pale, exclaiming, "Mark! I have terrible news!"

2 ~ SINKING OPTIMISM

"Evelyn? I didn't know you were still here. Are you OK?" asked Mark.

"I heard from the Florida state police," she replied. A slender woman who looked like she might blow away or snap in two if the next breeze were too stiff, Evelyn looked to be in her early fifties. Her shoulder-length hair—once dark—was graying around her face, which was nearly the same shade of gray. Her hands were visibly shaking, and she looked like she might faint.

"Why don't you sit down?" said Mark as Matthew abruptly rose from his chair and turned it around for her to collapse into. "And tell us what happened."

"Th-they've located a car in a w-waterway of some kind. The…the license plate is missing, b-but the number on the car, the one that identifies it," she stammered.

"The vehicle identification number, or VIN," supplied Matthew helpfully.

"That's it. The officer who called me said they're trying to get a look at it—to see if it's the car Greg rented. It's still underwater, so they don't know for sure yet. The water is too rough for divers, and he said they worked against it to feed cameras down there. They're trying to figure out how to secure the car with cables to pull it out. There's a danger of it moving out to sea. It matches the description of the rental car that Greg and Darya were driving, a golden-brown Toyota Camry. And there's…there's," she stammered. Taking a deep shuddering breath, she continued, "There are two bodies in it."

"Oh!" said Mark, sinking back into his chair with the impact of this news. Then, quietly, he asked, "Do they know whose?"

"It sounds like they're not sure if they're male or female yet," she said as her face turned an odd shade of green, and she looked as if she might be sick. "The car has been down there for a couple of days, and the fish have been…well, it's going to be difficult to identify the bodies."

"I'm so sorry you had to get that call. Would you like some water?" asked Mark, rising from behind his desk.

"I've got it," said Matthew, who was closest to the door outside of which was a water cooler with cups.

"The officer went into more detail than I needed to know," she replied.

Matthew handed Evelyn a cup of water. She took it in a shaking hand and sipped slowly, trying to regain her composure. "I didn't go into the medical field for a reason," she said apologetically.

"It's OK," said Matthew. "Some things you never get used to unless you deal with it daily. And I think that's mostly a good thing. It's one of many reasons I chose family medicine—in the little town of Peak—over the career as an emergency department physician in a big city like I was originally considering."

"Did they tell you when they might know?" Danbury asked. "If the rental car was theirs? And who was in it?"

"They didn't," she answered as she shook her head.

"There were four of them traveling together," said Matthew comfortingly. "And only two in the car found in the water. Maybe it's the same type of car but not the one they were driving."

"Where did they find it?" asked Danbury.

"In some place I've never heard of," said Evelyn. "They said it was northeast Miami."

"Sunny Isles?" asked Matthew.

"No. Some place called Haulover Inlet," she replied. "Somebody spotted the back end of the car. It floated up to the surface of the water and then submerged again."

"That's below Sunny Isles," said Matthew. "At the south end of the same island. It's called Haulover for good reason. That's why it's taking some time to secure the car and figure out how to pull it out. I don't think the channel is that deep, just turbulent. That's probably why it resubmerged."

That got a reaction from Danbury, who bolted out of his chair. "Give me the number," he said. "The one they called you from. And the name of the officer. Whoever you spoke with. If you can remember."

As Evelyn turned and looked blankly at Danbury, Matthew explained, "I'm sorry, Ms. Rawlins. I should have introduced you earlier. This is my friend, Detective Warren Danbury. Mark has asked us to help find the missionaries. If they are victims of some sort of crime in Florida." Matthew purposefully did not mention murder. "This is out of state, but otherwise fully in his wheelhouse."

"Oh," she said simply. "Thank you so much. That makes me feel better. And please, Matthew, call me Evelyn." She pulled a phone from the pocket of her skirt and tapped to access the requested information. Calling out the number, she apologized profusely for not getting the name of the officer.

"That's OK," said Danbury.

"I'm sure that was quite a shock to get that call," Pastor Mark said empathetically.

"I'm going to step out. Call him back. See what he can tell me," said Danbury as he left the office.

"He's the right person to make that call," Matthew explained soothingly to Evelyn. "I don't know if there's any sort of professional courtesy extended there, but he's got a stellar reputation here for solving cases and wrapping up investigations, air tight."

"Mark, is there anything they left behind that could help identify them? Anything with DNA on it?" asked Matthew. "Hair? A toothbrush? Even something like a tissue in a trash can?"

"If there were, it's probably long gone by now," said Mark. "They stayed with our pastoral staff over the first weekend that they were here. Ross and Ivan were with Bill, and Greg and Darya stayed with

Evelyn."

"Oh!" said Evelyn. "This is really gross, but what about hair in a shower drain?"

"I'm not a forensic pathologist, but that might work," answered Matthew, nodding.

"I'm embarrassed to admit this, but the shower in my guest suite hasn't been cleaned since they left. We use that space mostly for hosting missionaries, pastors from other places, and sometimes somebody down on their luck who needs a place to stay to get back on their feet. I haven't needed it since they left, and they were supposed to be coming back for one more night. I emptied the trash, but maybe there is still something there from Greg and Darya."

Mark simply said, "I'll call Bill and ask."

"Great. Meanwhile, maybe the Florida police can tell us something helpful, at least to rule out our missionaries as the victims," said Matthew mainly to Evelyn.

To Mark, who was busily tapping his phone, Matthew added, "If Pastor Bill finds anything, tell him not to touch it. Danbury will want to bag and tag it with gloves on, so as not to contaminate it if it hasn't been already."

"I'll relay that information," replied Mark.

"Then we need to check the box that Greg and Darya left behind. You still have it, right?"

"I do. That's a good idea," agreed Mark. "I'll make the call first."

"I'll see if Danbury has learned anything else," said Matthew and left the office with a feeling of relief. It was overly warm, stuffy, and crowded in there, he thought. Danbury was pacing the lobby, phone to ear.

"I'm on hold," said Danbury, sounding annoyed.

"Evelyn said she might have hair in a shower drain from Greg and Darya," offered Matthew. "Would that help to compare against DNA of the bodies?"

"It might," said Danbury. "If I ever get an answer. We won't have dental records. Or fingerprints on file. If their fingertips are intact.

Anything on the other two? The pastors in training?"

"I don't know. They were staying with another of the pastors on staff here. Mark is calling now to ask," said Matthew. Eyebrow raised and foot tapping, he stood in front of a wall of glass windows and doors staring pensively into the darkened evening down the well-lit sidewalk outside.

"Then we're getting the box they left here," said Matthew, turning back to the office as he heard Danbury's voice on the phone behind him.

"Yeah. Warren Danbury. Homicide detective. Raleigh, North Carolina. Right. Four reported missing." As Matthew disappeared into the office, he overheard that being followed by, "Uh-huh. Yeah. OK."

Pacing between Danbury on one call in the hallway and Mark on another in his office, Matthew felt like a caged tiger. That thought reminded him that he needed to get home and feed his cat, Max. He'd gone straight from his office to meet Danbury at the gym that Danbury's girlfriend, Penn, had recently opened. Then he had come to meet with his pastor, and he hadn't been home since that morning.

Checking his watch, Matthew saw that it was nearly eight. His stomach rumbled in protest and he realized that he hadn't eaten yet either.

Finally, Danbury strode purposefully into the office with an update. A forensic expert in Miami had done an initial assessment from video footage captured by the camera they'd submerged on cables. He believed both victims to be male. Both appeared to have been shot in the head, execution-style. Danbury had, Matthew noticed appreciatively, tried to phrase that in the least disturbing manner possible.

"That doesn't help us a lot," said Mark—who had put his phone down—in response to Danbury's update. "But it likely rules Darya out. Bill is going to search his guest bedroom and bath. He'll call us back."

"Hope he finds something," said Danbury. "What else you can tell us? About the missing missionaries."

"There are just the four of them, as I mentioned earlier," said Mark pensively. "Both Grygoriy and Darya Starkovich are well educated.

They're dedicated to their ministry and to each other."

Matthew nodded, remembering hearing them speak and then meeting them after the church service two weeks before. Greg spoke nearly flawless English, Matthew had thought admiringly. Darya seemed to struggle more, particularly with word choices, enunciation, and dialect.

"The Starkovich family includes four small children," continued Mark. "They were left in Ukraine with relatives. Neither of the two young pastors with Greg and Darya is married. Rostyslav Pavelko, Ross, left a fiancée behind in Ukraine. Ivan Domitrovich has been caring for his disabled father there. I hadn't met either of them before—I don't know much more about them."

"What can you tell us about the churches?" asked Danbury. "The last two on the itinerary?"

"I don't know much about those, either. If I'm not mistaken, Aurora Springs Chapel began supporting Greg and Darya's ministry last year. From what I can tell, that's a misnomer. It's a big contemporary church, not a small chapel. It's on the southern tip of Buchanan Island above Jacksonville, Florida. I haven't had any contact with the pastor there until now."

Mark knit his brows in concentration before he added, "I know nothing about St. Athanasius at all except that it's an Eastern Orthodox church. I studied the saint it's named for in an early-church-history class. Athanasius was critically important—fourth century, I believe— when the early church theologians were trying to solidify their understanding of the nature of God. They were struggling with the concept of one God in three persons, the Trinity. Athanasius taught that the members of the Trinity are one, and therefore, they're equally God. I think Athanasius was a contemporary of Arius who was determined that Jesus was not coequal with the Father. But don't quote me on that. That class was a long time ago."

"What about the box?" asked Danbury. "That Greg asked you to mail. Where is it?"

"It's in a big storage room in the original section of the church building. It's sealed, but it isn't addressed. Greg gave me the address to send it to."

"We'll need to open it," said Danbury. "Can I get that address? The texts from Greg. The phone numbers. For all four of them. Pictures of them. And the rental-car information. Do you have that?"

Pastor Mark nodded. "I can provide all of that."

"Do you know where they stayed? Thursday night?" Danbury asked.

"I don't, but the pastor in Macon might. I can call him back."

"I'll do that," said Danbury.

"Sure," said Mark, looking relieved to be getting help with the confusing situation. "His number is on the itinerary. I'll get the rest of that information for you."

"One more thing," said Danbury. "That last church. Do you know why they added it? It seems odd."

Matthew nodded his agreement. It seemed odd to him too—a missionary team that relied on interdenominational churches, like his, for support suddenly visiting an Orthodox church. Maybe they weren't seeking support. Why else would they go there, he wondered.

"That's a great question. From what Greg told me Wednesday, one of the other churches recommended it and made the connection for him. An Orthodox church, though," added Mark, voicing Matthew's thoughts aloud. "That's not their usual type of supporter."

"Which church?" asked Danbury. "Made the recommendation?"

"Greg said it was Aurora Springs Chapel," answered Mark. "The one that was supposed to be their last stop before returning here."

Mark pulled a pad and pen from his top desk drawer and slapped the pad down on his desk. Attacking it with the pen, he alternated scribbling on the pad with tapping keys on his computer keyboard and glancing up at the screen. Tearing the top sheet of paper off, he handed it to Danbury.

"That's the rental-car information and the address for the box," said Mark. He retrieved his smart phone from his desk, tapped it, and handed it to Danbury. "This is the last text message. You'll find the other three members of the mission team under that same chat. It's a group chat. It wasn't a private conversation between Greg and me. It's not much to go on, I know. But if you're willing to help, I'd be beyond grateful."

Finding missing Ukrainian missionaries in a heavy Russian-born population—what could possibly go wrong with that? Matthew thought sarcastically, immediately before agreeing to help.

3 ~ ARCANE UNBOXED

"I'll talk to my colleagues and staff about covering my patient load for a few days," said Matthew pensively.

He and Mark both turned to Danbury.

Nodding slowly, Danbury answered by way of taking charge of the situation again. "Let's see what we can learn here. Before rushing off to search. We need to know where to look. Doc, can you check the box?"

Matthew agreed, and Danbury added, "I'll call in a favor. See where the phones were used last. Find them if they're active. Or if they go live. And the rental car. It likely has a tracker on it. From the rental agency."

Matthew thought lots of people must owe Danbury favors. This was not the first time he'd heard the big detective say something similar about calling them in. He'd cashed in a few of those favors to help Matthew out a time or two over the past year since they'd become friends.

Mark said, "Let's go get that box, and we can bring it back in here to open."

"Mind if I hang onto this for a few minutes?" Danbury asked, indicating Mark's phone.

"Sure," Mark replied, nodding, as Danbury slipped out of the office.

While Matthew followed Mark out of the office in one direction, Danbury went in the other. Out through one of multiple sets of glass doors, Danbury headed for the well-lit parking lot and the black

Chevrolet Tahoe he drove.

Following Mark to the older section of the building to retrieve the mysterious box, Matthew realized that he hadn't been in this part of the building in many years—probably not since he was a child. He loved the old creaking wooden floor boards and the smell of lemon furniture polish. It had a nostalgic homey feel to it.

The box was less than a foot square—maybe ten inches, Matthew estimated—but it was completely covered in clear packaging tape. Picking up the box, he heard the creak of a floorboard behind him. Turning, he caught a glimpse of a dark-hooded shadow in his peripheral vision. The figure in the hallway passed by the open door of the storage room they were in. Then a loud bang reverberated through the old building that made both men jump.

"What was that?" asked Matthew softly, listening for anything further. It sounded close and not quite loud enough to have been a gunshot, but almost. It was unnerving coming from a part of the building that he knew was usually devoid of people and activities, particularly during the week.

"That sounded like the side door slamming. The one between the old sanctuary and the hallway to the offices."

Taking the box with him, Matthew rounded the corner in pursuit while Mark paused to relock the storage room door. Having passed the outside door on the way to the storage closet, Matthew searched his mind trying to remember if it could have been ajar. It had appeared closed, though he hadn't scrutinized it. There had been no reason to.

"Is anybody still around this time of night?" he asked Mark. Shaking the door handle—gently at first, and then more firmly—he found it locked. The door was solid, an older, thick wooden door, sturdily built and precisely fitted into the frame.

"No, not down here, and not this late."

The empty hallway was eerily and dimly lit; the floorboards creaking under Matthew's weight had lost their nostalgic feel. Given where the box had been stored, the concern of the owners for leaving it behind, and the bodies found in Miami that might be connected, Matthew wished he had gloves on as he carried the box back to the senior pastor's office.

"If somebody was in here and got spooked by our voices, they're long gone by now. Have you had any trouble with intruders or pranksters?" Matthew asked.

"Not that I'm aware of," answered Mark, shaking his head definitively as he found a pair of scissors in his desk drawer and handed them to Matthew. "You open it, if you don't mind. I know we need to do it, but I feel like I'm breaking a confidence somehow by opening it."

"Sure," said Matthew, who had never really gotten used to the feeling that he was snooping and intruding when helping Danbury to investigate took him into other people's private domains. Carefully, he ran one blade of the scissors along the seam in the box top. As he was repeating this procedure to cut the tape down the sides of the top box flaps, Danbury returned.

"Doc," said Danbury, tossing Matthew a pair of latex gloves.

Snapping them on, Matthew pulled back the flaps of the box. Mark moved his desk lamp, aiming it over the box, and they peered in. It wasn't full. On top, half sheets of paper were stacked. They looked like completed pledge forms for prayer and financial support.

Putting those aside on the desk, Matthew retrieved a bundle of four small T-shirts that professed their love for North Carolina.

"I gave those to him. Gifts for his children," said Mark.

"I thought I remembered them only having two children when they were here before," said Matthew. "Two very young children."

"Biologically, yes, they have a daughter and a son," answered Mark. "Last year they adopted two little boys who were orphaned."

"Oh wow," said Matthew, laying the shirts aside.

"I don't know why those weren't in his suitcase," said Mark.

"I'd bet this is why," said Matthew, holding up a clear-plastic, zippered bag containing a leather-bound notebook or journal of some sort that the shirts had been carefully wrapped around. It looked ancient. Gingerly, Matthew slid the book out of the bag. Clumsily in the gloves, he untied the leather cord that held it closed, and coughed as he opened the cover. It smelled musty, and the pages were thick paper, yellowed with age. Inside, there were characters and markings that were indiscernible to him.

Carefully, Matthew flipped through the pages. Except for two small sketches inserted in the text, everything else was handwritten in the strange lettering. One of the sketches appeared to be an ornate cross and the other maybe a shrouded person, though it was difficult to tell.

"That all looks Greek to me," said Danbury leaning over Matthew's shoulder for a closer look.

"It isn't Greek," said Mark. "I have a rudimentary grasp of Greek from my master of divinity program at Duke. These characters are different. Perhaps it's Ukrainian."

It wasn't until Matthew flipped to the end that there was anything discernible. The final two pages of the book contained intricately drawn, detailed ink sketches. Though of what, he wasn't sure. On the left page was an oddly shaped blob that Matthew thought vaguely resembled an elongated amoeba—or maybe an outline of the Statue of Liberty from behind and leaning severely to the left.

Rippled lines looped the inside edges of the figure—ragged rings— as if someone had thrown a rock into sections of the blob and the ripples radiated outward to the edge of the shape. Rectangular, square, and other odd shapes were strewn around the inside edges of the blob. One shape on the left near the bottom—where the feet would meet the base of the Statue of Liberty in Matthew's mind—was neatly circled.

The shape within the circle looked like a wrench to Matthew's imagination. Beside the circle but outside of the wrench was a string of characters. Like the characters in the rest of the book, they weren't from the Roman alphabet.

On the right page was a large circle enclosing rectangular and square shapes. It looked as though the circled area on left page was blown up in more detail. Still basically wrench-shaped in arrangement, it was made up of individual squares and elongated rectangles.

"If it is Ukrainian, I don't suppose you know anyone who could translate it?" Matthew asked Mark. "Could someone from their ministry back in Ukraine?"

While Mark pondered the question, Danbury spoke up. "I might know somebody. Can we copy it? The original should stay here.

Locked up securely."

"I'm not sure how secure it is here," said Matthew and explained the shadow and the loud bang that they'd thought was an outside door slamming, presumably by somebody on their way out of it.

"Ah," said Danbury. "We need to be careful about who sees it. The fewer, the better. It might be connected to your group's disappearance. Do you have a safe? Somewhere to lock it up?"

"I don't," answered Mark. "Maybe it should go in a lock box at the bank."

"Eventually," said Danbury, and he paused, rubbing his chin with his thumb as he often did when he was pondering something. "It needs to be somewhere safe overnight."

"Can you lock it up downtown at your precinct?" asked Matthew. "Even your desk drawer in a police station is safer than any other place here overnight. I have a safe, but my house has been broken into more times in the past year than most people's in a lifetime. So, I'm not volunteering."

"I can," said Danbury. He turned to Mark. "If you agree?"

"It's obviously safer there than here," said Mark, nodding agreement.

Matthew finished flipping backward through the pages. Closing the book, he sneezed violently as he lay it on the plastic bag beside the box on the desk.

"Who are you going to ask about translating it?" asked Matthew, recovering from the sneezing fit, as curiosity trumped his usual regard for Danbury's tendency toward extreme privacy. It was a professional contact—surely, not his personal life—Matthew justified to himself immediately before being proved wrong.

"A buddy of mine. From back in the Corps. Until he got recruited by a government agency. He studied languages. Middle Eastern languages, mostly. But he dabbled in Russian. I don't know how similar they are. Ukrainian and Russian. Maybe close enough."

"Ukrainian is Slavic, sort of a mix between Polish and Russian I'd guess," said Mark. "I learned a few words when I was in Ukraine. But I had Greg and Darya translate everything for me. And I didn't have to read or write any of it. I just had to get close enough on the pronunciation of a few basic phrases to be understood."

Danbury handed Mark a pair of gloves as he reached for the book.

"Oh sure," said Mark, pulling them on before picking up the book to examine it more closely.

From the bottom of the box, Matthew pulled two pens and a small lined notepad—a miniature legal pad—and flipped through the blank pages. He shook it, and when nothing fell out, he held it up to the light. "Is this yours?" he asked Mark.

"I don't think so. Why?"

"Because whoever wrote on it last presses down hard like you did when you wrote down the information for Danbury. We might be able to tell what was written on it last."

"Oh," said Pastor Mark as if this observation were a revelation to him. "I see."

"We could try the pencil trick on this unless you want to take it somewhere," Matthew said to Danbury.

"I can't take it to a lab. Not officially. This looks like a murder investigation. But it isn't mine." After considering for a minute more, Danbury said, "That pencil trick is as good as any. We can give it a try. Is there anything else in the box?"

"Nope," said Matthew, turning it upside down. As he was flipping the box upright, something fluttered from it to the floor. "And then again." Matthew stooped to retrieve a slip of paper in his still-gloved hand from where it had landed under the edge of Mark's desk.

Like the pages in the leather-bound book, the scrap of paper was thick and yellowed with age. It was frayed around the edges as if it had been torn from something else.

"I have no idea how to pronounce this," said Matthew. On it, were four words in a less-blockish handwriting than that in the book. The lettering, though, looked similar.

"B O P O N, maybe?" said Matthew, trying to make something from the first word.

"Is this one Greek?" he asked Mark hopefully.

"No, that's not Greek."

"I didn't think so but it might as well be. Maybe your guy can tell us," Matthew said to Danbury, laying it on top of the book.

"What do you need to see what was written on the pad last?" Mark asked.

"A dull pencil will work. The flatter and duller the better," Danbury answered.

"How's this?" Mark asked, handing over a pencil from his desk drawer.

"OK to break it?"

"Sure," said Mark and handed Danbury the pad he'd been writing on, "Here."

Danbury snapped the point off on the note pad and then bore down at an angle, rubbing it on the notepad to flatten and smooth it.

"Let's get the copier fired up," said Mark. "We can set it to send a file to my email account if we set it to scan as we print it. Then I can forward it to you or put it on a memory stick if you want it that way."

"Sure," said Matthew as he took the book and scrap of paper in gloved hands and followed his pastor out to the outer office. Mark rattled off his code to the copy machine, and Matthew began carefully scanning and printing pages.

Danbury pulled out his phone and tapped to enter the information that had been revealed from the pencil rubbing.

"What is it?" asked Matthew, peering in from the copier in the outer office.

"It's contact information. For a person named Alex Stevenson. Could be male or female. Phone number and physical location. No mailing address. But a building and room number. At a university in Miami. Probably a private school. I've never heard of it. Barclay University. Do you recognize this name?" he asked Mark and held his phone up to share the information he'd painstakingly typed into the small device.

"I don't," said Mark. "We can look him up. Or her."

"Right," said Danbury, tapping his phone.

After a moment, Danbury said, "He's a professor. Of antiquities and linguistics, specializing in Russian and Slavic studies. He's shown in two departments. Languages and history. He looks at least sixty. Maybe older."

"Antiquities?" asked Matthew. "Like some sort of specialized history of language, maybe. Somebody Greg might consult about this book. But he left it here, so that doesn't make sense. If that was it, he'd have taken it with him."

"I would think so," said Mark as Danbury's phone began to buzz.

"It's the pastor in Georgia. From the church in Macon. Returning my call," said Danbury and then into the phone, "Detective Danbury."

Danbury questioned the pastor at length about exactly when the missionary team left Macon and where they were planning to spend the night. After a series of interspersed "Uh-huh…uh-huh" comments and more questions, Danbury thanked the pastor.

"He didn't know for certain," reported Danbury. "He recommended a hotel to them. It's a localized chain. Safe and adequate. Nothing flashy. In a little town called Queen's Ferry. It's in Georgia. But barely. Northwest of Jacksonville. I'll check it."

While Danbury looked up the number, Matthew handed copies of the pages from the ancient leather book to both Danbury and Mark, holding one for himself. Matthew put the book and scrap of paper in the plastic bag and—along with the T-shirts and other papers—back in the box.

"I received the scanned copy," announced Mark, leaning over his computer and tapping keys to pull up the file. He glanced through it. "It's as clear as the copied version, which isn't saying much."

"Great," said Danbury, handing over a tiny device. "Here's a thumb drive. Copy the electronic file to it. I'll send it to get translated. From a secure server. When I get back downtown. I'll call the hotel in Georgia. Then we need to get the hair. From that shower drain. And see if the other pastor found anything. Or go look for ourselves."

"I'll call Bill back," said Mark.

When both calls were completed, Mark said, "Bill says they had forgotten to empty the trash from their upstairs guest bath. They don't use the upstairs themselves. There are tissues still in the trash can, and Ivan had a nose bleed the first night he was there. Probably due to the altitude changes from the flight over."

"Perfect," said Danbury. "The hotel confirmed check in. Thursday night. Two rooms. All four pastors. But they haven't checked out. Nobody has seen them. Not since Thursday night."

"Did they leave anything behind?" asked Matthew.

"The desk clerk thinks so. He's going to look. And call back to confirm." That seemed to cinch it for Danbury. "I'm between major cases now. I can take a couple of days off. Drive to Georgia tonight. Could you fly to Florida tomorrow morning?" he asked Matthew. "I can pick you up from the airport."

Danbury's credo was to eat when you could and sleep when you could because you never knew when you'd be able to do either again. The guy could put away massive amounts of food, and he functioned well on little to no sleep. Matthew had seen him do both multiple times over the past year, but to drive all night was extreme, even for Danbury.

"I need to talk to my colleagues, but I don't want to call them this late at night," Matthew responded. "So, it'll be at least midmorning before I'm free to travel, probably early afternoon."

"OK, Doc. I'll pick you up. From whatever airport. Wherever you can get a flight in. Let me know. One more thing," said Danbury, turning to Pastor Mark. "I'll need a car. Instead of a plane ticket. To drive down. My Tahoe technically belongs to you. The taxpayers." He grinned. "This isn't a case I'm assigned to. I need to leave it here."

"No problem. We can rent you one." Mark checked his watch. "I'm not sure what time most of the rental companies close, but the ones at the airport are open later, I think."

"They're open until ten. The big ones are. The one out Highway 70 is."

"I can collect the—ah—samples from the pastor's houses before I go home tonight, in case you need them, if that would help," offered Matthew as they discussed logistics.

"That would be great, Doc," said Danbury. "If Georgia's a bust. And nothing helpful was left. That'll be our best shot." He pulled gloves and evidence bags from a pocket of his black cargo pants and handed them to Matthew.

"Then I need to get home to feed Max. I can wrap up patient charts, pack, and book a flight for tomorrow," said Matthew, planning out loud. Refraining from checking his watch or the smart phone it was connected too, he felt exhausted listing it all.

"Max?" asked Pastor Mark.

"My cat," said Matthew. "Oh, and I'll need to talk to Leo about taking care of him while we're away. Leo is Penn's younger brother."

"Penn, Danbury's intended fiancée?" asked Mark.

"That's the one," said Danbury with a grin as Mark handed him the tiny thumb drive.

"We can talk about that soon too," said Mark. "I'm happy to meet with you to discuss it all. I had already agreed to that before I asked for your help. One isn't contingent on the other."

"Thanks," said Danbury, pocketing the thumb drive and picking up his copy of the book contents.

"I guess it's OK to leave the box in my office overnight," said Mark, glancing around. "There's nothing left in it but T-shirts, pledge forms, pens, and a note pad.

"All but the top couple of pages. Those should go with the book. The rest of the notepad can stay."

"Right. Of course," said Mark, tearing them of and handing those to Danbury. "One more thing. I'd like to pray for you and this trip before we all go in different directions. I'll go get Evelyn. She's waiting for us in her office."

As Mark left, Danbury turned to Matthew, looking concerned. "This isn't something I'm used to."

"It's like when I say the blessing over meals," said Matthew reassuringly. "And if you want Mark to marry you and Penn, you might as well get used to him praying over you. He'll do it a lot. This is his way of commissioning us to go find the missionaries and asking for our safety while we're doing it."

"Yeah, OK," agreed Danbury.

Matthew welcomed all the prayer he could get as he felt his trepidation building. It was more than dismay about the bodies found in the channel, the missing missionaries, or a trip back to Florida. There was something else troubling him that he couldn't quite identify—it was more foreboding.

4 ~ HEADING SOUTH

As he sat staring out the plane window late the next afternoon, Matthew marveled at how quickly his life could pivot from a normal day and week into something completely different. In less than twenty-four hours, everything had changed. His priorities were rearranged.

Puffy clouds morphed from one shape to another outside the window seat he occupied, but he barely noticed them. His mind returned to the evening before and the whirlwind of activity between then and sitting on this plane headed for Fort Lauderdale, Florida.

Max greeted him when he'd arrived home, happily wending and winding between his legs and making it difficult to walk to the pantry and retrieve the bin of dry cat food. Matthew had packed his suitcase and all of Max's belongings this morning. His patient charts were not only current but also detailed. Handing off his most urgent patients to his colleagues, he'd gotten his office manager and receptionist to divvy up the others to call and reschedule.

Yawning was a struggle under the surgical mask he'd opted to wear. Reports of the spread of the new SARS virus were sufficient, at least in his mind, to warrant a bit of precaution. Most people around him, he noticed, seemed unbothered by the tight quarters and proximity on the plane. A loud cough emanated from somewhere behind him, validating his decision.

After his own late night and early morning—with less than five hours of sleep in between—he wondered how Danbury had managed to drive all night. Matthew knew he should be thankful that his partners were supportive and encouraging of his commission to find the Ukrainian missionaries. Still, it felt irresponsible to be running out on them. He hated doing it, never wanting to shirk his share of the workload.

It was his girlfriend, Cici—during their regular morning FaceTime chat—who had raised the most objection to this trip. Cici was still in London. Finishing up a year-long assignment, she was helping some of her prestigious law firm's high-profile clients move operations to the United States.

Matthew pulled his laptop from the bag under the seat in front of him and opened a file to begin compiling the information that they knew so far. His methodical mind, trained to be so by his medical profession, preferred to order information and then study it to understand. Danbury had called midmorning to provide an update on what he'd learned, and Matthew wanted to capture that information.

Pulling the car from the channel had been delayed due to rough weather conditions. Particularly when the tide is going out and there are strong easterly winds, the resulting waves could be treacherous for small watercraft. Those same conditions prohibited pulling the car out earlier in the day. The medical examiner—who was standing by—determined from pictures brought up by the cameras the day before that both bodies were male. That ruled out Greg's wife, Darya, as one of the victims.

Luggage was left behind in the Georgia hotel room. While police officers from the two states were bickering over jurisdiction of potential evidence, Danbury retrieved samples from hairbrushes. Those could be compared for DNA matches. Technical teams from both Florida and Georgia scanned the area for blood residue and found none, which was somewhat relieving.

Because the missionaries' belongings were left behind, the text from Greg answering Pastor Mark on Friday was highly unlikely. They were due to have left the hotel Friday morning, but they hadn't. If it wasn't Greg who answered the text, then who had? And why? Why would anyone answer an incoming text message?

Maybe—Matthew postulated as his fingers flew over the keyboard—to disguise the length of time that the missionaries had been missing. Postponing alerting anyone that they were potentially in danger delayed an immediate search. Greg's group was due at a church near Jacksonville by lunchtime on Friday, so someone knew that they weren't where they were supposed to be. That information, Matthew added to the file as he created a timeline for the missing team.

Danbury hadn't specified how he'd found the hotel rooms when he entered them. Were there, for example, pajamas or sleeping clothes lying around, or had the missing occupants unpacked at all? Those details could determine whether they'd been missing since Thursday evening, early Friday morning, or sometime in the overnight hours in between. Matthew typed those questions to ask.

The team—according to Mark's inquiry and Danbury's confirmation—was seen by a whole church full of people in Macon on Thursday. They checked into a hotel Thursday evening. Their descriptions, Danbury was told by police who had initially questioned the desk clerk, matched the pictures Pastor Mark had taken of the team while they were in Raleigh. Danbury showed the clerk the pictures himself, to be thorough, and the desk clerk confirmed the match.

Neither the local police nor Danbury had found any identification left behind in the hotel room. What time did they check in, Matthew wondered. He added a note to ask. Nobody could confirm hearing from them since then, though it seemed likely that somebody had tried to make it seem as if nothing out of the ordinary were happening by answering the text Friday morning.

As he mulled that thought over and added a few more notes, Matthew was surprised to hear the announcement that he needed to stow his electronic device under the seat in front of him in preparation for landing. Glancing out his window on the right side of the plane, Matthew could see that they were over water, with the eastern coastline of Florida and the sun heading down the horizon beyond.

A brightly lit hotel—disguised as a giant guitar—loomed in the distance as they banked steeply before straightening out and quickly dropping out of the sky. Deep in thought, Matthew watched from the window as the plane taxied in, wended around to a gate, and slowed to a stop. He texted Danbury that he was on the ground as soon as passengers were told they could use their cellular devices. A thumbs-up icon appeared from Danbury as the passengers stood, ready to disembark. Because Matthew had packed mostly lightweight, quick-dry clothing in a carry-on bag—with his computer bag as his personal item—he didn't have to go to the baggage claim area.

Following the flow of passengers out into the main part of the airport and down an escalator, Matthew made his way out. It was appreciably cooler and less muggy when he stepped through the doors of the airport into the waning afternoon light on that late January afternoon than it had been on his last trip to the area in June. Pulling his phone from his pocket, he saw that Danbury had dropped a pin with his location. Matthew turned right, making his way down the sidewalk to a long pickup area marked at intervals with both letters and numbers. That, he thought, was a confusing system, and he was thankful for location technology.

"Hey, Doc," said Danbury as he popped open the rear gate of a big black Chevrolet Tahoe. It looked suspiciously like the SUV he drove at home in North Carolina, but for the bumper stickers from the rental agency. Matthew stowed his bags, climbed in, and buckled up as Danbury fought his way across multiple lanes of traffic to emerge into the lanes exiting the airport. "Good flight?"

"Not bad," said Matthew. "I was typing up some notes while we were in the air. I didn't ask earlier about the condition of the hotel room in Georgia and what you could tell from it. You said there was no blood and no ID left behind, right?"

"Right. No signs of a struggle. If that's what you mean."

"From the suitcases and the clothing, could you tell if they had unpacked? Or if anyone had slept in the beds? Or had they only checked in and hadn't managed much else?"

"Hard to say," said Danbury. "The rooms were likely searched. Professionally and carefully. Nothing looked disturbed. The beds were made. Maybe by housekeeping. They had been in. After the occupants didn't check out. They got charged for the next nights. Maybe the beds were never unmade. There were a few items in the bathrooms. Toiletry bags were out."

"And you got samples of hair from all four of them for the DNA testing?"

"I think so. I pulled sample from hairbrushes. I know which is Darya's," said Danbury. Then he clarified the information. "Pink sparkly hairbrush. The other is Greg's, by default. But Ivan and Ross,

I'm not sure which is which."

"I have the samples from the pastor's houses," said Matthew, nodding. "There's no guarantee who they belong to either, but Ivan had the bloody nose. Maybe that helps."

"I submitted the samples I collected. To the Florida police. In Miami. We'll get your samples to them too. As soon as they pull the car out. Hopefully, we'll know soon."

After a momentary pause, Matthew said, half to himself, "So, there's no way to know if they actually spent the night at the hotel."

"Right," answered Danbury. "The suitcases were opened. But not unpacked. They were likely rifled through. But carefully. Professionally."

"That could have been room service. And some people don't unpack their suitcases when they travel. Particularly not for one overnight."

"I don't."

That wasn't surprising, Matthew thought, from what he knew about Danbury and his ability to be ready to go anywhere at any time on very short notice. It was a result of the guy's military background, he assumed.

"For all we know, they could have come in, washed up, gone out to get dinner, and never made it back to sleep there," said Matthew.

"That's one possibility."

"Do you know what time they checked in?"

"They were there at three."

"Was that the earliest check in time?"

"It was. I asked. I also questioned the housekeeping staff. They know something. Nobody could have memories that short. They 'don't remember' making the beds. Or cleaning the rooms. They weren't offering any information."

"Huh," said Matthew pensively. "I wonder why not. Could they have seen something and been paid off not to talk by somebody?"

"Or scared off. Not to talk. Threatened."

"Maybe they were scared to get involved."

"Entirely possible," answered Danbury before turning his attention fully to the traffic, which was some of the most horrendous that Matthew had ever seen. They'd managed to get out of the airport traffic and onto I-95 headed south. Cars zipped in front—into places they didn't fit—and immediately braked. With all that chaos, it was a wonder that the traffic ever moved, and that anybody ever got where they were going—safely or at all.

"Hey, Doc, watch the navigation app?" asked Danbury, indicating his phone that was clipped to the dash. "I set the destination. But these roads down here, they dart off. Then they're blocked by traffic. Before the nav app tells you to go that way."

"Sure. It says you have two more miles before we exit I-95," answered Matthew before the automated voice announced the same information. He swiveled Danbury's cell phone slightly in the mounting device on the dash so that he could see it too. "We're getting off on 858, the road name is Hallandale Beach Blvd. Where are we going?"

"To Haulover. I want to see the car. If they can pull it out."

Matthew provided the navigation from I-95. After working their way down the coastline, they approached the end of the island toward the inlet and found a spot to park. Bright lights against the darkening night sky declared their proximity to the scene as they slid from the SUV. Danbury flashed his badge, motioned to Matthew, and explained their involvement to what must have been new police officers who were manning the entrance to a barricaded area. Both looked bored.

Miami, Matthew thought, probably had so many more occurrences of such circumstances that it wasn't nearly as remarkable as in the triangle area of North Carolina. Still, a camera crew was drinking coffee where they stood by the news van of a local television station. They had selected what must be the best vantage point from outside and off to one side of the barricade. A small team of people worked diligently—under huge lights that looked like highway-construction lighting—on a car, only the back of which could be seen.

Matthew followed Danbury to the water's edge. They watched from a safe distance as the car was slowly emerging from the churning darkish water that was partially lit by the tall work lights. Thick metal cables were attached from two industrial-sized tow trucks, anchoring the operation on either side and preventing the car from flipping. As the sedan leveled out on land, water poured from beneath and gushed from the open windows. A forensic team of two—already clad in white suits—circled it speculatively, photographing the exterior and waiting for the water to drain.

After what seemed to Matthew like hours but was probably less than ten minutes, the forensic team approached the car and struggled to open the front doors. Stepping back momentarily, as more water streamed out, they began photographing the interior. Matthew could see two figures in the front of the car, presumably pinned in place by seat belts. After photographing the scene to their satisfaction, the two figures in white cut the seat belts. Carefully, they slid the bodies onto what looked like plastic sleds and then out onto the waiting tarps under the bright lighting.

Matthew shifted, tapping first one foot and then the other as he watched the proceedings. From where he stood, he could see that the bodies were in less than pristine shape and he was happy not to need a closer look. A strong odor akin to rotting fish, but worse, began to emanate from the general direction of the car. The forensic team sported masks and clear face shields, but Matthew figured the smell was permeating that apparatus and probably singeing their nose hairs. That they were doing this by artificial lighting at night and not in baking Florida sun was probably a good thing.

Clad in khaki pants and the collared three-button shirt he'd worn to the office that morning, Matthew was wishing for the waterproof windbreaker jacket he'd packed in his carry-on bag. He didn't want to deal with the police officers standing guard to retrieve it from the Tahoe. The breeze off the water was stiff and chilling, but he'd been OK in worse. Danbury was prepared slightly better. Clad in gray cargo pants, a black T-shirt, and an open charcoal-gray windbreaker, he could at least zip the jacket against the wind if he chose.

The medical examiner approached the scene from off to one side— where he'd been leaning on a white van with large block lettering that announced his profession. After the bodies were fully photographed, the ME exchanged a few words with the forensic team and two local officers. The conversation was beyond understanding; Matthew barely caught a few words here and there on the breeze.

As the ME went to work and the officers stepped back to allow him space, Danbury approached and introduced himself to them. Flipping his badge open, he explained his interest, then began questioning one of the officers.

The bodies were both male, the guy responded, and they'd been in the water a few days, but likely less than a week. They both had what looked to be bullet wounds in their foreheads, which had been earlier photographed by the underwater camera. Not much else was known yet.

"I've submitted hair samples. To be compared for a DNA match. And I have additional samples. From North Carolina. To provide to the ME. If these are the guys we're looking for, they're from Ukraine. You won't have dental records. Nothing like that on file here. How bad are they? Will facial recognition match? Passport photos maybe?"

The guy shook his head. "Not likely. I'll tell him, though. And give him your DNA samples if you'll bring me those," he offered and then stepped up behind the ME while maintaining a respectful distance.

A couple of hours later—midnight had come and gone—and Matthew could feel the exhaustion seeping through his body into the core of his being. To his relief, Danbury returned from a conversation with the ME ready to go to the hotel.

"They collected DNA samples. From both bodies. It's on the way to the lab. The bodies will be transported soon. The ME confirmed bullet wounds. One in each forehead. And two to the chest. Bullets might be found. In the head wounds. There are no obvious exit wounds. Though a ballistic match is a long shot."

"Because you'd need the weapon to compare them to," supplied Matthew.

"Right. Or other crimes. That the weapon was used in," added Danbury. "The autopsy should begin tomorrow. There's nothing more to learn tonight. Let's get some sleep. And start fresh in the morning."

"Great," said Matthew, heading for the Tahoe. "Were they shot because they were in the wrong place at the wrong time? Or because they were specifically targeted? Maybe they wouldn't answer questions. Or maybe they didn't know the answers."

"There is another possibility," Danbury answered as they climbed into the big black Tahoe. "One we haven't acknowledged. Or discussed."

"Which is?"

"Their own motive. They could have had one. A reason to disappear."

"Maybe," said Matthew pensively. "If they were scared or threatened by somebody or something."

"Or they're in on it. Whatever it is."

"I guess that's possible, but given what Pastor Mark says about Greg, not very likely. Mark is an excellent judge of character. If he says Grygoriy Starkovich has integrity and is fully committed to his ministry in Ukraine and would never do anything to jeopardize that, I believe him. And that includes causing or condoning harm to his team."

"I'll take your word for his word," said Danbury with a grin, tapping his phone to pull up the navigation app and placing his phone on the dash holder. "That's the location of the hotel. I've already checked us both in. We're on the fourth floor. And across the hall."

"Great," said Matthew on a yawn. "Today already feels like several."

"Yup," agreed Danbury. "You should be used to that by now."

"Yeah, I should be," answered Matthew, remembering the murder cases he'd worked alongside Danbury in the past year and buckling up—both literally and figuratively—as Danbury pulled out onto the beach road and headed for the hotel.

*****

Reassuring Cici in their usual morning FaceTime conversation when she admonished him to be safe, Matthew promised, "I'll be careful, Cees." His eyes crinkled at the corners as he smiled warmly, addressing her by the name that only he called her. "You have my word."

After they'd said their goodbyes and he'd had his usual shower and shave, Matthew called his office to check in. Then he met Danbury in the hotel lobby for a quick breakfast. Danbury had gotten photos forwarded to him from the hotel rooms where the missionaries had left their belongings. Between gulps and bites, they scanned through the photos, passing Danbury's tablet back and forth.

"The only interesting thing I see here is what looks like Darya's nightgown thrown on top of her open suitcase. It isn't folded. Could she have worn it and tossed it there the next morning?"

"I wondered that too. Notice anything else?"

"Not from the photos," answered Matthew, scrolling back through them on Danbury's tablet. "Did you see something else in the hotel room that isn't in these pictures?"

"Nothing specific. It's just a feeling. Like there's something there. And I'm not seeing it."

"Huh," said Matthew, squinting at the tablet.

"Let's hit the road," said Danbury, picking up the tablet and tossing his paper breakfast plate and biodegradable plastic cutlery into the trash on the way out.

They climbed in the Tahoe, and Danbury entered the location in the navigation app on his phone—clipping it to the mount on the dash. Back on I-95, with a travel cup of coffee in hand, Matthew was once again navigating from the app.

"There's a lane opening to the right ahead. Move to that. We want exit 8-B at NW 103rd Street. Where are we going?" asked Matthew, realizing that they hadn't discussed the order of operations for the morning, merely what they knew so far, who they needed to talk to, and what they hoped to learn.

"To talk to a professor," said Danbury as he began to cross traffic, changing lanes.

"Ah, to see Professor Stevenson. That sounds like a good place to start."

Danbury nodded.

"He knows we're coming?" asked Matthew.

"He does."

"Did you tell him what we want to talk to him about?"

"Not specifically. I want to watch his reactions. In person. When I ask about Greg and Darya. Keep an eye on him. See what you think."

"OK, will do," said Matthew, returning his attention to the morning traffic jam.

When they'd gotten to the university campus, cleared the security gate, and managed to park, Danbury pulled his phone from the dash and began tapping. "Huh," he said.

"What is it?"

"A message from my buddy. From the Corps."

"From the guy you were asking about translating the book and slip of paper?"

"Yeah, but it's brief," said Danbury. "He says it's Russian. Not Ukrainian. The strings in the back. Around the drawings in the book. Those are numbers, spelled out."

"Numbers? Why not write them as numbers?" Matthew asked, immediately before answering his own question with a hypothesis. "Ah, because then anybody could read them."

"Russian numbers are written out," said Danbury. "Their numbering system. At least, he says he thinks so."

"Oh!" replied Matthew. "You have the strings of numbers?"

"He sent them. And the paper-scrap translation. He sent that too. But he can't get to the rest of it yet. He's on assignment. Somewhere in the Middle East. The strings of characters. They're mostly numbers. They look like coordinates."

"Read them off and I can search," answered Matthew, tapping his phone.

"Forty. Nine. Fifteen point six zero. North. Twenty-four. Nineteen. Twenty-one point zero zero. East."

"Huh," said Matthew, spreading his fingers to zoom in on the resulting view on the map. "It's on the edge of an island." Matthew corrected himself. "Or actually a peninsula." He pinched to zoom out and see the location. "In Northern Greece. It's a land mass that looks like"—Matthew hesitated and caught his breath.

"The land mass looks like what, Doc?"

5 ~ ANCIENT SECRETS

Studying the location on the map, and turning his phone slightly for Danbury to see, Matthew said, "The land mass looks like the Statue of Liberty from behind and leaning to the left."

"What?" asked Danbury, startled.

"It's what I thought the sketch in the back of the book looked like. I have the copies of it in my computer bag. They're sealed in an envelope, but I can pull them out to compare."

"No, I see it. It does look like the sketch."

"Mount Athos," Matthew read, then tapped his phone hurriedly to search. Reading the results aloud, he added, "It's an island of Greek Orthodox monasteries. The area that the coordinates point to—where the Statue of Liberty's toe hits the base—that's St. Simon Peter's Monastery. Or Simonopetra Monastery. It's what was blown up in the circle on the final page of the book. If those are coordinates, why a Greek Orthodox monastery?"

"That's what we need to find out. It's likely connected. To your missing missionaries."

"I can't see how," said Matthew thoughtfully. "Maybe it's related to the Greek Orthodox church that got added late to their schedule."

"What I was thinking," agreed Danbury.

"If Greg and Darya were protective of the box and loathe to leave it behind, there had to be a reason. It's too much of a coincidence not to be connected, and neither of us believe in those," said Matthew pointedly. "What did the scrap of paper say?"

"That's really odd," answered Danbury, glancing back at his phone. "It says, 'The raven croaks at midnight.'"

"What? Why would a raven croak at midnight—and why would anybody care if it did? Maybe it's some sort of coded message and it means something else entirely."

"That's possible. Let's go talk to the professor," said Danbury as he tucked the phone back in his pocket with the key fob for the Tahoe and climbed out.

The university building was an older light-brick structure that looked entirely utilitarian. A large rectangular cement front stoop was all there was of an entrance, and it had palm trees, standing like tall rigid sentinels on either side of double front doors.

"Upstairs, second floor," said Danbury as they entered, found a stairwell, and started climbing the concrete steps edged with scored metal strips "Two twenty-nine." Danbury turned right on the second-floor landing.

"Professor Stevenson?" asked Danbury, tapping on the doorframe of the open door.

"I'm Alex Stevenson, yes," answered a graying man with glasses who was seated behind a large desk. The desk—and every available surface in the room—was overflowing in all directions with papers, folders, magazines, books, and sections of newspapers that appeared to have been unceremoniously ripped out. Stevenson looked, to Matthew, exactly like a professor should—complete with a cardigan over a rumpled collared shirt.

Danbury introduced himself, flipping his badge open. "I called earlier."

When the professor merely nodded without rising from behind the desk, Matthew introduced himself and added, "Thank you for agreeing to meet with us."

"Of course. Come in. Pull up a chair and have a seat," he invited, still without getting up.

Having a seat was easier said than done. The chairs in the room were piled with file folders, books and papers, the detritus of years of research and teaching materials. Matthew removed a large canvas bag—which was full of thick books and heavier than he'd anticipated—from a chair and placed it with a soft thud on the floor. He pulled the chair in front of the desk while Danbury carefully moved a stack of papers and file folders to the floor before sliding a second chair in beside him.

"Now, what I can do for you?" asked Stevenson.

"We're looking for a missing couple. Grygoriy and Darya Starkovich," replied Danbury. "They left your contact information behind. Though probably accidentally. Did they contact you?"

The professor's face clouded over like the sun had disappeared behind his head. While they waited patiently, he seemed to be weighing his words carefully before responding. Finally, he replied, "I got a phone call from Mr. Starkovich, yes."

When it became apparent that elaboration wasn't forthcoming, Danbury prompted, "When was that?"

"On a Monday, I believe. A couple of weeks ago now, I think it was." Stevenson hesitated after the string of wiggle words.

As they continued to stare at him, Stevenson moved two stacks of papers and folders aside, adding them sideways on existing stacks to see a desk blotter. Cornered by black leather triangles, it had a paper center that was covered in scribbles at odd angles. It was more than Matthew could begin to take in, even if it hadn't been upside down from his perspective. How could this man function like that, he wondered.

Running his finger around the left side of the blotter, he finally announced, "Ah yes. It was the thirteenth of January."

That was the first Monday the Starkovich team was in the United States—the day they'd set out on their speaking tour—thought Matthew. Greg hadn't wasted time in contacting the professor. Whatever he wanted must have been important.

"Do you know Grygoriy Starkovich?" asked Danbury.

"No, I do not know him."

Something about that answer, the way the professor responded, tugged at the corners of Matthew's mind.

"Or his wife, Darya?"

"No."

"Did he tell you what he wanted? Why he contacted you?" asked Danbury.

"He asked if he could meet with me. He did not provide much information."

"Why did he want to meet you?"

"He said he wanted to consult with me about an item of minor antiquity."

"And did you? Meet with him?"

"No."

"Why not?"

"We were scheduled to meet on Saturday morning. That would have been the twenty-fifth of January," he added, this time consulting an old flip-style desk calendar. "But he did not arrive at the appointed time. Neither did he call to reschedule."

"Did he tell you what the item was?"

"He said it was a book that had belonged to a family member."

"He didn't say who?"

"He did not elaborate."

"You said you didn't know him," Matthew interjected. "You'd never met him or talked to him before the thirteenth of January?"

"No, I had not," said the professor, sliding his glasses atop his head and rubbing his eyes as if the discussion was giving him a headache. He was making this process harder than it should be. They were having to pry every tiny piece of information out of him, bit by bit. The guy could save them a ridiculous amount of effort by telling them whatever it was that he was withholding, thought Matthew in annoyance.

"You know who he is, though. Am I right about that?" asked Matthew, trying again to get at whatever the professor knew that he wasn't sharing.

"He told me he is a Ukrainian missionary in the US for a short time. He brought with him a book about which he wanted my opinion," Stevenson said stiffly.

When he again hesitated, Matthew said, "Professor Stevenson, all we want to do is find Greg and his wife and get them home safely. They left four small children behind in Ukraine who need their parents. Maybe you know something that can help us to locate them. Maybe you know things that you don't realize might be important in helping us to find them. Did he tell you anything else that could be helpful?"

After a lengthy pause, the professor finally said, "No, he did not tell me anything else."

"But you know of him, don't you?" Matthew prodded again.

In a hushed tone, Stevenson added, "Yes, I believe that I might know of him."

"And the book he asked you to evaluate—what do you know about it?"

"I also have an idea about the book that he was transporting."

Danbury leaned forward in his chair. "Please tell us what you know," he said softly and politely.

"I do not know anything definitively. I merely suspect. If what I suspect is true, you will not find Grygoriy or his wife alive. If I am correct, you need to stop looking for them, or you are endangering yourselves as well."

That was a harsh warning, Matthew thought, for an antiquated book with Russian writing that Greg didn't take with him from North Carolina to begin with. Matthew wondered why that was.

"Tell us," said Danbury simply.

Slowly and stiffly, the professor raised himself from his chair. He limped to circle the desk, closed the door behind Danbury and Matthew, and then back again. He was of a medium height and plump, as if he'd eaten well and exercised little. His wide hands clutching the arms of the chair, he grimaced as he lowered himself slowly and carefully back into it.

Taking a deep breath, and sliding his glasses back down onto his nose, Stevenson stared a hard, cold stare at Danbury and said between clenched teeth, "I believe Grygoriy Starkovich to be the grandson of Yuri Starkovich."

"Who is Yuri Starkovich?"

"If I am correct," Stevenson answered slowly, "nothing positive can come of that knowledge."

"Professor Stevenson," began Danbury, "we need to know what you know. We need to find the missionaries."

"Or at least to find out what happened to them," added Matthew. "If they have met with some horrific fate, as you seem to think, you must have a reason for thinking so."

Alex Stevenson mutely stared at them from across his desk.

"Ravens croaking at midnight," said Danbury, abruptly changing the subject. "That's the English translation. Of a Russian phrase. Have you heard of it?"

All blood and resulting color drained from the man's face, and he froze, unmoving.

Afraid that he was going to have a heart attack or stroke, Matthew leaned forward. "Professor? Are you OK?"

"Where did you get that phrase?" he asked, his voice low and hoarse.

"From something else Greg left behind. Probably also accidentally," answered Danbury. "What do you know about it?"

"You are asking dangerous questions," said the professor at last as his face regained some color. "I would kindly advise that you forget you ever heard that phrase and go back to your own affairs."

"Professor Stevenson, we can't do that," said Matthew. "We have to find the missionaries, and you know more than you're admitting."

"We will find them," insisted Danbury. "With your help. Or without it."

"I have knowledge, yes, but how it might fit this situation is purely conjecture," said the professor.

"Knowledge that could help us," prodded Danbury.

"Or get you killed," answered the professor.

"Who is Yuri Starkovich?" Danbury asked again, more insistently this time.

"That is not the right question," said Stevenson. "Correctly stated, the question is, 'What *was* Yuri Starkovich?'"

Matthew wondered how long Danbury would tolerate talking in riddles, which the professor seemed to prefer, over laying out the facts for them.

"OK," said Danbury patiently. "What *was* Yuri Starkovich?"

Taking a deep breath and rubbing his forehead again, the professor quietly answered, "Yuri Starkovich was a fierce and renowned KGB agent. He was operating prior to and during the beginning of what you call the Cold War with the Soviet Union. That is a misnomer. The conflict was quite heated, and the effects of it linger still. Yuri Starkovich was a brutal and ruthless man, not one you would want to cross in any way."

"You used the past tense, so I assume he's deceased?" asked Matthew.

"Presumed so, yes. He would be quite ancient were he not."

"That organization, the KGB, is no longer functioning. If both he and it are no longer operating, why can't you tell us what you know about it?" asked Matthew.

"KGB is no longer operational, that is true. But it has descendants, departments within the Russian governmental system today that are equally as dangerous."

"And you know all of this due to your research, your specialty as a language and antiquities professor?" asked Matthew.

"That is correct," said Stevenson, returning the glasses to the top of his head and rubbing his eyes again.

"But there's something else, isn't there?" prompted Matthew.

"There is," said the professor. Staring beyond them, he hesitated so long before answering that Matthew wasn't sure he was going to elaborate. Finally, he spoke again very softly. "I know this also because I knew Yuri Starkovich."

"Come again?" said Danbury.

"I knew him from KGB," replied Stevenson.

"You're Russian?" asked Danbury.

"No!" the professor answered vehemently. "I'm American. I defected and sought asylum many years ago."

"But you were part of the KGB?" prodded Danbury.

"I was a young agent during the Cold War in the late nineteen sixties, selected to be groomed to become another like Yuri Starkovich." The professor sighed deeply before he added, "I had not progressed far within the agency when I got on the wrong side of some treacherous people. My young family was in danger. I knew how it would work. My wife and my two daughters, still babies, would become targets. They would be used to control me. I had to get them out. And myself as well—or my extended family would become the next targets."

"How did you do that?" asked Matthew.

"I had the help of an older agent—one who I thought was working with this country—a double agent. I asked no questions at the time. I could not afford to ask. It would not help to know. I was not sure of his allegiance. But he got us here safely. Out through Ukraine, which was dangerous enough at the time, and into Canada. Then to the US where we sought asylum."

"Did you know Yuri Starkovich well?"

"No, I did not know him well. I feared him greatly. As did most people. I think very few people knew him well. But I believe that is why Grygoriy sought me out."

"You think he wanted information about his grandfather?" asked Matthew.

"Perhaps. I believe that the book, which was in his possession, had belonged to his grandfather. That is what I suspect, yet I do not know with certainty. If I am correct, his possession of that book put him in grave danger. There are people who would go to great lengths to see it—to possess it—and particularly to keep it out of my hands. If they have Grygoriy Starkovich, then I fear that they also now have the book. At which point they have no more use for Mr. Starkovich. He is expendable, and he will be treated as such."

Matthew glanced at Danbury—which seemed to go unnoticed by Stevenson—but neither of them said anything to dispute that assumption or disrupt the professor's thought process.

"If it is what I think it to be, it has been lost for many years and presumed destroyed," continued Stevenson. He hesitated. "In the wrong hands, it is incredibly dangerous."

"Why do you think Grygoriy Starkovich has this book?" asked Matthew.

"The name, Yuri's kinsman, the request to assess an item of minor antiquity. It all makes sense."

"What's in this book?" asked Danbury. "What makes it so important?"

"Information. I believe that it is a handwritten ledger, of sorts. It includes some arcane information, compiled over many decades last century. Now that information is mostly irrelevant after the end of the Cold War."

"Then why is it still valuable? Why would anyone want it so badly now?" asked Matthew.

"Because it is said to also contain information regarding the whereabouts of religious relics of a much earlier age. Immeasurably valuable artifacts, one in particular. Treasure known only to a few and accessible currently to no one. Except possibly whoever is in possession of this book."

"Treasure?" asked Danbury. "What sort of treasure?"

"Articles that were carefully hidden to be protected from merchants and treasure seekers. One is of incalculable value—both in terms of intrinsic value and equally as much in terms of the extrinsic."

"And the KGB had possession of it?" asked Matthew.

"I don't believe so, no. But KGB very much wanted to possess it. I believe Yuri Starkovich knew of its whereabouts. Or, at least, he thought that he knew. Then he disappeared under very suspicious circumstances and was presumed dead."

"If the KGB doesn't have this treasure, then who does?" asked Matthew.

"That, my friend, is the question. The relics are said to be well hidden in a church or religious site of some sort. Many people want to know that location. Many dangerous people want to know that very thing," said the professor, but then he said no more. He closed his mouth tightly, his lips a flat line.

"Then we need to keep it out of the hands of those dangerous people," said Matthew simply. "If it's well hidden now, it should stay that way."

Stevenson opened his mouth as if to speak, but then closed it again, though not as tightly as before. The professor's lips were literally visibly loosened.

"Tell us," was all that Danbury said.

"I did not trust Grygoriy Starkovich when he called. Why should I now trust you?"

How to answer that question, pondered Matthew. There were so many of his own questions running through his mind that he didn't know where to begin. The guy's speech patterns were perhaps those of a professor, but still odd in a way. He didn't seem to like contractions, for one thing, and his language sounded formal and slightly stiff. Old school. Maybe that was due to English not being his first language.

Why wouldn't this professor of language and antiquities tell them what he knew and whatever he suspected without having to drag it all out of him? Why didn't he trust Grygoriy Starkovich? And, most importantly, why would he have reason to believe that Greg and Darya weren't still alive? The one thing he knew that the professor—presumably—didn't yet was that Greg didn't have the book in his possession.

"We're not treasure hunters," answered Matthew honestly. "We want to find missing people, not ancient hidden treasure."

"That might be one and the same thing," said Professor Stevenson.

"If there's a danger of the treasure falling into the wrong hands, I will do whatever I can to protect it. I don't want to know where it is," said Matthew, and Danbury nodded in agreement.

"You say that now. Treasure of this caliber changes people," said Stevenson. "To possess an item of such incalculable value has driven honorable men to drastically dishonorable behaviors. I have seen it happen. It is a risky venture to pursue either the treasure—or the one who knows of its location."

"And you think Grygoriy Starkovich knows where it is?" asked Matthew.

"If the book he contacted me about is what I think it is, then yes. Surely, he must know if he has the book in his possession. I have personally never seen this book. I doubt more than a handful of people ever have. Unless Grygoriy Starkovich has shared it."

"That's doubtful, if he has it and knows what it is," said Matthew, refraining from looking at Danbury. Riveting his focus squarely on the professor, he tried to keep his facial expression neutral. He'd seen Danbury do exactly that many times and Matthew knew how unreadable Danbury's face would appear in this moment without having to look at him to see it.

"The existence of this book," continued the professor, who had apparently warmed to his subject now. "It was touted by some as a legend, merely the stuff of folklore. I think Russian officials worked hard to sell that concept. As I said, the intelligence it is reported to have contained—very likely in some sort of coded system—is probably irrelevant today. But the treasure. That could be exceedingly dangerous in the wrong hands."

"Due to its value?" asked Danbury.

"Correct. The primary relic would likely be destroyed. To sell the purest gold of which it is made and the jewels that adorn it. It could not easily be sold as it is. The destruction of such an artifact would be a great loss to the religious community, worldwide, and humanity. It is irreplaceable." He paused, frowning, the lines between his bushy graying eyebrows deepening. "In the wrong hands, the proceeds from the sale of the gold and gems would fund unimaginable hostility unleashed on the rest of the world in an attempt at domination. It could fund weaponry of mass destruction that would be amassed and engaged globally."

Matthew struggled to keep his face bland as his mind was wandering. He could hear the heavily mustached antagonist in an animated cartoon clip that he saw in his imagination saying, "Muahaha! I want to take over the world!" It sounded fanciful in the extreme to his logical mind.

"But," the professor continued and then hesitated. "Removal of this relic from the cathedral, church, shrine, or religious facility—wherever it is currently located if indeed it exists—is forbidden. Touching it is strictly forbidden, except by the approved, elect priests most likely of the Eastern Orthodox Church. That too, might be legend and folklore. Legend has it that any person who touches the relic is horribly cursed. None but the holy and pure may see it, and no one must touch it. I do not know who that includes or how that is determined, but that is the legend of the cross."

"The primary relic is a cross?" asked Matthew.

"According to the legend, yes. It is said to be an enormous gold-jewel-adorned cross. It stands taller than men and requires several to move it. Many people, though, are not deterred in the least by the curse and would risk that to possess the ancient treasure."

While Matthew pondered what that could possibly look like, the professor continued, softly, "And you were correct with your assertion that the KGB is no longer a functioning agency. But it is not entirely absent. It has evolved. First, as the FSK—the Federal Counterintelligence Service of Russia—and then as the Federal Security Service of the Russian Federation, FSB. I did wonder if Grygoriy Starkovich is a member of the FSB. As such, he will have been sent here to gather information and report back to the Russian authorities."

"He's a missionary," protested Matthew. "A pastor in Ukraine. He would never be an FSB agent, or operative, or whatever you call them!"

"Perhaps you are misinformed," answered Stevenson.

6 ~ PURPOSEFULLY ALTERED

"Then enlighten us," said Danbury calmly. "If you suspect missionaries. Why is that?"

"There was no regard for the church or any value assigned to religious affairs in the Soviet Union," began Professor Stevenson.

"OK," prompted Danbury when the professor hesitated.

"But that doesn't mean that the fallen Soviet Union and Russia afterward haven't been active on the religious scene."

"How so?" asked Danbury.

"If Russian governmental leaders had any true regard for organized religion or the church, perhaps they would have been more judicious in their exploitation of it."

"Exploitation? How has the Russian government exploited organized religion?" asked Matthew.

"They have infiltrated it. That was a common tactic of the KGB, to plant agents in churches to spy. That practice continues today."

"What?" asked Matthew incredulously. "But surely not here in the United States."

"Oh yes, particularly here in the United States where churches are prevalent, as is organized religion."

"But how is that possible?" asked Matthew.

Steepling his fingers in front of him on the desk, the professor leaned forward. Staring beyond Matthew and Danbury, he looked as if he were lecturing a class.

"As recently as 2007, the international Russian Orthodox Church was integrated into the Moscow patriarchate. This created a powerful intelligence operation in the US and other Western countries that is directed from the Lubyanka headquarters in Moscow. Churches in the United States are the one place where counterespionage services have no authority. Not within religious communities. Putin has taken full advantage of this knowledge, placing agents in churches as pastors and exploiting America's religious freedom. The agents spy from the altar. This tactic also exploits the trust of religious congregations, enabling pastors who are planted there by Russia to spy on and influence the west."

"Pastors? You're telling us that there are pastors in the United States who are Russian spies?" asked Matthew dubiously, one eyebrow raised and his foot tapping as he processed this assertion.

"Exactly."

"They're still doing it? Infiltrating church communities?" asked Danbury.

"Yes, most definitely. Especially now."

"In Orthodox churches?" asked Matthew, thinking of the Greek Orthodox church in Sunny Isles.

"Certainly, but not exclusively. They can be in any denomination. Soviet spies even managed to infiltrate Muslim communities back in the 1980s."

Dumbfounded, Matthew sat staring at the professor.

"Congregants would swear their pastor is a wonderfully godly man. Usually, the pastor spies are men," Professor Stevenson clarified. "And the church members would never believe that he could be anything other than genuine. Pastor spies are well trained, theologically educated, and fully prepared for their acting roles."

"Why target churches?" asked Danbury. "What's to be gained?"

"American politicians, entrepreneurs, and political activists attend churches," answered Stevenson. "Even if it is for appearances alone. It is quite easy to build relationships with them there—both influencing their thought processes and decision-making, and garnering political and corporate favors and information from them."

"Because pastors, as a profession, are trustworthy. Both conversations and confessions are confidential," said Matthew slowly, taking it all in. "That's unbelievable!"

"I do not disagree," answered the professor. "But I assure you that it is true."

"The missionary team from Ukraine that our church sponsors was visiting churches all over the eastern United States, southeastern mainly," began Matthew. "They had a full itinerary for the two weeks they were supposed to be here. More than halfway through their trip, they added a final church to the end of their itinerary. It's a Greek Orthodox church in Sunny Isles."

"Sunny Isles?" repeated Stevenson, in alarm.

"The pastor at that church says they never made it that far, at least according to a phone call from my pastor back in North Carolina. Neither did they make it to what was supposed to have been the last church on their tour, one in Aurora Springs, on Buchanan Island. Again, according to the pastor there," added Matthew, realizing that—like most people he knew—he'd have trusted the word of pastors implicitly. But perhaps he shouldn't have.

"I would not take his word for it," began Stevenson. "The Greek Orthodox Church has been heavily infiltrated by Russians."

"Interesting," said Danbury. He paused a moment before continuing. "We mentioned a phrase to you earlier. One translated from Russian. It alarmed you. And you mentioned the KGB. Why? What's the significance of the phrase?"

"I think your translation is a bit off. May I see it? Do you have it with you?"

"A picture of it," responded Danbury. Pulling out his phone and selecting the image, he handed it to the professor.

"Properly translated," said Professor Stevenson, studying the picture closely, "it is, 'the crow caws at midnight.'"

"OK," said Danbury as the professor handed his phone back. "What does it mean?"

"It is a coded message, though thinly veiled. You would have to study crows, or ravens in your translation. Crows do not caw at midnight, except under a very limited set of circumstances. Baby crows might caw at odd hours. Otherwise, either the environment has been disrupted—say by a newly installed light or source of new noise near their nest—or it is a distress call. As a distress call, it usually means their nest has been infiltrated by a predator."

"Infiltrated. Interesting," said Danbury, rubbing the stubble on his chin with his thumb.

"It was an SOS message," said Matthew. "A distress call for help?"

"Most likely, yes," said the professor. "Where did you get that phrase?"

Matthew looked at Danbury, not sure how much they should share with the professor.

"On the scrap of paper. The one in the picture," Danbury answered. "Old, torn, and yellowed. It fell out of something Grygoriy Starkovich left behind."

"Ah, something that he did not mean to leave behind," surmised the professor. "But he understood the meaning of the phrase?"

"I wish we knew the answer to that," said Matthew.

"How old is Grygoriy Starkovich?" asked Stevenson.

"Greg? I'm not sure," answered Matthew. "I'd guess maybe midthirties. Not over forty anyway, why?"

"His grandfather disappeared mysteriously in 1991, about nine months before the end of the Cold War was declared."

"It ended on Boxing Day, December 26 of 1991," Matthew supplied. "Yuri disappeared in March of 1991?"

"Right." The professor looked at him curiously. "But that was before your time surely?"

"Barely. But I'm a big history buff," explained Matthew. "How does this pertain to Greg Starkovich's age?"

"By your estimate of his age, he would have been a small child himself when his grandfather disappeared and was believed to have been killed. If he has Yuri's book in his possession, I would wonder how he obtained it, and when. And also, how much he knows of the meaning of its contents."

"If he was coming to consult with you about it, maybe not much?" ventured Matthew.

"Good point," said Danbury, nodding agreement. "Otherwise, why consult you?"

"It is a good question," said the professor, rubbing his eyes.

Changing the subject again, Danbury asked, "Does Mt. Athos mean anything to you?"

"Mt. Athos, you say?" asked Stevenson.

"Right," Danbury answered as Matthew nodded. "An island—a peninsula, actually—in northern Greece."

"Interesting that you should ask that. I know quite a bit about it. What is it that you want to know?"

Matthew was relieved that the professor had asked what they wanted to know—and not why they wanted to know it—as Danbury carefully answered, "Anything you can tell us about it."

Returning to what Matthew had come to regard as his lecture posture, leaning forward with fingers steepled, the professor began to answer the question and continued at length.

"It is a monastic island. Greek, of course, but only by location. Like the Vatican is a papal state in Italy—likewise—it is also a self-governed entity. By its proper name, it is called the Autonomous Monastic State of the Holy Mountain, the capital city of which is Karyes. It is not minuscule by island land mass standards. It is about a hundred and thirty square miles. That is about five times the size of Manhattan, New York," the professor added, as if they would have had no concept of the size without that comparison. "When I say it is monastic, I do not mean that there is a single monastery, or that it is at all eremitic."

"Eremitic?" asked Danbury.

"It is not designed for hermits to live in solitude for contemplation. Rather, it is designed for cenobitic monasticism, or communal living. Community is stressed, and it is regulated entirely by a religious rule, a set of religious precepts, if you will. There are multiple communal monasteries on Mt. Athos, and they all participate in governance. The communities totaled nearly two thousand souls at one time, though I believe those numbers have dwindled a bit over the past ten to twenty years. That is likely at least partially due to the ban of the female gender. No women are allowed on the island, nor are female animals of any kind."

"What?" asked Matthew, intrigued. "Why?"

"This edict was made in deference to Mother Mary," explained Stevenson. "The community feared that she would be less honored by the presence of females on the peninsula. The monks' vows of celibacy are in faithfulness to the Virgin Mary. They believe that she received Mount Athos as a gift—a private garden—from Christ himself."

Matthew and Danbury exchanged a glance. Matthew's mind raced ahead to wonder about bugs. Did they control the population of bugs to prevent females of that species as well? He knew it was a ridiculous thought and his offbeat sense of humor was asserting itself. But the whole premise that there should be no females of any sort on the island struck him as equally absurd.

Adjusting his glasses, the professor continued, "Mt. Athos, as a monastic society, was founded in the tenth century by a retired Byzantine monk named Abraham from Constantinople. When he founded the community, he changed his name to Athanasius and was then referred to as St. Athanasius the Athonite."

"St. Athanasius?" Matthew asked, sliding forward in his seat. Then he parroted what Pastor Mark had explained. "But I thought St. Athanasius was a contemporary of Arius in the fourth century, not the tenth, and he was known for arguing that Jesus was equal to God, in favor of the Trinity?"

"That's right," agreed the professor—the surprise showing clearly on his face as he seemed to regard Matthew with a renewed respect. "The name was likely reassigned from that earlier saint. The first St. Athanasius is far better known for his contributions to the formation of doctrine in the early Christian church. Most people will never have heard of the second one. Why? Is that important?"

"The church in Sunny Isles," answered Danbury. "It was added late. To the missionaries' itinerary. It's St. Athanasius Orthodox Church."

"Oh!" said the professor. "There is a much stronger tie there than I had imagined."

"How so?" asked Danbury.

"Sunny Isles, as you might know, has a large Russian-born population."

Danbury and Matthew both nodded. They knew. The senator in Matthew's church had hit a wall in trying to help locate the Ukrainian missionaries for that very reason.

"Monasteries on the Mt. Athos peninsula have been heavily endowed by several Slavic countries, particularly Russia, over the centuries," explained Professor Stevenson. "With that support, in the fifteenth century, there were about forty separate monastic communities there. That number has dwindled to about half that now, and some of the community buildings on the peninsula have been damaged by fire over the years. Patronage from the tsars of Russia continued into the nineteen century, expanding the monastic buildings and their properties."

"Interesting," was all that Danbury said as he rubbed the stubble on his chin with his thumb.

"Meaning that the monasteries on St. Athos are heavily allied with Russia?" asked Matthew.

"They are. Exceedingly so," replied Stevenson. "Men are currently allowed to visit the monasteries, and some are permitted to stay for short periods of time—a couple of weeks, perhaps. I have never been there myself, but from the reports of some of those visitors, I gather that the monks regularly chant about highly political topics."

"Such as?" prodded Danbury.

"Like protection and health for Putin, who has also funded projects there."

"Oh!" said Matthew, more fully understanding why Grygoriy Starkovich wanted to talk to Professor Stevenson. The man held a wealth of valuable knowledge. They hadn't mentioned the contents or the whereabouts of the old leather-bound book and he knew it would be unwise to share that information with anyone.

Instead, Matthew asked, "What can you tell us about the monastery of Simon Peter?"

"Símonos Pétras, or the Simonopetra Monastery?" repeated

Stevenson in something other than an English dialect. "It is located on the southwestern side of the peninsula. Atop a rocky cliff about two hundred and fifty meters, or well over eight hundred feet"—he clarified for his American audience—"above the sea. Built in the twelfth century, it is one of the more picturesque and impressive monasteries, seven stories tall, I believe. It has, therefore, been heavily photographed by both visitors and the curious alike. But only from outside the peninsula, mind you. From the water mostly. Photography is banned within."

"And its affiliation? Is it heavily Russian?" asked Danbury.

"It is an Eastern Orthodox monastery, yes. Eastern Orthodoxy is currently—and has been over the centuries in which religion has been recognized—the predominant religion of the Russian populace. It is, therefore, no surprise that Russian leaders have supported the monasteries of Mt. Athos. Roughly half of the world's Eastern Orthodox Church population lives in Russia, with much of the remaining adherents of that religion in eastern Europe. It is also the majority religion in Ukraine. Is Símonos Pétras of particular interest to you?" asked Professor Stevenson.

Dodging that question, Matthew asked, "Is it one of the monasteries that you have studied much?"

"Not as much as some of the others. My specialty, you see, is antiquities and languages. The Símonos Pétras Monastery was destroyed by fire in 1891—including the ancient texts and treasure it was said to contain—and along with that my reason for desiring to study it. There are reportedly only printed books stored there now. If any were of earlier time periods—true antiquities that were moved to that location after the fire—I would be interested in studying those. Some of the surviving monasteries are known to contain ancient writings and treasures. I am more familiar with those."

"I see," said Danbury. Thanking the professor for his help, Danbury rose from his chair and handed him a business card. "In case you think of anything else, call or text. Night or day."

"Certainly," said the professor. "You'll forgive me if I do not get up to see you out. I have not one but two bad knees much in need of surgery."

"No problem," said Matthew, moving to the door and repeating Danbury's thanks. As he opened the door, he heard a shuffling noise and then retreating running footsteps. Stepping into the hallway, he saw the nearby stairwell door swish closed.

7 ~ OVERLOAD

Danbury, too, had realized that someone was outside the professor's door, and he bolted down the hallway at a full sprint in pursuit. Matthew followed in his wake and held the stairwell door open, hearing running steps above him. By the time Matthew dashed up the stairs and caught up with him—two floors above the professor's office—Danbury was coming back down the hallway. He was checking doors and peering through the tiny windows in closed classroom doors as he went.

"What happened?" asked Matthew.

"He disappeared. I saw the stairwell door closing up here. Nothing on the floor below. Nobody was on the hallway. I think he went this way. He's not in the men's room. Or in any of the rooms that weren't locked. There are classes currently in three of them. They don't look disrupted."

"He? You saw a person?"

"A glimpse. From the back. A person in baggy jeans. And a black hoodie. With the hood pulled up. I assume he was male. Or a tall, slender woman. Wearing athletic shoes. Running shoes. They squeaked when he ran on the polished floors."

Matthew knew that Danbury was highly trained—both from his years in the military and more recently as a detective—to sum up a suspect immediately. Still, he had to ask as Danbury continued checking doors down the remaining shorter end of the hallway, "Maybe we check the women's restroom?"

Danbury gave him a look and turned on his heels after checking the last door. "Good idea, Doc," he answered with a smirk. "Right behind you."

"Oh no, you're the one with the badge," Matthew insisted. "That gives you permission to enter places."

"Yeah, OK," said Danbury as they made their way back down the hallway. Hesitating outside the door only momentarily, Danbury knocked and announced himself. "Police detective Warren Danbury. Is anybody in here?"

Pushing the door open, slowly, he repeated the announcement. When there was no response, he went in. Matthew saw him pushing each of the stall doors open before shrugging and coming back out.

"Coincidence?" asked Matthew, not believing it himself. "If a student was there to see the professor, why run?"

"Exactly," said Danbury. "Whoever it was didn't want to be seen."

"I wonder how much he heard?"

"If anything," said Danbury. "That office door is solid wood. But maybe sound traveled underneath. Or above. Let's go ask the professor about that."

As they descended the two floors together, Matthew realized that Danbury, too, was still listening for stealthy movements and peering—both up the remaining two flights of stairs and down three—for any movement. Back at the professor's door—which was standing open as they'd left it—Danbury tapped again.

"Did you forget something?" asked Stevenson.

"No. Were you expecting anybody? After we left?" asked Danbury. "Another visitor or appointment?"

"Not that I am aware of. Why?"

"There was somebody outside your door when we came out," said Matthew. "He ran, so we chased, but we lost him."

"Oh," was all Stevenson said, though he looked concerned.

"Is there anyone you know of who could have been listening? Anyone asking questions or lurking around lately?"

"Not that I have noticed," answered the professor. "Though I have gotten several calls lately that I thought were merely pranks."

"Prank calls?"

"Right. I answered, but no one was there, and the line went dead after I said hello a second time."

"How soundproof is your door? From the other side of it?" asked Danbury.

"I do not honestly know," said Stevenson. "I have never been outside trying to hear inside."

"Let's test it," said Danbury as he stepped back into the hallway. "Doc, you stand where we were. Talk in a normal voice. Then do it from the professor's desk."

"Got it," said Matthew—as the door clicked closed behind Danbury—and he looked around to find the spot he'd been standing in earlier.

"It's a great day to chase people around buildings in Miami universities," said Matthew in a normal tone of voice. "It's so much fun having them run away like that and then disappear."

"What did he look like?" asked the professor.

As Matthew slipped in beside him behind his desk, he responded, "We didn't get a good look. Danbury said the person had a slender build, either a guy or a tall woman. They were wearing baggy jeans and a black hoodie with the hood pulled up."

He paused, and Danbury opened the door.

"I can hear very little," said Danbury. "Without a listening device. I hear voices. But I can't make out words. Even with my ear to the door. It's solid."

"He can't have heard much unless he had a listening device," said Matthew, joining Danbury at the door. "Either that, or he was pretty brazen."

"Why do you say that?" asked Danbury.

"Because he ran after I opened the door," said Matthew. "Would he have stuck around that long if he'd heard us thanking the professor and realized we were preparing to leave?"

"Good point, Doc," said Danbury.

"You are a doctor?" asked Stevenson from where he sat behind his desk.

Matthew nodded and said, "I'm a general practitioner in a family medical practice in Peak, North Carolina. It's a little town outside of Raleigh."

"You have a most unfortunate name, then, Dr. Paine," he said cracking the first smile they'd seen from the man.

"So I've been told many times. If you have some new material, though, I'd love to hear it."

"I am the last person to criticize a name," the professor responded.

"Oh?" asked Danbury. "Why is that?"

"Close my very solid door, and I will tell you what no one else knows. Maybe it will help you somehow to find your missing Ukrainians."

"OK," said Danbury. Closing the door quietly behind him. "Why is that?

"Because I changed my name. I Americanized it considerably."

"What was the name you were born with?" asked Matthew.

Looking furtively over his shoulder as if someone behind the wall could be listening, he filled the distance between them softly with his voice as he all but whispered, "Aleksander Stepanov. And I trust your discretion with that information. It is not known here except by the top level of administration."

"Of course," agreed Matthew, nodding, and wondering why the professor had chosen to trust them with that information, now or at all.

"One more thing," said Danbury. "Are there cameras up here? Anywhere on this hallway?"

"No, there are not."

"On the fourth floor?"

"There are none on any of the hallways."

"What about the stairwells?"

"No. A camera is mounted over the front door at the entrance to the building. And there are cameras over each of the back doors. There are none internally."

"Thanks for your help," said Danbury. "Call or text. If you think of anything else."

"Certainly," he said, dismissively before turning his focus back to the computer screen that was perched on a little table beside him.

This time, Danbury pulled the door closed softly behind them.

"That was informative," said Matthew quietly as they descended a flight of stairs and went briskly around the corner of the downstairs hallway and out the front door. He shielded his eyes from the bright sunlight. "It isn't obvious yet how it all fits. Do you think he knows more than he's saying?"

"If he doesn't, he'd be the first," answered Danbury. Matthew nodded in agreement. From working with Danbury, off and on for nearly a year, he'd learned that everyone has secrets. Most people lie about one thing or another, all omit things—purposefully or not—and many twist the truth to portray themselves in a better light. Distinguishing who was lying, and about what, was a big part of the job of a police detective. There would surely be more lies and information withheld before they were finished. That, he also knew from working alongside Danbury.

"We're heading to the Eastern Orthodox Church on Sunny Isles?" asked Matthew as they climbed into the rented Tahoe. The January Wednesday morning was sunny, and the vehicle had been parked in the middle of a paved parking lot—all of which prompted Matthew to pull off his windbreaker jacket before donning his seat belt.

"Yep," was Danbury's terse response as he climbed in and buckled up. Matthew had learned to read Danbury well enough to both expect the fewest words possible from the big detective and also to know that a short brusque response usually meant that Danbury was still processing information or some new development. Without interrupting that thought process, Matthew looked up the address and programmed it into the navigation app on his phone, plugging it into the charger and placing it in the holder on the dash.

"OK, looks like we're going out the entrance we came in, but then off to the right. Not back out onto I-95, thankfully."

"Yeah, nearly twelve klicks north and east," replied Danbury, distractedly reverting to military terminology and apparently forgetting who he was talking to. "Traffic should be lighter by now." He obviously navigated well in his head without the map, thought Matthew as he glanced at the digital display and saw that it was after ten already.

As they left the university, there were rows of houses, mostly single-storied, with lots of stucco and gating, tall palm trees and shorter thicker fronds of tropical shrubbery. The residential area was neatly organized. The houses were close together and arranged along a gridwork of streets; some of the homes backed up to canals and narrow waterways. Matthew caught glimpses of boats and docks occasionally between the houses and at the end of streets.

The conversation they'd had with Professor Stevenson—a defected KGB agent who had changed his name to Americanize it—was replaying in his mind. He'd heard things that he would never have imagined to be true and learned a plethora of information. Was it all true? Did any of it fit together at all with their missing and presumed murdered missionaries? If so, how?

Turning, he posed those questions to Danbury. "I'm on information overload from that conversation, do you think it's all true?"

"No idea, Doc. But I think he thinks it is."

"How does any of it fit together with Greg, Darya, Ross, and Ivan? Is there anything there that gets us any closer to finding them or finding out what happened to them? And why did the professor trust us with some of that information—particularly his real name?"

"I was thinking about that. All of that," answered Danbury. "Playing with the pieces. Reconstructing the conversation. Comparing bits of it. You're right. It's a lot of facts. Some of it fits together. There's no solid evidence. It doesn't get us closer yet."

"If it does fit together somehow, then there should be a pattern. A picture should form. Or a timeline, or something concrete," Matthew added in frustration. "It seems like there's something there, just out of reach. We need to figure out what it is. Something that we're missing that'll make it all make sense. How do priceless forbidden relics, monks chanting to the health of Russia's leadership in secluded ancient Eastern Orthodox monastic communities, outdated KGB secrets, and Russian spies help us at all? None of that gets us closer to finding Greg and Darya."

After a moment's pause, Matthew continued, "What about the person you chased? If we can find that person, maybe they know how the pieces fit together."

"Maybe," said Danbury, checking the mirrors for what seemed like the hundredth time since they'd pulled away. "The pieces will fit eventually. We're missing some. Probably lots of them. Let's go find some more."

"I hope it's that easy," said Matthew, turning back to the navigation app. "It's only a little over seven miles away. But that doesn't mean much down here—time-wise—does it?"

"Nobody said easy," said Danbury. "We keep asking questions. Go where the answers lead us. Then ask more questions. The usual."

"Hopefully, we can get some answers," agreed Matthew before turning the volume up on his phone for the navigation app and settling in for the trip.

"You know, Doc," began Danbury. "There is another possibility. One you don't want to discuss."

"Which is?"

"Your missionaries are behind this. Greg and Darya. Ross and Ivan knew too much. Greg cut them out. Had them killed."

"What? No way! We don't even know for certain the bodies are theirs yet."

"It's possible. You heard what the professor said. About pastor spies. It's not such a stretch. Greg's grandfather was renowned KGB."

"Assumed renowned KGB. We don't know definitively that Yuri was Greg's grandfather," argued Matthew vehemently. "The name is the same, and the professor supposed that to be true. But how common is the name Starkovich in Russia and Ukraine? Is it like Smith or Jones here? I wish I'd asked Professor Stevenson that question."

"Maybe Greg is following in Yuri's footsteps. And he was pursuing people. Or information," continued Danbury. "We have to keep an open mind."

"You can keep an open mind. I'm still struggling with the idea of pastor spies. Greg and Darya did not disappear on their own. If the murdered bodies belong to Ross and Ivan, Greg and Darya did not kill them. The missionaries, at least Greg and Darya, aren't responsible for any of this. I can't believe that Ivan and Ross are either. They're victims, and we need to keep looking until we find them alive!"

"Here's hoping, Doc," said Danbury.

"And one other thing has been bugging me," said Matthew after a few minutes.

"What's that?"

"Why make an appointment to talk to the professor about a book that had been left behind? That doesn't make much sense."

"It doesn't," Danbury agreed.

"It turned out better for them in the long run," said Matthew. "If all of this is about that book, it's better that they don't have it with them, or they'd all have been dead in Haulover Inlet. Maybe Greg feared it might put them in jeopardy and decided to leave it behind."

Danbury grunted in response—taking the next four quick turns—without further comment. That landed them on the West Dixie Highway, which Matthew found ironic because they were heading east and toward a heavily Russian population.

8 ~ RELATIVE TRUTH

"Here's how I want to play this," Danbury said, breaking the silence and interrupting Matthew's tangled thoughts. "I know you're 'Notta Cop'"—he grinned, quoting Matthew's usual objection to playing good or bad cop—"but I could use your help."

"That's why I'm here," said Matthew. "Technically, I dragged you into this one. I'll play cop if it means that we can find Greg and Darya faster and all go home."

"Understood," said Danbury. "You know more about church. A lot more."

"OK," agreed Matthew, wondering where Danbury was going with that thought.

"You're the good cop. The one with empathy. And understanding. Of the church. And of preachers."

"OK," Matthew said again.

"I'm the bad cop if need be. The antagonist or devil's advocate," said Danbury. "The skeptic. About organized religion. The church, in particular. I'll gauge the situation. Before I say much."

"No problem," said Matthew. "I'm skeptical myself about most organized religion."

"Come again?" Danbury said, his head turning sharply toward Matthew at that comment.

"There are lots of denominations that are full of rituals and traditions," explained Matthew pensively, trying to put into words what he believed as he spoke it aloud. "And that's OK if they don't put the rituals ahead of the relationship. I don't know much about the Eastern Orthodox Church, though, I'll admit."

"You go to church, right? With your family. Almost every weekend. Isn't a church a church?" asked Danbury.

"Not at all. Churches are very different, as are denominations of churches. I attend every weekend that I can, but it's an interdenominational church."

"Meaning?"

"It means we try to focus on the main thing—following Jesus—and not arguing over peripheral things that don't matter."

"What peripheral things?"

"Things like whether communion should include wine or grape juice and be served in individual tiny glasses, dipped by the bread, or sipped from a chalice. Whether the bread should be wafers or pulled or cut from a loaf. That the carpet must be red and the fixtures gold. That sort of thing. Too many people waste way too much time and energy arguing over those things and totally miss the point. I fully appreciate that my church tries to avoid arguing over things that don't matter."

"That sounds complicated. Penn wants a church wedding. At least officiated by a pastor. Not a justice of the peace. Maybe we should elope," Danbury added with a tight grin that was almost a grimace.

"I'm sure Mark will explain what the church believes when you start premarital counseling. He's agreed to marry you and Penn, but that's always his stipulation—that you meet with him together several times before he does. He wants to be sure you know what you're getting into," said Matthew with a chuckle. "When Mark Kushner marries you, you're good and married. But he probably didn't have time to talk to you about any of that before we left."

"No," said Danbury. "He didn't."

"He'll explain it all to you better than I can. But I can play good cop," Matthew reassured him, answering Danbury's initial question. "I have no problem with that. For the record, I do believe that the underlying intent of sincere believers to connect with God is the same, regardless of the denomination and most traditions."

"Good to know, Doc," said Danbury as he accelerated from yet another stoplight.

Except for directions from the navigation app, the rest of the drive was mostly quiet—with each of them lost in their own thoughts—until they pulled up to a large ornate building. It looked more like a cathedral than a church to Matthew. "Wow!" he said, taking it all in. "Who knew this was out here on the Florida coast?"

"Not me," agreed Danbury as he parked.

"Did you contact them when you got to Florida?" asked Matthew. "Do they know we're coming?"

"I didn't, and they don't," answered Danbury. "Should they have? Do we make an appointment? With a priest?"

"I don't honestly know," Matthew answered with a shrug. "Let's go find out."

As they were about to climb out, Danbury's cell phone chimed repeatedly.

"Danbury," he answered. "Uh-huh. Wow, that was fast. Tell me," he said as he pulled the phone away from his ear and tapped the speaker function.

"A priority rush was put on this test. And the result is positive for two of the specimens submitted," Matthew heard a disembodied voice report.

"Which two?" asked Danbury.

"The matches were to the samples from the two males you said were sharing a hotel room. One Rostyslav Pavelko," said the voice, stumbling over the pronunciation. "And one Ivan Domitrovich. I'll run both against the bloody tissue to determine which is which."

"That helps a lot. Thanks for letting me know," replied Danbury. "I'm way out of my jurisdiction. I appreciate it."

"Professional courtesy," said the voice. "At the request of the captain. Testing is far faster when we have limited samples to run. You provided those, so the captain asked that I share the results with you. The autopsy won't happen until tomorrow morning. I'll let you know if we find anything interesting. The manner of death looks obvious with the gunshot wounds, so I mean anything else. I wouldn't bet on it, though, given the condition of the bodies and the fact that there was nothing personal on either of them. No ID, no wallets, and nothing else at all—not even a watch or ring. And nothing identifying in the car either."

"Thank the captain for me."

"Will do. You have a good one, now."

"You too," said Danbury before clicking to disconnect.

"That was fast. That was a lab tech. I can't believe those results are back," Danbury said to Matthew.

"And the DNA of the bodies matched Ross and Ivan," summarized Matthew, frowning.

"Right," said Danbury. "We found two of them. Not how we wanted."

"True, it is what we had assumed. We were treating that as part of our working assumptions."

"Now I want to know why. And at whose hand."

"And to find Greg and Darya before they end up the same way. If they haven't already," added Matthew solemnly.

"Let's hope not. We act like they're alive. Unless we learn otherwise," said Danbury. "Hope for the best. Prepare for the worst."

"I'll call to let Mark know," said Matthew as they climbed out of the Tahoe. "After we talk to the priest or whoever is in charge of the Orthodox church," he added, realizing that he had no idea who they'd be talking to.

"His Beatitude, Metropolitan Tikhon, the current Primate of the Orthodox Church in America, presides over the meetings of the Holy Synod of Bishops. Bartholomew the First of Constantinople is the ecumenical patriarch of the Greek Orthodox Archdiocese of America," said a helpful voice behind Matthew—a little too cheerfully—that made him jump. Startled, he had been totally unaware of anyone else in the parking lot. There were a few cars—including a Maserati that Matthew had a mere moment to appreciate before the interruption—

but he'd thought it was devoid of people.

Turning, Matthew was greeted by a small, wiry man who was probably in his late fifties. His light hair was thinning, and he was sporting wire-rimmed glasses. The guy was clad in a knitted scarf, gloves, and a parka as if it were cold at nearly seventy degrees. He wore a pair of athletic shoes that looked new and spotless. Apparently, they had interrupted his morning walk when they parked at the edge of a walkway that seemed to loop the facility.

"Ah, hello," said Matthew, introducing himself.

"Good morning. I'm Stanley Strausbaum, a member of the parish council here at St. Athanasius. Pleased to meet you," he said formally, offering a gloved hand to Matthew, who shook it. The name suited the man perfectly, Matthew thought, as he introduced Danbury.

"We need to speak with whoever is in charge locally, here at this church," said Matthew as Danbury muttered something indistinguishable under his breath, apparently morphing into bad cop mode already.

"That would be the Reverend Father Grossman, our resident parish priest."

"We need to talk to him. It won't take long," said Danbury gruffly.

Undaunted, Strausbaum pushed up his parka sleeve, checked a silver watch, and said, "He's with another member of the parish council until eleven, but you can wait if you'd like."

"We'd like," said Danbury.

"Please follow me, then," said Strausbaum, turning on his heel and heading toward the building. His feet were everted—turned out—which made him resemble a duck waddling along in front of them.

Matthew was glad the guy hadn't said, "Walk this way," because he wasn't sure that he could. He chided himself for those thoughts as he followed Strausbaum to a side entrance. The guy withdrew a key card from his pocket and swiped it in front of a reader mounted beside the door, which clicked in response.

Without quacking, Strausbaum held the door and said, "There's a very comfy waiting area outside the offices."

"Thanks, that would be great," answered Matthew as they followed him into the building and down a long corridor.

As promised, the seating area was comfortably furnished. After they'd settled in and refused drinks and snacks, Stanley Strausbaum left them to finish his morning walk. Matthew pondered the intricacies of the beautifully decorated but formal church setting as he tried to remember what Strausbaum had said about the church leadership in the US. It sounded highly structured, and he wished he'd thought to ask how that compared to the denominational leadership in eastern Europe.

Their wait was shortened by the appearance of two men talking together as they walked through what Matthew determined to be one of the inner office doors. Matthew and Danbury stood as they entered the sitting area.

"Oh. I didn't know anyone was out here," said the shorter of the two men. He wore a serious, but not unfriendly, expression on his pale face. His dark hair, cut short but not buzzed, was slightly graying at the temples. Matthew placed him in his mid to late forties.

"One of your parish council members, Stanley Strausbaum, showed us in and made us comfortable," replied Matthew.

"Ah yes, Stan. I'm Father Grossman." The shorter man extended a hand, which Matthew shook as he introduced himself first and then Danbury.

"This is Victor Pavlov, a member of the parish council here."

As they shook hands all around, Matthew thought, "That rings a bell. How are your dogs?" Relegating that comment firmly to his mind, he prevented it from slipping out of his mouth. Given his own ironic name, he tried never to comment on anyone else's unfortunate one—particularly strangers he didn't know at all.

Pavlov was slightly taller than Father Grossman, and his build was compact and solid. His face was angular and chiseled. Dark eyes under heavy brows somehow managed to look down an aquiline nose at Danbury and Matthew, both of whom had at least an inch of height on the man. He looked a bit like Boris Karloff. Or maybe it was more his voice—deep and resonant—that reminded Matthew of the actor from the old movies he'd watched with his friends at Halloween as a preteen. That had been a concession on the part of his parents because he wasn't allowed to see the newer horror movies. The older ones left more to the imagination, which, in his opinion, made them scarier anyway.

"How can I help you today?" asked Father Grossman.

"We'd like to talk to you about missionaries who were due to visit here last weekend but apparently didn't make it," said Matthew.

Victor Pavlov quickly excused himself and departed.

Turning to Matthew and Danbury, Father Grossman said, "Come on in and have a seat. I'll tell you what little I know, though I'm afraid it isn't much."

After everyone was settled, Matthew said, "I know the pastor of my church, Mark Kushner, already spoke to you on the phone about the missionaries who are missing." Though two of them were technically no longer missing, Matthew thought he'd save that revelation for later in the conversation to first gauge the pastor and then his reaction to that information if need be. Danbury looked on, but he was obviously reserving comment for the "bad cop" role if he deemed it necessary.

"He did," replied Grossman. "He called to inquire about their whereabouts, and I told him they were due to have been here. But they neither arrived on schedule nor at all."

"You didn't hear from them?"

"That's right. When they weren't here, I called the contact number that I had for Grygoriy Starkovich, and I got nothing. No answer, no voicemail. Merely a recorded message that the mailbox was full."

"Did you talk to them prior to that?"

"I spoke with Grygoriy briefly after Mike Fisher connected us. They were on the way to another church at the time. Grygoriy conferred with his group and called back to accept the invitation. That was it."

"That's Pastor Mike Fisher from Aurora Springs?" asked Matthew, remembering the name he'd seen on the list of pastors on the missionaries' itinerary. Mike Fisher was the pastor of the big church with the little name if he recalled correctly. "And he contacted you about the team visiting?"

"That's him. He's north of us, the lead pastor at Aurora Springs Chapel up on the southern tip of Buchanan Island. He recommended the Starkovich team to me."

"He did? Why?"

"That's a good question. He didn't say exactly, but I assumed it was because the missionaries are from Ukraine. They speak Russian fluently, and he knew that we have a heavy Russian population down here. I didn't ask him to explain. I thought it was an excellent recommendation."

"Do you know him well?"

"Mike Fisher?" he asked. As Matthew nodded, Father Grossman answered, "I don't know him at all."

"You don't? He contacted you, out of the blue, to offer to send a group of missionaries to share their work with you?"

"That's about how it worked, yes. He said we met at a convention a couple of years ago, but I must confess that I don't remember him."

"But you did attend the convention he mentioned? A specific one?"

"Oh yes. It was a three-day interdenominational council meeting in Tampa entitled, 'The Relevant Church.' A very beneficial discussion on how churches could better work together to reach the unchurched. Florida has a growing population, but churches are permanently closing their doors at alarming rates due to diminishing attendance. It's unfortunate, but the upcoming generations think that church is irrelevant and truth is relative. So, I supposed it made sense that he'd reach out to other pastors who had attended that conference to foster that interdenominational cooperation."

"When was that?"

"It would have been," said Grossman, reaching for a keyboard off to the left of his desk and turning to the monitor. After a bit of clicking, he said, "That was Monday morning. Last Monday, the twentieth."

"And then you spoke to Greg directly?"

"After I consulted with my parish council, I did. We met quickly Tuesday afternoon and voted unanimously to bring the missionaries here. One member was particularly instrumental in that process. Victor

Pavlov, who you just met."

"Instrumental how?"

Grossman hesitated but finally responded, "Financially. He offered to pay the extra expenses. Then I spoke with Grygoriy Starkovich, as I said, very briefly."

"When was that? When you talked to Greg?"

"Tuesday evening."

"Tuesday of last week? The same day your parish council met?"

"Right. The twenty-first. I knew we didn't have long to decide if we were asking the mission team to change their plans to include us."

"Had you ever heard the name Starkovich before? Are there any members of your church with that name?" asked Matthew.

"No, I hadn't. There are no members with that name. Or any visitors, to my knowledge."

"What did you talk with Greg about?"

"When I contacted him, he explained their program and tailoring their presentation to our parish council—what they usually presented and how long that took. Then he confirmed the change in plan with his team and called me right back to say that they could be here Sunday afternoon."

"And when they didn't show up, you called him?"

"I did. And then I called Mike Fisher up in Aurora Springs because I knew they were supposed to be there before traveling down here. He told me they hadn't been there either, and he didn't seem to know why. He said the pastor in Macon, Georgia, at the church where they'd been before they were due at his, knew nothing about it. They were in Georgia as scheduled, but then they weren't at Aurora Springs."

"You talked to Mike Fisher Sunday afternoon?"

"Right."

"And he had already contacted the pastor in Macon before that?" asked Matthew.

"He told me he had, yes. It's like the missionaries disappeared. I thought maybe they'd flown home early."

"They didn't," Danbury spoke up at last. "At least, two of them are still here."

"Oh. You've located two of the team?" asked Father Grossman, looking up hopefully.

"Yeah. They got hauled out of Haulover."

"Hauled out?"

"In body bags," said Danbury.

Matthew watched the father cringe visibly, and his face drained of color, turning a pasty shade of white.

"Oh! They're deceased?" he asked.

"As doornails," said Danbury, unbothered by the incorrect metaphor.

"That's horrible!" exclaimed Father Grossman, crossing himself. "Haulover is south of here."

"We know," said Danbury. "Not far at all."

"I'm so sorry to hear that," said Grossman, looking genuinely distraught. Matthew thought the priest was sincerely sorry to hear the news, and the information came as a complete surprise to him. Could he be wrong in his assessment? Given what Professor Stevenson had explained, if he was telling the truth about pastor spies, Matthew didn't know what to believe. Was this priest a well-trained actor? A Russian FSK agent spying from the altar?

"There was an accident?" asked Grossman.

"If you call being shot an accident."

"Oh!" exclaimed the father.

"Execution-style," added Danbury for effect.

Father Grossman blanched visibly, crossing himself again, and then asked quietly, "You said two of them?"

"Right. Rostyslav Pavelko and Ivan Domitrovich," said Danbury.

"And the other two? Grygoriy and Darya Starkovich?" Grossman asked, crossing himself again. It must be a practiced and somewhat subconscious habit, thought Matthew.

"We're searching for them," answered Matthew. "Hoping to find them alive. It's why we came to talk to you. To see if you could shed any light on their whereabouts. Anything at all you could tell us that might be helpful in locating them."

"I wish I could help you, but I really know nothing about them except what Mike Fisher told me. Is there anything I can do to help?"

"Call or text," said Danbury, rising from his seat and handing a card across the golden oak desk to Father Grossman. "If you hear anything. Or remember something. Anything might help."

"You must have a huge congregation," said Matthew, motioning out to the church building beyond the office. "But somebody might know something, or maybe they heard or saw something. Please let us know if you hear of anything like that."

"Certainly. I do hope you can find them, ah—alive," added Father Grossman. Matthew nodded in complete agreement.

9 ~ NORTHWARD BOUND

"Where does that leave us?" Matthew wondered aloud as they left the church building and wandered out into the pleasant warmth of the sun.

"Headed north. To Aurora Springs," Danbury responded to the mostly rhetorical question. "Good question about the last name, Doc. We need to ask them all that question. And watch closely as they respond."

"We're driving up to Buchanan Island now?"

"Yep. We need to do this in person."

"True," said Matthew, knowing it was what they needed to do but dreading the process of getting there. Driving in Florida was painful. "That's a long drive, and we've got to come back tonight. I need to call Mark to update him on what we know so far. That conversation will be hard enough. I don't want to ask for more hotel bookings too."

"We'll plan to come back tonight. It's about six hours. Each way. Florida is a long state. You're half way home from Miami when you hit the state line."

Matthew groaned, wishing they could keep going north. Forcing his thoughts back to their purpose for being there, Matthew said, "It is odd that Pastor Fisher contacted Father Grossman—who he didn't know at all—and offered to send missionaries to talk to the leadership team."

"What was your take? You think he was telling the truth?" asked Danbury.

"I was considering that. Before Professor Stevenson told us about the pastor spies, I would have said yes. I wouldn't have questioned it. But now—I don't know what to think. But then, Stevenson could also be wrong or purposefully trying to scare us away for some reason. Maybe he's the one behind their disappearances. He seemed to be open and honest after he decided to be forthcoming with the information. But that, too, could have been a ruse—his initial reluctance to talk to us."

"All good thoughts," said Danbury as he pulled out his phone and tapped the navigation app.

"About Grossman," began Matthew. "I wonder if he's heard rumors or overheard discussions in his church that he's not sharing with us. He seemed to be withholding something. I'm not sure what it was or how important it might be."

"No doubt. He's withholding something," agreed Danbury. "Everyone always is. Pastors and priests are no different."

"We do need to talk to Mike Fisher directly. You're right. In person is far better than by phone for reading reactions. Maybe he can shed some light on things. I hope so."

"It's half past eleven now. We need lunch. A drive-through. You OK with that? To eat on the road," added Danbury, sliding his phone into the holder on the dash.

"Yeah, that works," answered Matthew. "I can help with the driving. It's a lot."

Danbury shot him a look but didn't initially respond verbally. Matthew was happy riding or driving, but he thought he'd at least offer. He well knew how much the big detective preferred to drive. It was a control thing, Matthew assumed.

"We could be there before dinner time," said Danbury. "If I'm driving."

"We could be there by dinner if either of us is driving," replied Matthew, pointing at the navigation app.

"No offense, Doc. But you drive like a granny."

"I drive like a—what?" asked Matthew indignantly.

"Like a granny. Hearses pass you."

"What are you talking about?" asked Matthew, not amused at the quip. "I'm a great driver. I've never had a speeding ticket. But then, I don't have the badge or blue lights on my cars," he added a bit more snidely than he'd intended." He took a calming breath before he continued. "And I've learned that whenever somebody prefaces something with 'no offense,' it usually means something offensive is coming next."

"Touché, Doc," said Danbury, chuckling. "Good thing you don't offend easily."

Matthew had to laugh at that. It was true—he usually didn't—but neither did he forget.

"Would we find Fisher there? At the church around dinner time?" asked Danbury, returning to the discussion of their destination and the purpose for it.

"Maybe," answered Matthew, raising an eyebrow. His foot tapped the floorboard with the rhythms that were always running through his head, one in particular now. "Lots of churches have Wednesday night services—or sometimes Bible study groups meet. I'll check."

Pulling out his phone and searching for Aurora Springs Chapel, Matthew tapped and scrolled until he found what he was looking for. "They have Monday and Thursday night Bible study groups and a Wednesday night service at seven that they call the 'Midweek Refresh.' That's the right time frame if we can catch the pastor before that service."

"OK, let's roll," said Danbury, settling back in his seat and buckling up.

After a few moments of silence—as they pulled out and began scanning for the ever-elusive drive-through fast-food restaurants—Matthew was the first to break it. "Do you believe that some invaluable sacred, and cursed relic is the reason for the murders of two young Ukrainian pastors—and the disappearance of two others?"

"I've heard stranger things. Greed is an overwhelming motivator. The professor was right about that. So are political aspirations. Power struggles. And alliances."

"Professor Stevenson said he'd seen honorable men do

dishonorable things for treasure. I wonder if he meant that in general or in pursuit of this relic in particular?"

"You'd have to ask him."

"I think I will."

After refilling the massive gas tank on the Tahoe, followed by what seemed like an interminable wait in a fast-food drive-through line—which they had discovered were much scarcer in and around Miami than in the Raleigh area—they were back on the road.

Matthew placed a couple of calls, the first to check in with his office and the second to Mark Kushner to tell him the horrible news—that the two bodies pulled from Haulover Inlet were those of Ross and Ivan.

"Oh," said Mark, sighing deeply. "That's so very sad and disheartening. It's not at all the outcome I'd hoped for." He choked a bit on the words before recovering his composure and continuing. "I suppose I'm not entirely surprised. I'll need to contact their families back in Ukraine and inform them, I suppose."

"I guess so. Nobody here has mentioned contacting Ross and Ivan's families," said Matthew, glancing questioningly at Danbury, who shook his head to confirm that assertion.

"OK, I'll handle that," answered Mark sadly. "While I'm at it, maybe someone over there will have heard from them or can offer an idea about where they could be, or at least why they aren't where they're supposed to be. I doubt it, but I'll ask. You're continuing to search for Greg and Darya?"

"Yeah, we're still searching for Greg and Darya," repeated Matthew, wishing that he'd put the call on speaker so that Danbury could have heard that part of the discussion too. "And we've learned some interesting things about the book Greg left behind and the diagrams in the back. As well as the meaning of the phrase on the little scrap of paper that fell out."

Matthew explained it all, including their discussions with both Professor Stevenson and Father Grossman. Mark was appalled at the idea of Russian spies posing as pastors in American churches. It was something he said vehemently that he'd never encountered and hoped never to.

At least not that he knew of, thought Matthew cynically. When had he become so distrustful, he wondered, and how did Danbury keep from becoming that way? Maybe it was a realistic attitude he'd acquired and not a cynical one, he rationalized.

After promising to do all he could to find Greg and Darya, Matthew ended the call with Mark. Putting his phone aside momentarily, he pulled Danbury's phone from the dash. It was already attached to the audio system in the vehicle. Matthew began to search for a specific song on the streaming service that they both subscribed to.

Usually, they listened to pop music when they traveled together. They both knew, from past road trips, that their taste in music was disparate. Matthew preferred classic rock that made Danbury cringe. Danbury's first pick was older mournful country music—something that Matthew had never found appealing. They didn't bother dickering over who listened to what and how each detested the others' choice in music anymore. It was by unspoken agreement that they opted for pop. While neither would have chosen it first, neither did either of them object to it.

Matthew knew there was a pop play list on Danbury's phone that they could agree on, and he figured he'd get back to it momentarily. Unable to resist the temptation, though, he pulled up an old surf music song first.

"If I drive like a granny, then this is you," he told Danbury as he put the phone back on the dash and tapped play. The first strains of the song about a granny driving like a maniac and terrorizing everyone on the roadways near Los Angeles, California, began to fill the vehicle.

"Good one, Doc," said Danbury as he hit the accelerator right on cue and merged onto I-95 headed north.

"You might even say 'well played,'" said Matthew, and they both laughed at his bad pun.

*****

They'd gone through the pop music play list and switched over to the streaming service as they made their way up the Florida coastline on I-95. After crossing to 295, Matthew began to see signs for various exits to Jacksonville. Switching to the radio in the SUV, he surfed the local stations looking for one they could agree on. Weather. Political news. Commercials. More commercials. Finally giving up on finding any actual music, he turned it all off and leaned back in his seat.

"Antsy, Doc?" asked Danbury.

"Bored," answered Matthew. "And antsy too. There are so many things we need to know and so many people to talk to. Time could be running out for Greg and Darya, and it takes us a whole day to get up here and back to talk to this one person. It's frustrating."

"Welcome to Florida," said Danbury sardonically.

"OK, we get off 295 in two more exits. At least, that's something," said Matthew, paying more attention to the navigation system that had announced the upcoming exit. As he said it, the traffic slowed to a crawl and then stopped altogether. "You were saying about Florida?"

Danbury grimaced as the navigation app instantly added four minutes to their arrival time.

"We should still be there in a little over half an hour," said Matthew, pondering their next stop. "You didn't say much to Father Grossman. Were you reserving your 'bad cop' in case you needed it?"

"I was," Danbury confirmed. "And you asked all the right questions."

That, thought Matthew, sounded like high praise coming from Danbury. Instead of pointing that out, he asked, "How do you want to play this one?"

"The same way," said Danbury. "You can be friendly. Ask the questions. I'll observe. Unless we need a harder line. Or if you miss something."

"OK," said Matthew, leaning back, happy to see that they were moving again, albeit slowly.

The following half hour seemed interminable. Matthew drifted into the silence of his own contemplation, wondering how the next conversation would go. As they traversed Highway 105 along the St. Johns River, he caught spectacular views of it, sometimes between houses dotted along the roadway. Up the A1A highway onto the outer islands, they crossed a river bridge and finally landed on Buchanan

Island.

A few quick turns landed them on a looping beach road that sported long, tall buildings—which called themselves villas—on the water front. Whether privately owned condominium units or vacation villas, Matthew wasn't sure. The rows of buildings looked well maintained—the lawns and gardens neatly manicured. On the right between the buildings, he caught glimpses of cabanas on the beach.

"There, up ahead on the left," said Matthew pointing at a discreet sign peeking through the tree line.

They easily found a spot to park, and Matthew looked around the mostly deserted parking lot. It was dotted with a few cars here and there. "There's a sign that says, 'Office,'" Matthew said, pointing to the side of the building. The sign was lit from above with an arrow pointing the way. Beyond the sign was a lit walkway that disappeared between two larger sections of the jutting cream-colored stucco building. "It's not six yet, but maybe the pastor is here preparing for the evening service. We can go see."

"OK," was all Danbury said as he retrieved his phone from the dash, tucking it in the pocket of his black slacks. Climbing out, Matthew's legs were stiff after having been in the same position for so long. They welcomed the brief stretch as he walked to the building.

The door, above which a larger sign read, 'Church Office,' was locked. Beside it was a helpful placard indicating a button to push that activated an intercom system.

"Hi," said Matthew to the fuzzy female voice on the other end that asked how she could help them. "We need to speak with Pastor Mike Fisher, please. I know it's nearly time for the evening service, but we won't be long, and it's important," he added.

"Is he expecting you?"

"He's not. But, as I said, it's important."

"And you are?" asked the fuzzy female voice.

Wow, thought Matthew, before answering. He'd heard that churches were being much more carefully locked and protected but this one apparently had a dragon lady protecting the pastor too.

"I'm Matthew Paine, and with me is Detective Warren Danbury," he enunciated clearly and said patiently, though he felt anything but patient in that moment. "We're from North Carolina, and we need to speak to your pastor about some missing missionaries who were due to speak here last weekend."

A soft buzzer sounded, and the door clicked, "Come on in and to your right," the disembodied voice directed. Once inside, a small unsmiling woman—who looked like she could be quite pretty were she not so serious and hiding behind huge thick eyeglasses—motioned them into a sitting area. Plush carpet sunk beneath their feet. The chairs were shiny metal frames with upholstered gray fabric seats and low backs that didn't look at all comfortable. Glass transoms framed in shiny metal rims adorned the tops of lightly gray-stained wood-grained doorways that went off in all directions. All of the doors were closed.

In the middle of the room sat an imposingly large desk that clearly belonged to the woman, who had yet to introduce herself. The dragon's lair, Matthew thought, realizing that he was punchy after the long drive. The woman, though, couldn't have looked less like a dragon. She looked more like a frightened little mouse. A large and imposing mouse house, then, he amended in his mind.

"Have a seat," she indicated the upholstered chairs that were informally arranged in a sitting area. "I'll let him know you're here." She picked up a phone, poked a button on the base, and did just that.

"He'll be out momentarily," she said to them before turning to a computer screen. In front of her was a stack of cards that looked to Matthew like information cards completed by church visitors. She soon fell into a rhythm of clicking on the keyboard, flipping a card, clicking, flipping, clicking, flipping, until Mathew found himself lulled into tapping out a similar rhythm with his foot.

Finally, a door opened, and a plump man appeared dressed casually in slacks and a three-button collared shirt. He was all smiles, his beaming face round and slightly reddened, "Come in, come in." He welcomed them heartily, shaking their hands in turn and introducing himself. "I'm Mike Fisher, but many of the members here call me 'Fish.' It's kind of an obvious joke, but I do enjoy deep sea fishing and some surf fishing whenever I get the chance."

"Thanks for taking a few minutes to talk to us," began Matthew as Fisher motioned for them to sit. The seats opposite his huge desk of glass and steel were steel framed, upholstered in cream fabric, with slightly higher backs than those in the waiting area, but no more comfortable. The office was decorated in soft tones of beige and creams, and the walls were hung with trophies of the pastor's hobby.

A lengthy swordfish was mounted high on the wall behind Fisher's desk. Beneath it—on the wall directly behind the pastor—the requisite diplomas were hung. A Florida state flag in a stand occupied one corner, and a United States flag flanked the pastor on the other side in the opposite corner.

"I know you have a service coming up that you're preparing for and we hate to bother you before that, but we really need to talk to you," apologized Matthew.

"No problem. No problem at all. I'm sorry you had to wait. I was finishing my dinner. My wife brings it in to me on Wednesday evenings so I don't have to fight my way home and back before the service."

Matthew could have sworn he'd smelled stale food odors when he walked in. Recently consumed, though, he noted, it wasn't as stale as he'd thought.

"How can I help you, gentlemen? Louise said it was important."

Louise must be the assistant who hadn't introduced herself—the dragon mouse. Matthew amused himself briefly by picturing that creature in his mind before he got down to the serious business at hand.

"We're from North Carolina," Matthew said, including Danbury with a gesture. "We need to know anything and everything you can tell us about the missionaries who were scheduled to speak here last weekend. My church sponsored Greg and Darya Starkovich and their team to come over from Ukraine, so we're trying to find them and get them home safely."

The pastor leaned forward—eyebrows knit—a deep crease forming between them. With a look of concern on his otherwise jolly face, he said, "I don't know what to tell you. They didn't show up when they were supposed to, and I have been unable to reach them by phone. I told your pastor, Mark Kushner, as much when he called to ask about them. I wish I could be of more help, but I don't know what else I can tell you.”

“Let’s talk through the timeline of what happened, in what order, and what didn’t, OK?” asked Matthew.

“Certainly. If that will help.”

“Any small thing that you can remember might help,” replied Matthew. “They were due here, as far as you knew, on Friday around lunch time, right?”

“That’s right. We had a light lunch ready for them, with the staff and some of the members of the leadership team here to greet them. Dinner was being prepared for them as well, and then they were going to present to the church congregation that evening. They were due in shortly before noon.”

“Did you know where they were coming from?”

“I knew they were coming from Georgia. Macon, I thought it was before I checked the itinerary Greg sent to confirm that. I wasn’t sure if they were coming all the way down here the night before or if they were driving down Friday morning. I wasn’t aware of those arrangements until I called the church in Macon.”

“When did you call the church in Macon?” asked Matthew.

“Shortly after one on Friday afternoon. We first thought maybe they’d hit some rough traffic or another road delay. Our staff waited patiently for an hour or so. Some of the leadership team had other commitments—several had jobs to return to—so when they weren’t here by one, I told everyone to help themselves to the luncheon, and I started calling. First, I called all of the numbers I had for the missionaries, starting with Grygoriy, then Darya, then Rostyslav and Ivan.”

“You got no answer from any of them?”

“No. None of them answered. I was sent to voicemail for all four of them. I left messages for the two I could, Ivan and Rostyslav. Grygoriy and Darya’s voice mailboxes were full.”

“And then what did you do?”

“Then I found a copy of their itinerary and called the church in Macon. I got a voice recording there too, and I left a message. I was wondering if I should locate the pastor's personal number and try him on that. As I was considering that course of action, he called me back and apologized for not picking up my call. It seems that their office is closed on Friday afternoons, and there's nobody there to answer the phone, so he filters incoming calls."

"And when he called you back, what did he tell you?" asked Matthew.

"The whole missionary team had been there—all four of them—Thursday evening. What they presented was engaging and well received by his congregation. He said they didn't spend the night with any of his church members."

"Did he tell you where they did stay?"

"Not specifically, no. Just that they were staying at a hotel somewhere along the way."

"Were they planning to get hotel rooms after they arrived here? Or were they staying with members of your church Friday night?"

"They were staying in homes, of course. Our members were very excited about hosting them. But it was a quick overnight. They were planning to get up early Saturday morning to drive south. They were meeting with the leadership of a church north of Miami."

"They were due at St. Athanasius Orthodox Church on Saturday?" asked Matthew.

"No, Sunday afternoon was my understanding."

"But they were leaving here early Saturday?"

"That was their original plan, and Grygoriy told me they weren't changing it."

"Where were they going on Saturday?"

"He didn't say."

"They were going to the Sunny Isles church on Sunday," Matthew summarized. "That was the addition to their itinerary that you initiated?"

"I helped to facilitate that, yes. When Father Grossman contacted me and asked about them, I gave him a glowing recommendation of

Grygoriy and his team. They'd been here last year, you see, and our congregation was very moved by their presentation. Spellbound, even. We have been supporting them, in a small way, ever since. Our leadership team had discussed contributing more to their ministry in this next year, and I was looking forward to telling Grygoriy about that decision. I wanted to tell them in person. I hadn't mentioned it on the phone."

Matthew pondered where to begin to question that account. Before he did, Danbury jumped in. "Father Grossman contacted you? And asked about the missionaries?"

"He did, yes."

"Out of the blue?" asked Danbury.

Matthew struggled to control his facial expression—attempting bland and neutral—refraining from glancing sideways at Danbury. He'd never had a poker face. Anyone who knew him well could read his face easily. Banking on this pastor not knowing him—and therefore not having that insight—he stared imploringly at the guy, attempting to present a mask of neutrality.

"Well, not completely," replied Fisher. "He said we'd met at a consortium a couple of years ago. After I looked him up online, I remembered him, of course. I never forget a face. I often struggle with names—and I work harder on that—but I never forget a face. He was a quiet man, rather reserved and serious as I recall."

"He asked about the Gregs' mission team? Specifically?"

Nodding his round head, Fisher answered, "He did. He said he'd heard there was a team of missionaries coming here to share about their ministry in Ukraine and he was interested in hosting them for his parish council. I confirmed that they were coming here and told him a bit about them. I supposed he was interested because his congregation is Eastern Orthodox. If I remember correctly, his church is in the middle of a large Russian population. Many of them still speak their mother tongue, or so I'm told. As do Grygoriy and his team, as I understand it."

"He contacted you?" asked Danbury again, staring intently at the pastor.

"Yes, indeed, he did," answered Fisher, bobbing his head with an affable grin.

"When was that?" asked Danbury.

"It was a Monday, I believe. Yes, I'm sure it was Monday morning, January the twentieth," Fisher answered without consulting a calendar.

That matched what Grossman had told them, thought Matthew, but Fisher was either very good with dates without having to consult a calendar, or it was a well-rehearsed response. Maybe the two pastors were working together—but to what end? Mentally, Matthew added it to the list of things to discuss with Danbury later.

"Who recommended the mission team to him if you didn't tell him? How did he hear about them coming here?" asked Matthew.

"I believe he said he'd heard about it from one of his parish council members who had been visiting up here a couple of weeks prior and attended our church. We've been announcing the mission team's arrival and reminding our members to be sure to be here for several weeks now. Not that we needed to encourage attendance after last year. Word got around. But we wanted to build the buzz to ensure a large audience for them."

"And Father Grossman contacted you to ask about them, what they presented, their schedule, that sort of thing?" clarified Matthew.

"Yes, I was most happy to connect them."

"How did you do that?" asked Danbury.

"I called Grygoriy and explained the opportunity to add one more church to their agenda. I told him we'd help in any way we could, accommodating a change in schedule here if need be."

"When was this?" asked Danbury.

"Ah, I believe it was that same day, Monday, January the twentieth."

"The second Monday they were here in the US," provided Matthew. "A little over a week ago now."

"That's right."

"How was that request received?" asked Danbury.

"By Grygoriy? Oh, very well. Eagerly, though he sounded a bit out of it."

"'Out of it,' how?" asked Danbury pointedly.

"He seemed preoccupied, distracted—probably exhausted from all the travel. They had so many stops in a very short span of time. The presentations and answering questions in English—I would imagine that's very draining. As is travel in a foreign country. He did say that he thought it was an excellent opportunity, and he had wanted to get to Miami during this trip, but he wasn't sure how to manage it. I gave him the contact information that Father Grossman had provided."

"Which of his parish council members visited here? Do you know? Did he mention that?" asked Matthew.

"Let me see now," said Fisher pensively, screwing his mouth sideways in thought. "I believe it was the name of a famous scientist or something like that, but the name escapes me now. As I said, I'm not as good with names as faces."

"Pavlov?" asked Matthew impulsively.

"Yes, I believe that's it! I do remember it after all," said the pastor, nodding enthusiastically, obviously delighted that he'd come up with the name.

"Speaking of names," said Matthew. "Have you ever heard the name Starkovich anywhere else? Other than from Greg and Darya?"

"I can't think that I have," said Fisher, all smiles.

10 ~ THE FRAUD FACTOR

Further questioning of Mike Fisher turned up nothing new or helpful. Matthew and Danbury said their goodbyes and found a waterfront restaurant on the way south to have a sit-down dinner. After ordering their meal and being served drinks, they managed more than a stilted conversation between interruptions.

"We have two pastors contradicting each other's stories," summarized Matthew. "The very serious Father Grossman and his antithesis, the charismatic and gregarious Pastor Fisher. Some discrepancies in their stories are to be expected, but others are too glaring to ignore. Both pastors pointing to the other one—as to who contacted whom about Greg's team visiting St. Athanasius Orthodox Church—tops that list."

"One of them is lying. Obviously."

"I know," said Matthew, raising an eyebrow. There was a look of anguish on his face as his foot tapped and his knee bounced under the table in concentration. "I hate to admit that about two pastors, but one of them must be lying. I can't come up with any scenario where both stories could be true. Why would either one lie about who contacted the other first? Why is that detail important? Which one is telling the truth?"

"Those are the right questions."

"Or," began Matthew, remembering his thought when they were talking to Pastor Fisher, "are they in this together? Pastor Fisher answered immediately after I asked when he'd talked to Father Grossman. He didn't look at a calendar. Is he that good with dates? Or was that a well-rehearsed answer? If they were working together, wouldn't their stories match? The dates when they said they talked to each other agree, but that's it. Is one of them trying to implicate the other? Thinking about how to prove which of them is telling the truth is getting all mixed up in my mind with why the other one isn't. I'm tending to believe Pastor Fisher, but I can't pinpoint why."

"Other than the Russian connection? At St. Athanasius. And the denomination? The Greek Orthodox Church. Maybe it's about what you're familiar with. And what you're not."

"The big interdenominational church, yes, that's familiar—but the gregarious, extremely friendly pastor, that's not. You've met Mark. He's friendly and welcoming but he's an introvert at heart. He's been my pastor since I was born, so I guess he is my gauge for these things."

"Mark might help. If he can remember exactly what Greg told him. About when Fisher made the recommendation. And how."

"Maybe Greg meant that Pastor Fisher gave a glowing recommendation after Father Grossman contacted him and then set up the contact," said Matthew, still wanting to believe the pastors and loathing the obvious fact that to believe one is to accuse the other. Their statements were so diametrically opposed, but there weren't any logical explanations otherwise.

"Maybe."

"That would mean Father Grossman is lying, and that feels equally wrong," said Matthew miserably. "What we need are concrete answers. Could either of the pastors have known about the book—that Greg had it? If that's the case, then I'd be more inclined to believe Pastor Fisher over Father Grossman, given their church backgrounds and congregations. The fact that a large proportion of Grossman's is Russian-born doesn't bode well."

After considering for a moment, Matthew added, "I think you're right about why I tend to believe Pastor Fisher over Father Grossman. My background does influence that. And the location in the back of the mysterious book that's tied to the name of the church—it all points to Father Grossman being the guilty one."

"Is he? Or is it circumstantial?" asked Danbury, rubbing his thumb across the stubble on his chin. "We need to draw them out, somehow. Both pastors."

"You're right. Doing it quickly could make the difference in finding Greg and Darya alive. But how? We can't tell them what we know," said Matthew. He thought for a moment before continuing. "And then there's the Miami discrepancy. Fisher said Greg wanted to go to Miami, but maybe that's all Greg told him."

"If Greg told him anything."

"Good point," said Matthew. "When could Greg have told him? Pastor Fisher said that Greg was trying to work Miami in. Greg contacted Professor Stevenson as soon as they started traveling and arranged to be in Miami."

"According to Stevenson," said Danbury.

"If Stevenson's story is true, Greg's plan to be in Miami didn't happen because the Sunny Isles church was added to the agenda. He'd already scheduled to meet with Stevenson before whichever pastor recommended that he go to St. Athanasius. I wonder if Professor Stevenson could shed any light on this—beginning with how to know if a pastor is a spy in disguise, a 'well-trained actor,' as he said."

"That would be hard to know. Given what he told us earlier. How well they blend in. Know their material. Know their role. And how well they act it."

"I want to ask him if there's any way to figure that out. And for clarification on his comment about honorable men doing dishonorable things—if he meant this treasure specifically or in general. We need his confirmation that Greg set the meeting with him for Saturday morning, and when he did that. While I'm at it, I'm sure he can tell me how common the last name Starkovich is in Ukraine and Russia. I need to make a list of follow-up questions for him."

"We can go back in the morning," said Danbury. "I have a few follow-up questions for him too."

"Maybe that will help us understand what happened to them—to know why Ross and Ivan were killed and to find Greg and Darya alive. We're missing some major piece of this puzzle still," Matthew added, glancing around to affirm that they were truly isolated at their corner table by the waterfront. It was dark and late for a weeknight—after seven when they'd stopped for dinner—and the turbulence in the pit of Matthew's stomach this time was partially hunger.

A heat lamp glowed from above their outside table. Feeling the chilly breeze off the water, Matthew was thankful for both it and his lightweight waterproof windbreaker. He and Danbury were the only holdouts in the outdoor seating area. Diners who were finishing their meals outside when Matthew and Danbury arrived had since trickled out of the restaurant. Newcomers were mostly at the bar, and all of them were indoors.

Lowering his voice anyway, Matthew continued, "The book, the forbidden treasure, the location on Mt. Athos—we can't outright ask if either of them know about that. It's not like one of the pastors will volunteer that information. If they know about it, then they're likely involved. Which means they're behind Greg and Darya's disappearance and the murders of Ross and Ivan."

Matthew shook his head dismally. "Pastor spies! I can't believe that's true. But it's right in front of us. Clearly. At least, one of them is lying to us. Maybe both are. There's no other plausible explanation, though I've tried to come up with one."

"We need to talk to Pavlov. Fisher pointed to him."

"Yeah, he did offer that name as the link between the churches—getting Greg's team to speak at St. Athanasius Church. After I provided the name, he jumped on it. I know I shouldn't have offered that information. That was impulsive," Matthew added, holding up a hand to prevent Danbury from saying it first. "But when he said it was the name of a scientist, I figured there was a good chance it was Pavlov."

Matthew hesitated, considering that situation before conceding, "Maybe Pavlov is the missing link. Maybe he's behind it all—or he at least has knowledge of it. We can add that to the list of things to do in the morning, assuming that we can find him. That might be a good excuse to circle back with Father Grossman anyway—to locate Pavlov. I want to go back and talk to Professor Stevenson first, though."

"Good plan." Danbury nodded. "I'll check with the locals. The guys working the murder investigation. First thing in the morning. And the evidence from the hotel room in Georgia. I'd like a second look at it. And to have you look. I'm not sure who ended up with it. My guess is Miami-Dade. Murder usually trumps origin. In a custody of evidence dispute."

Danbury checked his watch, and—as if magically—the food arrived.

Matthew blessed it and they dove in. Seafood had always been a favorite of Matthew's when it was fresh from the coast. They made fast work of their meals, declined dessert and drink refills, quickly paid their checks, and got back on the road.

The return trip south to their hotel seemed longer than the drive up—probably due to the lateness of the hour, Matthew thought—because in reality, it was faster. The traffic wasn't an issue. There were a few places where it seemed to slow, but it never stopped completely as it had on the way north.

Traveling in relative silence—the music from the streaming service turned down in the background—each of them was lost in his own thoughts. Matthew's internal struggle raged on—the new conundrum in which he found himself. Having grown up in a church, he completely trusted Mark Kushner. It had never occurred to him not to. As his pastor, the man was human but dedicated. Matthew hadn't ever questioned Mark's intentions. He was inclined, he realized, to believe Mike Fisher. The uncomfortable realization was tough to admit. It was because the Aurora Springs church was more like the one he'd grown up in than the Orthodox church with which he was far less familiar.

Confronting his own prejudice made him uncomfortable and he realized that his judgment was impaired, or at least confused, by it. On the one hand, he trusted Pastor Fisher because Aurora Springs Chapel was like his own church—in terms of being more modern and interdenominational. On the other, that awareness made him lean toward trusting Father Grossman in an attempt at fairness. Frustrated, he knew neither was the right reason and his thoughts were tangled.

Aloud, Matthew confessed, "I know I have a bias from growing up in a church that's more like one of those we visited today than the other. That makes your perception more objective than mine. What are you thinking about who's telling the truth and why either of them would lie?"

"I was hoping you knew, Doc," answered Danbury with a chuckle. "That you'd figure it out. With your church experience. I was relying on it."

After a moment, Danbury added, "I have been thinking about the why. Why they'd lie about something that seems unimportant. Like which one contacted the other. That tells me that it must be important. We'll be closer to finding your missionaries. If we can figure that out."

"Huh," said Matthew, settling back in his seat again. "The why. If one of them is a fraud, then lying already comes easily to him. Maybe it's to conceal that fact, that he's a fraud. Or maybe it's to throw suspicion on the other one to keep us from finding Greg and Darya. Or from discovering the fraud factor."

They lapsed again into silence, but Matthew's mind was far from quiet.

11 ~ WHICH IS WHICH

Arriving back at the hotel at something shortly after one in the morning, Matthew and Danbury agreed to get an early start the next day. After a quick recap of their plans for Thursday—and mumbling terse good nights—they headed for their rooms.

Matthew quickly washed his face, brushed his teeth, and happily changed into his cozy sleep pants and soft cotton T-shirt. Climbing into the center of the big king-size bed, he sunk into oblivion where time, space, light, darkness, and reality no longer existed. His consciousness seemed to shift, and the haze in his mind was clearing.

Smelling brine on the soft wind, he knew he was near the sea. Matthew's view became that of a drone floating above the ocean, looking down on it. He saw the rocky cliffs of an island that he was slowly approaching. A structure hovered there, clinging to the edge of the cliff. The building was multi-storied and brightly lit in the early morning before dawn. The sun rose blindingly from behind the building. He was facing east then, Matthew thought, but he didn't need to shade his eyes as he drew nearer and nearer to the island.

A distant bell chimed once—deep and resonant—the tone wafting on a light ocean breeze and momentarily overtaking the consistent sound of lapping waves splashing on something hard. And that note—the note of the chime. He knew that he should know it, but he struggled to remember what it was. Frustration roiled within him as he searched his mind for the name of the note. Music was his serious hobby. Naming the note should have been an immediate recollection, an obvious one. A second chime filled the salty air with an equally sonorous tone, though louder and closer this time. All thoughts of logically defining it fled his mind, along with his grip on the angst caused by that futile effort.

By the volume of the richly pitched third sounding of the bell, Matthew knew it was much closer than the first two. He was floating nearer the edge of the island when his feet landed gently on a rocky outcropping. He found himself among a group of bearded men, robed mostly in long, dark sheaths. Some were hooded, and others had dark black hats. Compelled by an unknowable force to join them, he wasn't sure where he was going as he fell in line and climbed with them on a winding stone pathway up a steep hill.

Monks, he realized they were, as he heard them chanting in perfect synchronicity, their feet tapping the ground in a unified rhythm. At first, he had no idea what they were saying. Was it Latin? Or Greek? He wasn't certain, but then he could understand the meaning, if not the words themselves. Either the voices morphed into English, or his comprehension somehow expanded. He heard and clearly understood, "Hail Mother Mary, full of grace," before the voices melded again into something more musical. Rising, the chant spiraled upward into a crescendo, then a drop beat before the pattern began again.

As they climbed, a monk in front of Matthew stopped a man who wasn't dressed as the others. "No, my friend, today's ceremony is closed to visitors, to outsiders. It happens but once a year, and it is a sacred event. The brotherhood alone will enter the holy chapel today. Come back again tomorrow."

"Outsiders?" Matthew thought as the man angrily turned around. He caught a glimpse of the man's face, and there was something familiar about it. For a fleeting moment, the expression was something that Matthew knew he should recognize but couldn't quite grasp. Was it anger? Fear? With an unsettling familiarity, the face lingered in his mind.

The man ducked his head and began sullenly making his way back down the stone steps. Though he was disturbed by the man's face, Matthew's attention shifted, and he grew more concerned because he himself was an outsider. He, too, would surely be reprimanded and turned away. He was also an imposter—not dressed as the others, not chanting, or knowing the unfamiliar rhythms, the rise and fall of the notes, the cadence.

He looked down, and shock tensed the muscles throughout his body. A relaxing relief washed through him as he realized that he was clothed in a long black robe. His face itched a bit with the beard he felt there. He looked like he belonged, though the imposter syndrome he felt was tangible. Suddenly, he had the uncontrollable urge to open his mouth. And then do what, he wondered? As he fought the prompting, it was as if a kinetic force propelled his mouth open, and sound emanated clearly from his throat. The notes and rhythm, the cadence of the chant suddenly poured forth in perfect pitch—and he understood every word.

The seemingly endless wending line of monks gathered in front of a building that he understood was a chapel. It wasn't a grand cathedral, but it was a lovely building. Or maybe that was more a soul-deep feeling of peace and tranquility that was not at all based on the appearance of the actual building in front of him.

A reverent hush fell over the crowd as the doors were opened and the monks began filing in, silent-footed on the solid flagstone floors and utterly devoid of sound. The coolness of the place—and a sense of wholeness that Matthew couldn't have described if he'd tried—washed over him. There was an understood order to how the monks filed in and who sat where that Matthew innately understood without having to be told. He filed into a row of long bench seating about midway back in the chapel on the left side of a center aisle.

At the front of the chapel was an altar and, behind it, what appeared to be a raised platform. Behind that, the vaulted wall was ornately carved with panels and arches and scrollwork that he knew each had meaning, and he understood it all in the core of his being. Six iconic carved panels flanked the sides of a pair of ornately carved doors, three on each side, under the center archway. Those, too—and their exact placement within the array of panels—had meaning that he innately grasped. Archangels on either end, St. John the Baptist, and the patron saint of the island, St. Athanasius. The panels depicting the Virgin Mary and Christ Jesus were the most ornately carved with touches of gold, and those stood on either side of the center doors.

An undertone of a hum began as six monks took their places at the front around the raised platform behind the altar. As the hum increased in volume and intensity, two of the monks stepped forward and filled censors from somewhere beside the front area and began waving them in the air above their heads. A strong smell of mingled sweet herbs and sensuous spices that were born on the smoke—incense, Matthew assumed—reached long fingers into every corner of the room. He could taste it—sweet like honey—on his lips and in his mouth and throat.

Another pair of monks stepped aside to the left and retrieved a thick pole with a handle on one end. It looked heavy as they struggled under its weight. Holding the handle steady, they inserted the other end into the side of the platform behind the altar. Two remaining monks mirrored the process in unison with another handle on the other side of the raised dais. The hum of the monk's voices continued to build until it was nearly deafening, overpowering, but fulfilling somehow as the sound enveloped Matthew entirely.

Suddenly, everything but the motion of the monks stopped, and everyone simultaneously dropped to their knees on the chilly flagstone floor. The motion wasn't organized in any tangible way that Matthew could discern but he found himself amidst the others—in perfect synchronicity—dropping to his knees, his head bowed. The floor wasn't completely level; the rock had likely been roughly hewn. It was worn smooth from years of use. The room was silent except for a loud clutching noise of metal on metal—the handles grinding cogs as they were turned beside the platform—and what sounded like creaking wood.

As curiosity overcame him, Matthew peeked from under his hood, feeling like a child at Christmas in bed awaiting Santa but unable to prevent himself from trying to catch a glimpse. In this case, it wasn't Santa he saw. The floor of the platform had split in half and opened up. From beneath it, something so shining bright that it was blinding began to emerge. Matthew couldn't make it out at first. And then he knew. Understanding filled him. It was a massive gold cross, larger than he could have imagined—covered in patterns of huge gem stones of all colors—at least twelve feet high and probably seven feet wide.

Struggling to keep his jaw closed, Matthew watched it from beneath the edge of the hood of his black robe as it rose fully into place from the platform. It caught the sunlight filtering in from windows in the rear of the chapel at exactly the right angle to make its glow blinding. The gems, catching the sunlight, shot rainbows throughout the room, painting the plain stone walls in vibrant color and permeating every crevice of the room.

In unison with the others in the room, Matthew raised his hands and face to catch a mere glimpse of the glorious sight before falling prostrate to the flagstone floor. Feeling the refreshing cool moisture seeping up through it, he realized that there had been intense heat in the fervor of the preceding moment. He felt almost feverish and drained, sweating profusely.

How long he held this posture, he couldn't tell; the experience held such intensity that there was no concept of time. The chanting had begun again, and he was one with the monks as their voices rose and fell in perfect harmonized union from their spots on the floor. Then the room instantly became completely silent, as if the assembly were one, a single heartbeat shared by a multitude of men. All ceased the chant at that precise moment. From the front of the room, Matthew could hear one of the monks chanting and another answering, one and then the other. It formed a tight intertwining of first two and then four voices, like a perfectly braided cord.

What they were saying exactly, he now couldn't understand, but he knew that they were words of praise, of affirmation and acceptance, of thankfulness. In this moment of true worship, he shivered as comprehension washed through him, tangible and compelling. The four voices dropped to two, then grew quieter, less intense, decreasing in volume until they stopped altogether. Then the creaking and squeaking began again. Matthew peeked from beneath the hood that had dropped over his face to see the enormous cross being lowered back into the platform on the floor from which it had come.

As the silence continued, Matthew rose noiselessly from his prostrate posture on the floor to his knees and then stood in unison with the assembly of monks. He was shaking, he realized, both from the cold of the floor and equally as much from the experience when suddenly he jolted. His whole body went rigid and then relaxed.

Trying to regain his bearings, Matthew found himself sprawled on his back, a sheet twisted around him, in the exact middle of a king-size bed. "I'm in Florida," he muttered aloud. "I'm in a hotel room in Florida. What was that?"

He had no idea what time it was, but he knew he wouldn't be going back to sleep anytime soon, if at all. Propping himself up in bed, he felt completely refreshed as he reached for his phone—which had been charging on the nightstand beside him. It was five in the morning, and he was wide awake, contemplating everything he'd seen, heard, and experienced. It was overwhelming and not something that he could ever explain—in mere words—to anyone.

If that was a dream, he thought, it was the most vivid dream he'd ever had—and he'd had some that were quite realistic. It wasn't merely visual and perhaps auditory, like most dreams. It was experiential, a melding of all five senses and then some that he couldn't begin to describe. It was as if there were more previously unknown senses, deeply rooted in the core of his being, that had been stimulated in some way.

Matthew wondered what he'd been doing as he attempted to untangle himself from the sheet that was no longer attached to the bed at any point. When he crawled to the bottom to retrieve the blanket, he realized that his soft cotton T-shirt and sleep pants were soaked. He'd been sweating in his sleep with the intensity of it all. Or had he been sleeping? He shivered now as his body began to cool with the evaporating moisture.

What was reality anyway, Matthew mused. One world was imagined, but both were tangible. Both he experienced deeply. The dream world and the awakening from it felt so real that it left him wondering which was which. That thought led him directly to evaluating the pastors of the two churches again. Which was telling the truth, and which was lying to them? That, he fully intended to find out, one way or another. Giving up on going back to sleep, he propped up in bed with his phone.

Where was that place, he wondered, and tapped his phone to search. He'd learned about monks on an island from Professor Stevenson, an island that was mapped out with coordinates in the back of an old leather book that had belonged to a KGB agent. Could it be? Had he seen Mt. Athos in his dream, vision, or whatever it was?

Pictures of Mt. Athos were readily available. There were pictures of various buildings, monks, and one with shelves of skulls. He had no idea what that was about, but he caught his breath in astonishment as he scrolled through the images. There were pictures of the monastic community he'd virtually visited. It was the one that Professor

Stevenson had mentioned but said he wasn't as interested in because the antiquities had burned two centuries before.

There, before him on his phone screen, were pictures of Símonos Pétras, St. Simon Peter's Monastery. It was the one positioned where the toe touched the base of the Statue of Liberty leaning sideways. The view in the pictures was exactly as he'd seen it.

He'd been to St. Simon Peter's Monastery on Mt. Athos—of the second St. Athanasius—and fully experienced it in a vision. How was that possible?

12 ~ REALITY IS OVERRATED

Matthew didn't mention his vivid dream or his online searching during his briefer-than-usual morning FaceTime conversation with Cici at six fifteen, nor did he mention it during the quick breakfast and requisite coffee with Danbury at seven. He appreciated his quiet breakfast companion because Matthew was still processing it all himself. Mulling it over and turning it in his mind like one of the gemstones he'd seen in his dream, he was examining the facets, the prisms that caught light and cast it out in every direction.

After breakfast, Matthew dragged himself back to reality and went back to his room to brush his teeth and check in with his office. Specifically, he was concerned about two patients he had been intending to see that morning. Preoccupied, he pulled up the EMR portal of his patient records on his computer, answered questions, and made comments as if he were on autopilot. His mind was elsewhere, preoccupied with the dream from the night before and the results of his online searching. Checking his incoming messages, he was satisfied with the responses he'd gotten earlier from his staff about his directives on patients. Packing his computer in his satchel and taking it with him, he met Danbury at the SUV.

After climbing into the Tahoe, Matthew returned to pensively pondering what the dream could have meant. Danbury called one of the local homicide detectives with a list of questions, including asking for an update on the autopsy of Ivan and Ross and the location and any information about the luggage they'd left behind. After being on hold for several minutes awaiting answers, he gave up and called the medical examiner's office instead.

Half listening to the conversation on Danbury's phone speaker with the medical examiner, Matthew heard that there was little new information. The ME said he would be completing the autopsies on Ivan and Ross this morning, but he didn't think that they had been killed in the car. More likely, they were placed in the vehicle afterward. He explained that was hard to know definitively because both they and the car had been submerged for several days before they were found. No bullets were found—lodged or otherwise—in the car, though, so that lent additional credence to the theory.

The ME's best guess on time of death was three days. That, though, was hard to know definitively, given the rough water and the marine life activity. It might not have been quite that long, he explained.

Partially helpful as evidence were the two bullets that had been found still lodged in the bodies—the head shots, predictably. Those shots had been fired from a relatively close range but not directly in front of either of the victims. The ME said it looked like someone had used the two men for target practice. Hearing that made Matthew cringe, and it saddened him greatly as he struggled to shift his mind to happier subjects—any other subjects were welcome at that moment.

The medical examiner announced that he had an important incoming call that he needed to take, and he abruptly ended the conversation.

Paying little attention to that abruptness and not bothering to wonder what had taken precedence, Matthew easily shifted his focus back to the dream from the night before. Because it was so unbelievably vivid—involving all his senses and a feeling of such reality that he couldn't shake—it came readily back to mind. He realized that it had never been far from the forefront of his thoughts so far that morning. There was a lingering feeling that he'd lived it, not merely dreamed it.

Could he have somehow had an out-of-body experience and been transported to Mt. Athos in his trancelike sleep? It was Mt. Athos he had visited in the night—one way or another—of that he was certain. It had felt like an out-of-body experience, a transportation of his inner being to another place and perhaps another time.

As an osteopathic physician, he hypothesized, maybe he was more likely than most doctors to entertain the notion because all parts of the body are intricately linked, and the mind and soul by extension. But, no, that was too much of a stretch for his logical scientific brain. Still, he wished he could return to the very tangible feeling of euphoria from the experience instead of his current reality. He was in Miami to try to locate missing people while they were only missing.

He reeled his mind back in to another conversation on the car speaker between Danbury and one of the detectives, trying to focus on it. They were running ballistic searches in their databases currently, he learned, comparing the patterns that were made when the bullets were fired from the gun against the patterns on ammunition retrieved from other crime scenes. That would only be helpful if there was a match— if the weapon had been used in a previous crime and bullets left behind.

If they got lucky and found that match, Matthew knew the next step would be to review the files from the earlier crime and look for any helpful connections—if they were given access to them. So far, professional courtesy had been extended. That was likely because they thought Danbury had knowledge that could help them find Ross and Ivan's killer. There was no guarantee that would hold if they began to make progress on their own.

Maybe there was a slim chance of matching the bullets to a weapon used in an earlier crime, Matthew thought hopefully. Searching through the ballistics database was necessary but likely futile. The real challenge to making any progress on locating their killer from the ballistics would be in finding a weapon to match the pattern made on the 9 mm—nine by nineteen-millimeter parabellum—bullets. Those were common, Matthew knew. They were used prevalently by both law enforcement and citizens in the private sector who owned semi-automatic handguns. Needles in haystacks, he thought, might be easier to find than a single handgun to match a bullet pattern in Miami.

Shaking his head, he tried to clear the negative cobwebs that seemed to be taking over his thoughts. Those spiders needed to move on, he decided, trying to shift his focus to the positive. The most positive thing he could think of was that because Greg didn't have the book in his possession, he and Darya might still be alive. They could be used as pawns to get the book, and Matthew surely hoped that was the case. Not that their experience in captivity would be a positive one, but maybe they could still be located and rescued. That was the positive thought he decided to cling to, though his mind was a hazy mess this morning.

"The suitcases are still at the hotel in Georgia?" he heard Danbury ask the detective.

Apparently, Matthew learned from the detectives' response, there was a chain of custody battle going on between the two states. Georgia had possession of the articles left behind by the missionaries and Florida was still fighting to gain control of those items because they had two bodies to whom the luggage had belonged.

"I'm tempted to go back up. Have another look," Danbury told the detective.

"Fine by us. Maybe you can convince those boneheads to send the physical evidence down here, where it belongs—with two of the bodies it belonged to. We haven't managed it so far," the guy said before they ended the call.

"Interesting," said Danbury after he'd clicked to disconnect. "I would like another look. I still feel like I'm missing something. Long trek, though."

"Yeah, that's another six hours, or more, up into the edge of Georgia," said Matthew, stating the obvious. "Maybe Florida will win out, and they'll transport it down here. There is something to be gained, though, but seeing it exactly as they left it."

"There is. We have things to do here first. Ready, Doc?" asked Danbury, who had tapped to pull up the navigation app, plugged his phone in, and slid it into the holder on the dash.

"Yeah, let's go talk to the professor. Hopefully, he can shed some light on lots of things. Like how common Starkovich is, how to tell which pastor is telling the truth, and if the dishonorable things he's seen men do was specific to this treasure. It sounded pointed."

"It did sound ominous. Like a warning."

"It was the way he said it," agreed Matthew. "If he was talking about this treasure, specifically, then he likely meant it exactly that way. And he did warn us directly to go home and leave this alone."

They both knew that neither of them had any inclination to heed that warning.

Buckling up quickly, Danbury nodded before taking off. Because they'd been to the university before, Matthew's assistance with upcoming traffic shifts wasn't needed, and the trip was silent except for the navigation app giving orders. So lost was he in his own thoughts about his disturbing dream the night before that Matthew hadn't bothered to wonder what was on Danbury's mind until he spoke.

"Did Grossman send Pavlov? To the church in Aurora Springs. Maybe they were trying to bring Greg to Miami. If they knew about him. First, we need to verify that story. That Pavlov went to Aurora Springs."

"I hate having to check pastor's stories. It's not something I've ever considered doing before."

"They're just people," began Danbury, but then grew silent as he'd turned into the parking lot and stared straight ahead at the campus building. The front sidewalk was corded off with police tape. A familiar white van with lettering that read MIAMI-DADE MEDICAL EXAMINER down the side was parked in front of the main entrance. As they watched, two people dressed in white suits were maneuvering a stretcher from the back, onto the sidewalk, and up to the entrance of the building.

"This must be the urgent call. The one the ME had to take. When we were on the phone this morning," said Danbury.

"Now what?" wondered Matthew aloud as Danbury pulled into a spot and barely had the vehicle in park when he grabbed his phone, jumped out, and strode purposefully toward an officer by the sidewalk. Matthew followed. Danbury flashed his badge, identifying himself, and the officer got on the radio with someone inside the building before he would answer any questions. Somebody must have cleared them because they were told that a professor was found dead in his office early this morning—obviously murdered.

They wouldn't be asking Professor Stevenson anything today or any other day, Matthew realized in horror, as the police officer identified the victim to them.

"We met with him yesterday. Here in his office," said Danbury. "We came back with more questions."

"You were here yesterday?" asked the officer. "Here at the school?"

"Right," said Danbury. "Yesterday morning."

"Hang on," replied the officer, speaking into the device again and explaining that scenario to someone on the other end. "Go on up." The officer held the police tape aloft for them to duck under. "They're in the professor's office. Apparently, you know where it is."

Danbury nodded in response. Dashing into the building, they took the stairs two at a time up to the second floor. The hallway outside of the professor's office appeared to be organized chaos. Or maybe it was pure chaos, Matthew amended his thought process. Uniformed officers were at either end of the hallway.

One officer was tapping on a tablet while talking to two people who were hovering uncomfortably near the elevator—interviewing them—Matthew assumed. The two people they'd seen suit up in the white jumpsuits were maneuvering a stretcher into the office as a woman clad in a black pantsuit dodged them to come out. She carefully placed the lens cap on a camera and put it gently into the bag she carried.

"Yes, ma'am," said a guy in gray slacks and a worn beige sports jacket from where he was pacing the hallway with a phone to his ear. "OK, will do." As he put the phone in his pocket, he turned his attention to the woman with the camera.

"You got everything you wanted?" he asked.

"Until they remove the body. From a distance, of course. I did not contaminate the scene," replied the woman, seeming to anticipate the next question. She was tall in flat black shoes—probably five foot ten—Matthew estimated. Likely in her early thirties and close to his own age, she was also very attractive. Her piercingly dark eyes bore into the man as she answered him. A long dark ponytail swung behind her as she finished stowing the camera and leaned against the wall opposite Stevenson's office to wait.

"Of course. Thanks," the man—whose short-cropped hair and no-nonsense expression screamed plainclothes officer of some description—answered somewhat absently.

Danbury chose that moment to step forward and introduce himself and Matthew to the guy. "We've spoken on the phone," said Danbury.

"A couple of times."

"Ah, the detective from North Carolina. The one the captain told us to work with," the guy said rather pointedly, sizing Danbury up. "I'm Sergeant Rhodes."

Rhodes must have decided they passed whatever tests he was running them through in his mind as he reached out to shake their hands, "Good to meet you in person. I'd ask how I can help you, but I think it's the other way 'round, isn't it?"

"Maybe so," said Danbury. "We were here yesterday morning. Talking to Professor Stevenson."

"Other than the style of murder, tell me how this one ties in with the two men we pulled from Haulover."

"That's a longer story. What's the deal with this one?"

"Same MO. Triple tapped, one right between the eyes, two to the chest, medium range."

"As in, from within the office? But not directly in front of Stevenson?" asked Danbury.

"That's what we think so far. The ME will be able to tell us more after the autopsy. He's being tight-lipped about the TOD, though."

The time of death couldn't be more than twenty-four hours, Matthew thought, as Danbury said exactly that.

"Less than twenty-four," said Danbury, checking his watch briefly. "We were talking to him yesterday. About this same time."

"Maybe we can help narrow that down," offered Matthew. "At least whether he's been here all night. What do his clothes look like? Yesterday morning, he had on a dark beige cable knit cardigan sweater over a rumpled collared shirt that was a lighter cream shade with some sort of beige and green sprigged pattern. Tiny leaves or something. Brown pants—wide corduroy—and dark brown loafers, dark socks."

Rhodes' jaw dropped slightly at the precision of the statement, and Matthew caught Danbury's smirk out of the corner of his eye.

Rhodes replied, "Ah, the sweater is the same. I can check the rest. You can't see much of the front of the shirt as it is."

Matthew cringed imagining the scene within the office, feeling some level of responsibility for the professor's death, and wondering if the guy in the black hoodie had returned after they'd left the day before.

"He was draped over his desk," Rhodes clarified. "They're getting ready to transport him now.

"When was he found? And by whom?" asked Danbury.

"Five this morning. By a member of the cleaning crew," answered Rhodes. He apparently was growing impatient with the questions and answers all going one direction. "Now, care to explain why you were here yesterday morning and how this is connected to the other murders you came down to investigate?"

"We didn't know that it was. Until now. Seems likely, though," answered Danbury, rubbing his chin and the edge of his square jawline, which was devoid of stubble this early in the day, with his thumb.

"My team has worked with you, Detective Danbury, including you in our dissemination of information on this investigation. Your turn. What did Stevenson tell you?"

Clearly, Danbury had decided that it was time to explain at least some of what they knew.

"He shared his suspicions. We found Stevenson's contact information back home. Left behind by Grygoriy Starkovich. We assume. Probably not purposefully. We got it from a notepad. The second page. Under one that Greg had written on. We weren't sure it was important. We met with Stevenson. He confirmed that Grygoriy Starkovich had contacted him."

"What did he tell you about Grygoriy Starkovich?"

"He said that Greg set up a meeting. Then didn't show."

"But he did tell you something important," insisted Rhodes almost accusingly. "What were his suspicions that you mentioned?"

Apparently, thought Matthew, they could read each other's expressions. It must be some sort of cop-to-cop thing because he'd never learned to read Danbury's face when he was in "cop mode."

"It was about an old book. Greg wanted to talk to him about it. Told Stevenson it had belonged to a family member. He didn't see the book. Obviously. But the professor thought he knew what it was. Given that information. And Greg's last name. I think he was right."

"And what was it about?" prodded Rhodes.

"Stevenson told us about Greg's grandfather. Who he believed him to be. Yuri Starkovich. Stevenson thought the book had been his. Yuri was KGB during the Cold War. Known to be ruthless. He disappeared mysteriously. And was presumed dead. He was rumored to have had a book. One where he logged tactical secrets. About the Cold War. It was highly sought after. But those secrets would be useless now. At least according to Professor Stevenson."

"Then why kill the professor over it if the book isn't of any value anymore? Did Greg know something he shouldn't have known?" asked Rhodes.

"We don't know. Greg had to have known what the book was. Maybe not precisely. It was all in Russian. But probably still cryptic."

"Could the younger Mr. Starkovich read it?"

"Yes," answered Matthew. "He's fluent in Russian—as well as the Ukrainian language—and he speaks nearly flawless English."

"Then we can assume that he knew what he had," argued Rhodes. "But again, why is that important now if it was full of Cold War secrets and tactics?"

"The professor said it's a myth. The book's existence is a legend," said Danbury carefully. "He said nobody has seen it. But it's also rumored to have other information. Not about the Cold War."

Matthew watched Danbury's face, trying to read it like the sergeant had, as Danbury tiptoed around admitting their direct knowledge of the book. When Rhodes prodded with more questions and wasn't backing down on knowing the rest of the story, Danbury added, "It's said to contain valuable information. About ancient relics. Hidden. Forbidden to be found. Or touched. Or moved. He said the treasure carries a curse. Again, all legend. According to Professor Stevenson."

"And this book has information about the whereabouts of those ancient relics?"

"That's what he said," answered Danbury.

"That's motive for murder," said Rhodes.

"If the treasure exists," Matthew took up the explanation. "These artifacts are supposed to be beyond calculable value—accessible only by select members of the clergy of the Eastern Orthodox Church—and forbidden to everyone else. The book is said to contain information about the location of them."

Matthew paused there, unwilling to disclose the fact that they'd seen the book or that they knew its whereabouts. His mind whirled with the vividness of the dream juxtaposed with the reality of their current situation.

If the two missionaries and the professor were all killed to find the location of this treasure, Matthew reasoned—and he and Danbury thought they knew the location—then the more people who knew, the less likely the killer was to pursue a select few people. He tapped his foot in concentration. But—on the flip side of that logic—if the kidnapper and killer learned the location, then Greg and Darya were as good as dead. They would be of no further use to their captor. Matthew stopped talking.

"People have murdered for far less than treasure beyond value, cursed or not," said Rhodes.

"The professor was worried," added Danbury. "About it falling into the wrong hands. He said the gold would be melted down. And then sold. The proceeds would be used to wreak havoc. He mentioned weaponry. And worldwide domination. An attempt at that."

"And now he's dead," said Rhodes slowly. "But he didn't know where the treasure was—if it even existed—or if Grygoriy Starkovich knew where it was, right?"

"That's what he told us," answered Danbury.

"And he didn't know where this book is either, right?"

"He wasn't certain of its existence," answered Matthew, tiptoeing as Danbury had around the real issue before the sergeant could rephrase the question more directly. "He said the book was a legend, a story that he thought some people had worked hard to squash when Yuri Starkovich disappeared. Maybe they thought Yuri had hidden it instead of destroying it before he disappeared. Professor Stevenson didn't elaborate on that point."

"And the treasure? Did Yuri have that at any point?"

"That, I don't know," answered Danbury. "The professor said not. If he was to be believed."

"I see," Rhodes said pensively. "Why don't you come have a look, if you don't mind? As soon as they remove the body. See if there's anything missing in his office, that sort of thing."

Matthew resisted the temptation to laugh aloud at that request. Given the circumstances, laughter would be a wonderful release from the tension, but he thought it highly inappropriate. From what he remembered of the office, nobody—other than perhaps Professor Stevenson himself—would be able to tell if anything was missing or out of place. The office had been stacked with papers, heaps of detritus from decades of collection by its occupant. There was nothing that appeared to be organized about any of it and to know if something was missing was beyond imagination.

"We can have a look," said Danbury.

"I'll be right back," said Rhodes, disappearing through the doorway into the office.

"Good luck with that," said the woman with the camera without looking up. She was still leaning against the wall but with her phone out now, tapping away at it.

"Pardon?" asked Matthew, turning to her.

"I uploaded the pictures of the office to sift through them. It's a disaster. Somebody must have tossed it properly," she said, flipping her phone around so that Matthew and Danbury could see one of the pictures.

"Actually," said Matthew. "It looked a lot like that when we were here yesterday."

"Oh!" she said. "Oh wow."

From the doorway, Sergeant Rhodes motioned them in as the stretcher was being wheeled out with the black body bag zipped up tightly.

"The clothes are as you described," said the sergeant as they entered. "Unless he regularly sleeps in his office or doesn't change his clothes, he's been here all night." He looked at Matthew. "Nice observation."

Dipping his head in acknowledgment, Matthew replied, "I noticed because I thought he looked exactly like a professor should. The attire, the glasses, the messy hair, the whole package."

"Have a look around and tell me what you see. Or don't see," added Rhodes, handing them each a pair of gloves.

Snapping them into place, Matthew looked around and then went to the one place where he thought he might be able to tell if something was different. The desk blotter was soaked in darkened blood, and that tore at Matthew's heart.

Being in the business of improving and saving lives, he still wasn't used to being on the scene when one had been ruthlessly taken. He hoped never to get used to it. That was a big reason why he'd opted out of the emergency department, where he initially thought he wanted to work. He wanted to make a difference for good, but there was so much bad in the world in the way of that lofty goal.

"Hey, Danbury! Look at this," Matthew called, and Rhodes strode purposefully across the room to get there first.

13 ~ CRYPTIC MESSAGES

"Yeah, I see," said Danbury, rubbing his chin as Matthew pointed down to some familiar-looking characters scribbled on Stevenson's desk blotter.

"We noticed that," said Rhodes. "It's in blue ink. Most of the notes that we can still see on the blotter are in black. Professor Stevenson was clutching a blue gel pen in his hand when he died. The color matches whatever this is. He was probably writing it when he was shot. But it doesn't make any sense. Does it mean anything to you?"

"I think it's a distress call," replied Matthew, glancing at Danbury, who nodded his agreement.

"Why do you say that?" asked Rhodes pointedly.

"There was a scrap of paper that fell out of some of Grygoriy Starkovich's things. Not something he meant to leave behind, we're guessing," answered Matthew. "And this looks like the beginning of what was written on that paper."

"You found it in the hotel room?" Rhodes asked Danbury accusingly.

"No, at my church in North Carolina," Matthew defended him. "It's a sort of home base for the mission teams when they're in the United States."

Pulling off his gloves and laying them carefully on the edge of the desk, Matthew retrieved his phone from his pocket and selected the picture of the scrap of yellowed paper. "Here," he said, showing it to Rhodes.

"Can you send me that?"

Matthew looked at Danbury, who nodded. "Sure," he replied. Rhodes called out his contact number, and Matthew tapped it in.

"Now, tell me everything you know about it, starting with what it means."

"It's Russian," answered Danbury. "We got a rough translation. Professor Stevenson clarified it."

"Stevenson was aware of it," began Rhodes, and paused.

"He was," answered Danbury.

"This is most of it," said Matthew, pointing to the professor's scribbled note. "But, in its entirety, it's something like, 'the crow caws at midnight.' Stevenson thought that it was a lightly coded distress call. Maybe one Yuri Starkovich—who he thinks was Greg's KGB grandfather—left. But that's pure speculation."

"Huh," said Rhodes. "Maybe the killer can't read Russian. Otherwise, why leave it behind as evidence?"

"Maybe he didn't care because the distress is obvious," said Matthew. "But it's in Russian. I would think that the killer wouldn't want anyone to see it if it's connected. If it is, it might provide insight into who shot the professor and why."

"What I was thinking," said Danbury.

"Maybe he didn't see it," said Matthew. "How was the professor's body positioned?"

"Good point," said Rhodes. He looked out into the hallway. "Kelsey!"

"Yeah, Sarge?" said the woman with the camera, appearing in the doorway.

"Can you send me the shots of the body? Anything that shows how it was positioned on the desk and what was visible around it when the professor was found."

"Sure, I transferred a few pictures to my phone. Here you go," she said, tapping it.

Shortly, they heard a ding, and Rhodes tapped his phone to open the message.

"You're right," he confirmed after expanding the view and studying the screen. "It's a wonder this part wasn't soaked with blood too. The message was likely meant for you because the professor knew you'd understand it. Unless somebody else knows about it?"

"I don't know," said Danbury. "But we need to find out. Who the professor was closest to. Family nearby? Close friends?"

"We're checking into his background to notify his next of kin," said Rhodes. "Unless the university is planning to handle that."

"Let me know?" asked Danbury. "If you find anything interesting."

"Yeah," Rhodes answered, nodding and tapping his phone. "I have your contact information. When we know, you'll know."

"Thanks."

"Why would Stevenson think we'd come back, though? Or find out that he'd been murdered?" asked Matthew, then postulated answers to his own questions before anyone else could answer. "Maybe he knew we'd still have questions. Or there's something he still didn't tell us and he knew we'd figure that out eventually and come back to ask him about it."

"We don't know who Stevenson talked to. After we left yesterday," said Danbury. "Or what they might know about the scrap of paper. Or speculation about the book."

"Or who else might already know about either or both of those things," added Matthew.

"We're having his computer searched and getting his phone records," said Rhodes. "I'll have them concentrate on the past twenty-four hours. If he told anybody else—by phone, online message, or note—at least we'll know who and exactly when. Then there are your missionaries. Clearly, they know all about it, and their whereabouts are currently unknown."

"The professor mentioned a family, a wife and two daughters who he brought to the United States seeking asylum when he got on the wrong side of the KGB in Russia," said Matthew, ignoring the comment accusing Greg and Darya. "When they're found and notified, maybe they can shed more light on this."

"I don't know," answered the sergeant. "We've asked the university who was listed as Stevenson's next of kin and if there's an emergency contact that he provided. They were supposed to get back to us with that information. Nobody has been notified yet that I know of. But let me circle back with that contact from the school, put some pressure on, and see what I can find out."

While Rhodes made the call to an official for the university, Matthew wandered over to the window and peered out at the commotion on the sidewalk and in the parking lot below. A crowd had gathered beyond the police tape. They were probably mostly faculty, staff, and students, Matthew surmised. As he watched, a news truck pulled into the back of the parking lot and made its way to the front of the building.

A quick movement under the edge of a palm frond caught his attention. "Danbury," he said, pulling his phone out as he began snapping pictures. "Look, there's a slender figure in baggy jeans and a black hoodie. There. Behind that palm plant." Stepping back from the window, he pointed.

"Seriously?" said Danbury, sounding annoyed and appearing at Matthew's elbow to look. "He got away from me once. Not this time. Where are the back doors? Stevenson told us there were two."

"There's a back door at both ends of the hallway downstairs," said Rhodes, who apparently was on hold and pacing the length of the small office with his phone to his ear. "My team checked that they were locked when we got here."

"Can I get around the building? From back there?"

"You can, but," began Rhodes before Danbury interrupted him.

"Doc, watch him. Let me know if he moves," Danbury announced before bolting from the room. The door at the top of the stairwell whooshed and then clicked shut behind him.

"On it," said Matthew to the empty space where Danbury had been standing. Sergeant Rhodes began to ply him with questions from behind.

"When did he get away from you? Are you sure it's the same person?"

"Yesterday morning," answered Matthew over his shoulder while watching out the window. "Somebody dressed like that was outside this door when we came out from talking to Professor Stevenson. Even with Danbury's quick pursuit, the person got away. I'm not sure if it's the same person, but the slender body build is right and they're dressed the same."

"Yes," said Rhodes into his phone. "That's what I was asking. Correct."

From the window, Matthew could barely see the edge of the hooded figure behind the palm plant. After watching for a few minutes, he saw Danbury slip around behind the crowd, working his way toward the hooded figure. It's not as if he were exactly incognito, thought Matthew. At an inch or more taller than Matthew's six-foot-three frame, Danbury towered over most of the people in the crowd. But he was stealthy, and the black hood that protected the lone figure's face from being seen also prevented him from seeing Danbury's approach in his peripheral vision.

"Oh, I see," said Rhodes into the phone. "And she's where? OK, yes, please let me know."

Danbury had nearly reached the figure when the guy turned, spotted him, and bolted toward the other end of the building. Danbury must have announced himself as a police officer as he began pursuit because several people around him turned in obvious surprise, one of them jumping backward in alarm and directly into his path.

What happened next looked like a carefully choreographed dance. Danbury jumped to one side—narrowly missing a direct collision with the woman who had stepped into his path—but then he had to catch her. The woman twisted and—while trying to get her footing—lost her balance completely and nearly fell in front of him. Multiple thoughts ran through Matthew's mind as he watched. The big detective was much more agile on his feet than he appeared. He had been a star quarterback in high school, so maybe that's where the ability came from.

The woman's face, which Matthew could now see from his window spot above, was one of complete shock. Danbury set her back on her feet and dashed off, chasing the slender figure that had since disappeared around the corner of the building and out of sight. One of the police officers who'd been posted at the front door took off running behind them. There was no need to tell Danbury which way the figure had fled, Matthew thought sardonically. He'd seen it all up close and personal.

Pulling up the pictures he'd snapped on his phone of the hooded person, he zoomed in. The face was always obscured as the slender hooded figure got bigger. He had hoped to get at least the side of the face or something more to go on. Disappointed, he put the phone back in his pocket.

"Professor Stevenson's wife is deceased," said Rhodes.

"How did she die?" asked Matthew. "Did they say?"

"They said that she was killed in a car accident nearly two years ago. I vaguely remember that indecent, now that I think about it. It was a single-car accident that was never fully explained, but my team was called to the scene. I wasn't directly involved, but I'm pretty sure it was chalked up to her having a stroke or passing out at the wheel. There were no skid marks before she slid off the road in a curve. The report said she bounced off of a guard rail, then rolled down a steep embankment on the other side of the road into a creek or ditch or something."

"Oh," said Matthew. "Is there anyone else who should be notified?"

"The school is trying to find contact information for his daughters. One lives in Denver, according to his emergency contact information—but the phone number is old and out of service—and they're not sure about the other one." Rhodes scratched his head pensively before adding, "Now I need to hear exactly what happened in this office yesterday morning. All of it, in detail. Leave nothing out."

"OK," Matthew said with a sighing breath, giving up on holding anything out as he was being directly questioned by a police officer. As Rhodes plied him with question after question, Matthew told him about the entire encounter exactly as it had happened. Because they hadn't told the professor that Greg didn't have the book and that they did, Matthew didn't feel the need to share that information with the sergeant. He concluded, explaining his recollection as Danbury reappeared. The look on his face said he'd missed catching the guy yet again.

"No luck?" asked the sergeant, though Matthew wouldn't have bothered to ask.

"No," said Danbury between gritted teeth.

"I saw your dance down there," said Matthew, trying to lighten the mood. "You're pretty light on your feet."

Danbury grunted, ignoring Matthew's attempt at levity as he looked around the office like they might have missed something.

"You have no idea who that person was?" asked Rhodes.

"None," responded Danbury. "I've never gotten a look at his face. If it's the same person."

"Which seems more likely since he ran again," added Matthew.

Rhodes paced the length of the room repeatedly, and Matthew figured he was another type A personality who couldn't be still and think properly. "It could have been the killer. Watching the scene to see the result of his handiwork," said Rhodes. "But he got awfully close for that to be the case."

"Yes and no," said Danbury. "He was well concealed. But not likely the killer. It's not a coincidence. His presence here again today. Somebody is interested. Curious, for some reason."

"Wanting to know what the professor knows?" asked Matthew. "Or what we know? There was a hooded figure when Pastor Mark and I went to the storage room." He'd purposefully not mention why they were in the storage room or what it was that they were doing there.

"I was thinking that too. Maybe he wasn't following the professor. He might be following us. And we led him to the professor."

"What storage room?" asked Rhodes.

"One the mission teams use in my church building back home in North Carolina," answered Matthew, neglecting to explain further. "We saw someone similarly dressed dart out of the church building before we came down here. But I didn't get a good look then either. It was a shadow in a hallway that I caught in my peripheral vision."

Turning to Danbury, an eyebrow raised and foot tapping in

concentration, Matthew added, "I'm sure you've considered this, but if we're being followed, this person might not be the only one. The timing of us asking the professor questions and him immediately being murdered is too much of a coincidence. The guy in the black hood could be the killer, and he's been following us. If he isn't the killer, could the killer also have been following us?"

"Either is possible," said Danbury. "I haven't seen a tail. Not while we've been driving around."

"Have you been able to watch for one down here in this traffic?"

"Good point, Doc," admitted Danbury.

"Do you two need police protection?" asked the sergeant with a smirk.

"I have my own," said Danbury, indicating the gun strapped to his waist under his shirt.

"And the license to carry it," said Rhodes pensively. "And you?" he asked Matthew.

"I don't. I mean, not with me. I have two handguns at home and the concealed-carry license in North Carolina. The license is with the guns in a lock box. But I flew down, and I didn't bring them."

"You might want to fix that," said Rhodes.

"Do you have any recommendations on where to go? I'll have to get my paperwork sent. It transfers to Florida."

"Yeah, I know a guy. I've got your contact information. I'll send you his name and number. He should be able to contact your NC Sheriff's office and get the permit validated," said Rhodes.

"Thanks," said Matthew.

"There are no security cameras," said Danbury. "Not in the hallways. Or in stairwells." He looked at Rhodes, who was wandering back out in the hallway to consult with the woman he'd called Kelsey and two uniformed officers outside the door. "Let us know if you see anything from the cameras over the outside doors."

"Do you think there's anything else to learn here?" Matthew asked Danbury.

"Nothing jumps out at me. In looking around. If it weren't so messy," Danbury began and trailed off as his gaze methodically took in the office, section by section.

"Yeah, it'd be a lot more obvious if something were out of place or missing," Matthew finished the thought for him. "OK, so what now?"

"Back to Sunny Isles. Let's talk to Grossman again. That was next, anyway. Then track down Pavlov. See what he can tell us."

"With no help from Professor Stevenson," added Matthew sadly.

"Maybe we don't need him. Lies are hard to maintain over time. When questioned repeatedly about them. They lead to more lies. This conversation will be different. Confrontational. We need to catch Grossman in the details. Twisting a fact. Something we know. We don't know much definitively. But enough to test him."

"That's an interesting plan. Like what?" asked Matthew.

"We have no crime scene. Not for the missionaries. But we do for the professor. We have a conflicting story. We'll start there. Get him to defend his. That Fisher contacted him. And not the other way around. Speak up, Doc. If you have any thoughts. On how to go about that."

"OK," said Matthew, who had slipped behind the professor's desk. "I know Rhodes promised us access to photos of the scene, but I want my own picture of the scrawled message and what's visible around the edges of the rest of the desk blotter. The professor seemed to have used it as both a notepad and a calendar. Maybe there's something here that'll be helpful." He hoped so. They needed information, and they needed it yesterday, he thought.

"Good idea, Doc. Nothing I saw there meant anything. Not yet. But maybe it will. Let's check in with Rhodes on the way out," Danbury said, indicating the sergeant pacing the end of the hallway, deep in a conversation on his phone.

As they approached, Sergeant Rhodes finished his call and turned to them. "What's next for you?" he asked.

"We're going to go back and talk to a pastor—Reverend Father Grossman—at the Eastern Orthodox Church. It's St. Athanasius, over in Sunny Isles," answered Matthew.

"The church that the Starkovich team never made it to?" asked the sergeant.

"One of them," said Danbury. "There's a discrepancy in stories. Between Grossman and another pastor. Both claim they were contacted. By the other pastor. About Greg and Darya visiting Sunny Isles."

"Ah. Should I sit in on any of that? Or send an officer with you?" asked the sergeant.

"I don't know yet," answered Danbury. "Not sure there's anything to learn. I'll let you know if we do. There's a member of the parish council. A guy by the name of Pavlov. We want to talk to him. Fisher indicated a connection involving him. Fisher is the pastor at Aurora Springs. It's a large church on the southern tip of Buchanan Island. He's the pastor who says Grossman contacted him. He said Pavlov visited there. And then recommended the missionaries to Grossman. And then Grossman contacted him. Grossman says that Fisher contacted him. Out of the blue. Both stories can't be true."

"How are you planning to figure out which is true?" asked Sergeant Rhodes.

"We're working on that. We're hoping to trip him up. Demand details. Expose inconsistencies in his story. Or the timeline. We're open to ideas. If you have any. Maybe talking to Pavlov will help. If he admits to being at the church in Aurora Springs. And if he told Grossman about it."

"Sounds like a long shot," said Rhodes. "And I can't spare the manpower right now anyway. Keep me posted, though, if you get anything useful. Keep me in the loop."

"Will do," said Danbury. "You do the same. Any progress on locating next of kin. Computer and phone records. Anything on the outside cameras."

"Yeah, that was the captain on the phone. His directive is to work in tandem with you. Full transparency."

"Great. Thanks," answered Danbury as they all shook hands. Danbury and Matthew wandered back downstairs, out of the building, and passed through the throng of curious onlookers.

"No comment," said Danbury as one of the news crew stuck a

microphone in his face and fired off a string of questions about what had happened on the school campus, when, and to whom. A second reporter was making her way around the rented Tahoe in Matthew's direction, but he ducked his head and climbed in as he heard the beep from the key fob in Danbury's pocket unlocking it.

"Wow," said Matthew with a grin. "Your paparazzi is tenacious."

"Reporters," answered Danbury, pointing to the nearby news van that had been joined by two more. "Are pushier than cops," he agreed as Matthew shot him an accusing glance at missing the attempt at levity again.

The reporters seemed to have rattled the big detective, Matthew thought, glancing sideways at Danbury. Superman had kryptonite after all, he surmised. Either that, or he was so deeply entrenched in his own thoughts that he completely missed the lame attempt at a joke.

Matthew turned his focus back to the professor, pondering who could have killed him and why. Was it because someone had overheard them or found out the man's true identity in some other way? Was it because Greg had contacted him? Did they think he had Greg's book or knew what it contained?

Or was it—Matthew thought with a shudder—that he and Danbury had led someone straight to Professor Stevenson? Were they the reason that he was dead now?

Of course, he reasoned, they weren't the direct cause of death because they hadn't shot the man. But Matthew was still haunted by the fact that the professor had been killed sometime after they'd left him the day before. He hadn't gone home last night, so how long after Matthew and Danbury left had he been murdered? There were classes taking place in rooms along the hallway with students all over the building. Other professors had offices in the building, presumably, yet Rhodes said nobody had heard anything.

How was that possible? That could mean that the professor was killed later the evening before when the building was deserted. Even a silencer on a gun made a noise, Matthew knew. Which either meant that nobody was in the building or that somebody somewhere had heard something and they hadn't come forward. Or maybe somebody saw or heard something, and they didn't yet understand the relevance of it.

He pulled out his phone to study the picture of the desk blotter. Zooming in, he checked the sections of it that were still visible around the edges where the blood hadn't fully obscured the ink. There were dates and names—which he assumed the police would be looking into—that were maybe student appointments or meetings with his colleagues. Notes about a departmental meeting were still mostly visible, enough so for Matthew to figure out what it was.

There were much earlier dates with notes, maybe for lectures he was working on. And there was one section of doodles. As Rhodes had said, all but the Russian lettering was in black ink. Was there a reason for switching to the blue? Or was that the first pen the professor could reach when someone showed up at his office door, and he was pretty sure he knew what was coming next? Had he recognized his killer? How much time had it taken him to jot those first few characters of the distress code on the desk pad?

"When will they know the time of death?" Matthew asked aloud. "And will they tell you when they do?"

"Not until after the autopsy. Likely a time range. Even after the autopsy. They were tight-lipped about that. They should have been able to tell something. From the rigor mortis. Or lack of it. The stage of rigor he was in."

"Sergeant Rhodes seemed surprised when I asked about Stevenson's clothing. I assumed, at the time, that he was surprised that I had noticed what the professor was wearing the day before. But what if that wasn't it?"

"Meaning?"

"Meaning that maybe he thought the professor had been shot this morning and not at some point yesterday, and his surprise was actually over the fact that the clothing I described was the same."

"He did pause. Said he'd check."

"True."

"But good observation, Doc. You might be right."

Settling back in the soft leather seat for the drive out to Sunny Isles, Matthew's mind began to wander, and it easily returned to his realistic dream from the night before. It was like the difference between watching a movie in a theater and being in an experiential attraction at a theme park where the scene was three-dimensional, your seat moved, air blasted your neck, and something moved under the seat behind the back of your legs. It was on a whole other level.

The man who'd been turned away had bothered him ever since he'd had the dream or the vision—whatever it was. He'd caught a mere glimpse of the guy's face in the dream, but he'd known then that he should know who the man was. It still wasn't coming to him. He tried to recall what the man had looked like, but the image was fuzzy and his face elusive.

14 ~ ACCUSATIONS DENIED

"Do you think the professor's murderer is the same person or people who killed Ross and Ivan?" asked Matthew after they'd driven in silence for a while. "It's the same method—the shot pattern is the same—but they didn't move his body."

"It's highly likely," said Danbury. "My guess? The bullets will match. But the killer doesn't care. He didn't bother to change methods. Or hide it. Why doesn't he care? That's what I'm wondering."

"Huh," said Matthew, nodding in agreement with Danbury's assessment. He pondered why the murder method hadn't been changed, why the body hadn't been moved, and why the murderer didn't seem to care about any of that. "It's almost like the guy is saying, 'I'm cleaning house. If you keep chasing, you're next, and I want you to know it.' Maybe he didn't care that the Russian distress code was left." Matthew shivered at that thought.

"That's possible," said Danbury. "Let's see who's left behind. Stevenson's next of kin. Rhodes will pursue that angle. It might help to know who that is. Their story. If they fit into any of this. And if so, how."

"I haven't gotten a text with the information about the gun from Rhodes," said Matthew, checking his phone again. "I wonder if he's already forgotten about it?"

"I've got a spare," said Danbury. "Locked in the safe. Back at the hotel. It's yours for the trip. We'll get it later. I wasn't offering it in front of Rhodes. Not after you admitted that you didn't have your permit. They can look it up, though. If it comes into question."

"I do have it," said Matthew suddenly. "I have a picture of it in my phone."

"Close enough," said Danbury.

Matthew nodded slowly, unsure if he was relieved or concerned with that development. He'd only ever fired his guns on the shooting range and in competitions. He wasn't excited about carrying a weapon because he knew that to pull it out meant to be ready to fire it. But he was less excited about being hunted by a killer who obviously both carried and knew how to use a weapon—being caught needing a weapon that he didn't have.

"Thanks, Danbury," he said, and his thoughts moved to the process ahead. How could they set up the pastors and the parish council member to determine if they were telling the truth? Could they possibly catch one of them in a lie? And in some way that was obvious enough to know for certain without blatantly accusing them of lying. Maybe that's what it would take. And maybe rightfully so.

The parking lot of St. Athanasius Orthodox Church was less populated on this Thursday morning than it had been the morning before. One lone car occupied a spot up near the building, and the back bumper of a second one could be seen protruding from the far end of the building.

"How do you want to play this?" asked Matthew as Danbury rolled the Tahoe to a stop under a tall, spindly palm tree. "Maybe it's time to lose the good cop entirely. I mean, whichever pastor is lying is most likely responsible for the missionaries' disappearance. Or at least he's knowledgeable about it. We need a definitive way to get at that information. Otherwise, it's a 'he said, he said' situation," said Matthew, with one eyebrow raised and tapping his foot in concentration.

"We might still need Good Cop. In case this guy wants to talk. If he knows something and isn't responsive to Bad Cop. He might be directly involved. Or, if he's protecting someone else. Then Good Cop is sympathetic. We lose that angle if we lose Good Cop."

"OK," agreed Matthew as he unbuckled his seat belt and prepared to slide out. "'Notta Cop' is retired for this trip, I guess. Good Cop it is then."

"We need to know about Pavlov. If he was in Aurora Springs. If he made that connection. That's one string to tug. To help unravel the lies," said Danbury as he grabbed his tablet from the back seat and slid out of the Tahoe, locking it behind them.

"Sounds reasonable to me," agreed Matthew, shading his eyes from the sun as they strode purposefully toward the church building.

After pushing the button to alert the church staff of visitors, the door was opened by a young man. Matthew guessed him to be in his very early twenties. He was short and slender to the point of being almost gaunt. His sandy-blond hair was shaggy and hung down into his face, which was pock-marked as if he'd had a severe case of acne as a teen. Hazel eyes peeked out at them from under the hair and behind oval-shaped glasses.

"We're here to see Father Grossman," said Matthew. "He's not expecting us, but it's important. We met him yesterday morning."

"I see," said the guy after Matthew had introduced himself and Danbury. "I'm his assistant, Albert Ness. Come on in, and I'll check his schedule this morning."

As they followed him down the hallway that they'd traversed behind Stanley Strausbaum the morning before, Matthew wondered where the assistant had been then.

"He has a couple in with him now, but it looks like he has a half hour after he's finished meeting with them if you want to wait?" said Ness from a desk in the corner. The desk was behind a large potted fiddle leaf fig tree that looked very happy to be growing there. It was as if the guy was hiding behind it. Still, he hadn't been there the day before. Though the desk was barely visible, Matthew was sure he'd have noticed had there been a person sitting behind it.

"We'll wait," said Danbury, pacing a few laps across the office before he dropped into a chair beside Matthew. Matthew's foot was tapping, and his knee was bouncing. Waiting—especially when there were more people to talk to and more information they needed to learn—wasn't his strongest suit.

Ness, meanwhile, went back to whatever he was doing almost noiselessly in his corner. Matthew's mind returned to the vivid dream and the man's face, which he couldn't quite see anymore, and who he thought he should know. It still haunted his mind, even though he could no longer see it clearly. Now was as good a time as any, he thought, to try his new approach to finding who was behind the missing and murdered missionaries. He stared intently at Ness's face, taking in every detail of it.

Ness wasn't the guy from the dream, Matthew swiftly concluded, and he pulled out his phone to update a document he'd been using to log the dates and times the people they talked to were providing. It was the file he'd created on the plane. He'd moved it into an online document so that he could access it from anywhere and shared it with Danbury.

To the file, he'd added entries for Professor Stevenson, Father Grossman, Stanley Strausbaum, and Viktor Pavlov with physical descriptions and the information they provided. In the file already were Pastor Fisher and his assistant, Louise. To this list, he added Ness with a physical description but not much more. He added the picture from Stevenson's desk.

Glancing over at the big detective, he saw that Danbury was on his phone.

"Penn says hi, Doc," said Danbury under his breath. That sounded too much like a good cop, Matthew figured, for him to say it out loud.

After what seemed like an eternity of waiting, Matthew got up and asked Ness for a restroom. It was more a way of trying to engage with the guy and maybe have a quick look around than anything else.

"Take a right outside this door, then a left down the second hallway, and it's on the left," answered Ness without looking up.

So much for engaging, thought Matthew as he nodded briefly at Danbury and stepped out into the hallway. It was deserted and bright morning light filtered in through the window panels that ran across the top of the wall the length of the hallway. It was shaping up to be a beautiful day, Matthew thought, as he wandered down the hallway. He took his first right, then left at the second hallway, then passed the restroom to see what he could see. Closed doorways lined the hallway. Double doors at the end begged to be opened, so he obliged.

The doors opened into the side of the church sanctuary, and he caught his breath in surprise. Inside, the same bright morning light was filtering in from a bank of windows somewhere above, and gold sparkled everywhere he looked. An ornately carved golden altar stood to his left with a more ornately carved and painted vaulted wall behind it. On either side of a doorway were six beautifully painted panels of biblical figures.

As Matthew audibly gasped—both at the beauty and the familiarity of it—he heard a soft sound behind him. He turned, startled, to find Stanley Strausbaum watching him closely. The guy seemed to appear noiselessly. Maybe it was the eversion of his feet. Did ducks make noise when they walked? Matthew thought not.

"Beautiful, isn't it?" Strausbaum asked. "Quite breathtaking in this morning light."

"It is," agreed Matthew. "I was admiring the painted pictures on the wall behind the altar."

"Those are the six icons that are consistent across Eastern Orthodox churches," said Strausbaum, eagerly. "They can be carved three-dimensionally or painted—as you see here—but they're usually in the same order. On the far left is the archangel Michael. To his right is a depiction of either an event that's particular to the location or a patron saint. In our case, that's St. Athanasius, for whom the church is named. Then the Virgin Mary, of course. On the other side is Christ Jesus himself, then St. John the Baptist, and on the far side, that's the archangel Gabriel."

Matthew immediately noticed that both archangels looked ferocious and nothing like the cherubs that were often depicted as angelic. Each of the panels was beautifully painted with more gold detailing on Jesus and Mary than the others.

A similar version of these six panels had been in the chapel on Mt. Athos in his vivid dream. Those had been intricately carved, the only paint being the touches of gold on the depictions of Mary and Jesus. What had been in the panel unique to the location in the dream? Try as he might, he couldn't recall.

Had he ever seen the icons before in real life, he wondered. He couldn't recall a time when he had. Wanting to stay and soak it in, he'd already been caught somewhere he thought perhaps he wasn't meant to be, so he turned back to Strausbaum, feigning embarrassment, and asked again for the restroom.

When Matthew returned to the office a few minutes later, Strausbaum was nowhere in sight. Ness, without looking up from his tropical corner, said, "Go on in. Your associate went in with Father Grossman."

"Thanks," said Matthew, opening the door and stepping through. Danbury was seated across from Grossman and staring holes into the priest, but quietly. Neither of them spoke.

"Good morning," said Matthew. "Sorry to disturb you again, but we had a few more questions."

"So I've been told," said Grossman, staring back at Danbury, his gaze neither hostile nor defensive. It was more banal, as if he endured interrogations of some sort regularly, and this one was no different. Had Danbury asked him anything yet? Matthew wasn't sure, but he took the seat beside him.

"We went up to talk to Pastor Mike Fisher yesterday after we left here."

"That's quite a trip," responded Grossman, turning to Matthew. The corners of his mouth turned upward, and his eyes softened slightly.

"It was," agreed Matthew. "And it left us more confused than anything else. Pastor Fisher told us a different version of your story about how the missionaries we're searching for came to be invited here to speak to your parish council." That, thought Matthew, was the politest way that he could manage to state the fact that somebody was lying.

"Oh? And what was that?" asked Grossman.

"He says that you contacted him out of the blue and asked about them coming down here."

"That makes no sense," answered Grossman. "How could I have known they were visiting his church without him contacting me and telling me?"

"He says a member of your parish council was visiting his church a few weeks back and heard the announcement about them coming there and mentioned it to you."

"If any of them did visit, they didn't tell me about it. But you're welcome to ask them if you'd like?"

"Can you provide a list with their contact information?"

"Certainly. There are five of them."

"There are only five parish council members in a church this size?" asked Matthew, amazed. His own sizable church in North Carolina had more elders on the consistory than that.

"We hold to the minimum requirement to avoid dissension. We have discussed expanding that number, but we have no definitive calling to do so. Unless the current members become overwhelmed with their role."

"Yes, we'd like the list and permission to contact them," said Matthew. "Mr. Strausbaum was here. He came up behind me and startled me. Again. Does he work here?"

"Stan? No, but he lives nearby, and he walks most mornings. The church is on his route, and he often laps the parking lot a couple of times before he continues his walk. Sometimes, he stops in for a drink of water or to say hello. He works from home—with some sort of accounting consulting business—so you should be able to find him there easily."

Clicking an intercom on his desk, Grossman asked Albert Ness to print a list of the council members with their contact information.

Matthew wondered if he could politely ask Grossman not to contact anyone on the list so that they'd have the element of surprise when they talked to them. He didn't want to give them time to corroborate stories if there were tracks to cover or stories to get straight.

Danbury had been quiet through this bit of the discussion, allowing Matthew to get what they needed before becoming confrontational, but he continued to stare holes in Grossman. There was an awkward silence until Ness responded through the intercom that the list was waiting for them when they came out.

Matthew thanked Grossman, but before he could manage to phrase anything else politely, Danbury spoke up.

"Don't contact them. Don't tell them we're coming," he said gruffly.

"I hardly think that's fair," responded Grossman. "I'm trying to be helpful in giving you their personal information without their consent. The least I can do is tell them that I've done so and to expect to hear from you."

Matthew thought that was reasonable, though it could potentially make their job in ferreting out the truth a bit more difficult.

"Fine," said Danbury. "But don't warn them."

"Warn them?" asked Grossman.

"I think Danbury is asking if you'd mind not telling them, specifically, what it is that we want to talk to them about," clarified Matthew.

"Ah," said Grossman, leaning back in his chair with his elbows on the arm rest and steepling his fingers in front of him. "You want the element of surprise to ensure that they don't have time to change their stories. I understand. Neither they nor I have anything to hide, so I will agree to that."

Danbury grunted his response before picking up his tablet and beginning to grill Grossman with questions, often accusingly. After asking differing forms of the same questions repeatedly about how and when the contact with Fisher had happened, exactly what they discussed, and how Grossman had proceeded to contact Greg afterward, Danbury finally seemed satisfied that the answers weren't changing.

Then he shifted to Grossman's whereabouts the previous day and night. He clicked the tablet to take down the details and time frame that put Grossman in the company of someone somewhere all afternoon, evening, and night.

Having exhausted the half hour that Grossman had between meetings, and surely much of the man's patience in the process, Matthew thanked him.

"I apologize for the inconvenience," said Matthew. "I hope you understand that our priority is to find the missionaries alive. We need to find Greg and Darya before they end up like Ross and Ivan if it's not already too late." He grimaced.

"I do understand," said Father Grossman. "And it is as I've said.

I've neither withheld nor embellished any information. Ask the parish council members, and they'll tell you the same. I'll have Albert call them and tell them merely that you wish to speak with them, nothing more." He picked up the phone instead of the intercom and punched a button to relay that information.

"Thank you," said Matthew as he stood and followed Danbury to the door. "One more thing. What can you tell us about the saint that the church here is named for?"

"St. Athanasius?" asked Grossman, looking surprised by that question. "Of course. He was a critical voice in the theological formation of the early church. A few centuries after our Lord's resurrection, the church was attempting to define both itself and its theological foundations. Athanasius was an avid proponent of the equality of the three persons of the Trinity, one God in three persons. The Father, Son, and Holy Spirit. These persons are distinct, but not separate. They are one God, in essence or nature, if you will. The Father is the unbegotten Fountainhead of Deity but the Son and Holy Spirit are equal to the Father. Athanasius was vocal about that equality in direct opposition of other followers of Jesus who claimed that He was not equal to the Father."

"And when was this?" Matthew asked for clarification as Danbury shot him a questioning look.

"It was the fourth century AD, Anno Domini, after Jesus was resurrected. Not immediately afterward, but at a critical time in history, as I said."

"Thank you for that explanation, Father Grossman," said Matthew.

"I feel so enlightened," muttered Danbury under his breath.

"Certainly," Grossman replied as they said their goodbyes, slipped out, and closed the door behind them.

Two men were waiting in the sitting area. As Matthew approached the tropical corner, Ness motioned to the men and said, "Go on in. The father is expecting you now."

"Here you go," said Ness, handing Matthew a page containing five names, addresses, and phone numbers. "I hope this helps you find the missionaries. I was looking forward to meeting them."

"Thanks," said Matthew. Then he asked, "Have you ever heard the name Starkovich before?"

"You mean the name of the missionaries, Greg and Darya?"

"Right. Had you heard it before you heard about them?"

"No, I hadn't."

"Where were you yesterday?" Danbury asked. "You weren't here."

Ness looked surprised, but then he answered calmly. "I work part-time here, though I hope to eventually be hired on staff. I'm currently a full-time student working on a divinity degree."

"Oh," said Matthew. "That's great. Where are you in school?"

He wasn't, however, prepared for the answer.

"Barclay University. I'm a little more than halfway through my program."

While Matthew recovered from that surprise, Danbury didn't miss a beat. "Do you know a Professor Stevenson?"

"I know of him. He's highly acclaimed, an expert on ancient manuscripts, I hear. But I haven't had him for any classes, so I only know of him from a distance. Why do you ask?"

"Because he was murdered," said Danbury gruffly, without softening the response at all.

"Oh!" said Ness. "That's awful. I hadn't heard that. When? How? Where?"

"You've never had him as a professor?"

"I haven't."

"Have you ever talked to him?" asked Danbury without answering any of the questions he'd been asked. "About anything?"

"I don't think I've ever actually met him in person. He doesn't, or I guess didn't," Ness corrected himself, "teach the languages I'm learning about—Greek, Hebrew, and Aramaic. His classes aren't on my list of requirements, but I could have taken an elective with him when I was an undergrad. Now I wish I had. I could easily have fit that in back then."

"You have an undergraduate degree from Barclay?" Matthew pursued.

"I do. A pretty useless one, but now I'm focused. I know what I want to pursue, and I'm doing it."

"You've been a student there how many years?" asked Danbury.

"Seven. I took a little longer with my undergraduate degree than I had intended," he responded, looking embarrassed. "But, like I said, I'm focused now. I have less than a year left in the program."

"That must be expensive," said Danbury. "It's a private school, right?"

"It is," answered Ness. "And that's a big part of the reason I'm working here part-time. Father Grossman went to the parish council to arrange funding for me to complete this program. If I serve here for five years after graduation, I don't have to pay it back. And I'm more than happy to do that anyway."

"You must be very thankful to Father Grossman," ventured Matthew.

Ness nodded, smiling beatifically from under the shaggy hair, until Danbury interjected, with an edge to his voice, "Dedicated, even. You'd do anything for him."

Ness looked surprised at the comment and said, "Yes, I suppose I would."

"Cover for him. Lie for him?" asked Danbury.

"What? No, never! He'd never ask me to do that. Or give me any reason to have to!" insisted Ness.

"Where were you yesterday?" Danbury repeated, holding the tablet awkwardly to enter the answer. "Afternoon and evening, specifically."

"I was on campus all morning. I came in here for four hours, from one to five, and then I was at home studying all night."

"Can anybody confirm that?" asked Danbury.

"My roommate was in and out," said Ness, looking concerned. "He can tell you when he was there that I was. Am I a suspect for something?"

"Everybody is a suspect," answered Danbury. "What's your roommate's name? And number?"

"His name is Charlie." Ness turned a few shades paler as he quietly gave Danbury the phone number he'd requested.

"Is he a student at Barclay too?"

"No, he works for a machine shop, tool and die. It's owned by one of the parish council members on the list here," and he pointed to a name, Kevin Anderson.

The irony of the type of business wasn't lost on Matthew. He thanked Ness and followed Danbury out into the brightness of the late morning sun realizing that he had more questions now than he had when they went in.

15 ~ MAKING THE ROUNDS

Because it provided the ability to question two people in one place, they agreed to begin with Anderson's Tool and Die. The office was on the edge of downtown Miami—that they had determined to stay as far away from as possible later in the day during the heaviest traffic hours—which also made it the perfect place to start. Working their way back from there would be far easier this time of day, they'd agreed.

Feeling a bit like he was making his way between patients in his office, trying to ask all the right questions and diagnose issues from the answers, Matthew joined Danbury in questioning members of the parish council from St. Athanasius Orthodox Church.

As the good cop, he politely asked a receptionist behind a metal counter with a chipped and cracking laminate top at Anderson's Tool and Die to speak with both Charlie and Kevin Anderson.

"Oh, Albert Ness said that you were coming, but he only mentioned that you wanted to speak with Kevin. Let me get him first, and then he can tell you when Charlie goes on break," she said, pushing a button on the phone and relaying that information to someone on the other end.

Matthew thanked the woman, then turned to survey the room. It was glass-walled on three sides with a long, narrow area in front of the big metal counter that spanned nearly the width of the room. The area would get hot in summer, Matthew thought, no matter how darkly tinted the windows were. Off to the right in the front area were two chairs and a small bench, all metal-rimmed and upholstered in some variety of bright orange vinyl. Truly utilitarian, Matthew thought; it didn't look at all comfortable.

Behind the counter, metal shelves ran along a back wall. On the shelves were what he assumed to be jigs and fixtures of all shapes and sizes. Under each one was a piece of paper, a form of some sort. Realizing that he'd never stopped to consider what a tool and die maker did, he turned back to the woman and asked.

"We manufacture dies, mainly. They're precision tools or metal forms that our customers use to work with metal and other materials."

"And they're made to certain standard sizes?"

"Some are, but most are custom manufactured. We ship all over the United States and into Canada," she said, indicating a stack of boxes on the end of the counter that had been assembled and taped on one end.

"How big can you make these dies?" asked Matthew.

"How big do you need one?" the woman asked and grinned at him.

Danbury, Matthew noticed, was looking impatient through this exchange, and his face changed to be completely unreadable as a man came through a door behind the counter and motioned them around it.

"I'm Kevin Anderson," he said. He looked at Matthew. "You must be the detective."

"No, I'm Matthew Paine. This is Detective Danbury," he replied, studying the man's face closely. Nothing triggered any memory from the dream the night before. The man was probably in his late fifties or early sixties. Matthew was certain he'd never seen him previously—in his dream or otherwise. The face in the dream was elusive, though. It was an expression on the face that stood out in Matthew's memory, and it was that which he thought he'd recognize if he saw it again. This face showed no familiar expressions.

Introductions completed, they followed Anderson through the doorway that he'd come through and into a noisy concrete hallway, turning right into an office. Anderson closed the metal door soundly behind them and offered them both seats.

"That's better," he said. "Now, what can I help you with?"

"We're looking for missionaries who were due to speak to your parish council at St. Athanasius last weekend, but they never made it," said Matthew, getting right to the point.

"Oh yes, I understand two were found dead, and the other two are still missing," said Anderson, nodding sadly. "How tragic. I was looking forward to hearing from them. They were supposed to meet with us last Sunday afternoon."

"When did you find out that they were coming to talk to you?" asked Matthew.

"Father Grossman contacted us Monday evening. Monday of last week. Actually, it was Albert who contacted us to see if we could meet on Tuesday," he clarified. "We quickly scheduled a meeting for the six of us on Tuesday afternoon."

"The parish council members and Father Grossman?" Matthew asked.

"Exactly. The discussion was quick, and we all agreed that we'd like to hear about the ministry in Ukraine. The timing worked out well because the missionaries were coming this way."

"Were they already planning to come to Miami?"

"That, I don't know. Father Grossman said they were coming to Florida. I'm not sure where."

"You all met at the church on Sunday?" Matthew prompted.

"We did."

"And you didn't know that they weren't coming?"

"Not until they didn't show up."

"What happened after you got there?"

"We waited around for a bit, ate pastries. I drank more coffee than I should have, and then we used the time to discuss some other parish business. We finally gave up about an hour later, after Father Grossman couldn't get an answer from them."

"Did anybody else know them? Anybody in your group?" asked Danbury.

"Just Father Grossman. He didn't really know them either. He shared what he'd learned about them. Nobody else mentioned knowing anything about them, why?"

"We're trying to be thorough in our questioning," answered Matthew. "We're looking for the two who are still missing, Greg and Darya Starkovich."

"Have you ever been to Buchanan Island?" asked Danbury. "Or Aurora Springs Chapel?"

"I haven't," said Anderson. "I hadn't heard of the church until Father Grossman told us he'd contact them to see what he could find out about the missionaries and if they could maybe come at a later time."

"Are you Russian?" asked Danbury pointedly.

"What?" asked Anderson, surprised. Then the wrinkles around his eyes crinkled, and he chuckled. "No, my family has been here for generations. There are a lot of Russian-born members of St. Athanasius if that's why you're asking. I'm not one of them."

"Have you ever heard the name Starkovich before?" asked Matthew.

"No," he began slowly. "I don't think I've ever known anyone with that name before. Or even heard it before last week."

Danbury followed up with the same basic line of questioning, elaborating on a couple of the questions Matthew had asked and doing so much more pointedly. The answers remained consistent and the answerer unfazed, even when asked for an alibi for the previous night and evening. His wife, he assured them, could vouch for his whereabouts all night after he arrived home from work at six thirty the evening before.

"Thank you, Mr. Anderson," said Matthew formally.

"Kevin," he said. "Call me Kevin."

"Kevin, we'd also like to talk to one of your employees," began Matthew.

"First name, Charlie," said Danbury. "Roommate of Albert Ness. Last name unknown."

Kevin Anderson provided his last name and excused himself to go find Charlie and bring him in to talk to them.

"What do you think?" asked Matthew quietly. "Does he know more than he's saying?"

"Doesn't everybody?" asked Danbury.

Footsteps echoing back down the hallway beyond the partially open door halted that discussion, and a slender guy with red curly hair followed Anderson hesitantly back into the office. His light blue eyes swept Matthew and Danbury in an inquiring glance and then back at Anderson. Matthew saw every constellation in the night sky in the guy's freckled face. The Miami sun probably didn't help that any, he thought.

After introducing them, Anderson said, "I'll leave you to chat with Charlie. I don't want there to be any thought that my presence influenced his responses to your questions in any way." Then he slipped out and closed the door soundly.

Charlie looked a bit panicked as he glanced around the room, searching for a place to be. Finally perching on the edge of the desk, he said, "Kevin said you wanted to ask me some questions. What do you want to know?"

Thinking that the guy was already worried enough, Matthew started questioning him about Albert Ness.

"How long have you been roommates?"

"Nearly two years. We rent the place cheap from parents of a friend of ours. They bought it for him, and then he graduated from college and moved away."

"How long have you known Albert?"

Charlie's face scrunched in concentration. "I think about fifteen years. We were in the third grade together, and we've been friends since then."

"You're both from this area?"

"Yes, sir."

"Call me Matthew. You can skip the sir."

"OK."

"Can you tell me where both you and Albert were last night?"

"Um…he was there studying when I got home about a quarter to six. Traffic, you know. I got off work at five."

Yeah, Matthew knew all too well. "And then what?" he asked. "Were you in for the night?"

"No, I didn't want to pay for food to be delivered, and we were out of everything. I showered and went back out to the store and got stuff. Bread, peanut butter, eggs, cheese, milk—like that. Nothing fancy."

"How long did it take you to shower?"

"About five minutes."

"And then you went to the store? How long did that take?"

"The market where we go is close. I was gone less than an hour. Maybe forty-five minutes, maybe less."

"And then you went straight back home?"

"Yeah, I bought ice cream. I went straight back."

"OK, so you were back by maybe quarter to seven?"

"Yeah, probably at least by then."

"And then what?"

"I hung out and made sandwiches for both of us, ham and cheese. Then I went to my room to watch some TV. Albert was studying at the bar in our kitchen. We don't have room for a table, so we eat there or on the coffee table in front of the TV if he isn't studying. But he was, so I went to my room."

"Albert was there studying all evening?"

"Yeah, he got up and got something to drink, like that. But he was studying all night. He had an exam this morning."

"And you were both there for the rest of the night?"

"Albert was. A buddy of mine stopped by, but we couldn't game with Albert studying, so I went to his place."

"How long were you gone?"

"Probably a couple of hours."

"What time was that?"

"Umm, maybe eight to ten? I know I was home by ten thirty because I set the alarm in my room for in the morning then and decided to call it a night."

"And Albert was still at home studying at ten thirty?"

"Yeah."

Danbury—who had been tapping his tablet to update the timeline—began with the same questions Matthew had run through but asked a couple of them more brusquely. When Charlie started to squirm, Matthew would have been inclined to back off, but Danbury doubled down instead. Like Kevin Anderson before him, Charlie's story never changed, no matter the angle Danbury came at him.

"Thank you, Charlie, I think we're done," said Matthew. As Charlie—looking greatly relieved—got up and headed to the door, the guy visibly cringed when Matthew said, "One more thing. Does the name Starkovich mean anything to you?"

"Umm, I don't think so," said Charlie, over his shoulder, only half turning but obviously wanting to bolt from the room after Danbury's questioning.

"Have you ever heard it before?"

"Nope. I don't think so," said Charlie, clinging tightly to the door handle as if he could use it to project himself from the room faster that way.

"OK, thank you," said Matthew.

After thanking Kevin Anderson again for his time and cooperation, Matthew followed Danbury out, and they climbed back in the Tahoe. "Who's next?" Matthew asked.

"Lunch," said Danbury. "Lunch is next."

"I like that plan," agreed Matthew, checking his watch to see that it was already after one. A quick search on Matthew's phone yielded a highly-rated Cuban sandwich and coffee shop nearby. Conversation was limited as they ate in the crowded and overly warm café. The one thing they could agree on was that, so far, nobody but Father Grossman was ruled out as having killed Professor Stevenson, and that was only if the alibis he'd provided all checked out. Anderson's wife couldn't be forced to testify against him—even if he wasn't telling the truth—so there was little point in following that lead with their limited resources, they decided.

As they were finishing their lunch and the coffee that Matthew had insisted on getting—and then praised until Danbury got one too—Danbury's phone sounded.

"Danbury," he answered, collecting his trash from the table and throwing it away on the way out the door. "Tell me."

16 ~ INTERROGATION FATIGUE

After they'd climbed in the Tahoe, Danbury grunted a few uh-huhs, thanked the caller, and put his phone down on the console.

"That was my buddy. Who checked the phone records. For the missionaries." Danbury paused to admonish, "And that never happened. Unless somebody specifically asks."

"Got it. I know nothing about that," he said agreeably. Then he asked, sardonically, "Could the guy who didn't look see the phone records?"

"He did. It took some work. But he got them."

"And?"

"He found the last location. For all four phones. They were triangulated from cell towers. It isn't exact."

"Yeah?" Matthew prodded.

"It puts them near the hotel. The one they checked into on Thursday. Up on the Georgia-Florida state line."

"Could he see the last time they were used or at least powered on?"

"Yeah. About eight that night. Greg's phone was used on Friday. Same general location."

"OK, so that's eight at night on Thursday, January the twenty-third, for the other three phones," clarified Matthew, using his phone to add that information to the timeline in the online file they shared. "And nothing else on Greg's after Friday?"

"Right."

"So, something likely happened about eight that night."

"Looks that way, Doc," said Danbury, starting the Tahoe and clipping his phone to the dash with the address of the next parish council member they were going to question programmed into the navigation app.

As they began the route, Matthew's phone dinged, and he saw an incoming message. "Rhodes sent me the information about where to get a handgun," he told Danbury.

Texting back, Matthew explained that he had a picture of his concealed-carry license on his phone and asked if that was sufficient or if he would need the guy to contact the Wake County Sheriff's office back home. Watching the screen, he saw the dots of an incoming message, but then they disappeared. Rhodes was probably beyond busy today, he thought, as he pulled up the address on his phone.

"We're not that close to this location, but they don't close until eight. Maybe we can still get by there today."

"Good plan," said Danbury distractedly. Before they could discuss it further, his phone sounded from the dash. He clicked to answer it on the car audio system. "Danbury."

They heard Rhodes' voice sounding like it was very far away. "Yeah, the picture of the concealed-carry license should be OK. He can always check it with the sheriff in North Carolina if he needs to."

"Great, thanks," said Matthew, wondering why Rhodes called Danbury's phone to deliver that news to him.

"We have some footage you might be interested in seeing. Two sets of it. One from the cameras above the doors around the building where the professor was killed. And one from the office of the hotel where the missionaries were staying up on the Georgia line. I haven't seen either one yet, but I'm headed back to the office to look now. You might want to stop by and have a look too. You'll be able to recognize people I won't. It sounds like there are quite a few people coming and going on both videos, so this could take a while, especially since we don't have an accurate time frame for either event."

"I did get more," said Danbury. "It might help now. With the video from the hotel. All four phones were triangulated near the hotel. Not pinpointed. Three were last active around eight. The night of Thursday, January the twenty-third. Grygoriy's was last found Friday. The twenty-fourth. In that same area."

"When were you going to tell me?" asked Rhodes accusingly.

"I just did. I got that ten minutes ago. Or less," said Danbury, sounding annoyed.

"Oh," was all Rhodes said in response.

"Any idea what's on the hotel video?" asked Danbury. "The vantage point, at least?"

"It's the feed from the hotel office, but it's supposed to catch a little of the parking lot through the window. I don't know if it's useful, but at least we have a narrower time span to look at. Thanks for that," Rhodes added, sounding slightly contrite. "You can stop by the office this evening. It's being processed in, and it'll be uploaded for viewing with a tech who can clean it up some, probably by seven or so."

"OK, got it. Thanks," said Danbury and clicked to disconnect.

*****

Nearly two hours and two more interviews questioning parish council members later, Matthew was feeling discouraged. He could identify neither of them as the face from the dream. They both told variations of the same story about inviting and then waiting for the team of missionaries. Both had alibis for the evening and night before. Neither had ever heard the name Starkovich prior to the week before.

"We're getting nowhere fast," said Matthew. "We're spinning our wheels."

"Sometimes we do, Doc," replied Danbury. "You know this by now."

"Yeah, I guess I do. Sometimes, we've gotten lucky, but other times, we've put in a lot of time and turned up nothing helpful. Like right now. Who's next on the list?"

"I thought maybe your friend. Stanley Strausbaum."

"My friend?"

"He seems to gravitate to you."

Matthew chuckled. "That's true. He's sneaked up on me twice now. He walks like a duck, so you wouldn't think he'd be all that stealthy, but somehow, he is."

"Yeah, I noticed. He has an odd walk."

"It looks painful to me, like it should put his entire leg out of balance all the way up his hip and into his lower back. But I'm not a Podiatrist, so maybe it's fine. You've got his address set in the nav app?"

"Yep," was all Danbury said before they set off again.

Arriving at a low house that was arranged in a U-shape around a lovely tropical landscape, they climbed out and approached a garden gate.

"Do we go through to the door, or," began Matthew, before noticing a button to the right of the gate. Pushing it, he heard lilting chimes from somewhere within. A few minutes later, Stanley Strausbaum appeared at the door and waved them in. Matthew glanced at him, but he was already certain that the face in the dream didn't belong to Strausbaum. It was more rounded, somehow. A mere glimpse of the face began to present itself to Matthew's mind, but it was as just as quickly gone. Frustrated, he opened the gate.

"Come on in, Gentlemen. I'm finishing up a business call, and I'll be right with you." Strausbaum had earbuds in, and he pressed a button on the cord and said, obviously not to his present company, "Yes, but that was the other line item. This one doesn't apply."

After they made their way through what looked like a tropical rainforest, Matthew and Danbury stood awkwardly in the entrance of the house on inlaid tile floors. Matthew glanced around. The décor was simple but ornate at the same time—quite a decorating feat. The walls, stucco inside and out, were an off-white shade with a glazed pearlescent appearance.

White wicker furniture with splashes of color on cushions and pillows occupied a brightly lit sun room off to the right. It was to this room that Strausbaum motioned them to have a seat while he disappeared into the room beyond. It would be this room, Matthew assessed, that would stick out on the front of the house to make the right side of the U-shape from the outside perspective.

The wicker creaked under Danbury's weight, and he shifted forward on the seat, looking concerned. Strausbaum's voice carried clearly from the next room, and the discussion was all about line items, cost margins, and a tax issue. Ten minutes later, Strausbaum reemerged apologetically and sank into the wicker love seat opposite the two chairs that Danbury and Matthew occupied.

"My apologies for that. If it hadn't been important, I'd have excused myself from the call."

"No problem," said Matthew. "We are interrupting your work day."

"Well, the end of it," said Strausbaum, checking the silver watch under his shirt sleeve. "I start work at six thirty, walk at eight this time of year, and then finish up about four. Anyway, Albert said you'd be stopping by. What can I help you with?"

"We have some standard questions for you," said Matthew, and he began with those about the parish council inviting the missionaries and proceeded through Strausbaum's account of what had transpired when they didn't show up. It sounded very much like the three versions they'd already heard.

"Have you ever been to Buchanan Island, north of here?" asked Matthew.

"Oh yes, but not for several years," said Strausbaum. "I should go back in the spring. It's a lovely location."

"Have you ever been to Aurora Springs Chapel there?"

"No, I'd never heard of it until Father Grossman said they'd contacted him about the missionary team from Ukraine."

"What about the name Starkovich? Had you ever heard it before?"

"Starkovich?" Strausbaum asked, the question seeming to catch him off guard and jolt him initially. Then he grinned easily. "Heard it before? I'm not sure I can pronounce it correctly now."

"So that's a no?" asked Danbury.

"No, I'm not familiar with the name," said Strausbaum, and Danbury took over the questioning process, putting the little man through the paces of restating and reconfirming his account of the events until Matthew thought he could see the wire-rimmed glasses fogging over.

"Are you ever at Barclay University?"

"No, I've never been there, why?"

"And you know nobody there?"

"I know that Albert Ness is a student there. Otherwise, not that I know of unless some of our church members went there."

"One more thing," said Danbury, rising to his feet. "Where were you yesterday evening? And last night?"

"Right here," said Strausbaum and began, unprompted, to give a detailed account of his evening. "I worked until a little after four, read a book I'm struggling with for a couple of hours, poured a glass of wine, and turned on some classical music. I fixed dinner, ate dinner, cleaned up, did a few household chores, checked my mail and answered a couple of important messages, organized for this morning, and went to bed around ten. And, no, I know of no one who can corroborate that information. I live alone."

That, thought Matthew, was an oddly specific and readily available and detailed account. It was as if he knew it was coming, and it had been carefully rehearsed. Still, there was no one thing that he could find wrong with it, so he thanked Strausbaum.

"Did you enjoy your tour of the church this morning?" asked Strausbaum.

"Oh, the look into the sanctuary?" asked Matthew, wondering why Strausbaum had brought that up. "It's beautiful."

"Do come back for the services this weekend. It's even more lovely then."

"I'm sure," said Matthew noncommittally. "I'm not sure what our weekend plans are yet, but thank you for the invitation."

"You're most welcome. Have a wonderful evening," said Strausbaum, closing the door behind them.

The sun was starting to wane in the late February afternoon, and Matthew was thankful to have only one more interview to conduct.

This one, though, they'd saved for last because they'd been told by Ness that Pavlov—the parish council member they'd most wanted to talk to—had been traveling and wasn't due back in town until after three.

It was nearly four now, Matthew noted, and he hoped to find Victor Pavlov home and willing to talk. They were silent as they climbed in the Tahoe, and Danbury tapped the address into the navigation app on his phone.

"Ah," he groaned. "It's only two and a half miles away. But this says it'll take thirty minutes."

"Yeah, welcome to Miami," Matthew said, thoroughly tired of both the cliché and the reality it represented.

He wasn't sure whether to be happy or annoyed when they pulled up to a short, gated driveway on their right twenty-five minutes later. They weren't there long enough for him to decide.

"Hang on, Doc," said Danbury, but the warning came too late to keep Matthew's shoulder from slamming into the door as Danbury veered sharply left. He made a U-turn at the end of the driveway, and the tires squalled as he stomped the gas pedal and went back in the direction from which they'd come.

"What the," Matthew began to ask as Danbury maneuvered a second turn.

His fingers white on the steering wheel as he held on through the second turn, Danbury yelled, "Get down, Doc!"

17 ~ PURSUERS PURSUED

Matthew barely managed to slip sideways out of the shoulder harness of his seat belt that was clutching him tightly and bend at the waist to duck beneath the window sill when he heard the pop of gunfire. He knew that bullets had penetrated the front window on Danbury's side of the car and whizzed over his head. Glancing up, he saw Danbury's gritted teeth and the determined look on his face as he maneuvered the Tahoe out of the second turn—without spinning out—and hit the gas pedal.

"Call Rhodes," said Danbury. "Send him our location."

"On it," said Matthew, sounding like Danbury in that moment as he rose and slipped the seat belt back on his shoulder. "Are you hit?"

"I'm OK. But I'm not giving them another shot," he said, backing off some on the speed. From the safer distance, he followed the bigger black SUV from which the shots had been fired into the afternoon traffic. It was distinctive; the chassis was raised, and the tires were wide. It was a Hummer—already an environmental pariah—that had been souped up somehow and Matthew was amazed that it had maneuvered the first turn. He knew exactly why it hadn't followed with the second one. It wasn't built with the agility for sharp turns. Neither was it crafted for speed. At the next corner, Danbury gunned it to slide into a spot where he technically didn't fit to make a right turn a few cars behind the massive Hummer.

"What happened?" asked Matthew as he pulled up Rhodes' contact information and shared his location, ongoing, then tapped to call him. Danbury kept the huge black Hummer in sight but hung back behind a couple of cars to stay out of immediate bullet range. Nobody seemed to be shooting at them anymore, but the vehicle wasn't speeding away either, Matthew observed. He wondered what that meant.

"You know the tail we didn't have? I spotted one and doubled back. Thought I'd pursue. But so did they. And they're armed. Heavily."

"Oh," said Matthew as he caught a voice saying, "Rhodes," from his phone, and then he heard himself explaining the situation quickly and calmly. It was as if he were disconnected from it all, almost like in the vision from the dream the night before—except that he knew this was real.

"I've got a unit headed your way," Rhodes reported after a momentary hold. "They'll be coming up on your left in about three blocks."

"Thanks," said Matthew.

"When you see them, back off," instructed Rhodes. "And let them pursue."

If it were up to Matthew, he'd be more than happy to do exactly that. He wasn't sure how Danbury felt about it after being shot at. Before he could wonder, it all became moot. They were approaching a bridge, and the Hummer slowed in front of them, almost to a stop. It shot across the oncoming lane of traffic—off onto the shoulder of the other side of the road—and then did exactly what it was built to do. It climbed up and over the low concrete wall, crawled down the riprap beside the bridge on the other side, and disappeared into the early night.

Is there water down there? Matthew leaned over to look as he and Danbury, along with the police cruiser, drove onto the bridge. As soon as it could make the maneuver, the cruiser spun a hundred and eighty degrees and went back to the edge of the bridge, lights flashing. Danbury waited for an opening in the traffic on the other side of the bridge, then made the one-eighty and went back across, pulling behind the police car on the edge of the road.

They parked where the hulking Hummer had gone off the road. Cars whizzed by, even with the police cruiser—lights flashing— stopped there. The two officers were out of the cruiser, and jumping sideways down the embankment, weapons drawn. Danbury's face was taut and grim, Matthew noted, but he didn't get out of the vehicle.

"Are you OK?" Matthew asked.

"Mostly," said Danbury and then confessed that a bullet had grazed his left arm. "Good thing there's a doctor in the house," he weakly attempted to joke.

Removing his jacket gingerly and carefully pulling his shirt over his head, Danbury turned and twisted in the seat so that Matthew could see his upper arm. Turning the dome light on in the vehicle, Matthew began to evaluate the wound.

"The good news is that it's a superficial wound. It isn't deep enough to have damaged muscle, and it never got anywhere close to bone. The bad news is that it's sliced and bleeding. You need a few stitches to close it up cleanly," said Matthew. "And when was the last time you had a tetanus shot?"

"I've got no idea, Doc."

"Then you need one of those too. Here, hold this on the wound and keep pressure on it to staunch the bleeding," said Matthew, folding Danbury's shirt and placing it gently on the wound, then pushing down firmly.

"I'm not going to the ED," said Danbury, wincing with the pressure.

"What time is it?" Matthew asked, picking up his phone to check it and realizing that Rhodes was still there.

"What's happening?" he heard Rhodes demand.

Tapping to put the phone on speaker, he updated Rhodes on the situation and explained that two officers were in pursuit, but on foot, down the embankment beside the bridge.

"There's a backup unit on the way," said Rhodes. They heard muffled conversation and the noise from a police radio as he asked for a location from the second police vehicle.

"Is there water down there?" asked Matthew when Rhodes was back on the line. "We haven't gotten out to go look. We have a situation here ourselves."

"There is, eventually, but there's a service road that runs along the waterway at that location. My guess is that they made their own ramp down to that road. But it's steep. That took some skill."

"Or a lot of practice," said Danbury.

"What's your situation?" asked Rhodes.

"Danbury was grazed by a bullet. It's not deep, but it could use some stitches, or at least wound closure strips, and a tetanus shot. But he's refusing to go to the emergency department."

"Don't blame him, there," said Rhodes. "How about you patch him up, and I'll get you in the back door for the shot?"

"Hey! I'm right here," said Danbury, objecting to being discussed as if he weren't.

"And the back door deal is the best offer you're going to get," said Rhodes. "You should really consider getting it stitched up."

"Yeah, OK," grumbled Danbury. "I'll get the shot. Doc, you can do the wound closure strips. Unless they'll let you stitch."

"I don't think professional courtesy extends quite that far if we're going to a hospital," said Matthew. "And that's not something I do regularly anyway. Somebody who does is likely to do a cleaner job of it."

"Nobody else is sticking needles in me," said Danbury, sullenly. "Except for that shot."

"There's a small emergency treatment center close by," said Rhodes. "And there's a pharmacy, one of the big chains, across the street, so you can get whatever you need. Tell you what, I'll meet you. It's not far from the precinct. I'm on my way there now. I'll text you the address."

"Ah, an ambulatory emergency department," summarized Matthew.

"Hey, Rhodes," began Danbury.

"Yeah?"

"We're going to need a police report. This is a rental vehicle. It's got bullet holes. At least in the windshield. I haven't looked at the outside."

"No problem. I can get that paperwork for you. We'll bring the vehicle in to see if we can retrieve the bullets after you get taken care of."

"Thanks," said Danbury, and Matthew clicked to end the call and then to see the address Rhodes sent.

"OK, out," demanded Matthew as they heard sirens. A second police cruiser approached and parked behind them on the shoulder of the road.

"Out where?"

"You're not driving like that," said Matthew. "Granny or not, I can get us there safely. Get out."

As Matthew opened the door and slid out, he heard Danbury's sharp intake of breath.

"What is it? Are you in pain?" asked Matthew, in professional medical mode.

"Doc," said Danbury and pointed at the seat back behind where Matthew's head had been. There, in the headrest, was a bullet hole. Both men stared at it in horror, and neither one spoke as two uniformed police officers approached.

"Everybody OK here?" asked one of them while the other ran along the side of the road and disappeared down the embankment. "We have a bullet wound, right?"

"Minor one," said Danbury, looking meaningfully at Matthew.

"We're going to get that looked at now," said Matthew.

"We'll meet Rhodes afterward. Give him our full statements," said Danbury. "And let your tech guys have the car. They can remove the bullets. See if they're a match."

"A match?" asked the officer.

"To two murders," answered Danbury grimly.

"Oh. Looks like you got lucky," said the officer, motioning to the windshield. "Take it easy out there."

"Thanks, Officer," said Matthew as that officer, too, started toward the embankment. How much could they really do on foot, he wondered. He walked around the Tahoe and saw a mark across the hood where a bullet had traveled and two holes in the windshield in addition to the one in the corner of Danbury's side window.

They had gotten lucky. It was far more than luck, Matthew realized, as he paused to thank God for their safety before he climbed behind the wheel and clicked the address on his phone that Rhodes had sent him.

"You good?" asked Danbury.

"Yeah, let's roll," said Matthew, quoting Danbury with a wan grin in an attempt at normalcy.

They set off in silence as Matthew's mind raced with multiple thoughts at once. Who were those goons? Where had they started following from? Were the goons trying to keep them from talking to Pavlov? Were they the same ones who had killed Ross and Ivan? Had they taken Darya and Greg? Or were they hired by the same person or part of the same group or organization, somehow? Had they meant to hit him and Danbury with those shots? Or the vehicle? Or just scare them off?

Matthew cringed at that thought because clearly, they had aimed at the occupants, not the vehicle. Would the police officers be able to determine where they'd gone? Was there any hope of finding them? Where did the service road by the edge of the waterway go? Was it a familiar escape route for them? What were they normally escaping from? Police? Other thugs?

Before he could vocalize any of those questions, Danbury said, "Did you get a look at them?"

"No. Did you?"

"The passenger. It was only a glimpse. Not enough for a sketch artist."

"There were two of them?"

"Yeah, at least two. The driver wasn't shooting at us. Not that I saw. It was the passenger. He was hanging out of the window. I thought maybe you'd seen him. When they spun around."

"I'm not sure that I wish I had," said Matthew honestly. "If I never see them again, it'll be too soon. Where did you first notice them following us?"

"I think we picked them up early. Right after we left Strausbaum's."

"Did they follow us there, or did they find us somehow and try to prevent us from getting to Pavlov? If they were with us earlier, I'm assuming you didn't see them?"

"I didn't notice them earlier. And I was looking. I spotted the car after we left Strausbaum. Even then, I wasn't sure. They were doing a good job. In all that traffic. They stayed back. I made a few lane changes. To see what happened. I thought I'd lost them. That they weren't following us. I didn't see them for a while. Until we hit the driveway. Then they came tearing down the street. I didn't want to be trapped at the gate. Or inside it if that was their plan. I spun on them. But they spun too. It took that second spin to end up behind them. That was my goal. To turn the tables."

"Yeah, that was some impressive driving," said Matthew.

"It's why I rented this Tahoe. Like the one I drive at home. I'm used to it. And the way it handles."

"I was a little too busy ducking to fully appreciate it."

"Good thing," said Danbury.

"They're long gone, aren't they? The police won't be able to find where they went," said Matthew dismally.

"Likely true."

"I wonder if that bullet will match," said Matthew. "The one in the headrest with those from Stevenson, Ivan, and Ross?"

"What I was thinking too. It's possible. Depends on how many 'they' there are. But I wasn't going to say it out loud."

"Why not? We need to know what we're dealing with and be prepared. I want that gun now. Maybe another Glock 19 like the one I have at home. Not that I'd have been able to do much with it back there, with all that motion. I wouldn't have fired it out of the window like that idiot did in a residential area with all the traffic anyway."

"Yeah, second stop. After getting fixed up, and the shot. Before the precinct. It's near there, right?"

"I think so," said Matthew, realizing that he was a bit turned around and feeling unusually directionally impaired. "What about the rental?"

"I'll call the company from the precinct. They'll bring another one. We'll hand over the police report. They can't argue with us. Not at a police station."

"Good plan," said Matthew. "And we talk to Pavlov when?"

Danbury looked over at the digital clock on the dash instead of letting go of his arm and pulling his phone out. "Depends on what we find on the video from the hotel. I wanted to talk to them all today. Might be tomorrow."

"We talked to four out of five," said Matthew. "And their stories all line up without sounding rehearsed."

"True. But it's that fifth one. The name that Fisher jumped on when you said it. He's the one I wanted to talk to. And the only one we didn't manage."

"And you think that's by design," said Matthew. "That he's maybe behind all of this and doesn't want to talk to us?"

"It's possible. You don't?"

"I'm not sure," said Matthew slowly. "It's a lot of coincidence if it wasn't somebody's intent to keep us from talking to him."

"Too much coincidence," answered Danbury.

They rode in silence as Matthew picked his way through the traffic with three speeds—stop, wait, and go slowly. Finally, he found the pharmacy across the street from the ambulatory emergency department and left the car running to dash in and get the wound closure strips and some large bandages. Then he turned into the parking garage of the ambulatory emergency department. Driving through it and out the other side to reach the back of the building, he thought maybe it wasn't as late as it felt. It got dark early in late January. With what they'd been through, time was momentarily difficult for him to grasp.

True to his word, Rhodes was waiting for them literally at the back entrance, which Matthew had circled the building in search of.

"OK, Danbury, let's get this done."

18 ~ BLURRED LINES

After getting Danbury's tetanus shot and stitches—which Matthew had managed to convince him to do—they made a quick stop by the gun shop. With Rhodes preparing the way for the purchase, that process was surprisingly quick and painless. Matthew briefly felt the weight of the Glock 19 in the new holster at his waist until they entered the police station. Without a badge, he had to check it at the door before he could go through the metal detector to enter the building and get his temporary visitor badge.

Inside, they gave their statements. The process of trying to remember exactly what he'd seen was frustrating because it all happened so fast and unexpectedly that Matthew could recall very little of the details. He didn't see the driver or much of the behemoth Hummer—except from the back—and he hadn't been aware that there was a passenger who was the one shooting at them.

Danbury's statement had been only slightly more enlightening. There wasn't a license plate visible on the back of the vehicle. It had been either covered or removed. The hulking Hummer, however, was distinctive in the size and breadth of the tires as well as the way the chassis perched atop them. It wouldn't be difficult to spot, and it couldn't be easily hidden.

While they were waiting for the tech to finish cleaning up the video from the hotel office, Danbury called the car rental company to explain that the vehicle was currently in a bay at the police precinct. He told them that it was being gone over by a forensic tech team—why that was—and requested a replacement. Matthew was happy to overhear that Mark had apparently added the insurance package on the vehicle rental. There would undoubtedly be lots of questions, but at least there were no complications.

The tech team worked to remove the bullet from the passenger side headrest and to search for others. Danbury saw only the one weapon—which Matthew hadn't seen—but they were being thorough in case there had been more than one.

The gathering in the room awaiting the video viewing was somber.

Though they'd found where the massive black Hummer went after it disappeared down the embankment, the officers had been unable to follow its path afterward. The road under the bridge only went one way. With that—and water on one side of it—escape options should have been limited. Going by car around to the street below, they discovered myriad side streets, alleyways, and canals running off it.

It was disappointing. But then, the driver of the big Hummer seemed to know exactly where he was going when he drove down the steep embankment to begin with. Why would he not know the best escape route from there, they reasoned as they discussed it all.

"OK, I think it's as good as it'll get," said the guy at the video controls. "I'll put it up on the big screen." Matthew and Danbury followed the gaze of the others in the room to the right-side wall that wasn't a wall at all. It was either one very large screen or multiple panels filling the wall. From his vantage point near the left wall, Matthew wasn't sure which.

There was no sound. As the video began to run, Matthew's mind drifted back to Pavlov—the one St. Athanasius parish council member they had most wanted to talk to and the only one they'd been unable to reach. The grainy picture ran on without anything exciting happening for a while as Matthew considered who would want to keep them from talking to Pavlov and why. The most obvious answer was that the guy was involved in the murders, and he didn't want them to discover that. Was that the case?

Before he could ponder that thought further, one of the officers who had been in the first patrol car chasing the Hummer pointed and said, "There! Stop."

Into the right edge of the screen had wandered a small, huddled group of people. There were four of them.

"Where did they come from? Can you back that up?" asked the officer.

"I can, but they came into the edge of the picture. It's not like I can zoom out to see more."

"Yeah, yeah," said the officer, "OK, never mind. Go slow. Half speed, maybe."

As the four wandered from the bottom right of the screen toward what was obviously the glass windows of the hotel office, there were indeed three men and a woman.

"Is that the group you're looking for?" the video technician asked.

"It looks like them. Do they get closer?" asked Matthew.

"No," said the tech. "They turn outside of that window and then walk off the screen to the left in about three, two, one," and he paused the video as the group had begun to turn, their faces grainy but still visible from a frontal view.

Their faces weren't entirely clear, but Matthew nodded. "Yeah, that looks like them. Are they heading to their room or away from it there?"

"To their room," said Danbury, who had been there already. "Probably from their car. There's a larger parking lot. Off to the right. On the other side of the windows."

"Is that…," asked Matthew, pointing.

"Is that what?" asked Rhodes.

At the same time, Danbury nodded and agreed. "It is. Coincidence?"

"Maybe," said Matthew.

"What?" insisted Rhodes again.

"Darya," answered Matthew. "It's not pulled up, but I think she has on a black hoodie. It's a dark color, for certain."

"Like the person you've chased a couple of times now?" Rhodes asked.

"Yeah, but it's not like dark hoodies are unique or unusual," said

Matthew.

"The build is right," said Danbury, leaning forward. "How tall is Greg?"

"Probably five foot eleven, maybe six feet, but not any taller than that," said Matthew.

"She's nearly as tall. Unless she's wearing heels, she's probably five foot ten," offered Rhodes.

Matthew was wracking his brain, trying to remember what he'd seen her wearing at church the morning they spoke to the congregation. He'd met them in the lobby afterward, but he hadn't been paying attention to their clothing, particularly not Darya's feet. "I think," he said, managing a vague recollection, "that she had on low-heeled boots when they were at our church a couple of weeks ago."

"I think those were in her suitcase," said Rhodes, reaching for a file folder on a low table beside him and flipping through it. "Yeah, there was a pair of brown, low-heeled women's boots in one of the suitcases."

"OK, so we know what she isn't wearing in the video then," said Matthew. "Unless she changed them as soon as they got back to the room. But dark hoodies and her build are common. The skulker could be anybody. If it were Darya, why would she run?"

"Good point, Doc," said Danbury.

"Let's keep going and see who comes by next," said Rhodes. "We know people do, but they were a blur before this was cleaned up." He motioned to the video.

"It's still blurry," said the other officer in the room.

"It's all kind of a blur," muttered Matthew under his breath as he sank back into the chair. The adrenaline from the earlier car chase, shooting, getting Danbury tended to, and arming himself was running out. Exhaustion was settling in its wake. They would need to eat something soon. It was already well after seven, and Matthew could feel himself fading.

They watched, in slower motion, as a couple walked by. Arm in arm, the couple was clearly in a hurry to get to their hotel room and not at all what the team assembled was looking for. The video was running at double speed again until another officer in the room called out, "There!"

As the tech ran the feed backward, the video slowed and Matthew noted the time stamp, seven forty-five. He could see two obviously male figures walking by the office at a fast pace. The darkness of the night was complete, so he couldn't make out details, but one of the men was heavier set than the other. Both looked intense.

"Timing-wise, from the last use of their phones in that area, that's about right," said Matthew.

"I wish we could see where they go after that!" said Rhodes in frustration.

"And where they came from," added Danbury. "Maybe a lifted black Hummer with wide tires. That looks like a city block on wheels."

"Do they come back by?" asked Matthew, leaning forward.

"I think one does later," answered the tech, running the video at double speed again. A few minutes later—about five minutes after eight, Matthew noted—one of the guys did walk back by. His face was averted, as both had been earlier, away from the office window and therefore not visible to the camera within.

"Huh," said Danbury.

"Do you want me to start over?"

"Not yet," answered Danbury. "Keep going."

"OK, what are you looking for?"

"That!" said Danbury, and the guy froze the video. Pixelated as it was, the city block on wheels that Danbury had mentioned was clearly passing the front of the hotel office. Eventually, the hulking black shape of the Hummer reappeared—heading back out the way it had come—moving more quickly by the office window this time. Then all was dark outside again.

"Two guys took four people out in that and then killed two of them?" asked Matthew incredulously.

"It would appear so," said Rhodes.

"Likely at gunpoint," added Danbury, rubbing the stubble on his chin.

"But they don't all fit," insisted Matthew. "Unless they were shoved in the back. Hummers only seat four, maybe five, but that's it. There isn't a third row of seating in them." An admitted motor head, Matthew tended to keep up with trends in the car world, though usually the racier sort.

"That it?" asked Danbury.

"Not quite," said the tech. Immediately afterward, a white panel van drove in. Seven minutes later, it drove back out.

"Now that makes more sense," said Matthew.

"Yeah," said the tech. "Nothing else interesting happens that I could see. At least not for the next ten hours or so, until daylight. A few people pass in the early morning hours, but they look like workers coming in to the hotel and travelers heading out with suitcases and luggage."

"Can I get a copy of that?" asked Danbury.

"Sure," said Rhodes. He looked at the tech. "I'll provide a list to send that out to. And we'll add the footage to the files for our two murder victims."

"What's down that way?" asked Matthew—who had not physically been to the hotel—pointing to the left, the direction the missionary team had last been seen heading in.

"Nothing much," said Danbury. "Dumpsters. The back of a pool around the corner. It's a back entrance."

"This isn't the front of the office that we're looking out of?" asked Matthew. "I had assumed that it was."

"It isn't, no," answered Rhodes. "It's the bank of windows along the back of the inner office. The only other camera in the office is at the front desk. There's no outside view at all from there. Just the check-in counter. We saw two of the men check in around three. That video was unremarkable. Nobody followed them into the office."

"Those dumpsters were searched, right?" asked Danbury.

"The Georgia guys said they searched the dumpsters," answered

Rhodes. "The Florida team didn't. At the time, we only knew that the missionaries were missing and that they were headed to Florida, not that any of them had been murdered here. Or murdered there and dumped here," he clarified, reverting back to what Matthew knew to be Danbury's first rule of investigation—never to assume anything.

"OK," said Danbury. "We need to get back up there. To that hotel."

"And we need to talk to Pavlov," said Matthew.

"I want a word with him too," said Rhodes.

"When's the autopsy? On Professor Stevenson?" asked Danbury.

"First thing in the morning," answered Rhodes. "It's been moved up due to the tie to the two earlier murders."

"Right now, I need food," said Matthew, holding his stomach to keep it from growling loudly.

"Food now. Pavlov in the morning. Autopsy results. Then we travel back north." Danbury summarized. "We need a car."

"There's a replacement waiting for you out front," said the guy at the technical controls. "I got a message about that a little while ago from the front desk. The rental agency delivered it, and their guy is waiting for the one you drove in to be released to them."

"Good luck with that," Danbury said with a grin. "Could be a long wait. Ready, Doc?"

"More than ready," answered Matthew, his stomach growling on cue as he stood and pulled his jacket from the back of the chair. "But why Pavlov in the morning? Nobody would be expecting us to go back there tonight. If Rhodes is there with officers standing by, neither would they be likely to try to shoot us again."

"You make a good point," said Rhodes. "Why put off until tomorrow"—he began the cliché, then completed it with a grin—"what they're less likely to see coming tonight."

"Good plan, Doc," agreed Danbury.

Medically minded, Matthew had realized months before that the logical thought processes from one profession easily transferred to the other. As a physician, he used the clues provided by his patients and their symptoms to diagnose and treat their conditions—or refer them to the right specialist who could. In the world of a detective, the process was much the same sort of reasoning, merely applied a little differently.

"There's a place near here," said Rhodes. "It's a Cuban café."

Matthew bit back the comment in his mind, announcing that they'd just eaten at one of those places because, hungry as he was, he could have eaten nearly anything.

"They have great sandwiches. The beef is sliced thin, then piled up thick. Or you can get it with pork."

"Sold," said Matthew, leading the way out of the room.

*****

After a quick dinner and a full tactical discussion about approaching Pavlov's house for a second time that day, they paid their bills and offered the appropriate amount of praise for the food to the family that owned the little café. Then they headed out to meet the marked police cruiser that Rhodes had summoned to the parking lot.

The replacement SUV provided by the rental agency was also a Chevrolet Tahoe. It was so nearly identical to the one they'd been in when they were shot at, that the only thing missing—to Matthew's relief—were the bullet holes. Climbing into it still made him cringe. Why black again? Wouldn't dark blue or green work as well, he wondered.

Aloud, he asked, as they made their way out of the parking lot and back toward Pavlov's street, "We're following Rhodes in this time?" It was a detail that hadn't been specifically discussed—which car was going in first.

"We are. The police cruiser will follow. Park at the curb outside. Another will patrol the area while we're inside. It looks like a compound in there. Behind the gates. And all the high fencing. We're treating it as such."

Matthew nodded in the darkened car that was lit rhythmically by the streetlights placed at intervals as they made their way down what had become a residential road. Approaching the house from the other direction this time, they waited by the curb to make the left turn into the driveway behind Rhodes. His car was tucked into the short bit of driveway at the street outside the gate.

Whatever Rhodes had said into the box at the brick gateway managed to get them access. One side of the gigantic metal gate swung open.

Danbury pulled across the now mostly deserted street and in behind Rhodes' unmarked police cruiser. They made their way, slowly and carefully, through the gate before it swung closed behind. The driveway wasn't long. It wound through palm trees on either side that were lit from beneath. The fronds waving in the breeze looked ominous, thought Matthew, but maybe that was the kind of day he'd had.

They parked in a circular drive behind a Maserati that Matthew was admiring and wondering why it wasn't in a protected garage. Normally, he'd have taken the time to look it over, appreciatively. But tonight, they had other business to attend to. The old Maserati song that was older than he was began running through his head as the three of them—Rhodes, Matthew, and Danbury—assembled on the wide tiled porch.

They stood under a portico that extended upward to a second story, which was rare in most areas of Miami. White cylindrical columns supported the ceiling from which hung a massive light fixture that brightly lit the porch and beyond.

That light fixture must be heavy, thought Matthew, stepping aside from directly beneath it as the door swung open. A small graying man in a black suit opened the door for them and wordlessly beckoned them in. Were he not with two fully armed police officers, Matthew would have hesitated longer before crossing the threshold. He chided himself for jumping slightly when the door slammed shut behind him.

A cool marbled entryway extended to the second floor with a small balcony overlooking it all. Standing there above them was the man who had reminded Matthew of Boris Karloff in the old movies. Studying the man now, he thought it was probably as much the voice as anything else. The dark eyes, slightly sunken, peering from beneath thick brows, enhanced that image.

Matthew tried to shake off the feeling that Pavlov was creepy because of his own assessment of the man's appearance. If he'd had to describe him in a single word, he wasn't sure if the word would be haunting or haunted.

19 ~ PROMOTING UNDERSTANDING

"Come in, gentlemen," said Pavlov as he made is way over to and then down a wide curved staircase on the right. "I did think you were coming earlier today."

"We were," answered Danbury. "Until we were ushered away."

"Ushered away? By whom?" asked Pavlov.

"No idea," said Danbury. "We hoped you could tell us that."

"I was expecting you," said Pavlov, rounding the newel post and offering his hand to Danbury and then to Matthew to shake. Danbury introduced himself, Matthew, and Rhodes. Pavlov nodded curtly at Rhodes. "No one here should have asked you to leave."

"They didn't exactly ask," said Danbury.

"Please, come this way where we can talk comfortably. Can I offer you anything? A bourbon, perhaps? A Cuban cigar?"

As they followed him down the center hallway and into a light-wood-paneled library, they all politely declined. Matthew kept his comments about assuming that would be vodka to himself as he perched on the edge of a leather chair.

Assessing Pavlov without staring at him, Matthew realized two things. The first was that this was not the face of the man in his dream. That face, he was certain, wasn't as angular and chiseled as Pavlov's. It was more rounded. The second thought was that if this man didn't look and sound like Boris Karloff—and if he smiled occasionally—Matthew might not think that he could be a murderer. If he looked less the part of a monster from old horror movies, his innocence wouldn't be so much in question. Those thoughts were unsettling because he knew that they were stereotypical thoughts that shouldn't have a place in his mind.

"Now tell me," said Pavlov. "Who ushered you away earlier today and why?"

Matthew watched his face carefully, as he was sure both Rhodes and Danbury were doing. Danbury explained that they'd been chased and shot at as they were turning into the end of the driveway by the gate.

"Here?" asked Pavlov, appearing to be both surprised and alarmed. "Someone shot at you in front of the house here?"

"Just down from it," answered Danbury. "You know nothing about that?"

"Of course not!" insisted Pavlov vehemently. He did look a bit taken aback, but why could be explained in myriad ways. That he'd been called out or that the attempt was unsuccessful were both plausible explanations if he were involved. That something like that had occurred in front of his house when the targets were coming to see him was also a possible reason, were he innocent of it all. Would he tell them which if he were asked, Matthew wondered and doubted it.

"You didn't hear anything?" persisted Danbury.

"Not that I recall. What time was that?"

"At dusk. Almost five," answered Danbury.

"I was in the kitchen at the back of the house about that time," said Pavlov. "I was talking with my cook about a menu for the rest of the week. He didn't hear anything, or he'd have said something. You're welcome to ask Hester who you met when you came in. He runs the household and would have been the only other person here at that time. The cleaning service had been here, but they would have been gone, as was the gardener, by that time."

The popping noises had been quiet for the damage they'd done and the more extensive damage they surely could have done, thought Matthew. The weapon was likely silenced, therefore making it entirely possible that Pavlov hadn't heard it from the back of his mansion of a house.

"Nobody else was here?" asked Danbury.

"No, I live alone," responded Pavlov, and Matthew noticed a downward tug at the corners of his eyes as he said it.

Rhodes asked to speak with Hester, and Pavlov called him in. If Danbury was a man of few words, Hester was nearly mute. He provided mono-syllabic answers indicating that he'd gone to check the call box at the front gate at about four forty-five, but he found nobody there. Afterward, he'd returned upstairs and didn't hear gunshots.

That was odd, thought Matthew, because they'd never made it to the call box. After Hester was dismissed, he asked Pavlov about it, "Hester mentioned the call box. We pulled into the end of the driveway a little before five, but we never made it up to the call box to let anyone know we were there. You have to push the button for that, right? Someone pulling up into the end of the driveway doesn't trip anything and notify you?"

"Precisely," said Pavlov. "Driving up used to trigger a camera system and a notification in the house. I've disabled that because so many people choose to turn around there, where the end of the driveway is wider where it meets the street. I regret to hear that you had such an eventful evening earlier." He looked down at his hands folded neatly in his lap. "What was it that you wanted to talk to me about?"

"A group of Ukrainian missionaries is missing. My church in North Carolina sponsors them and brings them here to present their ministry to other churches in the US," said Matthew. "That's what we stopped by St. Athanasius to ask Father Grossman about when you were leaving his office yesterday."

"Ah yes, I did hear you mention that you wanted to talk to him about that. Have they been located? I'm assuming not if you're here to talk to me about them now."

"Two of them have been," said Danbury. "We're investigating their murders."

They all watched Pavlov's face as he was given this information. An odd look passed over it that wasn't quite readable. If Matthew had no preconceived ideas about the Russian population at the church— and had Stevenson not told them about pastor spies—he might have thought it was fear. Maybe it was, he thought, attempting to keep an open mind.

"I'm so sorry to hear that," said Pavlov. "I was looking forward to meeting them and hearing about their ministry. They serve mostly families—children's ministry and camps, right?"

"Mostly," answered Matthew. "Though they work with all sorts of people, lead Bible studies and worship, and help anyone they can who needs assistance. Or at least they did. They leave behind four small children." He'd added the last because Pavlov's interest in that aspect of the ministry hadn't escaped his notice. "We need to find them, we hope alive, and return them home to their children and their mission. What can you tell us about the arrangements you made for them to speak to your group at St. Athanasius?"

"Not a lot," said Pavlov. "Father Grossman called a meeting and we briefly discussed it. Bringing them to speak to us was a unanimous decision. We all wanted to hear more about their ministry in Ukraine."

"We were told that you were particularly interested in it," said Matthew. "Why was that?"

"Ah, I do have a personal interest that goes beyond the church's involvement and support, yes. My grandparents, my mother's parents, were from Ukraine. I still have some distant relatives there who I don't know much about. I've become interested in my family ancestry recently, and I'd been meaning to reach out to them. I want to learn more. I thought perhaps getting involved in the ministry of this missionary group might be a good start to connecting with that part of my heritage."

That reasoning sounded benign enough, Matthew thought.

"How did you learn about the missionaries? That they were coming to Florida?" asked Danbury.

Pavlov looked genuinely confused by that question, "I told you. There was an urgent called meeting of the parish council of St. Athanasius Orthodox Church. Father Grossman apologized for the abruptness and lack of notice, but timing was everything in this case. He'd found out about the availability of the mission team, and he said they were only due to be here a couple of days before returning home."

"You knew nothing about them before then?" asked Danbury.

"No. That was the first I'd heard of them, but we all wanted to learn more and hear from them directly."

"Were you at a church up north of here? A few weeks ago. Did you hear about them there?" persisted Danbury.

"No," said Pavlov, looking confused. Genuinely or not, Matthew couldn't tell as he continued. "I travel a good bit, but I haven't been to any other churches in years. Who told you that I had?"

"You were away last night, right? Overnight?" asked Danbury.

"That's right. I left yesterday around lunchtime. I met with financial consultants in the Keys about an acquisition down there. Then I returned late this afternoon. I was home around four, I think. Maybe a little earlier."

"Does the name Alex Stevenson mean anything to you?" asked Danbury.

"I don't think so. Should it?"

"How about Aleksander Stepanov?"

"No, who are they?"

"They're one and the same," replied Danbury. "And he was murdered. Probably last night."

"Ah, so you were checking to see if I had an alibi," said Pavlov, leaning back into his chair, his face seeming to pale. "I do, and I can provide it if you'd like. I'd appreciate your discretion because the acquisition I'm working on has not been made public. If the wrong people heard about it, that would be the end of it."

"Your alibi can account for last night? And this morning?" asked Rhodes, speaking up.

"They can, yes. We had a late dinner, then drinks while we worked on some details and logistics. I met them for breakfast, and we signed the paperwork this morning to pursue this opportunity. I'll get you both the hotel information and their names and contact numbers," said Pavlov, rising and going over to his desk. Pulling out a pad and pen and consulting his phone, he jotted the information down while they waited.

"Thank you, Mr. Pavlov," said Rhodes.

"Of course. Is there anything else I can help you with?" Pavlov asked, handing Danbury the piece of paper he'd jotted the information on. "I'd very much like to know that your missionaries are found and headed home to be with their family and continue their ministry."

"There is one more thing," said Matthew. "Would you mind giving us a minute?" he asked Danbury and Rhodes.

Rhodes looked surprised at the request, but Danbury nodded to him reassuringly. Standing, he said, "Sure. We'll wait outside. In the car."

"Shall I call Hester?" asked Pavlov.

"We'll see ourselves out," said Rhodes.

"As you wish," replied Pavlov.

That, alone, spoke volumes in Matthew's mind. Would Pavlov be so relaxed with two detectives wandering through his home unescorted if he had something to hide? If he did, it must be well hidden, Matthew concluded.

When they were alone, Matthew leaned forward and said, "Thanks for providing the alibis. I'm sure they're checking those now."

"No problem. You have something else you wanted to discuss with me?"

"I do. It's kind of personal, which is why I asked them to leave. You don't have to answer anything I ask you, and it's all off the record. Obviously."

"OK," said Pavlov slowly and apprehensively, settling partially back into the leather chair opposite Matthew.

"Earlier, when we were talking about your living situation, you said that you live alone."

"I do."

"This is a huge house."

"It is a lot for me to ramble around in alone," answered Pavlov, and Matthew observed the downward turn at the corners of his eyes again. "But I don't have any plans to move yet."

"You mentioned the ministry for children and families that the missionaries provide in Ukraine when you said you'd wanted to meet them and learn more about what they do."

"That's right. I looked them up online after Father Grossman told us what the urgent meeting was about. So that I could make an informed decision about welcoming them here."

"They do lots of other things too, but you seemed particularly interested in that family facet of their ministry."

"Yes, I suppose I am."

"As we came in, I noticed portraits of a beautiful woman and two small children," said Matthew. "Hanging along the hallway."

When Pavlov merely nodded sadly but didn't respond to what wasn't really a question, Matthew tried again. "Are those portraits of your wife and children?"

"Yes," he answered quietly.

"Where are they?" Matthew asked as gently as he could.

"They're deceased," he responded so softly that Matthew barely heard him.

"I'm sorry to pry into your private life, Mr. Pavlov, but this could be related," said Matthew. "How long ago did they die?"

"Nearly two years ago now," he replied, his eyes filling with tears that he tried to blink back before one managed to slide over his chiseled right cheekbone and down to his chin, unchecked.

"May I ask how?"

"They were in a car accident."

"Was anyone else involved, or was it a single-car accident?"

"Just my wife's car."

"How did it happen?"

"She went over a bridge right after a curve in the road."

"Were there skid marks?"

"No," said Pavlov, jerking his head around to look at Matthew. "How could you possibly know that?"

"Do you have any enemies that you know of?" persisted Matthew.

"I've made a few, certainly. Sometimes, business acquisitions don't go exactly as the original owners had intended or preferred. I've had a few who were angry with me."

"Enough so to kill your family?"

"No!" said Pavlov. Then he calmed himself. "I hardly think so."

"But you suspect that somebody did kill your wife and children, don't you?"

"It was never confirmed, though I pushed them to investigate it further."

"Why was that?" asked Matthew.

"I think her car was tampered with. As you say, there were no skid marks where she went over the bridge. They found nothing chemically altered in her body. She wasn't drugged, and there were no signs of a stroke or heart attack, seizure, anything like that."

"I don't believe that there's a way to prove someone recently deceased suffered a seizure," said Matthew pensively. "Those signs are often not very specific."

Pavlov nodded. "There was no history of any of that. She was perfectly healthy. They didn't find cancer or anything else that might have caused a change in how her body responded to stimulus."

"That sounds like a pretty thorough autopsy," said Matthew.

"I insisted that it be so," said Pavlov. "They ruled it an accidental death, saying she could have been distracted by one of my children from where they were restrained in the back seat," he said, choking on the words. "They couldn't get out of the car. After it went over the bridge and into the water."

"I'm so sorry to have asked these difficult questions," said Matthew, trying to put himself into his professional medical mode as if he were talking to a patient. "It sounds like it's related to the current situation. Did you receive any threats or instructions to do anything you might not have wanted to do?"

"How could you possibly know that?" asked Pavlov, leaning forward in his chair.

"I didn't until you just confirmed it."

"Oh," said Pavlov.

"Do you know who threatened you?"

"No, I never did know."

"What did they ask you to do?"

"It wasn't what they'd asked me to do. It's what they demanded that I not do."

"When was that?"

"It started about a month before," he began but couldn't finish his sentence.

"Before the tragedy?" Matthew finished for him and Pavlov nodded, ducking his head to avoid eye contact.

"What did they demand that you not do?"

"I'm not even sure how anyone knew about it. I wondered that at the time."

"Let's start with what they wanted you not to do and then move on to who knew about it. But first, would you talk to Danbury about it? I'm not sure how you feel about Rhodes," said Matthew, having sensed some unexplained animosity there.

"I remember Rhodes. He was involved in the investigation when," he said and couldn't finish that sentence. He shook his head to clear the thought. "I don't trust Rhodes. Like the others, he was far too quick to dismiss my wife's death as an accident. Or, really, worse still, as her own fault."

"Would it be OK to bring Danbury in? You can trust him to listen and hear what you're saying."

"I suppose so," answered Pavlov, shrugging consent. The solidly imposing man had shrunk considerably back into the chair, and his chiseled features looked sad to Matthew now, not at all intimidating and not angry or monstrous.

Pulling his phone out, Matthew texted Danbury and then said to Pavlov, "I'll go let him in if that's OK."

Pavlov nodded his assent.

20 ~ CONNECTIONS

Matthew quickly explained what he'd learned to Danbury before bringing him back into the library. Pavlov still sat, sunken in the leather chair, staring into the stratosphere beyond where the present company existed.

"Mr. Pavlov?" said Matthew gently as he and Danbury settled into chairs. "We need to know whatever you can tell us about the demand you mentioned that you not do something, what that was, and who else knew about it."

"Yes, of course," said Pavlov as if he'd suddenly realized they were still there. "You really think this is related to the current situation?"

"I do," said Matthew.

"Could it help to determine who killed my wife?"

"It might. That was nearly two years ago, but the evidence was all logged, as were the findings from the autopsy that you insisted be thorough," answered Matthew, looking over at Danbury, who nodded his confirmation of Matthew's assessment.

"I knew then, and I know now, that it wasn't her fault. She was a careful driver. And our children behaved in a car. They were five and seven, of rational ages and beyond the years of having tantrums for no apparent reason."

"OK, so help us to prove that," said Matthew. "Tell us everything you can remember about the demand that you received."

"It was March of 2018," began Pavlov. "I was negotiating the purchase of some waterfront property north of here, below Fort

Lauderdale. It's on a canal off the river and highly desirable. I planned to develop it with apartments, condominiums, shops, and such—to create a community. I wanted to see the property for myself, so I toured it. Not with a real estate agent or with anyone who would tip off onlookers—if there were any—as to my purpose for being there. Just my wife and I. We had a nice lunch and then went for a walk. She didn't know the true purpose of the walk by the water that day."

"And then what happened?"

"When we returned to the car, there was an envelope in the driver's seat."

"Your car wasn't locked?"

"It was. I am certain that I locked it, and I remember unlocking it for us to get in it."

"And then what?"

"I saw the envelope, and I was curious, of course, so I opened it. There was a note inside with a message that sounded like a veiled threat."

"Do you still have the note?"

"No, I tucked it into my pocket at the time. I told my wife it was a bill I had forgotten to pay, as if I'd dropped it myself, and tried to change the subject to get her mind off it. She'd no doubt noticed my apprehension over it, but I didn't want to alarm her. At that point, I didn't think there was reason for concern. Later, back at my office, I shredded it."

"What did it say?" asked Danbury, apparently unable to leave the questioning to Matthew any longer.

"It had three words, 'Don't do it.'"

"That was all?" asked Danbury, looking over at Matthew.

"Yes."

"Was it handwritten?" asked Danbury.

"No, it was typed. Or printed from a computer. It wasn't handwritten," said Pavlov in obvious irritation at his inability to explain it.

"But that wasn't all, was it?" asked Matthew.

"No," said Pavlov. "That was the first one. I didn't know what it meant then. Not at first. The only clue was contextual—where I was and what I was doing at the time I received it."

"There were more?" Matthew asked gently.

"Yes, two more."

"You don't have either of those either?" asked Matthew.

"No," said Pavlov. "I destroyed them. Shredded them all."

"Tell us about the second one," said Danbury.

"When and how did you get it, and what did it say?" Matthew amended the question in more detail as Pavlov seemed confused and unable to determine where to start.

"The second one came to my office. It was in an envelope with the address typed but no stamp or any sign that it had been mailed. It was two sentences, also sounding like a veiled threat. I don't remember the exact words, but they basically told me to back off from my purchase of property along the canal because it wasn't safe."

"It wasn't safe?" repeated Danbury.

"That's what it said. Those words I remember because I pondered their meaning. That could be taken more than one way. It could have been the property itself that wasn't safe or the transaction, somehow."

"You didn't know which it was then?"

"I didn't. And I can tell you I very much resented being told to back off from it. I was arrogant, I know, and my wife and children paid dearly for that mistake." Pavlov choked out the last few words and paused before adding, "As have I."

"And the third. It was also a note?" asked Danbury.

"It was. I found it in my mailbox at home. Like the others, it was in an envelope with my address typed, but no stamp or other indication that it had been mailed."

"Sending you a message," said Danbury. "They knew where to find you."

"I thought so too, but as I said, I was ready for a fight, and I thought they'd picked the wrong guy to try to threaten. Obviously, I severely underestimated them."

"What did this one say?" asked Matthew.

"It was more specific," Pavlov answered, then paused. "It said that I had one week to pull my offer on the property along the canal, or the consequences would be dire. Something along those lines." He shrugged resignedly.

"But you didn't?" asked Danbury.

"I did not, no. I thought the sender a coward because they were hiding behind the notes. I didn't give it much credence at the time."

"Now you think it was related?" asked Danbury.

"I know that it was."

"Why?"

"Because my wife and children died a week and a day later. The day after, I didn't pull my offer on the property."

"Did you pull it? Later?" asked Danbury.

"I did. I was crushed. Destroyed. They were my world. I had no desire to develop the property after I lost them. If it weren't beneath the airport, I'd have considered putting a house there myself."

"It's south of the Fort Lauderdale Airport?" clarified Matthew.

"It is."

"Who bought it? And what did they do with it? Do you know?" asked Matthew.

"As much as there is to know," responded Pavlov. "It hasn't been developed. It still has warehouses there along the canal, as it did when I was looking at it. The company that bought it is some sort of shell corporation. I began digging into it because, initially, I didn't care if they came back for me or not. I had already lost everything I loved most and I thought I had nothing left to lose. Eventually I decided to drop it and try to move on with my life."

"Can you give us that information?" asked Danbury. "The location of the property. And whatever you found. On the shell corp."

"Sure," said Pavlov, rising from his chair and moving listlessly back to the desk. Pulling out the pad and pen again and consulting his phone, he jotted the information down and then tore the sheet off and handed it to Danbury.

Matthew reached for it, took a picture of it with his phone, and handed the paper back to Danbury.

"I hope this helps you find the bastards who killed my family," said Pavlov. "I had an inkling." He paused.

"An inkling of what?" prodded Danbury.

"That someone within the police department was involved somehow. Or at least bribed to look the other way. I told them about the notes I'd received. But when I couldn't produce them, the police responded as if they'd never existed at all. They didn't take them seriously."

"Who else knew? About the purchase offer?"

"That's the thing," said Pavlov. "Two other people knew that I'd made an offer on that property. My lawyer knew, and a property real estate agent knew. It was all done anonymously, as are most of my transactions. If other entities learn that I'm interested in a property or an acquisition, the prices tend to go up. Perception is that I have deep pockets and access to deeper ones, so the prices get jacked up. Sometimes, it's blatantly done outright, and others, it's done by someone else placing higher bids until I go higher. Usually, that other entity then disappears."

"That's not ethical, and I'd assume it's not legal either," asserted Matthew.

"But still, it happens."

"You mentioned deeper pockets," said Danbury. "Any we should know about?"

"There aren't any, really," said Pavlov. "I have gotten loans for some of the transactions over the years, but all legally acquired and above board."

"No shady business partners?" asked Danbury.

"Not that I'm aware of. When I work with partners, they're those that I've known and worked with for years."

"Did any of them know about your offer to purchase the property along the canal?" asked Matthew.

"No. I had not contacted anyone to partner on that venture," said Pavlov. "I do have a list of potential partners I might have contacted when it was time to design and build the community."

"Are you on good terms with them? All of them?" asked Danbury.

"As far as I know."

"Are there any you're not on good terms with?"

"How do you mean?"

"Any disagreements? Strong differences of opinions? Parting of the ways? Anybody think they got short-changed? Or had expectations that weren't met?"

"No one that I can think of," said Pavlov slowly, contemplating.

"Any chance you can share your list of potential business partners with us?" asked Matthew.

"And any others you've worked with in the past," added Danbury. "Say, two to five years ago."

Pavlov considered this for a moment and then said, "I suppose I can do that. I'll need to get by my office to compile that information. I'll print it for you if you promise to destroy it afterward. I'm not sending it electronically. I don't trust that it won't get intercepted by someone."

"We can pick that up in the morning," said Danbury.

"OK, I'll have it ready by eight. I usually go into the office early when I'm in town," said Pavlov and rattled off an address. Danbury handed back the paper from the notepad, and Pavlov added his office address to the bottom of it.

After they thanked Pavlov for his time and the information, Hester showed Matthew and Danbury out formally. Rhodes was waiting by his cruiser, looking both impatient and annoyed at having been literally left outside of the discussion.

"Well?" he demanded.

Danbury laid out the information that they'd gleaned from Pavlov. He mentioned the promised list of partners but excluded the claims that the police department had been involved in covering up the earlier death of Pavlov's wife.

"You think it's connected?" asked Rhodes when he'd finished.

"Don't you?" asked Matthew.

"Sounds like it might be," admitted Rhodes.

"Have you been through Stevenson's office? Any of the contents?"

"Just scratched the surface on that," said Rhodes. "Most of what we've found so far is academic resources. There's very little in the way of personal effects in his office, files, memorabilia, or anything like that."

"Look for notes," said Danbury. "Anything threatening. Stevenson didn't mention that to us. But the death of his wife is too similar. Very much like Pavlov's. And the same time frame. Pavlov denied knowing Stevenson. By either of his names. There's no way to prove otherwise. Or that Pavlov got threatening notes. But if he did, maybe Stevenson did too. Before his wife was killed. It would help to know what they wanted from him. If Stevenson was also threatened. And if he saved the notes."

"Yeah, makes sense. I'll pass that along," said Rhodes.

"Have you reached his daughters yet?" asked Danbury.

"One of my officers did this afternoon. They found the daughter who was the emergency contact in Denver. She said she'd convey the information to her younger sister, who lives outside of Tucson."

"Did she have any idea who might have wanted to kill her father?" asked Matthew.

"She clammed up when they asked her that. She insisted, too strongly, that she had no idea. She said she hadn't seen her father since shortly after her mother's death. She talked to him about once a week."

"Sounds like she knows something," said Danbury.

"Or maybe she suspects something, but she's too afraid of what she thinks she knows to talk about it to the police," added Matthew.

"That's a strong possibility," agreed Rhodes, nodding slowly. "She's flying in tomorrow morning to deal with her father's house and to make funeral arrangements as soon as his body is released from autopsy. I'm not sure about the younger sister, but I'll be sure to talk to whoever shows up."

"What time does she get in?" asked Matthew.

"I'm not sure. Why?"

"I'd like to talk to her. I'm not a police officer, so I'm less threatening. Like with Pavlov, people will talk to me who won't—for whatever reason—talk to you."

"OK," said Rhodes. "I can't argue with that. Pavlov did talk to you. Where are you going now?"

"Back to the hotel," said Danbury. "To pack."

"Pack?" asked Matthew. "I was planning to look up this information that Pavlov gave us about the canal property and shell corporation."

"Yeah, we're on it," said Rhodes. "I called that information in. I also want to check the reports after his wife's death to see if the story he gave us then matches what he told you."

"Good plan," said Danbury. "We can go see the property in the morning. After we check out of the hotel. Get the list from Pavlov. And talk to Stevenson's daughter."

"We're heading north again?"

"We need to. We got corroboration here. Either they planned it all very carefully," began Danbury.

"Or they're telling the truth, and Pastor Fisher isn't," Matthew completed the thought.

"Exactly," said Danbury.

"Whatever we find," said Matthew solemnly. "I hope it's connected enough to the reason that Greg and Darya disappeared to lead us to them in time."

"Yeah, me too, Doc," said Danbury. Matthew was disturbed by both the look on his face and the tone of his voice. For once, the big detective was clearly readable. Danbury didn't hold out much hope of finding them alive. And for the first time since they'd arrived in Florida, Matthew felt discouraged. He was exhausted—both physically and emotionally—but the disturbing feeling that he was losing hope went deeper than that.

21 ~ TOSSED ABOUT

"Danbury!" hissed Matthew as soon as he opened the door to his hotel room and switched on the light. Backing carefully out of the room without touching anything, he felt all tiredness ebb immediately from his body like a weak current. An electric jolt of adrenaline kicked in, replacing it.

"What is it, Doc?" asked Danbury. Staring at his phone, he had paused in front of his door without opening it. Matthew pointed wordlessly into his room. Danbury stepped behind him and peered in.

"Somebody has been in here," said Matthew, realizing the magnitude of the understatement. His suitcase was upended in one corner, the contents thrown all around it. An upholstered chair was flipped over. The cushion, thrown across the room, was slit open, and the stuffing ripped out. Sheets, towels, pillows, a duvet, and he wasn't sure what else were strewn all over.

"I'll check mine," said Danbury, slipping back across the hallway and tapping his key card above the door handle. Opening the door slowly and peering in, he noticed Matthew's inquiring glance. "Nope. I'm good. It's just yours."

Matthew groaned as Danbury tapped his phone. "Calling Rhodes. There won't be fingerprints. But just in case. Danbury here," he said into the phone and then explained the scene before them.

"These aren't pros," added Danbury. "Not like the hotel in Georgia. That was methodically searched. Carefully. Without disrupting it. This one was tossed. They didn't care that we knew it." After a pause, he said, "OK, we'll wait for them. And sit tight."

"Walk in carefully," said Danbury sympathetically, clicking to end the call. "Can you tell if anything is missing?"

"There's nothing valuable here. I have my computer." He indicated the satchel that was slung over his shoulder, which he'd brought in from the Tahoe. "And I've got the Glock with me." Matthew patted the holster under his shirt.

Stepping carefully over the debris and into the center of the room, Matthew turned slowly, taking it all in. The room that had once been so neat and orderly looked like high winds had blown through it, leaving nothing that wasn't nailed down in the place it had previously occupied.

The mattress and springs of the king-size bed, that he'd looked forward to immediately sinking into, leaned at odd angles against the far wall. The mattress had been ripped open—the inside padding strewn all through the boxed base it had been resting on—as had the bottom of the box springs.

Nudging the bathroom door open with his elbow and clicking on the light the same way, Matthew saw a similar disarray but on a smaller scale. His toiletries littered the counter and floor, flung about here and there. The leather bag that had contained them was turned inside out and dropped on the floor. There were no towels in the bathroom at all; they had all been thrown out into the bedroom.

"One quiet, restful night would have been so nice," muttered Matthew.

"Last night wasn't quiet?" asked Danbury, having overheard.

"It should have been," responded Matthew—noncommittally—still unready to discuss the vivid dream, or vision, or whatever it was that he couldn't name from the night before.

"Did I miss something? I didn't hear anything."

"No, the noise was all in my head," responded Matthew. Then, changing the subject, he asked, "What do you think they were looking for? There was nothing exciting to find in here. Why my room and not yours? How did anybody know which was which?"

"Good questions," responded Danbury. He walked to the end of the hallway, which their rooms were near, looking up at the corners of the ceiling and then opened the exit door, scanning the landing within. After repeating the process at the other end of the hallway, he announced, "I'm going down to the front desk. There are no security cameras on this floor. But I've seen them. By the front doors. Behind the front desk. In the elevators. And at the ends of the hallway downstairs. You coming, Doc?" he asked.

"Yeah, I guess so. Rhodes is sending officers?"

"He is. They won't be in a hurry. They'll want a look. And a statement. To file an official report. But there's not much they can do. Nothing that we can't," he added, releasing the door with a swoosh behind Matthew.

At the front desk, Danbury flashed his badge and identified himself to the guy behind it. "Warren Danbury. Homicide Detective from North Carolina. We have some questions."

"How can I help you, Sir?" asked the well-dressed man professionally. His teeth were perfect. Their whiteness stood in stark contrast to the deep brown of his flawless complexion. The guy should do toothpaste commercials, Matthew thought.

"You're Samuel Dixon?" Danbury asked, motioning to the guy's name tag. Tapping to enter that information on the tablet, he pulled from the backpack that he was still lugging around with him. When the guy nodded affirmation, Danbury's fingers flew over the tiny electronic keypad.

"How long have you been here?"

"Today?" asked Dixon. As Danbury nodded and he responded, "Since six. I'm on shift until two a.m."

"The rooms on the fourth floor. They were cleaned today?"

"Certainly, Sir. Any rooms that were vacated today or occupied last night were cleaned."

"Do you know what time that happened?"

"The fourth floor is usually serviced after lunch, but I can look if you need a specific time."

"That would be helpful," Matthew answered as Danbury nodded.

"Can I ask what this is regarding?" asked Dixon as two uniformed officers came through the glass doors behind them.

"We'll get to that. In a minute," said Danbury, turning to the officers as all identified themselves and flashed badges. He briefly told them what had happened and that he was in the process of talking to the front desk attendant.

"Carry on," said one of the officers with a smirk that Matthew wasn't sure how to interpret. "We'll listen in and get the information for our report. Then we can go see the room. Like you said, I doubt we'll find anything. We'll look to be thorough."

Danbury rejoined Matthew at the desk and waited impatiently for Dixon to finish with a call on which he was obviously scheduling a reservation for somebody.

"OK," said Danbury. "You were going to check the time. When the rooms got cleaned."

"Oh right," said Dixon. "Is there something I should know about?" he asked, looking nervously past Matthew and Danbury at the two police officers who were standing, hands folded in front of them, listening to the conversation.

"You've had an intruder," answered Danbury.

"Oh! In one of our guest suites?

"Yes, 421. Mine," answered Matthew.

"Only the one room?" asked Dixon.

"As far as we know," answered Danbury.

"Was anything valuable taken?" Dixon asked, obviously concerned.

"No, I don't think so," answered Matthew, leaning forward on the counter. "There was nothing valuable in the room to take. It was ransacked, though."

"Ooooh," said Dixon. "I need to write up an incident report and call the hotel manager to let her know."

"After we're done," said Danbury, holding up a hand.

"OK," answered Dixon dubiously. "She will likely want to be here if the police go into the room, though."

Taking a deep breath, Danbury said, "Go ahead. Call her. We'll wait."

"What do I tell her?" asked Dixon, picking up the handset to the desk phone. "That a room was broken into and—ah—disturbed?"

"Right. She needs to come now. To be here when the police look."

"When did this happen?" asked Dixon, struggling with his professional demeanor.

"That's what we need you to tell us," said Danbury impatiently.

"We just found it," said Matthew. "Before we came to talk to you. We've been gone all day since early this morning, so we have no idea. Likely after the room was cleaned, though, which is why it's important that we know when that happened."

"And to see your security footage," added Danbury. "See if anyone stands out. Coming or going."

"She'll definitely want to be here for that," said Dixon, poking buttons on the phone and talking in a clipped brisk manner to the person on the other end of the call.

"She's on her way," said Dixon, replacing the handset. "She told me to cooperate with you fully."

"Thank you," said Matthew, trying to coax the guys' helpfulness. "Can you see what time room 421 was cleaned?"

"Oh, right," said Dixon. Pulling over a keyboard, clicking it, and studying a monitor, he said, "It looks like it was between two and four. There were six rooms on that floor that got cleaned. One person serviced all six. He started at the other end of the hall where the other four were. So, it was probably at least three before he got to your end, maybe later."

"OK, three or so," said Danbury aloud as he tapped his tablet to enter that information. "Who was here at the lobby desk during that time?"

"There were two people here from ten this morning until six tonight when I arrived, at least officially. We usually overlap a little to hand off anything that needs attention."

"Can you reach them?" asked Danbury. "I need to ask them some questions."

"I can," said Dixon, checking his watch. "I hate to disturb them this late, though."

"We wouldn't ask if it weren't important," said Matthew. "We're here looking for a team of missionaries who are missing."

"Were they staying here?" asked Dixon in alarm.

"No, but the intrusion is likely related," answered Matthew. "It's important that we find the missionaries before it's too late. Figuring out who searched my room might help."

"Just a few questions," said Danbury. "It won't take long."

"OK," agreed Dixon as he leaned forward and aggressively poked buttons on the phone, including the speaker button.

"Hello?" answered a sleepy female voice.

Dixon identified himself, explained why he was calling, and introduced Danbury. Then Danbury took over.

"Did anybody ask for information today? About a guest? About anybody staying here?"

"No," said the voice. "And we wouldn't have given them that information if anybody had, unless the guest had asked us to do so."

"No inquires at all? About Matthew Paine? Or Warren Danbury? Or Dr. Paine? Or Detective Danbury?"

"No, nothing like that."

"Did you notice anything unusual today?" asked Danbury.

"Unusual, how?"

"Like somebody hanging around. Maybe watching the lobby area. Somebody who isn't staying here. Or didn't belong. Maybe listening in. To whatever was happening at the front desk. Or discretely watching guests."

"Not that I can remember," she answered. "If they were, they weren't obvious about it. We do have little partitioned workstations around the corner from the front desk for our guests. That's our complimentary office eSpace. Each work area has a monitor, keyboard, and charging station. So, it's common for them to be in use. Anyone sitting there could probably hear what's going on at the front desk. Did you check in to the hotel today?"

"No. We checked in on Tuesday," said Danbury.

"We didn't call the front desk, so no conversation could have been overheard," added Matthew. "We left early this morning, and we were gone all day today. Nobody followed us in—at least not today."

"That doesn't help, then. If there was nothing specific to have been overheard. I'm sorry," she said. "I wish I could tell you something useful, but it was an ordinary day, nothing exciting at all."

"You didn't have any internal conversations? Like with the cleaning staff?" asked Matthew, trying to be exhaustive and beginning to feel exhausted instead.

"Not about the fourth floor. We had a toilet leaking on the second floor and called in plumbers. That's the only thing I can think of that was at all exciting. Even that isn't so unusual. We've used that same plumbing service since before I started work there about five years ago. The two guys who came out are brothers, the owners."

"And the rest of your staff," prodded Danbury. "They all showed up? On time. No replacements?"

"Yes, they were all here; and, no, there were no replacements. The breakfast staff was cleaning up when I came in at ten. They left shortly before eleven. The housekeeping staff all arrived on schedule and left as they finished their floors."

They thanked her and moved on.

A second call was placed to the other employee who had been on the day shift. A male voice that sounded far less sleepy yielded nothing further. A final call obviously woke the guy who had cleaned the rooms. The guy's English was spotty, and Matthew knew that his own Spanish was worse. After a few attempts to communicate, he asked them to hold on, and he called someone else to the phone.

A young female voice identified herself as his daughter. After a few back-and-forth bits of translated conversation, she verified that he'd cleaned both rooms on the far end of the fourth floor shortly after three p.m. that afternoon. He'd clocked out at four thirty.

During that call, a disheveled woman arrived, obviously hastily dressed in wrinkled slacks and a blouse that was half tucked in and had some sort of stain on the left shoulder. Her hair was pulled back in a messy bun.

Dixon introduced her as the hotel manager. Coolly and calmly, she escorted the two officers, Danbury, and Matthew, to the fourth floor to examine Matthew's room. A sharp intake of breath when she walked in belied her calm veneer. She was obviously shaken when she saw the destruction. Her eyes darted around the room, from the lamp thrown to the floor and broken to a full-length mirror—into which the desk chair had been hurled—that lay shattered on the floor outside of the bathroom door.

Danbury was watching her, taking it all in. "The intruders didn't find anything," he said as the two officers donned gloves and began to sift through the debris.

"What were they looking for?" she asked, her face ashen in the overhead lighting.

"I'm not sure," said Matthew. "But there was nothing valuable here, thankfully."

"Then you won't be submitting a claim?"

"A claim?" asked Matthew.

"Against our insurance, for anything destroyed or stolen."

"Oh. I hadn't thought about it, but no. If my clothes are all here, they can be washed. Some of them needed to be anyway." He motioned to the heap on the floor beside the upended suitcase.

"I'll get them run through our laundry service. At no charge, of course," she clarified, blowing out a breath of obvious relief.

"When we're done," said one of the officers over his shoulder from where he was kneeling beside the pile of clothing—carefully pulling each piece apart and sifting through it. Turning to Danbury, he asked, "Are you thinking nothing was taken because there was nothing valuable here to take? Or is there another reason?"

"Several reasons," said Danbury, rubbing the stubble on his chin with his thumb. "Another hotel room was searched. Last week. Probably related. But that search was professional. Not ransacked, and nothing was destroyed. This one wasn't done by professionals. And these searchers were angry. Likely because they didn't find anything. Not what they were looking for. Or anything of value to make their effort worthwhile."

"Oh?" asked the manager curiously.

"This goes beyond searching," answered Danbury. "The destruction of the room. There's emotion in that. Anger. Not calm cool professionalism. This was an amateur job. Or a deeply personal one."

"I agree," said the officer who'd been sifting through the clothing. "Amateurish and angry. I see both here."

The other officer, who'd just gotten off of the phone, announced, "I just updated Rhodes. Given the other situations that you've been investigating, he asked us to evaluate this incident thoroughly."

22 ~ LONGEST DAY

"This pile can go to the laundry," said the officer who'd been sifting through the heap of Matthew's belongings. He held out the pile of quick-dry shirts, pants, sleep pants, soft T-shirts, boxer briefs, and socks. What Matthew wouldn't give to slip into those soft sleep pants and T-shirt and the nearest bed, he thought, reaching for his clothing.

"May I?" asked the manager, interrupting to take the clothing. Pointing to the laundry bag that clung to one end of the ironing board, which had been thrown from the closet across the room, she asked, "And can we have that?"

"Sure," the officer said. Matthew stuffed his clothing—beginning with his boxer briefs and socks—into the bag she'd picked up. It quickly overflowed. The manager expertly draped two shirts over her shoulder and a pair of pants over her arm, making her look a bit like a robotic coat rack.

"I'll take these downstairs to laundry," she said. "And get them ahead of the morning queue. They'll be ready by seven."

"Thank you," said Matthew wearily.

"We need to see your security video," Danbury said. "Can you get that set up? Everything from three this afternoon. All angles from all cameras."

"Yes, of course," she answered, turning on her heel and walking purposefully from the room as if not looking made the mess cease to exist. "And we'll move you to a fresh room. Do you want to relocate to another floor?"

"No, thanks. If there is a room available, this floor is fine," he answered, the tiredness evident in his voice. He'd happily slip into another bed on that floor and likely not have any trouble dropping into a deep sleep. Taking one last glance at the room, Matthew could relate to it. He'd been tossed about too, since he'd arrived in Florida. It felt more like weeks than mere days, he thought, as he turned and followed the manager out and down the hallway.

"We'll be finished here soon. There's not much to process. No fingerprints or footprints that we can verify. Somebody wiped it clean," the other officer called after them. "Then you can move the rest of your things to the new room. We'll want to see that security footage too."

"Yes, yes," she muttered, making her way briskly back down the hallway and onto the elevator with Matthew and Danbury in her wake. "I'll pull a couple of monitors in from the guest eSpace area and get you set up in my office."

Matthew wasn't excited about spending more time watching hotel security footage. Danbury was apparently thinking the same thing as he said, "More hours of boredom. Maybe interrupted by something exciting."

"Paint peeling, grass growing," echoed Matthew as they trudged along behind the manager. "We should get popcorn. How much hotel video can you watch in one day?" he asked rhetorically.

"Technically, that was yesterday," said Danbury, checking his watch.

"True. Dixon will be leaving in an hour if there's anything else we need from him."

"Don't think so," said Danbury as the elevator doors opened behind the downstairs lobby desk.

He wasn't excited about looking through more video, but Matthew did want to know who had violated his space and why. He had a few ideas about that because nobody in Florida but he and Danbury knew that the fabled notebook—which Greg had brought from Ukraine—was safely locked in a police building in Raleigh.

*****

Nearly two hours later, they'd zoomed through most of the video feeds captured from eight cameras. The first six were located exactly as Danbury had described—one over the front doors, one behind the front desk, and one in each of the two elevators. Cameras at both ends of the first-floor hallway were mounted over outside doors—which also positioned them over internal doors at the stairwells. The external doors—the manager explained—were locked to the outside and exit only. Two additional cameras—one by a back entrance that staff used, and one by the door to the pool and small gym area—completed the hotel surveillance package.

Danbury and Matthew were watching one video feed on a monitor, and the two officers were each watching two others. All of them were wearying of the task, zooming through the feeds at accelerated rates until they saw motion or people enter the screen, then reversing and slowing to watch. The hotel wasn't densely populated during the week at the end of January, but guests were leaving and returning around the dinner hours.

As Matthew and Danbury were watching video from the camera above the outside back door, the staff entrance, they slowed to study three women leaving in a group around three thirty. There was nothing remarkable about the women or their exit, so they moved on. A short, stout, youthful-looking man waddled out shortly before four. Then a small, wiry man with dark hair—the guy they assumed had cleaned their rooms—left at four thirty-one, exactly as he'd said.

They sped up the video, then slowed it again to watch Dixon come up the sidewalk, swipe a badge, and enter shortly before six. They sped through a short bit of boring footage until the door opened, and a woman stepped out. Looking around, she moved briskly along the sidewalk to a car waiting at the curb.

Before they could speed up the video feed, the door opened once more, and a man came out. Holding a cigarette, he paused to light it without looking around before stepping all the way through the doorway and walking briskly away. As the door slowly closed behind him, a hand reached out from the wall beside the door and held it ajar.

The arm swung the door open, but the body it was attached to hugged the wall of the building. Mounted above the door, the camera captured the sidewalk approaching it, but its angle wasn't wide enough to provide a view of the wall on either side of the door. Whoever held the door had come along the darkened wall, not up the lit sidewalk. There was a limited view of two figures slipping in under the cover of baseball hats that were pulled down low.

The door closed slowly behind them, and Danbury paused the video. "We've got something," he said to the two officers. As they and the hotel manager crowded behind, Danbury reversed the video feed and they watched that whole sequence again. One entered, two left, then two others slipped in. Something about the arm holding the door niggled at the corners of Matthew's mind, but the video image was dark and grainy. He couldn't pinpoint what was bothering him about it.

"They not only knew where the camera was, but how it was angled," said one of the officers. "Did you see them come back out?"

"Not yet," said Danbury. "They came in at six twenty-two. We'll watch for them leaving. Get that time stamp. Then we'll go check that area. It's behind us here, right?" he asked the manager, thumbing beyond the door of the office in which they were all sitting.

"It is," she answered, nodding.

"It opens directly to the outside?" asked Danbury.

"Yes," she said, nodding. "But between here and that outside door, there are doors to the laundry facility and to the kitchen area where our staff prepares the breakfast buffet. And there are two storage rooms where supplies are kept."

"Let's see if we can find them leaving," reiterated one of the officers. "And then, as you say, Detective, we'll go check those staff areas and around the door, inside and out."

Danbury fast-forwarded through the rest of the footage and saw nothing after that point, no coming and no going through the rear door. The two officers got back on their monitors and zipped through footage until one said, "Here!"

Two men—both broad shouldered and otherwise lean—came through the stairwell doorway on the ground floor at the end of the hallway that was closest to Matthew's room upstairs. Both still donned the baseball caps pulled low over their faces, and both stared at the floor as they went down the hallway, providing no view of their faces at all. The color of their hair, cropped short, was difficult to determine from the video feed in the shadows of the hallway. Zooming in didn't help because they were too far away from the cameras at the other end of the hallway, and the image pixelated.

The camera behind the desk in the lobby captured their backs as they were leaving through the lobby shortly after seven that evening. There were no guests visible in the lobby. Dixon—whose back was to the camera behind him—was holding the phone between his shoulder and ear while tapping the keyboard in front of him. He didn't look up as they passed by him.

It was already well after dark as the two men walked away from the building, their backs to it, toward the parking lot. As the officer zoomed through the video, they saw that nobody came or went through the front entrance for the next twenty minutes afterward. Families began returning, presumably from their dinners, after seven thirty, and some revelers came in much later. There were no obvious witnesses to give a description of the two men unless, Matthew thought, somebody had seen them in the parking lot.

"Well, we know they came in shortly after six," said one of the officers. "By the back door. And left nine minutes after seven through the front entrance. Somebody might have gotten a look at their faces. Or seen them moving around the hotel. How did they get up to the fourth floor without us catching them on either of the cameras on the ground floor?"

"Oh," said the hotel manager, dully. "There's a dumbwaiter in one of the storage closets. It houses all of the cleaning supplies and the carts that our housekeeping staff uses. It opens into storage closets on each floor beside the ice machines and snack area."

"And a master key?" asked Danbury. "To get in the rooms?"

"There shouldn't be any keys in the storage rooms," said the manager. "Unless somebody got sloppy and left one on a cleaning cart."

"Is there any way to check? If somebody used it, it won't likely have been returned to the cart."

"If one is missing, housekeeping will have to request a new one this morning."

"Let us know if that happens?"

"OK."

"They weren't worried about being seen leaving," said Matthew. "They walked straight out the front doors."

"They weren't carrying anything incriminating that they were worried about getting caught with," said the police officer. "But still, it was bold. They obviously knew where all the cameras were. They had to have known that we'd look at the video. They didn't seem to care."

After checking the staff areas accessed from the back door, finding nothing amiss, and learning nothing new, one of the officers said, "Well, I think we've done all we can tonight."

"Are you finished in here?" she asked Matthew and Danbury hopefully, motioning to her office door. With one hand on the doorknob, she was poised to turn off the light and close the door behind them.

Drawing a deep breath of regret and trying not to think about the bed he wouldn't yet be dropping into, Matthew said, "Not quite. I want one more look at something on that video."

"OK, will you lock up on your way out?" she asked. "I need a couple of hours of sleep before my daughter wakes me up. She's usually awake by seven and always hungry. I don't know who coined the phrase 'sleeps like a baby,' but whoever it was had obviously never had one."

"Sure thing," said Danbury. "We won't be long."

"Thank you. I'll be back in at nine if you need anything else."

The underlying message, Matthew understood, was "Don't call me again until then."

"OK," said Danbury, sitting down in front of the makeshift monitor that he and Matthew had been working from earlier. "What did you want to see, Doc?"

"The back door feed when the two guys came in."

"OK. Why?"

"I'm not sure. Something about it bugged me."

"OK, pulling it up. To see what bugged you," said Danbury.

"It's the hand that held the door. The wrist and arm, really. Hold it there," said Matthew, eyebrow raised, as he turned his head, looking quizzically at the screen. "Can you zoom in? Even if we lose some clarity?"

"Sure, Doc," said Danbury, manipulating controls to zoom in on the extended arm as it darted from the shadows and prevented the door from swishing closed.

"There! That's it!" The image was grainy, but Matthew's brain had finally made sense of the unclear pattern. It was a distinctive one that—once he'd seen it—he couldn't unsee.

"That is what?" asked Danbury, looking confused.

"It's a tattoo of a snake's body wound twice around the guy's right wrist! See? There!" Matthew exclaimed, leaning forward and pointing at the image on the computer screen. "The tail is below his wrist on top of his hand, and the rest of the snake disappears up his arm under his sleeve."

"Yeah," said Danbury, thumbing the stubble on his chin. "I see."

23 ~ BY MORNING LIGHT

It was the last day of January. Matthew awoke to the sound of the alarm on his phone. He'd had only four hours of sleep after gathering his few belongings and switching rooms in the middle of the night. It was at least restful sleep, he thought. If he'd dreamed at all, he couldn't remember it. Unwilling to think about the horrific and seemingly unending day in between—being shot at, his ransacked room, and the snake tattoo—he willed his mind to return to the vivid dream from the night before.

Did the man who was turned away in the dream have a snake tattoo on his arm? Trying to remember exactly what he'd seen, he couldn't recall the man's wrist. Maybe he hadn't seen the guy's wrist. Who was the man in the dream, and why did it still seem important to figure that out? It was one more question in a growing list of them. There were so many more questions than answers; it seemed that every time they got one answer, it raised at least ten more questions.

His natural optimism was stronger this Friday morning, though some of it was forced as he talked to Cici on FaceTime. She knew him as well—in many ways—as he knew himself, and she could read him expertly. He didn't want to upset her by talking about all the events of the day and night before. Cici was across an ocean in London, and there was nothing she could do to help. She would worry, he knew, and he wanted to spare her that. What he wasn't admitting to himself was that she'd also likely petition him to go home, and he wasn't prepared to do that. Not yet.

Trying to ban all thoughts of being shot at and the ransacked room from his mind, he shifted his focus during their usual morning chat.

Instead, he entertained her by showing her how he was working on his unreadable face. "I've about got it down now, Cees," he said, trying to show no emotion and keep his face straight in the process. Face of stone, he told himself, trying not to grin at her.

"You can't do it," she insisted, laughing at his antics. "You have the worst poker face I've ever seen!"

If she only knew, he thought, as they professed their love, said their goodbyes, and disconnected to get on with their day—her afternoon and his morning.

Packing—after showering and shaving—was easy because he'd flown in with a carry-on suitcase and a few clothes. Those had been brought up for him from the laundry as soon as he called the front desk. He'd washed the quick-dry shirt he wore the night before in the sink and hung it on the desk chair in his new room. It had managed to dry in the few hours overnight.

Pulling out his computer, he went through his patient records, leaving a few notes and answering questions from his office staff on their voicemail. Checking his watch, he decided to spend a few minutes searching for a couple of things on his computer before going down to breakfast.

He'd been overly optimistic in thinking that this would be a quick trip. Finding people in Florida was difficult, and it took time—but he hadn't been willing to admit that to himself. Neither had he considered that they might not find them at all—and he was still unable to come to terms with that possibility—though the thought tugged annoyingly at the corners of his mind.

When Matthew arrived in the hotel lobby, Danbury was characteristically earlier. The big detective was already in the process of scarfing down a huge breakfast from the buffet. A small bag that Matthew had seen before in Danbury's Tahoe in North Carolina sat at his feet by the table—his go bag that was always packed and ready. Danbury looked up, nodded in acknowledgment, and went back to shoving massive amounts of food into his mouth faster than Matthew could imagine chewing to swallow.

Rolling his own travel bag alongside the chair across the small round table from Danbury, Matthew realized that he was hungry and went to investigate the breakfast options. A cup of coffee, heaped with sugar and cream, was first on his agenda. He considered that habit to be one of his vices.

He sat down at the table, blessed his food, and dug in—though less aggressively than Danbury had done.

"I hope the police are having better luck than I did with the owners of the property on the canal," said Matthew between bites. "I searched this morning, at least in the online public records. The shell corporation that Pavlov told us about, Preservation Reserve, is a ghost company. The name tells us nothing about its purpose, and ownership is listed under yet another company named Liberty Conservancy.

"Subsidiaries are listed under Preservation Reserve, but they're not functional—as far as I can tell. They're all named similarly. It's like somebody looked up synonyms and incorporated long strings of empty companies under related names. There's nothing about any of them online except their incorporation under the parent companies."

"We can check in with Rhodes. First thing this morning," said Danbury, wiping his mouth with a napkin and tossing it onto his empty paper plate. "I was planning to do that anyway. Then get the list from Pavlov. See if there's anything interesting."

"I hope whatever we learn will bring us closer to finding Darya and Greg. It all seems to be related, but how tenuously is any of this connected to their disappearance? I wonder if chasing down who killed Stevenson's wife and Pavlov's is the best use of our time."

Before Matthew could say more or Danbury could reply, they heard the vibration of Danbury's cell phone.

"Danbury," he said, pulling his phone from his jacket pocket and tapping to take an incoming call. Between pauses, Matthew heard uh-huh a few times and then, "Which airline? Yeah, we'll bring it by. Anything on the canal property? Or the shell corp? Preservation Reserve. Yeah, we found that too," he said, glancing over at Matthew. "Anything else?"

Matthew assumed the caller to be Sergeant Rhodes. They threw their trash away, gathered their bags, left their key cards on the desk in the lobby, and made their way out to the Tahoe. Danbury finished the call, and Matthew patiently waited for him to share what he'd learned from it.

As they climbed into the SUV, Danbury summarized quickly for Matthew. "Stevenson's daughter is on a plane. The older one. Out of Colorado. Arriving in Fort Lauderdale at ten thirty. The other daughter will be in this afternoon. Out of Nevada. Nothing yet on the shell corp. Or the canal property. Rhodes has a forensic tech guy digging into both. Stevenson's autopsy is in an hour. They're not expecting any surprises."

Getting situated and buckling up, Danbury added, "Rhodes pulled the case files. On the deaths of both wives. Stevenson's and Pavlov's. There are similarities. He had to take another call. So, I don't know what they found yet. I told him we'd share Pavlov's list. He'll share whatever he's found."

"We're going talk to the daughter when she lands?" asked Matthew.

"Yeah. What I was thinking."

"Good. Maybe she can tell us something to tie it all together. I hope she's not in danger here."

"What do you mean?"

"Stevenson said that he defected all those years ago because he knew that not to would be putting his family in danger. His wife was likely murdered, presumably for something Stevenson either wouldn't cooperate with or to ensure that he did. If we're right about that, then if his daughter knows anything, that could put her in danger."

"We need to know what she knows."

"Unless it's something she doesn't know that she knows."

"Doc, you hurt my brain sometimes," said Danbury, rubbing his head in mock pain. "Maybe she doesn't know anything. But I agree. We need to get her to talk to us. About her mother's death. See if she knew anything about it. Investigated it at all. Or knows if her father did. The timing of his death isn't a coincidence. He was killed after Greg contacted him. Specifically, after talking to us."

"But his wife died nearly two years ago. If she was murdered, how does her death fit into any of this?"

"It must, somehow. We need to keep an open mind. Follow the

leads. Assess the relevance. You're right. It doesn't fit yet. Unless Greg and Darya were involved then."

Matthew felt the irritation rising at Danbury's mention of their possible guilt again. They weren't guilty of involvement in something as horrible as murder. They couldn't be, could they? Aloud, he said, "Greg hadn't contacted the professor two years ago. At least not that he mentioned."

"Yeah, that might be key. The things he didn't tell us. Obviously, there was more. Like his wife's death."

"Maybe he didn't see the connection."

"Maybe. But Stevenson wasn't stupid. He understood lots of things. Probably most he didn't tell us. We were barely getting started. Mining the information he knew."

"That's not a comforting thought," said Matthew. "What we don't know could kill us. Literally."

"What we do know might do it first," said Danbury, making Matthew grimace.

"Pavlov's office, police precinct, Stevenson's daughter at the airport, canal property, and then to talk to Pastor Fisher and finally recheck the hotel room in Georgia, I assume," he muttered the order of operations for the day, not as a question but as a summary. Tapping his phone, Matthew found and entered the location of Pavlov's office into the nav app and clipped the phone to the dash.

"Right. We have agreement here. From everybody we've talked to. Their stories all match. On Greg and Darya. How they were coming to be here. But the stories weren't contrived. We go poke the pastor. That should be loads of fun. The conversation with Fisher."

Matthew wasn't looking forward to more intently grilling a pastor, but he knew it was necessary.

Looking up from his phone, Danbury pocketed it. He started the Tahoe, pulling out of the parking lot without further comment. The voice of the navigation app sporadically interrupting the background hum of engine noise and traffic sounds was all that was to be heard as both Danbury and Matthew were lost in their own thoughts. The interior of the SUV was otherwise quiet.

After a quick trip in and back out of the building that housed Pavlov's offices, Matthew was surprised that they weren't sent up to see him. Instead, the receptionist asked to see their ID. When she was satisfied that they were who they said they were, she handed them a large sealed envelope.

Matthew marveled that Pavlov trusted people to handle sensitive information but not technology to send it securely. It was odd that Pavlov didn't insist on personally handing the information to them. Maybe he had talked about his family's death enough the night before and he was in avoidance mode today. That was understandable, thought Matthew, realizing that he'd come to believe Pavlov's account of the situation with the missionaries. That also meant that he believed the guy was innocent and not the monster from old movies at all.

Unsure when his assessment of Pavlov's story had changed, Matthew reminded himself to keep an open mind. Danbury opened the envelope and slid out two printed pages. Peering over his shoulder, Matthew read the list.

None of the names, people or businesses, were familiar to him. That wasn't surprising, given that he neither operated in that business development world nor lived and worked in Florida. Also not surprising was that neither Preservation Reserve nor any of its subsidiaries appeared there.

"Let's roll," said Danbury, shoving the pages back without comment on them. Matthew settled in as they made their painstaking way through heavy traffic to the police station. After checking in and getting passes at the reception desk in the front lobby, they were directed to a small office occupied by Rhodes, who was on the phone but motioned them in.

Matthew could feel himself tensing as they waited for Rhodes to finish a call that sounded like it was about Stevenson's autopsy. Inactivity when there was so much ground to cover made his foot tap and his knee bounce as much in impatience and anticipation as in nervous energy.

Finally, Rhodes ended the call and spun his chair slowly around to face them. "As we thought, there's nothing unusual in Stevenson's autopsy results," said Rhodes as if he were merely continuing a conversation that they were in the middle of. "The only surprising thing was that there was no ID on Stevenson's body. No wallet, no keys, no personal effects. We haven't found any in his desk drawers or anywhere else in his office. Did he have a briefcase? Book bag? Backpack? Anything that you noticed in his office when you were there?"

Matthew hadn't thought to notice that. He searched his memory, trying to recall exactly what the office had looked like when they'd walked in the first time. It was a mess with books, papers, and folders stacked everywhere, that much he clearly remembered. What had been where or what might have been missing on their second visit wasn't as obvious.

Danbury spoke up. "There was a satchel. Beside his desk. It was brown. Probably leather. Beat up. From what I could see of it."

"There was!" agreed Matthew, impressed with Danbury's memory. The satchel had been behind the side of the desk where he'd been seated across from Stevenson. He knew that Danbury was often better at taking in details at a scene that wasn't yet the scene of anything because he seemed to scan and catalog all that he saw when he was investigating. Matthew knew that he himself was better at seeing the potential relevancy of things in scenes that were already scenes, connecting dots that didn't seem, on the surface, to be important.

"I thought it was a trash can at first," added Matthew. "But I remember it now. It was a brown messenger bag. You didn't find it when you answered the call about his death?"

"No," Rhodes responded simply.

"Interesting," said Danbury. "It was taken."

"I guess you didn't see what was in the satchel?" asked Rhodes.

"No idea," said Danbury. "I only saw the edge of it."

"We'll call the university administrators and see what they can tell us," said Rhodes, tapping a button on the phone to set the speaker function, then tapping in a number from a file that was open on his desk.

"Hello, office of the director of the Barclay University School of History, Artifacts, and Archives Department," said a firm female voice.

That was a mouthful, thought Matthew, and he wondered how many times a day the woman repeated it.

"Hi, this is Sergeant Rhodes of the Miami-Dade Police Department. I have a few questions about Professor Stevenson. Who would best know about his habits and routine?"

The woman seemed to consider for a moment, then rattled off a male name, said she'd connect them, and put them on hold. After making the necessary introductions, she excused herself, leaving them on the line with a bored-sounding man who had little inflection in his voice. Matthew sincerely hoped the man wasn't a professor teaching classes. The guy could quickly cure any case of insomnia, were that the case.

"How can I help you?" he asked after the initial introductions.

Rhodes succinctly explained that Professor Stevenson had neither identification nor any personal effects on his person or in his office when he was found. He asked what items the professor would normally have and how he would carry those.

"He carried a tablet in a computer bag. His keys should have been in his pocket along with his wallet. He had no ID, you say? No badge, nothing?"

"That's right."

"That's a problem. Thank you for calling it to my attention. He was issued an ID badge with a readable chip that permitted access to the buildings on campus—his office and the classroom buildings. It also enabled his access to a rather sensitive research facility. Just a moment, please," he said, and they heard a muffled conversation in which he called out to someone named Janice and asked that she immediately contact the security department to deactivate Professor Stevenson's badge.

Matthew thought that was something that should have been done immediately when the body was discovered; he marveled that it had taken a call from a police sergeant to point out that necessity.

"Can you also check to see if it's been used since his death?" asked Rhodes.

"Sure," he said, muffling the call again and calling out to Janice to also have security report back on the usage history of the professor's badge over the past two days.

"And we're going to need to know what's in that research facility," said Rhodes.

"Ah, it's um," hedged the voice, now fully alert. "Artifacts."

"What kind of artifacts?"

"From archaeological digs," the voice responded after a pause. "Some of our students participated in excavations and artifact preservation two summers ago. Our students—under the direction of our staff of course—are still cleaning, dating, and categorizing the collection while researching the likely origin and importance of each item. It's quite a long process. We're honored to have that collection here. We were part of a cooperative, and we jumped through lots of hoops to have some of the less important pieces shipped over after the trip. Those will be shared on tour with museums around the country after they have been researched and properly cataloged. Probably next year this time."

"Where were the digs?" asked Matthew.

"Ah, mostly in Greece," the man seemed to hedge in answering.

"Any particular part of Greece?" Matthew persisted.

"Two islands, or peninsulas, in the northeastern part of the country. They're like three fingers reaching south into the Aegean Sea."

"Was one of them Mt. Athos?" asked Matthew.

"Ah, yes and no," said the voice, sounding surprised. "Mt. Athos is one of the three fingers I mentioned. But archeological activity in that area is strictly forbidden. There are two others to the west of Mt. Athos where the excavations took place. We sent two groups of students. They worked on one peninsula for a month, and then the groups switched places to work on the other."

"Let me know if that facility was accessed with Professor Stevenson's ID badge, specifically since his death," said Rhodes. "Would you be aware if anything had been disturbed or removed?"

"Ah," hesitated the voice. "I don't know. The students clock in and out, leaving copious notes about what they accomplished during their shift on the articles they're working on. But the artifacts aren't exclusively assigned. They're all being formally cataloged. We do have lists of what we were allowed to bring back, but not necessarily who's been working on what or exactly when."

"Let me know that too," said Rhodes. "Whatever you can tell me about those lists and particularly if anything has been disturbed or is missing." He provided his cell phone number.

The voice on the phone—sounding less bored and much more agitated now—agreed.

"One more thing," said Matthew. "What type of artifacts? Are we talking pottery? Statues? What exactly? Are these items valuable?"

"Some of both of those, yes, though mostly shards and pieces, some of which can be reassembled. And some ancient writings. But valuable? Do you mean intrinsically or extrinsically?" asked the voice. Before anyone had the chance to answer that question, he answered it himself, "They're extremely significant, historically. I'm not talking about precious metals, coins, or gemstones. Those items, if they were found, would have been left in Greece. But historically, the artifacts our students are working on are rare and therefore exceptionally valuable."

"Contact me as soon as you have any of that information available," said Rhodes. When he'd gotten verbal agreement, he disconnected the call.

Returning to the conversation in the room, Rhodes asked, "You showed Professor Stevenson the note that you'd found, right? That little slip of paper with the odd writing on it. You didn't send it to him? Print it for him? There was no way he could have put anything about it in that satchel?"

"No, we only showed it to him," answered Matthew. "He knew immediately what it was, though, and didn't seem very surprised to see it. If it was in his satchel, he rewrote it himself. Like on the desk pad. We didn't tell him anything we didn't have to tell him to get him to answer our questions. Mainly, we wanted to know why Greg had scheduled to meet with him, when he'd done that, and if Stevenson had any idea about where Greg and Darya might be now."

"You're going to the canal-front property when you leave here?" asked Rhodes.

"Planning to see Stevenson's daughter first," said Danbury, checking his watch. "And then the canal property. Why?"

"I sent officers up first thing this morning to look at that property, but they didn't find anything. They said it was a warehouse district, and there wasn't anything going on there. It looked deserted. Several fences were closed and locked. The buildings that weren't surrounded by fencing were locked up tight."

"Huh," said Danbury, rubbing the stubble on his chin with his thumb. He'd apparently decided to stop shaving since they'd arrived, and Matthew was noticing at least a day's worth of blondish growth. "I still want a look. To see it for ourselves. Makes you wonder what's going on there. If it's tightly locked up and seems to be deserted. Here." He handed the envelope from Pavlov across to Rhodes.

"It is odd that it's locked up but deserted," agreed Matthew. "After killing a woman and two children to get it, if Pavlov told us the truth, you'd think somebody would be using it. If Pavlov was right in his assumptions."

"Do any of those mean anything to you?" asked Danbury after Rhodes had scanned both pages, copied them for his use, returned the original copies to the envelope, and handed them back.

"Not at first glance," said Rhodes as Danbury and Matthew stood. Checking his watch, Rhodes asked, "You're heading up to the airport now?"

"Yeah. We need to get going. Traffic and all," added Danbury, making his way to the door. "Your guys are picking her up?"

"They are. But you can talk to her at the airport before they bring her back here if you're quick about it."

"You said she still talked to her father regularly but she hadn't been back since her mother's death, right?" asked Matthew.

"That's right. Why?"

"And the other daughter, the one from Nevada? Do you know how often she talked to her father?" asked Matthew. "Or the last time she was here? Any details about her life now?"

"She hadn't talked to him in several months. And she was last here when their mother died. Both sisters agree on that detail. They've only seen each other twice since then. Over the holidays the past two years. The younger sister in Nevada isn't married. The older one in Denver is. Neither have children," summarized Rhodes. "Why?"

"Just making sure I have the facts straight before we go talk to her," answered Matthew.

After the usual abrupt goodbyes, Matthew and Danbury left, handing over their guest badges and retrieving Matthew's Glock on the way out.

It was a beautiful day, already above seventy degrees—nearly seventy-five—Matthew noticed as he checked the weather app on his phone. Sixty to eighty was the range for the day. This was nothing like North Carolina weather in late January, he thought. He'd shed his light jacket earlier and was carrying it over one arm. Slipping it into the back seat of the Tahoe, he was glad to have a short-sleeved, dry-fit shirt on as he climbed into the hot vehicle that had been parked in the sun and dropped his window. A light breeze that was blowing in from off the water was slightly chilly and refreshingly welcome.

They had programmed the navigation app on Danbury's phone and started out for the airport in Fort Lauderdale when their trip was interrupted.

24 ~ SIGHTINGS

"Danbury," he said, tapping his phone to answer the incoming call on the car system.

"Arabella Bosch's flight has been delayed," said Rhodes. "Her connecting flight got canceled due to some weather, and she won't be in now until at least one this afternoon. Maybe closer to two."

"Arabella?" said Matthew. "Is that a Russian name? It doesn't sound like one to me."

"It's probably British. Her parents changed it when they immigrated here. She goes by Bella, or probably Dr. Bosch to us. She's also a physician, so you should have some common ground. I'll let you know as soon as we find out exactly when she's due in, and we're headed back that way."

"Thanks, Rhodes," said Danbury, tapping to disconnect the call, pulling the phone from the holder on the dash, and handing it to Matthew. "Reroute us, Doc?"

"To the property on the canal?"

"Right."

"OK," said Matthew, tapping to end the current route and searching the map for the approximate location. "Got it." Clicking to open the music app, he selected a pop music playlist he knew they agreed on before sliding the phone back into the dash holder.

Music filled the Tahoe as they headed north up the Florida coastline. The drive was smoother and faster now that most people were already at work, school, or their destination for the day.

Directions that were being spouted from the navigation app were easy to follow, so Matthew allowed his mind to wander. Two things that had been tugging at the corners of his mind now demanded his attention. He chose to consider the least disturbing of the two first. Relaxing his mind, he tried to remember what the man's face in his dream looked like to determine why he'd thought it was so important.

Maybe, he thought, it had merely seemed important in the dream, and it wasn't so in reality. Or maybe he'd only known the person in the dream, and the guy wasn't real outside of that hazy world. He didn't think that was the case. As he pondered that possibility, he felt the vehicle slow.

"Hey, Doc," said Danbury, pointing down a row of buildings that looked drab and industrial. Rows of stacked shipping containers lined the other end. Tucked between the buildings and the containers, they could barely make out the back end of a huge black SUV chassis that was jacked up on a wide wheelbase.

Matthew's mind began to race with the other thing that his subconscious had wanted him to consider but that he'd tried to ignore. He flashed back to the drive when they were going to talk to Pavlov the evening before. He'd tried not to think much about the bullet that went into his headrest instead of his head when Danbury had seen the gun and warned him to duck. Seeing the Hummer from which that shot had been fired, though, brought it all back into sharp focus.

The thought he'd been trying not to acknowledge finally pushed its way fully into his mind, front and center. Had they been aiming specifically at him, or was it a misplaced bullet from a moving vehicle? The thought was unsettling, to say the least, and Matthew shuddered as he stared down the long row of buildings at the back end of the vehicle.

"This could be a trap," said Matthew.

"Very likely it is," said Danbury, who had already pulled his phone from the holder on the dash. Looking all around him—particularly in the direction from which they'd come—he backed up with the rear of the vehicle facing the water to easily see in every other direction. Closing the music and navigation apps, he left the phone on speaker, pulled up his call list, and tapped to call Rhodes.

Identifying himself, he explained where they were and what they were seeing. "We're at the docks," he told Rhodes. "The property Pavlov told us about. At the warehouses. The black Hummer is here. The one that shot at us. It's parked. At the west end of the row. We're on the east end. We need to check it out. But I'm not going solo. Not without backup."

"Smart. Hang on. I'll send a couple of units in," Matthew heard Rhodes say before giving that directive—apparently on another device—and arguing with somebody in the process. "Yes, I know that's Broward County," said Rhodes. "I'll notify them next, but get the units rolling now!"

Matthew knew Danbury well enough to know that he was having trouble sitting still and waiting. The most likely reason that he wasn't finding the best route in after notifying Rhodes was Matthew himself being in the vehicle. Danbury had looked truly shaken by the bullet hole in Matthew's headrest the day before. Somehow, he'd seemed far less concerned about the bullet that had grazed his own arm.

Nearly in unison, Matthew and Danbury drew their weapons from their holsters—both aimed them between their feet at the floorboard in front of them. Matthew decided to ponder how he felt about acting like the police officer he'd never wanted to become later—but not right now. Now, he needed to focus. Heads swiveling back and forth like the big bobblehead toys of celebrities and other personalities, they were watching all directions except the water behind them. Danbury was checking that in the rearview mirrors in his sweep.

Matthew felt a cold sweat building at the nape of his neck as they listened to Rhodes explaining their presence and that of the incoming police units to someone. "Yeah, I know it's Broward County!" he said again. "It's your county. That's why I'm notifying you that there's a suspicious vehicle parked there. Whoever was driving and the passenger from yesterday are wanted for questioning in a shooting. Consider them hostile, armed, and dangerous!"

After a few minutes, they heard distant sirens, and then all was quiet again. Matthew could hear the water lapping against the bulkhead behind him as the gentle breeze blew it in. It was the kind of day that he'd have loved to savor, except that there wasn't time for that. He was on his guard, watching around him. To his surprise, he realized that he was ready to aim his Glock at anyone holding a weapon. Aiming his weapon also meant being ready to fire it at anyone who might begin shooting at them again.

He didn't take time to ponder that either as four police cars drove into sight.

"They're here," said Danbury into his phone. The line was still open with Rhodes, though they hadn't been conversing on it at all for the past five minutes, at least.

"OK, they've got you," confirmed Rhodes after a few back-and-forth exchanges. The four police vehicles pulled into the parking lot at the far east end of the row of buildings and stopped nearby. They were hidden—for the moment—by the buildings, with only Matthew and Danbury still visible from the other end. Two police cars were marked as belonging to Broward County, one was marked from Miami-Dade, and a fourth was clearly a police cruiser, but it wasn't marked at all.

The hulking Hummer at the end of the buildings slowly moved forward—either behind or into a building—and disappeared.

"Did it go into the building?" Matthew asked as Danbury explained to Rhodes that it had moved from their sight line.

"I've got two officers in the unmarked," said Rhodes. "And one in the marked if you want to join, Detective."

"Yeah, will do. I'll leave eyes here," he said, nodding to Matthew. "There are fences between. Nobody can get this far. Not in a vehicle." He started the Tahoe. Angling it forward, then turning, he backed it directly alongside the end of the building, mirroring the way the huge Hummer had been parked at the other end.

Rhodes was barking out orders over the other device, which sounded like a police channel with loud static between the bits of conversation. The unmarked police cruiser reversed direction and moved slowly back down the short street. It turned left to head west onto the road that paralleled the canal and toward the other end of the row of warehouses where the Hummer had been parked.

"OK, Doc, we need your eyes," said Danbury as he poked his phone to conference Matthew's in on the call with Rhodes. Matthew clicked to accept the call, muted it, and put it on the speaker function as

Danbury continued. "They'll know that you're here. But they already do. Let us know if you see anything. Or anybody. Any movement."

Matthew nodded.

"One of the Broward County cars is staying with you to watch your six," explained Rhodes, apparently forgetting for the moment that Matthew wasn't law enforcement. He did understand the lingo, though, and answered affirmatively in kind.

Danbury reached up without looking at his hand and turned off the dome light in the vehicle. Releasing his seat belt, he ducked and slid from the driver's seat—which was visible to anyone watching down the row of buildings—over the console into the backseat, which wasn't visible from the other end of the warehouses. He slid out of the vehicle through the rear door. How the big detective had managed that maneuver so smoothly and effortlessly, Matthew couldn't imagine.

Resisting the urge to put all his focus on the other end of the building, Matthew clicked to unmute the conversation on his phone and continued to monitor his surroundings. As Danbury slid into the marked Miami-Dade police cruiser, both it and one of the Broward County cars pulled out to follow the unmarked car. Left with the other Broward County car and not alone, Matthew was relieved that he had their company.

"Here, put this on," Matthew heard the officer with Danbury tell him.

"Thanks," said Danbury, and the phone was muffled.

Meanwhile, Rhodes was giving orders to the unmarked car at the other end of the row of buildings.

"Slowly, make a pass. Get a good look, then circle back."

"Got it, Sarge," responded a voice. Though the car was only maybe a quarter of a mile away at most, Matthew realized that he was hearing the voice across multiple devices—both Danbury's and Rhodes' phones. "It's all still," the voice reported back. "Looks deserted, if we didn't know better."

"Maybe they weren't expecting us to come back today," said Rhodes. "But we don't have the element of surprise now if we ever did."

"What next?" asked another voice over the staticky radio.

Rhodes was instructing the occupants of both cars to get into place and be ready to move in on his orders when a sound made Matthew react and then wonder later why he'd done exactly as he did. The roar of an engine and screeching tires drew his attention away from the buildings toward the incoming road. Instead of getting down and ducking, he leaned across the vehicle and placed his weapon on the open window sill. Draped awkwardly over the center console with his right elbow on the steering wheel, he steadied his aim at the oncoming car.

It wasn't the behemoth Hummer. This time, it was something smaller and sportier—faster and much more agile. Before he could do anything else, the Broward County cruiser that had been parked at an angle behind him closed the distance and filled the gap between himself and the oncoming sports car.

As the popping sound of shots being fired filled the air, Matthew ducked beneath the window sill on the driver's side. He didn't have a clear shot at the approaching car, and he wouldn't have taken it anyway, he realized. There, he lay prone, sprawled over the console but beneath the line of the open window.

"Sit rep! What the hell is going on?" he heard Rhodes demand and something about a code one-oh-one as other shouts of codes and confusion rang out over the police radio.

As quickly as it had started, the shooting ceased, and the squalling tires reversed direction. Heading out the short side road, the vehicle went east—at least according to the reports on the police radio. Afterward, the airwaves erupted with demands for updates and the less-than-calm voice of one of the Broward County police officers in the car beside Matthew.

"Shots fired!" Matthew heard. That was followed by a cacophony of radio noise. The eruption of voices was difficult to comprehend, except that Matthew distinctly heard the nine ninety-nine code called out before, "Officer down!"

Without pausing to think through his actions or motions, Matthew rolled into the driver's seat, flung the door wide, and jumped out in one fluid motion. Opening the back door of the police cruiser, he slid in across the seat. The officer behind the wheel had been hit in the neck with a bullet. There were bars behind the driver that prevented Matthew from reaching him. He slid out of the back door on the driver's side of the vehicle, yanked open the driver's door—pulling his dry-fit shirt over his head as he went—and dropped onto the door sill.

Matthew wadded his shirt, stuffing it into the wound—that was already pouring blood—and pushed hard. Though he couldn't tell how deeply the bullet had penetrated or exactly what had been damaged in its wake, that area was an extremely dangerous place to take a hit. An artery had likely been at least nicked.

"Don't unbuckle him!" he barked at the other officer as the driver's dark head lolled to one side, and his normally dark complexion was draining of color. "Come around from behind!" he yelled. When the officer had slipped in beside him, Matthew said, "Hold this here, push down like this, but don't move his head. Hold it steady." Taking the guy's hand under his, he demonstrated exactly what needed to be done.

With the officer holding the wadded shirt in the wound, Matthew quickly began to assess the injured man. He was still breathing, but that would change quickly if help didn't arrive immediately. He saw no other bullet wounds.

"We need transport! Stat!" yelled Matthew into the stratosphere, not knowing who could hear him or on what device as he checked vitals on the injured officer.

The next few minutes were critical, but they dragged like hours. He had to make quick decisions to assess the risks involved in treatment and try to save a man's life. Move the officer to his back on the ground to administer CPR and risk potentially life-ending neck injury—or hold steady and do what he could from there? It wasn't the sort of decision that any first responder ever wanted to have to make because it could go deadly wrong in so many ways.

As he was deciding he was out of time and needed to move the officer, he heard sirens approaching from behind him. Two paramedics sprinted to the car, one of them with a bright orange backboard under his arm.

"Dr. Matthew Paine," he identified himself and began summarizing the injury and the state of the officer as he slid out and stepped aside, instructing the officer in the back seat not to move until the paramedics told him to do so. The paramedics were on top of the officer, assessing, reporting, and planning aloud before Matthew was completely clear. They'd managed to slide the injured officer out and onto the waiting board. One of them had relieved the officer in the back seat of holding pressure on the wound. Matthew's shirt had been so long ago soaked with blood that it was impossible to tell that it had once been a shirt at all.

He watched in horror as one of the paramedics called a code blue, and the other ran to the back of the ambulance.

"Get him to the ambulance!" Matthew yelled as he grabbed one end of the board. With the help of the uninjured officer, they lifted the backboard and ran with it for the ambulance. Sliding the backboard into the ambulance, Matthew relinquished his hold on it and jumped backward. The paramedic on board ripped open the officer's shirt, attached leads to his chest, and yelled, "Clear!"

Before he knew what he was doing, Matthew had climbed into the back of the ambulance. He took his shirt and something else that the other paramedic handed him before the guy jumped out and ran for the front. Matthew held pressure on the wound as best he could for what seemed like an eternity—but was probably only a fifteen-minute trip to the nearest hospital—while the paramedic in the back with him started an IV and monitored his vital signs.

A second shock to the heart brought the officer back, yet again, before they lowered him from the ambulance, and he was whisked away. The officer would be transported directly to the operating room and a waiting team of surgeons, Matthew hoped, as he stood shivering in the shade of the canopy over the emergency department drive-through.

"Dr. Paine?" said one of the paramedics and handed him a sage green scrub shirt. "Here, I have an extra."

"Thanks," said Matthew. He knew that he was shivering because of the adrenaline, not because he was cold.

It was nearly eighty degrees and barely shy of noon, he saw from his smartwatch. It was caked in dried and drying blood, and Matthew pulled it off, stuffing it into the pocket of his slacks. If it was functioning, then must that mean he had his phone on him somewhere? He thought he'd dropped everything in the Tahoe when he'd jumped out, but he found the phone in his back pocket.

Pulling it out, he saw that he was still connected to a call, and there was lots of conversation, none of which he'd heard at all while tending to the injured officer during transport.

"Danbury?" he said into the phone.

"Hey Doc," he heard Danbury call out. "Can you hear me?"

"Yeah, we're at the hospital."

"Did he," began Danbury, but then stopped. There was so much noise in the background that Matthew wasn't sure he'd have heard anything else anyway. When it got momentarily quieter, Matthew answered Danbury's unfinished question.

"I don't honestly know. I'm sure they ran him directly into surgery, but he coded twice before we got him here. It'll be a miracle if he pulls through this," Matthew added and shivered again. "But we did our best. There's nothing else we could have done that we didn't do."

"I'm glad you were there," was all Danbury said in response.

Rhodes interrupted, and Matthew begged off, disconnecting the call on his phone and stuffed it back in his pocket. As the paramedics loaded a stretcher onto the ambulance and prepared to leave, Matthew stepped over to thank them and asked the taller guy who had given him the scrub shirt how much he owed him for it.

"Keep it, Dr. Paine. It belongs to the company," he said, pointing to the logo on the pocket. "I didn't buy it myself. And you more than earned it. I'll tell my supervisor that it was collateral damage."

Grinning, the guy jumped into the passenger seat of the ambulance, and it pulled away. Matthew marveled at the guy's ability to return to a normal state so soon after the emergency they'd been through. Or had he really done so, Matthew wondered. Coping mechanisms were a necessity for a job like that.

There were good reasons why Matthew had changed his career course from the emergency department doctor he'd intended to become when he'd chosen to be a family physician instead. He couldn't imagine how stressful that job would be, day in and day out, or how much toll it would take on the health and well-being of those practitioners. Somehow, they learned to compartmentalize it, but he'd never completely mastered that during his clinical rotations through the ED in medical school.

He knew how to shift into a professional medical practitioner mode. It was like a tunnel vision where he saw nothing but the patient—evaluating the issues, prioritizing them, and treating them as best he could. It was the aftermath—shifting out of that mode having dealt with critical conditions like the one he'd just handled—that he'd never been able to walk away from completely. Genuinely admiring those who somehow managed to cope, he knew it was rough on those practitioners.

He remembered a seasoned ED nurse he'd met during one of his rotations. She had told him—when he asked how she managed to stay positive and focused, day after day—that it took a toll on her. Some of the patients they'd lost, she said, you never forgot. The worst, she explained, was when they lost a child. Sometimes, late at night, she'd confided, she could still hear the anguished screams of the parents.

Stepping into the sunlight, he continued what he'd been doing the whole way into the hospital—that one thing he knew could make a difference. Fully acknowledging his mortality and the limitation of his abilities, he bowed his head slightly and prayed fervently for the officer who'd been shot. He didn't know the guy's name, but he prayed for strength and healing for the officer. For the OR doctors—in whose hands the guy's life now depended—he prayed for wisdom to make all of the right decisions at the right time. For the man's family, whoever they might be, he prayed for peace in the face of tragedy and deep personal pain.

Raising his head, Matthew was thankful for his life. He paused to wonder how he'd so quickly gotten into the crosshairs of ruthless murderers yet again. It seemed to be a knack he'd perfected in the past months, nearly a year, since he'd been working alongside Danbury. Life was fleeting and precious, he thought, pulling his phone out and checking the time. He didn't want to call Cici because he knew she'd be ready to jump on the next plane and fly home. At that moment, what he wanted was to talk to someone who would pray with him.

Tapping his phone, he called one of the few people he knew would answer immediately.

"Matthew, how's it going down there?" he heard the familiar voice after the second ring.

"Not so well." Explaining what he'd been through, he asked for prayer for the officer whose life literally hung in the balance at that very moment.

25 ~ TO KEEP GOING

After Mark Kushner had prayed with him on the phone, Matthew felt a peaceful relief sweep over him. He'd done what he could do, and it was out of his hands. Letting it go and leaving it in God's hands was easier now. After refusing to come home without Greg and Darya—despite Mark's concern for his well-being—he disconnected the call and saw a text that had come in from Danbury.

"On the way. Drop a pin. Have your Glock."

"Thanks. At the ED entrance," Matthew texted back and then tapped to send Danbury his location. What he didn't do was look more closely to see where that location was, exactly.

Matthew saw a thumbs-up emoji as he wandered into the building and asked for a restroom. The receptionist in the lobby looked alarmed at the blood coating his hands and arms.

"It's not mine," he reassured her. "I rode in on that last ambulance. I'd ask for an update, but I'm a physician, and I know HIPAA laws prohibit sharing that information with me, even if I did know the police officer's name. I'm looking for a restroom to wash up."

"Right over there," she answered, pointing. As she said it, the Broward County officer who'd been in the passenger seat of the car rushed up to the counter behind him.

"Hi, I'm…" he began to the receptionist and then recognized Matthew. "Oh, you're," he began again and faltered. Words weren't his strong suit today, Matthew thought, but who could blame him? This guy, the younger officer of the two, had been shot at and then acted as a human plug to try to keep his partner alive.

"Yes, I rode in with the other officer. I'm Matthew Paine, a doctor from North Carolina. I'd shake your hand, but I was about to go wash up." Looking down, he saw that the young officer hadn't managed to do that yet either. It appeared that he'd tried to wipe his hands off on something, but they were far from scrubbed clean.

"Is h-he…I mean, d-did he…," the officer stammered, unable to ask the question that Matthew, too, wanted answered.

"I don't know," Matthew answered honestly. "We got him this far, but he was in rough shape. I'm sure they rushed him straight into surgery." He decided not to sugarcoat it, but neither would he mention that the guy had been shocked with the AED twice. Using an automated external defibrillator more than once on anyone—particularly someone who was losing that much blood—was never a good sign. They had started fluids on the way, but they couldn't give him blood until they'd gotten him to the hospital.

"Thank you, Doctor. I mean it. Thank you. With your help, maybe he has a chance. Without it," the guy said and paused.

"You're welcome," said Matthew as the officer turned to the receptionist.

"I'm looking for information on my partner, Diego Acosta."

So that was his name, thought Matthew, and he made a mental note of it as he wandered in the direction the receptionist had pointed. He heard her say, as he walked away, "I'm sorry, Sir. Police partner or not, the doctor there already told you more than I'd have been able to unless you're a relative."

Scrubbing his hands and arms up to his elbows with hot, soapy water, Matthew wished he could scrub the memory from his mind. Pulling his watch and phone out of his pockets, he scrubbed those with a soapy paper towel and carefully wiped them clean and then dry. He replaced the watch on his wrist and noted the time. It was after one in the afternoon, and he couldn't tell if his stomach was empty or if it had done so many flips that it was growling in protest. The former, he decided, as he tossed the wad of paper towels in the trash.

He caught his reflection in the mirror as he was turning to leave the restroom and realized that he had smudges of dried blood down one side of his face. Yanking out more paper towels, he soaked them in hot water, added soap, and scrubbed that too. He rinsed and dried his face—satisfied that he looked as calm and collected as he was likely to—and strode purposefully back through the lobby and out the front door.

The younger officer was nowhere in sight, nor did Matthew see any police vehicles parked out front as he wandered to the edge of the entrance and perched on a stucco wall. He had no idea which direction he'd traveled, nor did he know where he was currently sitting.

Pulling his phone from his pocket, he decided to rectify that. He was in Fort Lauderdale, proper, north of FLL, the Fort Lauderdale airport that was above Dania Beach, where he'd been when the shooting had started. The drive up was so frenzied that somebody could have told him he'd ended up almost anywhere, and he'd have believed them.

His mind wandered back to the thought that he'd had earlier. Somehow, he'd begun acting like a police officer. Or maybe it was a detective he was acting like after nearly a year working alongside Danbury. Exactly when that transition happened, he wasn't sure, but he wasn't excited about it. When people had asked him as a child what he wanted to be when he grew up, "policeman" had somehow never made the list. That hadn't changed over the course of his life. And yet, here he was.

It was, he supposed, after being shot at multiple times that he started to react more like a detective and less like a physician. There were times over the past year when he was certain that he had been the target on the wrong end of a weapon. This time, though, he wasn't positive the shots had been aimed at him. The thing that troubled him was that he wasn't certain that they hadn't been either. Had he been the intended target either time he'd been shot at?

Was the first incident when he'd ducked, and his headrest had taken the bullet a lucky shot? Or was it aimed at him? And if he was the intended recipient of the bullet, why? Was there something that somebody didn't want Pavlov to share with them? What, of all that Pavlov had told them, was somebody trying to keep them from learning? It had to be something far more important than Pavlov not connecting the missionaries to his church in Sunny Isles.

Surely, Matthew thought, nobody would go to that much trouble to keep them from confirming that. If he was right about that, what else could it have been? What had Pavlov told them that was so important? Or what hadn't he told them that he should have?

Finding no satisfactory answers to any of those questions, Matthew mentally moved on. Was the second shooting specifically targeting him, and the police car intercepted the bullets? Was it randomly aimed at whoever was intruding on the warehouses because there was something there that somebody didn't want seen? Or maybe the police officer was targeted for some reason. If that were the case, what could that reason possibly be? He intended to find that out. The officer was from Broward County, not Miami-Dade, for whatever that was worth. The warehouse was in Broward County.

As Matthew pondered all the possibilities, his thoughts were interrupted by the black Chevy Tahoe pulling into the looped drive alongside the wall on which he was perched. Danbury handed over the Glock, grip in and barrel pointed away from them.

"What's the latest from the warehouses?" asked Matthew as he slipped the weapon into his holster. Momentarily, he breathed a little easier. He was finally able to disconnect his mind from the shooting scene as they pulled away from the hospital. Reconciling himself to the fact that he'd done all he could and the officer's fate was long since out of his hands, he fleetingly wondered if it had ever truly been there, to begin with.

"They're getting a search warrant," responded Danbury. "That shouldn't be too hard. After the shooting. There's definitive cause. Rhodes is in the loop. He'll keep us posted. He wants to talk to you. To get your statement."

"OK, I can call him in a minute. I have a few more questions first. What about the black Hummer?"

"Disappeared," said Danbury. "Likely into the end unit. In the row of warehouses. It's all under surveillance. Until they get the warrant."

"Ah, good," said Matthew, nodding. "This Tahoe is OK? It wasn't shot up this time?"

"It wasn't," answered Danbury. "Just the police car."

"Interesting," said Matthew, with an eyebrow raised and his foot tapping on the floorboard in concentration.

"How so?"

"I have been wondering, after the bullet in my headrest on the other vehicle yesterday, if that was an accident. I mean, shooting with any accuracy at a moving target while in motion yourself would be difficult, at best."

"True. I've seen a couple people do it consistently. But they've practiced. A lot."

"They weren't aiming for me this time if the police cruiser took the spray of the bullets. There were multiple shots fired. I'm not sure how many. I ducked under the window sill and lost count."

"Right," Danbury said slowly, encouraging Matthew to continue.

"All in the police car," said Matthew, half to himself. "They couldn't have been shooting at me, not this time. After I call Rhodes, what's next?"

"Food," said Danbury. "I'm hungry."

"You're always hungry," Matthew said with a chuckle. "But I am too. Breakfast was a while ago."

"And then back to the airport. To meet the first sister. We're picking them up."

"How did you convince Rhodes to let us do that?"

"They're not suspects. They need rides," said Danbury simply. "He consented to letting us pick them up and bring them to Miami. I think he's low on manpower. After this last incident. We can question the sisters on the way. But then he takes over. We get the drive. And that's it. Anything we learn, we tell Rhodes. That's the deal."

"Ah. What time are their flights coming in?"

"Two and three thirty," said Danbury. "FLL and MIA airports. Respectively."

Tapping his phone, Matthew saw that they didn't have much time to get up to Fort Lauderdale. He located a café nearby and pulled the address up on Danbury's phone. Then he called Rhodes.

"Ah, Dr. Paine," he said. "I need to get a statement from you. And I need to inform you that I'll be recording it. Tell me what happened as best you can."

"I heard the roar of a medium engine and the squall of tires and turned to see a car coming at us from the service road from the east. It was a low sedan, a Mercedes, or a BMW," Matthew said, then hesitated, searching his memory. "It was a BMW. I remember the double kidneys."

"Double kidneys?" asked Rhodes.

"You know, the twin grills on either side of the center on the front."

"Oh," said Rhodes. "What color was it?"

"That's the thing," said Matthew. "It shouldn't be hard to find. It was a metallic purple."

"Purple?"

"Right. These people don't travel incognito, do they? Why would anyone who wanted to remain anonymous drive a massive Hummer on a widened wheelbase or a metallic purple BMW? Those stand out—they don't blend in."

"Good point. The Broward County guy didn't get a good look at it from the passenger seat. He said it all happened fast. It was there, and then it was gone."

"Pretty much," answered Matthew. "It roared in, spun, and the shots started popping. I ducked down behind the window sill and heard the tires screeching back out to the street. The car headed back out the way it had come in. Then I heard the call go out on the police radio—I guess through my cell and probably from the car beside me too—that an officer had been hit. I jumped out, ran over, and started to work on the officer, Diego Acosta."

"That's it?"

"That's it. The car roared in quickly, fired the shots, and then back out just as fast."

"Did either of the Broward officers fire back?"

"I don't think so, but I don't know for sure. I ducked when the shooting started, and I didn't look again until the car was gone."

"Did you see the driver? Was he the one shooting?"

"No. The car spun in so that the passenger side was facing us. There must have been a passenger who was shooting." Matthew concentrated on replaying the scene in his mind. "There were two guys in the car. I didn't get a good look at either one of them. They had on ball caps, pulled low. They were dark hats, like black, charcoal, or navy."

"They were both male?"

"That's my impression, yes, but I didn't see faces. I suppose either or both could have been women. I don't remember seeing hair hanging out of the ball caps, but it might have been. I didn't get a good look."

"OK, anything else?"

"Nothing that I can think of."

"I'll get this typed up, and I'll need you to sign it at some point."

"Sure," said Matthew, wondering how their plan for the day could go sideways so fast as they finished the call.

From the Cuban café, they ordered sandwiches to go, grabbed bottles of water, and piled back into the SUV to make their way to the airport.

"How are we finding her when we get there?" asked Matthew between bites.

"Rhodes," said Danbury, swallowing hard. "He told Dr. Bosch where to go. An exact location."

"Huh," said Matthew thoughtfully, "Does she know we're picking her up?"

"No."

"How will we find her? And convince her to come with us?"

"She gave Rhodes a description. Shouldn't be too hard to spot. Pink-plaid suitcase."

"Pink-plaid?" asked Matthew, crinkling his nose in surprise.

"Yup," answered Danbury as they both returned to attacking their sandwiches.

Traffic thickened the closer they got to the airport, and it was after two as they were pulling to the curb of the passenger pickup area.

As she'd promised, Bella Bosch approached the numbered and lettered spot that Rhodes had specified, pulling a shiny pink-plaid suitcase on four wheels along beside her. Strapped atop it was a matching soft-sided leather bag. The woman, too, went with the suitcase, Matthew thought. Clad in a pale pink skirt and jacket, she walked confidently toward them in spiked heels of the same color. He'd heard Cici refer to the color as blush, but he wasn't sure why it wasn't plain light pink.

"You want this one?" asked Danbury.

"OK," answered Matthew, slipping from the SUV. "Dr. Bosch?" he asked, approaching the woman.

"Who's asking?" she responded in a defensive, no-nonsense tone that didn't at all match the soft pinkness of her appearance. Bright blue eyes sparkled up at him from a serious face, oval with a pointed chin. Streaked blonde hair brushed the tops of her shoulders.

"Dr. Matthew Paine," he said, extending a hand. "I'm a GP in a family practice in North Carolina. And this is Detective Warren Danbury." He thumbed over his shoulder to the driver's side of the SUV. "Sergeant Rhodes from the Miami-Dade police department sent us to pick you up."

Dubiously, she took his extended hand. Her handshake was firm. Her short nails—painted a shade of light iridescent pink like her clothing—glistened.

In her other hand, a pink face mask dangled. She, too, had traveled cautiously with the news of the spreading SARS virus, Matthew thought. He'd flown down in a surgical mask, given the tight quarters on the plane and in the airports, particularly in Florida. He wondered, briefly, where she'd acquired hers. Surgeon's masks were almost always the same boring shade of light blue or white. Dismissing the thought, he reached for her bag, "Can I take this for you?"

"I suppose," she answered, rolling it forward and stepping to the curb. "Your detective has ID, I assume?"

Smart woman, Matthew thought, not to take his word for any of it. "He does," he responded as Danbury held it up through the open window and flipped it open for her perusal.

"We're from North Carolina," said Danbury. "So is the badge."

"A badge is a badge," she answered, nodding, with a slight shrug as she slid the rolling bag toward Matthew and then followed him to the back of the Tahoe.

After it was properly stowed, Matthew asked, "Would you like to ride shotgun?"

"I'm fine back here," she answered, opening the door behind the one Matthew was holding for her and slipping into the back seat behind his.

Skipping the small talk, Danbury dove into a quick introduction of their search for the missing missionaries as he pulled away from the curb. Making his way slowly out of the passenger pickup area, he maneuvered into the creeping flow of traffic exiting the airport.

"What's your specialty?" Matthew asked, trying to break the wall of ice between the seating rows.

"I'm a podiatric surgeon," she replied. "And don't bother with any of the foot jokes. I've heard them all by now."

Matthew laughed out loud at that. "Sure, if you don't make any jokes about my name."

"It's a deal," she said softly and lapsed again into silence.

"My condolences on the death of your father," said Matthew. "I'm sorry for your loss." He couldn't see her face without pulling down his sun visor. It had a mirror on it that he thought might be intrusive as he heard a muffled sniffle from the back seat.

Softly, Matthew added, "And I'm also sorry for the questioning that you're about to undergo. We're not sure it's related, but your father was killed right after we visited him. We were asking for information about the Ukrainian missionaries Danbury just told you about. Your father said Grygoriy Starkovich had contacted him and set up an appointment to talk about a book of minor antiquity, a book that had belonged to a family member of Greg's. I think that was how your father described it."

When she didn't respond, Matthew asked, "Does that name mean anything to you? Starkovich?

"I don't believe so. Should it?" she asked.

Changing his angle and deciding to get right to the point, Matthew asked, "You had reason to believe that your mother's death wasn't an accident, didn't you?"

"What has that got to do with this?" she countered sharply.

"Maybe nothing," answered Matthew honestly. "But there's another person we've talked to whose wife was also killed around the same time. He was convinced that it wasn't an accident because he was indirectly threatened. We think we know why—what it was that they wanted from him—but your father didn't tell us anything about the circumstances surrounding your mother's death."

Crickets would have been far noisier than the silence in the back seat.

After waiting a few minutes for a response, Matthew gently prodded, "It would help us to know if you have any idea if she was targeted. If your father was threatened by anyone prior to her death. Or prior to his own."

As the silence was unbroken, Matthew was happy, for once, that the traffic was heavy on I-95 headed south. The trip would take some time. He didn't want to push and upset her, but neither did he want to lose the chance to learn something from her if the deaths were related to the murdered and missing missionaries. Their time was limited. Danbury glanced over meaningfully, and Matthew reluctantly flipped down the sun visor to read the mood in the back seat.

Bella Bosch was sitting rigidly upright, staring stonily out of the window beside her. There were no tears. She looked angry more than anything else, he thought.

"Dr. Bosch?" he prompted. "We need your help."

From the mirror on the visor, he saw no reaction. Glancing over at Danbury, he decided he'd had enough of the silent treatment. Though normally soft-spoken and not confrontational, Matthew knew there was a time for everything. And they were running out of it. He had to get whatever information might help them to locate Greg and Darya out of her before they reached the police precinct.

Taking a deep breath, Matthew began with a more pointed approach, hating having to do it. "Dr. Bosch, do you want to know who killed your parents and why? Do you want their murderers to answer for that? Or would you rather leave them on the loose to kill other peoples' parents and loved ones too?"

26 ~ RECONCILED

"Of course, I want to know! And they should absolutely pay!" Arabella Bosch retorted hotly from the back seat of the Tahoe. "But that'll never happen. And I don't want to be next! My dad was inquisitive, and he challenged the status quo. You see where that got him. He and Mom survived for many years, but even he couldn't fly under their radar forever."

"Who? Who was he running from? Whose radar was he flying under?" asked Matthew.

"Probably nobody's," she said sadly. "I'm sure they knew where he was the whole time."

"Who?" repeated Matthew.

"The Russians," she said so quietly that Matthew barely heard her.

"If they knew where he was," Matthew began. "What changed?"

"What do you mean?" she asked, still staring out the window.

"If they knew where he was and under what assumed name, but they had left him alone until now, why now? What changed two years ago if your mother's death wasn't an accident? What was the catalyst? And what made them come after him now?"

"I wish I knew."

"You have no idea? No guess?"

"Not really."

"Then tell us what you do know. From the beginning. How old were you when your parents defected to the United States?"

"I was tiny, too young to understand any of it."

"When did you learn about your true heritage?"

"When I was a teenager. I wanted my birth certificate to get my driver's permit, and Mom had put me off every time I asked for it. My sister and I went searching for it. We were snooping through a lock box and found some old documents from when my parents entered the country. Those forms showed that they'd changed our names. Our new names were listed, our original names redacted. We demanded to know who we really were and where we came from."

"And your parents told you then?"

"We left them little choice."

"What did they tell you?"

"Only that they were seeking a better life for Aleah and me. They'd escaped some dangerous people to come here and start over."

"They didn't tell you who or what they'd run from?"

"No. Not then, they didn't. They told us our story up to a point. When we pressed them to explain, they flatly refused. Later, they confessed that they thought the less we knew about the circumstances of where we'd come from—why and how—the better it would be if anyone ever did come after us. I objected and told them we needed to know to be on the alert if they thought someone might."

"When did you find out the rest of your story?"

"Eventually, as we became adults, they told us little bits of what my father had left behind—what he was being groomed for, really—and why my parents had chosen to come here. He'd gotten on the wrong side of somebody in the KGB, and he was living in fear for our lives."

"And you were never approached by anyone? Nobody ever asked you any questions when you were growing up here?"

"Not that I ever remember, no. I thought I was being followed once or twice more recently, but I was never sure. I had hoped that was my imagination working overtime. But now I doubt that," she replied, blowing out a deep breath, apparently reconciled to the idea of telling them what she knew.

"When and where was that?"

"In Denver, a couple of months before my mother was killed."

"Two years ago?"

"Right."

"Why did you think you were being followed?"

"It was nothing concrete at first. Just a feeling. I'd seen the same man several times. Maybe he lived and worked nearby. But maybe not," she said ominously.

"He never approached you directly?"

"No. I saw him at a distance, usually. On the sidewalk in the park where I was jogging, walking by outside the office complex where my practice is. The closest he ever came was in a coffee shop in Denver. I felt eyes on me. You know that feeling like somebody's watching you, staring at you? When I turned around, I'm sure I saw him duck his head and look away. And I'm nearly positive it was the same guy I'd seen before."

"Would you recognize him if you saw him again?"

"Probably, even if his arm is covered. Definitely, if it isn't."

"His arm?"

"He's a blond guy with short-cropped hair, deep-set hazel eyes. Grayish, I guess. He's a medium height."

Nothing too remarkable there, thought Matthew, and then she continued.

"He has a tattoo of a snake wound around his wrist and up his forearm. I'm not sure how high up his arm it goes. The cuffs of his shirt sleeves were flipped up maybe twice. The tail of the snake hung below his wrist on the top of his hand."

After a quick intake of breath that he hoped she didn't notice, Matthew looked over at Danbury, exchanging a glance of understanding. "A snake?" Matthew asked. "He had a snake tattoo on his arm?"

"Yes."

"Left or right?"

"Pardon?"

"Which arm? Did you notice?"

"Oh, it had to have been his right arm with the way he was facing."

"And you saw all of that from a distance?" asked Matthew, incredulously.

"In the coffee shop, there's an angled mirror above the counter behind the baristas. I watched him from the side in that mirror until he left. He got his order, then glanced my way twice more before he went back out to the street. I lost him after that. I don't know where he went, and I didn't see him again. If he was still watching me after that, he was doing it a lot more stealthily."

"What can you tell me about your mother's situation? Did you know she was in any danger?"

"Not until after the fact, no. She had told my dad that she thought somebody was following her, but she never got a good look at them. Neither of my parents told me about it at the time. I overheard Dad telling the police after she died. She kept seeing this gray sedan everywhere she went. At first, she thought she was imagining things. Gray sedans are prevalent. But then she started paying closer attention. This one had heavily tinted windows, which still isn't uncommon. She never saw the license plate on the back, and there wasn't one on the front."

"That was here in Florida?" asked Matthew. Heavily tinted windows were—as she'd said—common in Florida. Neither Florida—nor North Carolina—required license plates on the front of vehicles. He wasn't sure how many other states didn't.

"Yes, it was here. All over Miami," she answered with a shiver. "She said it was a sleek, gray, four-door Mercedes. I don't know what model. But she noticed the emblem on the front."

"The Mercedes badge?" clarified Matthew.

"Right. That."

"Did anybody approach her? Ask her anything? Threaten her in any way?" Danbury asked, peering at her in the rearview mirror and joining in the questioning.

"Not that I know of."

"How did she die?" Matthew gently asked, wanting to hear her version of what Rhodes had told him earlier.

"In a car accident. At least, the police ruled it as an accident. I was never sure. The more questions I asked, the less sure I was. Dad wouldn't talk about it."

"Why weren't you sure?"

"It was a single-car accident, just my mom in the car. There were no skid marks, but her car went off the road down a steep embankment and flipped over several times. It landed upside down in a deep ditch. It was dark, and they didn't," she began and then choked.

"Take your time," Matthew said soothingly.

"They didn't find her car immediately. Not until the next morning. If they had, she might have been saved. If only someone had seen the car go off the road or spotted it down in the ditch."

After a long pause, she continued, "Ever since then, I've wondered what really happened. The authorities hypothesized that it could have been suicide, which I outright rejected. There were no signs. She was perfectly fine on the phone with me the night before. She didn't mention going anywhere that next night, so I'm not even sure why she was out. They think it happened around nine, but that's conjecture on the part of the medical examiner. She wasn't found until the next morning when Daddy started looking for her."

"I'm so sorry," said Matthew, feeling the pain emanating from her words.

"Daddy thought she'd gone to bed early. They had separate bedrooms. He didn't know she wasn't home until he couldn't find her the next morning."

"And your dad?" asked Danbury. "Was he threatened?"

"Probably."

"You don't know for sure?"

"I don't."

"Why do you think he might have been?"

"I overheard him on the phone once the weekend of my mother's funeral service. He was angry. I could tell by his voice, though he was talking in hushed tones. He was insisting to somebody that he wouldn't alter the translation of text on some artifact—he was refusing to do that. Whatever he'd authenticated was the real deal, as was his translation, and he was swearing to it. Insistently."

"You don't know what that article was?"

"I don't. He didn't say. Or, if he did, I missed it."

"Do you know who he was talking to?" asked Matthew.

"I have absolutely no idea."

"When was that service?" Danbury asked.

"It was the weekend after my mother died. We're coming up on the anniversary of her death in March, so nearly two years ago. It would have been," she hesitated, pulling her phone out and tapping it. "The weekend of March 17 and 18, 2018. I don't remember which day I overheard the phone call. I was in shock over losing Mom so suddenly."

She drew a deep breath before continuing, "I was a bit of a daddy's girl growing up, but my mother was the glue that held our family together. Daddy could be the typical absent-minded professor sometimes. OK, more often than sometimes. He'd forget special occasions, like birthdays. He regularly forgot things my mother had told him—things like where we were going or what we were doing when, or with whom."

She stared steadily out the window as if she were seeing something other than the scenery along the interstate that was moving slowly by.

"How often did you talk to your parents, to your father?" asked Matthew.

"Mom called almost daily when I went off to college. Then Aleah left for school three years later and I know Mom called her regularly too. I guess it was more like two or three times a week before she died. Sometimes she called, and sometimes I called her to check in. For Dad, it was as if we had more to talk about when we were home—but like we almost didn't exist when we were away. I've made the effort to call him regularly—usually weekly—but Aleah is mad about it and says he can bloody well call her if he wants to talk."

"When was the last time you talked to him?" asked Matthew.

"Last week. On Wednesday. We talked for about fifteen—maybe twenty—minutes or so that evening."

"The evening of Wednesday, January 22?" Matthew asked.

"That's right."

"What did you talk about?"

"Daddy always told me about what he was doing professionally—at the university, in his research, or his speaking engagements. He wasn't all that interested in the social scene when Mom was alive and planning things. He avoided social obligations altogether after her death."

"If he didn't have much of a social life, then he had no close friends?" Matthew asked.

"Not outside of the university, no."

"What did you talk about on Wednesday? Was there anything unusual?"

"I'm not sure I'd call it unusual, but he was excited. I could hear it in his voice. He didn't fully explain, but it sounded like he'd had a couple of developments. One involved a project his students were working on. They'd discovered something with an artifact they were cleaning, researching, and cataloging. They'd called him in to have a look. He said he thought they were right about their assessment, but he had more to do to validate it."

"Was that at the research building? Anything to do with artifacts they'd brought back from a summer trip a couple of years ago?" asked Matthew, purposefully leaving out a few details to see if she'd fill them in for him correctly.

"He didn't elaborate," she said, much to his disappointment.

"You said a couple of developments," Danbury chimed in. "What was the other one?"

"Somebody called and wanted to see Dad about a relic or artifact, and he thought he knew what it was. It must have been particularly ancient, rare, or valuable. He'd have been more likely to get excited over something unusual than monetarily valuable, though, knowing him."

Last Wednesday, remembered Matthew, was the same day that Greg had called Mark to tell him that they were adding the church in Sunny Isles to their agenda, changing their flight home, and wouldn't be returning to North Carolina before flying out for Ukraine. He had also asked Mark to mail the sealed box home for him during that call. Greg had contacted Professor Stevenson by that point, which meant that Stevenson already knew about the book before he spoke to his daughter.

That must have been at least half of what had excited the professor, Matthew thought. The guy hadn't sounded excited about it when they'd met with him. But then, he had also thought he'd been ghosted when Greg didn't show up for the meeting they'd scheduled.

One other question pushed its way to the forefront of Matthew's mind. If that book was so valuable, he understood why Greg didn't have it in his possession as they traveled around the US. Why would he bring it in the first place and then risk mailing it home to Ukraine? Wouldn't that be equally as risky? Or maybe more so. That was a question he hadn't yet discussed with Danbury, but it seemed an important one.

Maybe Greg didn't know its importance. He could read Russian, so he knew exactly what it contained far better than they yet did. Why wouldn't he treat it as something valuable? Maybe because the Cold War had ended, and he thought the contents were too antiquated for anyone to care about anymore.

To Bella Bosch, Matthew asked, "He gave you no clue? He said nothing at all that would help to identify the item or artifact?"

From his vantage point in the vanity mirror, he could see her face screw in concentration. "I'm trying to remember, specifically, what he said, but his exact words are eluding me."

Matthew gave her space to ponder until, finally, she said, "It was something about an article of minor antiquity that needed to be analyzed and safe guarded, I think. He said it wasn't terribly old but that he was excited about seeing it. Something like that. He dealt mainly with antiquities, so if it wasn't old, I don't know what it could have been."

Glancing at Danbury, Matthew said, "That sounds important. Did he mention being worried about anything?"

"No."

"Did he sound worried?"

"Not that I could tell."

"He didn't mention being threatened or noticing anyone following him?"

"No, nothing like that."

"Did you talk about anything else?"

"He asked when I was coming home again, like he always does. I told him maybe over his spring break, like I always do," she added, choking on the words. "It was mostly an empty promise. But I wish I'd meant it back in the fall when I told him maybe I'd come home over the holidays. Because now…" her words slurred and didn't finish the sentence.

Matthew flipped his mirrored visor up to give her some privacy. Locating the small stack of napkins from their take-out lunch in the console, he handed them over the seat to her.

"Thanks," she snuffled and blew her nose softly.

As they pulled into the police precinct, Matthew said, "Thank you, Dr. Bosch. Believe it or not, that was very helpful. If you think of anything else—any little detail—it might be important. Please contact us."

He selected one of the business cards from his wallet that he'd already jotted his cell phone number on and handed it to her. Danbury did the same.

"OK," she said, taking them and tucking them into a pocket on her fitted pink suit jacket. "I will if I think of anything that might help. Are you getting Aleah and bringing her back here too?"

Matthew glanced at Danbury, who nodded his affirmation. "We

are," Danbury said. "Thank you for talking to us."

"I'm going to have to go through this all again with the police, aren't I?" she asked.

As Matthew slid out to retrieve her bags, he heard Danbury respond, "Very likely so."

She looked reconciled to her fate as she thanked them for the ride and trudged into the police station with her bags in tow. Matthew felt a sudden rush of sorrow for the woman. She'd lost both parents quickly and prematurely, and he was concerned for her safety now too.

"We need to know if her father's badge was used to access that research building after his death," said Matthew as he slid back into the vehicle and closed the door. "It's one of many things we need to know."

"It is," agreed Danbury before tapping his phone to call Rhodes and provide the promised update about what they'd learned from Dr. Bella Bosch. Matthew tapped the navigation app on his phone and selected the address to get them to the Miami airport. Picking up Aleah meant having to do that all over again, which Matthew wasn't looking forward to.

27 ~ BURNING QUESTIONS

After picking Aleah up at the Miami airport, Matthew questioned her at length—with Danbury interjecting a few questions here and there—all the way to the police precinct. Her responses were far less enlightening than her older sister's. She hadn't been in touch with their father nearly as often. Aleah, it seemed, had been a Mama's girl growing up.

Admittedly not a psychiatrist, Matthew thought he read resentment toward Professor Stevenson in the tone underlying the words of his younger daughter. Did she hold him responsible for her mother's death? It sounded that way to him.

Returning to the police station with Aleah, they stepped inside. Sergeant Rhodes met them in the lobby and introduced a fit, young, uniformed officer. The guy was apologizing profusely for questioning her there instead of somewhere more comfortable as he guided her through the doors into the interior of the station.

Rhodes handed Matthew a printed copy of the statement he'd provided about the drive-by shooting. While Matthew read through it, Danbury filled Rhodes in on their conversations with Professor Stevenson's daughters. Mostly, it was a discussion about what Bella had told them rather than the less-enlightening conversation with Aleah.

As Matthew signed his statement, he was happy that he'd provided that information so quickly in the aftermath of the incident. It was accurate—and he could think of nothing that he'd left out—but it had all happened so fast that it was beginning to be a confused tangle in his mind a few hours afterward. The statement provided clarity on the order of events that he might not have been able to reproduce now.

A single impression had been solidifying itself in his mind since the incident. The police cruiser must have been the target of this shooting. This time, he didn't think it was the Tahoe he occupied.

"Do you know anything about the officer who was shot? Diego Acosta?" Matthew asked Rhodes, handing the paperwork back to him.

"You mean his condition?"

"Well, yes," said Matthew, not appending, "that too." He was concerned about the condition of the officer, of course. But he was also curious about the officer's life before the shooting.

"He was in surgery, last I heard. I guess that's a good thing. If they were still working on him, then they hadn't lost him. But that was over two hours ago."

"Do you know anything about him, either personally or professionally?" asked Matthew.

"No, he's from Broward County. I've crossed paths with some of them, but not Officer Acosta. At least, I don't recognize his name. Why?"

"What about the other officer who was in the car with him?"

"I don't know who that was. I'm sure it's in the report, though. I can get it if it's important to know."

Matthew realized that he didn't know the guy's name either. He'd heard the name of the officer who'd been shot, but he hadn't been introduced to his younger partner. "Huh," was all he said.

"Why?" Rhodes asked again.

"Because it wasn't like when we were shot at yesterday, and the bullet went into my headrest," he began, and a chill crept up his spine at the thought.

"The shooting at the warehouse was different," Matthew continued. "Acosta pulled the Broward County car alongside the Tahoe I was in. He blocked the bottom half of it from the incoming car before the shooting started. The top of the SUV was exposed, but all the bullets fired hit the police cruiser and none went over it into the Tahoe at all, right? It makes me wonder who they were aiming at and why. And if Acosta saw the gun or how he knew to cover me when the purple car came tearing into the warehouse parking area."

"All good questions," answered Rhodes, shifting to stand mostly on one foot and scratching his head. "It's worth asking about both of those officers."

"Any update on Professor Stevenson's badge?" asked Danbury, changing the subject. "Was it used after his death?"

"I still haven't heard back from Barclay University about that yet. I need to get one of my team to follow up," said Rhodes.

"Let us know?" asked Danbury. "When you do."

"Yep," said Rhodes, starting to move around Matthew and Danbury back toward the interior door. "Will do."

"One other thing," added Matthew before Rhodes could get away. "Bella Bosch seems to know a lot more about Professor Stevenson than her sister Aleah could ever have forgotten. She might well know things that she doesn't know that she knows—at least things that she doesn't know are important. Maybe some of them go back to her childhood and emigrating here. You've got a protective detail around her, right?" Matthew asked, one eyebrow raised.

"Better than that," said Rhodes, looking annoyed that Matthew had asked. "They'll be staying with one of our officers who volunteered the use of two spare bedrooms in her bungalow. The cottage will be under rotating surveillance while they're there. The sisters aren't staying at their father's house or in a public hotel."

"Great. I'm relieved to hear that," said Matthew, thinking that he could personally vouch for how safe that wasn't.

"You're heading up north now?" Rhodes asked.

"We are," answered Danbury, checking his watch. "It'll be late when we get up there. I want to talk to Fisher. At Aurora Springs Chapel. And get another look at that hotel. Where the missionaries were. That argument over jurisdiction. It might have paid off. If nothing has been removed yet."

"I don't think it has. At least, not that I know of," said Rhodes. "Safe travels. Try to avoid getting shot at." He smirked at Matthew.

"Keep me updated."

"Will do," said Danbury. "You too." They nodded sharply to each other and went in opposite directions—Matthew and Danbury out through the front doors and Rhodes through the double doors into the interior of the building.

As they climbed in the Tahoe, Matthew saw from the dash display that it was already after four thirty. Traffic would be a nightmare. It would all be heading out of Miami with them, he thought, as he suggested, "We could travel up the coast instead of on the interstate."

"Good plan," agreed Danbury as he handed over his phone for Matthew to set the location and choose the route. "Traffic heading north out of Miami will be rough. No matter which way we go."

Studying the map, Matthew said, "We'll head up US 1—which is Biscayne Blvd—then east on 826 above Haulover to A1A and up the coastline."

"OK."

That accomplished, Matthew clipped the phone to the holder on the dash and sighed as he noticed the time required to get to Aurora Springs. It would be late, as Danbury had told Rhodes, but they had plenty of time to discuss what they knew so far.

As Danbury backed out of the parking spot and turned out to head north and east, Matthew called his office to check on patients, answer a few questions personally, and talk to both his office manager and his most trusted nurse. Returning his cell phone to his pocket absently, he was thinking about how he still hadn't told Danbury about his dream. For whatever it was worth, the dream seemed to add a new layer of uncertainty—it felt like all they had were questions—and very few answers about any of it.

"This will be a long trip," groused Matthew. "But we need time to discuss everything anyway and try to make some sense out of information that seems completely unrelated. It must be, somehow. I have so many questions."

"Yeah, me too," said Danbury, rubbing the stubble on his chin.

"Let's start at the beginning and reconstruct the timeline," suggested Matthew. "Maybe if we run through who told us what about when—whether any of it is true or not—it'll help us to form a better picture of what could have happened to Greg and Darya and why. Then maybe we can figure out where they are."

"OK, Doc. Shoot," said Danbury after maneuvering the turns necessary to set them on US 1 headed north. Traffic was indeed thick, and they inched slowly along between stoplights.

"I guess the first thing that happened was Greg leaving the box containing the book behind at the church in Raleigh. I get why he thought having it with him would have been risky. And he was right. But why would he risk mailing it home to Ukraine? Wouldn't that be equally as risky? Or maybe more so. I mean, maybe Greg didn't understand its importance."

"He could read Russian. He knew what it contained."

"Yeah, I considered that too. He knew then—better than we know now—what's in it. Given that, why wouldn't he handle it more carefully? Maybe because the Cold War ended, and he thought the contents were too antiquated for anybody to care about anymore. Or maybe because he thought that was the best of several bad options," added Matthew, posing the answers to the question that he'd been contemplating.

"But if he brought it all this way to show it to Professor Stevenson, why not take it to him?" Matthew continued. "Had he tried to make an appointment with the professor and been unable to at the point when they left North Carolina? Maybe Greg had copies. Or pictures. Of whatever he thought was important."

"Possible," agreed Danbury. "Pictures could be deleted. Copies destroyed."

"Right," said Matthew. "He probably wouldn't have wanted to destroy the book itself, even if he knew that his grandfather was KGB and potentially a horrible person."

"Maybe there was more."

"More what?"

"It's leather-bound," said Danbury pensively, pulling forward from a red light. "It might have layers. Maybe there's something in the binding."

"That's true," answered Matthew. "We weren't looking for that then. You left it at the precinct, right?"

"Yeah, I did."

"Could somebody there look?"

"I'll ask. At this next stoplight," said Danbury, braking and pulling his phone from the dash. He texted something and returned the phone to the clip on the dash before pulling through the light and continuing to the next one.

"Monday, January twentieth," said Matthew, opening the online document that he'd created with the timeline on his phone.

"We need to back up," said Danbury. "I know you don't want to admit it. But Grygoriy Starkovich was hiding something."

"Yeah, the notebook."

"Something else."

"What do you mean?"

"When did he schedule to meet Stevenson?"

"The first Monday that they were traveling, January the thirteenth."

"To meet in Miami when?"

"Saturday morning, January the twenty-fifth."

"That's six hours south of Aurora Springs."

"OK."

"When were they due back in Raleigh? Originally?"

"Saturday night. January the twenty-fifth."

"That's a twelve-hour drive. In the best of traffic. From Miami back to Raleigh. After the six hours south from Aurora Springs."

"Yeah," prompted Matthew, beginning to see where the big detective was going with this.

"How could he be in both places? In Raleigh. And driving back from Miami? He didn't tell Mark they weren't coming back. Not until after the addition of St. Athanasius. But he wasn't planning to be back in Raleigh. Not since Monday, the thirteenth. Why didn't he tell Mark?

Maybe he orchestrated this whole thing."

"What?" asked Matthew in alarm. "To what end? I mean, what would he gain from that? He had the book in his possession already, and he must have had at least some idea of what it contained. Otherwise, why contact the professor at all? We only have Professor Stevenson's word that Greg called him on the thirteenth and scheduled to meet on the twenty-fifth."

"We can't check that with him. Because he's conveniently dead."

Matthew hadn't thought of that, he realized, probably because he hadn't wanted to think about it. "There must be a logical explanation," he said. "One we haven't uncovered yet. We need to keep working on it."

Danbury was silent, so Matthew continued with the timeline. "Father Grossman and Pastor Fisher agree that they spoke to each other about Greg and his team being in Florida. And they agree on the day that happened. But each of them says the other made the contact. Father Grossman says he called Greg Tuesday evening—the twenty-first—after an impromptu meeting with his parish council members that afternoon. The council members all agree that they met on Tuesday."

"Greg called Mark Kushner the next day," said Danbury.

"Yeah, he called Mark on Wednesday to tell him they weren't coming back to North Carolina. It was then that he asked about mailing the box back. That same evening, Bella talked to her father, and she said he was excited about an artifact that he'd learned about and something that his students were working on. Two separate things. But she says that he didn't explain either of those in detail. We're assuming the artifact was Greg's book. What if it wasn't? What if it was a coincidence? What if he hadn't just scheduled to meet with Greg?"

"That's possible," said Danbury. "But how likely?"

"OK, let's go with the more likely scenario that it's connected. The professor was excited about seeing Greg's book—or at least pictures of it."

"Anything else on Wednesday?"

"Not in my notes. Thursday, Greg's team was at Christ Walk Church in Macon, Georgia. They left there that afternoon and checked into a hotel north of the Florida state line. We know they made it that far. Nobody has definitively heard from them since.

"Somebody responded to Mark's text on Friday near that hotel in southern Georgia, but only by text. Maybe it was Greg, though the hotel security footage suggests that it wasn't. Why would somebody else answer a text as if it was from Greg? We're assuming it was to delay anybody knowing the missionaries were missing. Maybe that time is important, somehow."

"That's likely," said Danbury.

"Then they were due at Aurora Springs on Friday to attend a luncheon for them, and they never showed up."

"According to Fisher."

"Pastor Fisher told us and Father Grossman that he called them and couldn't get an answer from any of their phones. His calls went to voicemail, and most of the voicemail boxes were full. He also said that he called the church in Macon and was told nothing seemed out of the ordinary when they were there."

"And then Saturday."

"Professor Stevenson said that Greg had scheduled to meet with him Saturday morning, he assumed about the book. They were due in Sunny Isles to meet with the parish council at St. Athanasius on Sunday. Father Grossman said he called Pastor Fisher when they didn't arrive, and that's when he learned that they hadn't been in Aurora Springs either."

Considering for a moment, Matthew said, "Nobody, so far, can account for their whereabouts definitively after Thursday. The surveillance video corroborates the assumption that they've been missing since then. The bodies of Ivan and Ross were found the following Monday, the twenty-seventh. They'd been dead at least two days, and the ME thought probably three. That puts their deaths most likely on Saturday, maybe as early as Friday."

"Plenty of time to question them."

"And either they wouldn't cooperate, or they didn't know

anything."

"Either could be true. Unless they did."

"You mean they gave the killers what they wanted and then were disposable because they were no longer useful?"

"It's one possibility."

"If that were the case, what would they have told or given their killers? If we're assuming the book was what the killers wanted, then maybe they had pictures of it or printed copies. Like you suggested earlier."

"The big unknowns. What did they want? Was it the book? If it wasn't, then what? If it was, did they get it? Or copies of it? But if they did," said Danbury, hesitating. "Then why kill Stevenson?"

"If this is all about that book and they didn't get pictures of it, then visiting Professor Stevenson makes sense. They wanted to know what he knew about it."

"Maybe. Or maybe they wanted his help. Deciphering what it meant."

"As in, they got pictures of the contents of the book but couldn't understand it?"

"Right."

"If it wasn't the book they wanted, then we're back to square one in figuring this out."

"Let's back up," said Danbury. "Nearly two years ago. Two women were killed. We know why one was."

"Pavlov's wife was killed because somebody wanted that wharf property—the warehouses on the canal. At least, that's what we think they wanted. That's according to Pavlov's account, if that can be trusted."

"That would suggest storage. And shipping. Likely something illegal. Maybe that wasn't all."

"Assuming the deaths of the two women are related somehow, we don't know what they wanted from Stevenson when his wife was killed. Bella Bosch overheard an intense phone conversation of her father's, the weekend of her mother's death. It was about some article that the professor was insisting that he hadn't altered and wouldn't provide false information about somehow. He could have procured it, sold it, or verified it for somebody. She didn't admit to knowing anything more about it—merely that the timing was odd for that heated conversation."

"And the guy with the snake tattoo," added Danbury. "Bella said she saw him following her. About two years ago."

"If it was the same guy," Matthew said. "If not, and there's more than one guy with a snake tattoo up his arm, then is it a gang? A group affiliation?"

"Or an allegiance to something," said Danbury.

After a few silent moments as they crept through the traffic, Matthew added, "Let's assume this is about Greg's grandfather's book. The notebook or journal—whatever you want to call it."

Before Danbury could respond, his cell phone dinged. Matthew glanced up to see an incoming text from a name he didn't recognize. Danbury told his phone to read it. The message reported that the notebook binding contained nothing hidden. It was a single layer of leather that had been affixed directly to a paper interior, with neither anything in between nor any writing on either layer. The texter apologized for having to pull it apart to verify that.

"Well, there goes that theory," said Matthew, taking a deep, frustrated breath before considering another idea. "If there had been something hidden in it somehow, could Greg have been carrying it? He left the book behind, but what if he had more than pictures or copies of it?"

"It's possible," answered Danbury. "There could have been something else. That we don't know about yet."

Following another contemplative silence, Danbury said, "Let's go back to what we know. Or what we've been told. Stevenson said the information would be antiquated. Too old to be useful."

"If it was all original," said Matthew, grinning because he knew that it would annoy Danbury that he wasn't letting go of the theory that there had been more to the book than what they'd seen.

"What we saw was," said Danbury. "Or somebody did a good job of making it look like it."

"To our untrained eyes, true," conceded Matthew. "And there'd be no point in altering or adding text unless you were trying to throw off something or somebody with it."

"Let's go back to the timeline," said Danbury.

"We left off with Ross and Ivan. They were likely murdered on Friday or Saturday. The group was due in Aurora Springs on Friday, but they didn't make it that far. According to Pastor Fisher's account, but we can confirm that with members of the church if we need to. A text went to Mark Kushner from Greg's phone on Friday," summarized Matthew from his notes.

"They were due to meet in Sunny Isles on Sunday, which they didn't do, according to several people from St. Athanasius Orthodox Church. Father Grossman also said that he hadn't heard from them. Greg was to have met with Professor Stevenson on Saturday, according to Stevenson, which also never happened."

"Greg didn't mention that meeting to Kusner? The meeting with Professor Stevenson?"

"I assume not. Mark didn't mention it. I'm sure he would have if he'd known. The plans for Saturday hinge on what Stevenson told us. There's no way to corroborate that information," answered Matthew, pondering momentarily before continuing.

"Ross and Ivan's bodies were found on Monday and pulled out on Tuesday, then identified. You arrived down here before dawn on Tuesday, and I came in that evening. From there, it's totally insane," added Matthew, drawing a deep breath.

"We talked to Professor Stevenson, Father Grossman, and Pastor Fisher all on Wednesday. Which was good because we knew where their stories intersected and where they didn't mesh at all. But there's something you don't know about Wednesday night."

"What's that, Doc?"

"I had what was either an extremely vivid dream or a vision. It was all-consuming. I woke up in a cold sweat, tangled in the sheets. I assume I'd been moving around in the bed, like in the dream. Though maybe not exactly so."

"So, that's it."

"That's what?"

"What you've been preoccupied with." Matthew glanced at him in surprise as Danbury added, "Tell me."

Matthew drew another deep breath, trying to figure out where to start, and then dove in. Beginning with seeing the southwestern end of Mt. Athos Island from a distance shortly before sunrise—and later looking up pictures of it that were exactly as he'd seen it—Matthew explained the man being turned away, the chanting, the rituals, and the enormous gold cross that was raised from the floor.

"I don't know what any of it means," he added. "One of the monks told the guy he turned away—the guy whose face has haunted me—that this ritual was done once a year and only the brotherhood could attend. I looked down in the dream, and I was clothed as they were in long black robes—and I'd grown a beard! I reached up to scratch my face because it was itchy."

Danbury was silent as Matthew continued, "But the most troubling part has been the face of the man I saw. I'm not sure if it was his face or an expression that crossed it in the briefest instant—but there was something I know I should recognize there. And I don't. I can't determine who he was or why it's important to figure that out."

"Interesting, Doc," was all Danbury said. "Your dreams have been right before."

Turning his head sharply toward Danbury—trying to remember if he'd ever shared that and thinking that he hadn't—Matthew answered, "They have. The really vivid ones have all told me something important. And this is the most vivid one I've ever had—fully immersive—involving all five senses."

A silence followed as both men were lost in contemplation. Finally, Danbury broke the silence, "It's after six. We need to find dinner."

Matthew laughed aloud. Trust Danbury to be thinking about food. The guy could always eat.

"That's your credo, isn't it?" asked Matthew. "To eat when you can and sleep when you can because you never know when you'll be able to do either one again."

"I didn't make that up," said Danbury. "It goes along with expressions like fubar. And hours of boredom interspersed with moments of sheer terror. And Whiskey Tango Foxtrot. It's a military thing."

"Oh," said Matthew. "I thought it was a Danbury thing."

This time, Danbury laughed. "I guess it is," he agreed. "I took it to heart."

Searching on his phone, Matthew found a highly-rated restaurant on the water where they stopped for a sit-down dinner instead of grabbing food on the run. A further query located a hotel in Aurora Springs, and he made a reservation for the night while they were waiting for their meal.

Sitting on an outdoor deck under a heat lamp overlooking a waterway between the island they were traversing and the ocean, Matthew spotted dolphins. Rhythmically surfacing in graceful arches and then submerging again, there were at least four of them. The rising moon caught the slickness of their bodies that shimmered each time they surfaced.

"They're so intelligent," said Matthew appreciatively, enjoying the view immensely.

"So are sharks," said Danbury ominously.

28 ~ FINS

Matthew fought his way through a haze of exhaustion when his alarm brought him back to reality the next morning at six. It was a Saturday, so Cici might not initiate a conversation with him quite as early, he thought. It was also the first of February and nearly Valentine's Day. She was on the other side of an ocean, he thought dismally. Maybe he'd send her something nice as a gift. He made a mental note to figure out what that might be. She was too practical to like cut flowers because she hated it when they died. He would come up with something, he reassured himself.

Having showered, shaved, and packed up first, he figured he'd FaceTime her before he and Danbury set out for the day.

"Good morning, sleepyhead," she greeted him. "You're up early on a Saturday. It's what, six thirty or so your time?"

"Good afternoon, Cees," he said, staring in awe at how her strawberry-blond hair looked like spun gold when the light was behind her as it was now. She was sitting in front of a large glass window. "Where are you?" he asked.

"At a coffee shop," she said. "The internet connection was down this morning at my flat. I had some things I needed to do, but I didn't want to use my phone as a hotspot or go to the office to do them."

"Ah," answered Matthew, thinking that his next activity should be getting online himself and checking his patient records before joining Danbury downstairs. He told her about driving up the coastline the evening before and that they were in northern Florida, beneath the Georgia state line.

"Oh, you're halfway home then," she smiled brightly at him. "Are you finishing your trip?"

"Not yet," Matthew sighed with a sudden homesick longing for more than Cici but also for North Carolina and his life there. "We still haven't found Greg and Darya."

"Are you any closer?"

"You would think so. But I don't know that we are."

"I would think so, yes. How long will you stay? I mean, if you don't find them soon, how long will you continue to look?"

"At least another few days. I need to get home to patients and my real job soon. I'm doing all I can from here to update records, answer questions, and advise my staff. I know my colleagues are more than capable of dealing with them, but there were a couple of patients this week that I really wanted to see and follow up with myself."

"I'm sure," she said, nodding as if she genuinely understood.

They finished their conversation, professed their love, and said goodbye. Then Matthew pulled out his computer and went through his patient records, updating a couple and checking to see which patients had scheduled appointments the following week. He was admitting to himself that he was both homesick and sorely missing Cici when his phone dinged, and Danbury texted that he was in the lobby, ready to go.

"On my way," Matthew texted back.

There was no breakfast, continental or otherwise, at this hotel, so they checked out and went in search of some. Over plates of eggs benedict with crab cakes and pecan waffles, Matthew searched for a home address for Pastor Fisher.

"He probably won't be at the church today," he said. "He'll likely be there a good bit of tomorrow, so why would he be today? But we'll find him. That, I know."

"We will?" asked Danbury dubiously.

"Yup. We should be able to find him easily enough if he's at neither of those places," assured Matthew.

"How's that?"

"Did you see the pictures hanging beside the door inside his office? In one of them, he's posed beside a boat at the end of a dock. In another—looking out toward the water from the shore—there's a long dock behind him. The names of both the boat and the dock are in the pictures."

"Oh?" said Danbury, looking impressed that Matthew had noticed those details. "I saw the pictures you're talking about. But I didn't study them."

"Good thing I did then," said Matthew, appreciating that he'd noticed something Danbury hadn't.

After they finished their breakfast and began the search, Matthew was proven right about all three things. Fisher wasn't at the church. Nobody answered the door of the lovely home at the address they'd found for the pastor. Inquires at the dock—aptly and redundantly named the Long Dock—provided them with the information they needed. Fisher had gone out on the *Great White*—the boat in the picture inside Fisher's office door—that morning. Likely, they were told, it wouldn't return until at least three that afternoon.

"What do we do until then?" asked Matthew, eyebrow raised and foot tapping. "We can't sit around, as much as I'd love to soak in the scenery." It was a beautiful spot there on the water and a beautiful day to enjoy it, but Matthew was anxious to make progress with the search and then head for home. The day was sunny but several degrees cooler in the northern part of Florida. With the breeze blowing off the water, Matthew was thankful for his jacket. Perfect weather if you were on vacation, he thought.

Checking his watch, Danbury said, "Let's go back up to the hotel in Georgia."

"How far away is it?" asked Matthew.

"Forty-five minutes. Tops," said Danbury. "We're almost in Georgia here. Queen's Ferry is barely over the state line."

"Yeah," said Matthew dismally. "And halfway home."

*****

Searching the hotel rooms again and questioning the staff and the local officers who had first been called to the scene turned up no new information. It confirmed that the rooms held nothing informative—neither identification of the occupants nor anything valuable. That, Danbury said, was telling. The local police swore they'd removed nothing. The logical conclusion was that the rooms had been professionally and carefully searched, as they had assumed. More than identification had likely been removed, though it was frustratingly impossible to know what else might have been.

It was shortly after three that afternoon before Matthew and Danbury made their way back to the dock in search of Pastor Fisher. When they arrived, they were told that *Great White* had come in earlier. Owner, crew, and all occupants were already gone.

"You're looking for Fish? I mean, Pastor Fisher?" asked a sun-scorched man who was spraying down a boat a few slips away from where *Great White* was now tied securely in its spot.

"We are," answered Matthew. "We really need to talk to him."

"Ordinarily, I wouldn't give away anything about the pastor, but if you really need him, I can tell you that he's probably back at the church by now. If he's not, he will be soon."

"How do you know that?" asked Matthew.

"I attend the church," the man answered. "And I know Fish usually goes over there on Saturday afternoons and runs through the sermon for the next morning a few times. Usually before dinner. You can probably catch him there now."

"Do you know anything about the missionaries who were supposed to speak at your church last weekend?" asked Matthew.

"The ones from Ukraine?"

"Right."

"I know we were all looking forward to hearing from them. I missed them last year. Everyone who heard them then was really excited about them coming back. It sounds like the main guy is really a character."

"You mean Greg?" asked Matthew.

"Yeah, that's his name," said the guy, pulling the hose around and dropping it in neat loops on the dock.

"How long have you attended Aurora Springs Chapel?" asked Matthew.

"Most of my life," answered the man. "It was just a chapel when I was a kid. It expanded some with a new building when I was a teenager. The big new building isn't that old. Maybe ten years or so."

"How long has Pastor Fisher been there?"

"About three years, I think. Something like that."

"Oh, so he's a recent addition to the church," said Matthew.

"Yeah, I guess you could say that."

"Is he from around here? Did he go to the church and then begin to pastor it?"

"No, I think he moved up here from somewhere south. Down near Miami, I think."

Matthew and Danbury exchanged a glance, and Matthew thanked the man before they headed for the church, which was a short distance away. The parking lot was empty except for one lone car, a sedan, that was parked by the curb of the building outside the entrance that said "Office."

Danbury pushed the call button, and they waited. Then Matthew pushed it again. As they were ready to go in search of any alternate entrance that might not be locked, a scratchy male voice answered. They identified themselves, and the door clicked open for them. Pastor Fisher met them inside and escorted them to his office.

As before, the man was affable and welcoming. He had an aw-shucks manner about him that Matthew could find no better way to describe in his mind than that. They followed the pastor back to his office.

"Now, how can I help you, gentlemen?" he asked, smiling broadly and motioning for them to take seats on the other side of his massive glass and steel desk. "I can't think of anything I haven't already told you, but I'm happy to try."

Before Matthew could get a word in at all, Danbury began drilling the pastor about the statement he'd given before. The man stood by his story, repeating what he'd told them previously. A member of

Grossman's church had visited his, he insisted, though he admitted that perhaps he'd had the name wrong. And Grossman most definitely contacted him about the missionaries coming to Florida, and not the other way around.

"And you're sure," said Danbury. "That it all happened exactly that way?"

"I'm a pastor," said Fisher, as if that put him beyond reproach. He puffed out his chest but grinned. "Of a huge and constantly growing church congregation. Why don't you go talk to that pastor down in Sunny Isles with the church named for the patron saint of the Grecian Peninsula?"

Matthew shifted forward in his seat. At that moment, he realized there were at least two significant problems with Fisher's statement. Due to his own experience growing up in a church that genuinely followed Jesus—with a pastor he considered a second father figure—he'd put pastors on a pedestal. All pastors. Simply because they claimed the title. He assumed that he was not the only person to do so.

"You mean Father Grossman?" asked Matthew, watching for a reaction. Fisher merely nodded.

"Pastors are people," said Danbury, perfectly stating Matthew's current thoughts. "Some are honest. Some aren't."

With that statement, Matthew saw the briefest flash of something on the pastor's face that wasn't affable at all. It was more than annoyance. Hostility, maybe? Anger? Fear? The expression was there and then it was gone so quickly that Matthew struggled to identify it precisely.

Realizing that they'd get nothing further from Fisher about the missionaries, Matthew watched and listened as Danbury changed his approach. Zeroing in on the pride the pastor had exhibited in his hot retort, Danbury asked, "How long have you been here? The pastor of such a large church?"

"A little over three years," answered Fisher. "And we've grown exponentially since I arrived."

"Where were you before here?" asked Danbury.

"I was at a smaller church for about four years. I went to seminary as a second profession, really. My master of divinity came a bit later in life." He motioned to the wall behind him.

"Where was that church?" asked Danbury.

"South of here," he answered evasively with a smile and noncommittal wave of his hand as if it were a trivial question. "Now, if you will please excuse me," he said, oozing politeness and charm, "I have a sermon to prepare for in the morning. I was working on it in the sanctuary before you arrived. I need to get back to it and then get home before my wife burns my dinner."

They excused themselves, and he walked them out. Matthew thought it was a bit overdone, but the man pulled the outer door closed behind them—instead of waiting for it to close by itself—with a decisive thunk. He heard the click of the lock engage.

The parking lot, Matthew noticed, had a few more cars in it. He wondered, as a passing thought, where the people were.

"Fish?" asked Danbury as they made their way back to the Tahoe. "Or shark?"

"I'm leaning toward shark," answered Matthew. "He comes across as very friendly and inviting, but there's something hard and harsh beneath that. I caught a glimpse of it when you were grilling him. I can't quite place what that was or why it bothered me so much. But you're right. There were other more obvious things. Several red flags."

"Such as?" asked Danbury.

They hesitated beside the Tahoe as Matthew said, "He talks about growing the church membership, not growing the members in their faith individually. That is a prideful thing that set off warnings in my mind. I know it's a thing with pastors, the size of their churches."

Danbury grinned but said nothing.

"I remember hearing Mark Kushner say that he'd once spoken at another church, and when he was introduced, they said he was the pastor of a church of 350 and not 3,500. He said it bugged him, and he had to fight with himself not to correct it when he began to speak."

"Was that what set you off? You reacted to something he said."

"Partially. But I think the real kicker was what he said about talking to Grossman."

"What's that?" asked Danbury.

"He said Grossman's church was named for the patron saint of the Grecian Peninsula. From what both Mark Kushner and Professor Stevenson said, the original St. Athanasius lived centuries before the second one that Fisher was talking about and wasn't connected to Mt. Athos in any way. Stevenson said that the fourth-century St. Athanasius is far better known. He was credited with arguing for some of the foundational underpinnings of the Christian church, so pastors would surely have heard of him in their studies."

Eyebrow raised, he paused, then added, "The tenth-century St. Athanasius is the one who is credited with founding the monasteries on Mt. Athos, the Greek peninsula. Would most pastors have ever heard of the second Athanasius? Was the second as well known as the first? I can call Mark and ask him."

"Ah," said Danbury. They climbed into the Tahoe, "He's been at the church only three years. Where was he before? He didn't answer that directly. He ducked the question. Twice. And seminary later in life. What was he doing before?"

"I'd like to know that too," agreed Matthew, his foot tapping in concentration.

As they sat in the gathering darkness in front of the church in the Tahoe, discussing where to go next, Matthew caught a glimpse of movement. A panel van—that appeared to be empty—had parked a spot over from them. The windows of the cab were heavily tinted, but not enough to prevent him from seeing a skulking figure backlit from a streetlight across the parking lot through them.

"Hey, Danbury," he said softly, pointing beneath the sill of his window toward the figure that seemed to have a hood over his head. "We have company."

"A guy in a black hoodie. No way that's a coincidence. Somebody is still following us."

"You have got to be kidding me!" Matthew hissed under his breath. "But you're right. The build does look like the person you've chased twice now." He refrained from mentioning that the big detective had also lost the person as many times.

Reaching up slowly, Danbury turned the overhead light off so that opening a door wouldn't trigger it. They both slid out of their seats. Danbury said, "Hang tight, Doc. I've got this." He slipped quietly behind the Tahoe, and Matthew waited silently. Danbury had made his way around the parked van, announced his title, and told the person to stop. Apparently, that admonishment was wasted, and the chase was on again.

As he stood by the Tahoe wondering what he should do and if there was anything he could do, Matthew suddenly felt complete clarity on one thing that had been bothering him. The face of the man in his dream. The one who had been turned away from the trek up to the chapel at the monastery as an outsider. It all became clear.

Suddenly, Matthew knew exactly why he recognized the man, though the facial expression was new. The dawn of understanding washed over him. The unfamiliar brief flicker he'd caught on the face in the dream was the same as he'd just seen. Hatred. The facial expression in both cases was the same—complete loathing.

Wanting to shout that he knew who was lying—who the pastor spy was—he pulled his phone from his pocket instead and began tapping it aggressively.

"I know who's behind this!" he texted Danbury and clicked to send. Continuing the message, he texted, "The man from the dream!" and clicked to send again. "But that's not who you're chasing," he began to text. Before he could click to send that or explain what he'd finally figured out, he heard a soft sound behind him.

Startled, he began to turn. He caught a mere glimpse of the white van with a door open. Then he felt the pressure of a large body and hot, rank breath on his neck as he was grabbed from behind. Before he could react to something put over his nose and mouth, he smelled an odd odor beyond the halitosis as his world went completely black.

29 ~ THROUGH THE HAZE

Matthew's head felt fuzzy. Focus was impossible—his mind hazy. There was something on his face and in his mouth, neither of which could he work free by moving his head. He couldn't breathe well. Trying to regain a sense of time and space seemed impossible. Where was he, and how long had he been unaware of the world around him? He was lying on his side, he determined. On a cold, hard surface.

There were voices coming and going, at least in his mind. Were they real? Could he hear people talking around him? But what were they saying? He couldn't understand their words, and concentrating to try wasn't working.

One familiar voice stood out in the cacophony. But that wasn't possible. It couldn't be. There were so many things wrong with Matthew hearing that voice at this moment. Worst of all, he couldn't understand anything that the voice said. It was speaking in an unfamiliar language, though the voice itself sounded exactly like the voice of his childhood best friend, Justin.

Could it be? Or was he dreaming vivid dreams again? It had to be a dream, yet it felt real enough. He wiggled his fingers and toes, though both his hands and feet were bound. No, this wasn't a dream, he reassured himself. He could hear voices audibly in the physical world.

Could you know the core of someone—the person they are deep in their innermost being—and not know peripheral but important things about them? That they spoke an unfamiliar language which sounded like guttural gibberish? He wondered through the haze of his mind if this could be possible. Justin had grown up down the street when they were young. They had continued to be close friends over the years.

Their childhood friend group still teased them about living parallel lives. Both were accused of being geeks, and they were definitely more reserved than the other friends they'd grown up with. They had similar preferences and experiences, even during periods when they weren't constantly or directly in touch.

Matthew supposed he and Justin had lived parallel lives, at least to a point. Their general worldview—convictions and beliefs—those had remained closely aligned through the years, though their professions couldn't be less similar. Justin had gone into the military to get through college and then joined one of the governmental alphabet soup agencies. Matthew assumed it was the CIA because Justin traveled internationally—being gone for weeks or months at a time—and nobody knew where he was or when he'd return most of the time.

The summer before in Miami, Matthew had seen Justin in action as both a super geek technologically and a genius, tactically. Miami. Something about that word was hauntingly familiar. Matthew stirred, pulling against whatever bound his hands and feet so tightly behind him. His body was stiff and sore—his movement entirely restricted. The floor was cement, he decided, and there was an echo. He was in a big, mostly empty, building of some sort.

As he was trying to stretch against his constraints, an unfamiliar voice speaking whatever that language was, came nearer. He felt a jab in his thigh—like a bee sting with something much larger than a stinger—and his body began to feel tingly and his mind numb, fading again into blackness.

*****

Light began to dawn like the sun burning through the mist of a foggy morning. Matthew smelled something dank, musty, moldy, and definitely stale. He tried to open his eyes but they were too heavy. Or were they merely heavy? There was something covering them and his face.

He heard a voice he knew—though the language it spoke was anything but. There was something familiar about both the voice and the odd language. Matthew was struggling to place either one.

Something was loosened from behind his head and pulled over it.

His eyes felt too heavy to open, but he tried. A blur of faces swam in front of him. The faces of three men stared back, though their features weren't clear.

As he blinked to sharpen his focus, the face in the middle stared intently at him. It was a tanned face with a rough, dirty-blond beard and scraggly longish sun-streaked hair. That was new. But the blue eyes that stared out from under sun-bleached eyebrows as the face came fully into focus were entirely familiar.

"Justin," Matthew tried to speak.

The head shook imperceptibly—the familiar face expressively stern in warning—and the eyes, blinking tightly twice, spoke volumes of warning.

"Just in case…," Matthew croaked, praying for divine intervention and surprised at his ability to shift what he'd started to say so quickly. What he didn't have, however, was an eloquent end to that sentence. He'd thought to say, in case he didn't survive this ordeal, to tell his family he loved them. As quickly, that thought was refuted in his mind. His attachment to anyone or anything when he was in this situation could put them in harm's way.

"Just in case what?" asked another face to the right, gruffly but in nearly flawless English. "What?" the guy reached over and prodded Matthew with his fist.

He hesitated, and his eyes fell on the outstretched arm of the guy who was punching his shoulder. The detailed tattoo of a snake's body wound twice around the guy's wrist and up his forearm. From behind the guy's elbow, the head of the snake appeared, open-mouthed, and it writhed and moved back and forth with his bicep.

"Water. I need water," Matthew croaked, stalling for time and struggling not to stare at the snake tattoo. The fog in his mind was clearing. Was this the same guy Bella Bosch had seen in Denver? Was it the guy who'd ransacked his hotel room? Or—as he and Danbury had discussed—was the tattoo one that a group of people had in common? Either way, he was struggling not to fixate on it.

"Do you know who we are?" asked the guy with the snake tattoo who, in Matthew's fuzzy mind, had become merely "Reptilian." The guy was like the archnemesis of a superhero, Matthew mused, amazed that he could find even an iota of humor in the situation.

Matthew was sure that he saw the guy in the middle—Justin—barely shake his head and blink twice.

"No," he answered in a whisper. "Water?"

Turning to the guy on his left, Justin said something in the unfamiliar language. The other guy retrieved a bottle of water from across the room somewhere, opened it, and thrust it in the general direction of Matthew's mouth. Sloshes of it landed in his mouth as the rest dribbled down his chin and down the front of his shirt.

Swallowing hard, Matthew tried to capture as much of the liquid as he could manage. Between gulps, he caught a whiff of an offensive odor and hoped it wasn't his own breath. The smell was familiar.

"You are the pastor from North Carolina?" asked the reptilian guy.

Matthew looked between the three faces to see the response from the guy he was convinced was Justin nod ever so slightly and blink once.

"Yes," answered Matthew, catching on to the blinking cues.

"What were you going to say earlier?" prompted Reptilian. "Just in case what?"

"In case I don't make it out of this alive," answered Matthew, but faltered.

Justin stared meaningfully at Matthew but spoke with a heavy accent in a calm, unaffected voice when he replied, "We are not going to kill you if you do exactly as we say. You will do as we ask?" He blinked hard once.

"Yes," Matthew answered without hesitation now. He'd have responded that way in this situation regardless of the blink.

"We have his agreement," said Justin in English but with an accent that Matthew was starting to get used to.

"Da," said Reptilian, and then added something that Matthew couldn't understand.

"Where am I?" asked Matthew, looking around. The walls were dark, and the floor definitely concrete. It was, he thought, very likely a storage room in a warehouse of some description.

"You do not need to know," answered Justin brusquely, blinking twice.

"OK," agreed Matthew, feeling a calm wash over him that he knew he wasn't controlling. "What do you want me to do?"

"You will know when you need to know," answered Justin. His voice was harsh, but the expression on his face—that only Matthew could see as he leaned forward—was intentionally soft and reassuring. He said something in the guttural language, and the guy on his left thrust the water bottle into Justin's hand.

Justin leaned over and carefully held the bottle to Matthew's lips, allowing him to drain the rest of the water from it before Reptilian jabbed a needle into his right thigh.

The faces began to blur quickly as Matthew's mind faded into blackness again.

*****

Exhaust. The smell was strong, and the air stagnant and heavy with a musty smell in addition to the pungent smell of the fumes. Light. It was breaking through the darkness. Matthew's mouth and throat were achingly dry, and his arms, now tied in front of him, were sore and strained. He was propped up on his side, not fully sitting upright, but no longer lying flat either. His feet, at least, had been freed and were no longer bound. The cold, hard surface he vaguely remembered had been replaced by something slightly softer and warmer. A cushion of some sort.

Fighting to the surface of awareness, Matthew was bumped and jostled. He must be in a vehicle of some description, he determined. A car? Trunk of a car? Truck? The fumes negated a train, and the movement didn't feel like a plane. He remembered that he was in some sort of danger. He heard a siren coming, and his hope for survival rose only to be quickly dashed again as the first-responder vehicle passed by and he heard it fade into the distance.

Looking around him, Matthew figured he was inside a large van or panel truck of some sort. Low makeshift seating lined either side of it. They were in motion by the feel of the bouncing and jolting, though there were no windows to see out of except one transom above what Matthew thought might be the driver's cab. Through it, weak light filtered. It was a panel van, he surmised.

Searching through the haze of his memory, Matthew tried to determine where he had last been. He fought to understand how he'd ended up in a panel van in transit, heading to an unknown destination for an unknowable purpose. There was a purpose—he vaguely recollected—and his mind struggled to recall it. The guy who'd told him they weren't going to kill him had confirmed it. Was that guy Justin? It had to be unless his best friend had an evil twin.

They wanted something from him, but what? They hadn't told him. And they had called him a pastor. What was that about? Had they awakened him merely to gauge his willingness to cooperate with whatever it was that they wanted? How could Justin possibly be involved in all of this, whatever it was?

As he looked around, trying to get his bearings, a familiar face looked back at him. Initially, Matthew couldn't place it. A single word came to mind when he tried: Reptilian. But what did that mean? The guy reached over, untied a bandanna, and removed the gag from his mouth.

"You want food?" Reptilian asked.

Was he hungry? He must be, though he had no way of knowing how long he'd been unaware of what was going on around him. There was a vague memory of being grabbed from behind. He'd been standing by the Tahoe, and Danbury had run off to chase the slender figure in the black hoodie. Had he caught him? And what time had that been? Nearly dinner time. It was dark then. And now it wasn't. He'd missed at least one meal, he determined. Before he could answer about the food, his mind swung back to a more pressing question. If they weren't going to kill him, were they going to torture him in any way for information? Had Justin somehow prevented his death?

"Yes," he whispered softly, his mind still whirring with questions and his throat dry and sore. "And water," he croaked.

"OK," said the guy. As the guy reached over to untie his hands, Matthew immediately understood why he'd associated him with a reptile. This was the guy with the snake tattoo. This time, he couldn't help but stare at it.

"You like that?" asked the guy. "It's a viper."

"Oh," said Matthew, because what else could he say?

"Here." The guy stuffed a cheeseburger into his hands, now freed. What Matthew really wanted to do was rub his wrists and try to return the feeling to his fingertips. He nearly dropped the burger, but he suddenly realized that he was hungry. Resisting the urge to shove the whole thing into his mouth, Danbury-style, he bit off a small piece and began to chew. It felt like gnawing on a newspaper because his mouth was so dry.

"Water?" Matthew asked again.

"Here," said the guy again, handing over a cup with a lid and straw from a well-known fast-food chain.

With his other hand, Matthew took the drink. That, he attacked. Root beer, he decided partway through when he came up for breath. A large burp came burbling up from his empty stomach. At first, he tried to squelch it. Then he realized that he was in the back of a boxy van with a guy sporting a snake tattoo. Why fight it?

When he'd downed the burger and the rest of the tall drink, he realized that he had another problem. How would they feel about a restroom break, he wondered. When he asked, the reptilian guy merely said, "I will ask."

Pulling out a cell phone, he called somebody and spoke in the unfamiliar guttural language that Matthew now remembered hearing earlier. "Da," the guy finally said, returning the phone to his pocket.

"We will stop," he said to Matthew. "Twice. As soon as we find a good place. The first time, you sit still. And make no sound. Can you agree? If not, I will tie you back." He held up the rag that he'd removed from Matthew's mouth previously.

"I'll be quiet," agreed Matthew, nodding, not wanting that gag back on for any length of time.

"You will get out, relieve yourself, and you will not run. Understood?"

Matthew nodded.

"Do exactly that, and we will not shoot you. Then we will be on our way."

In another fifteen minutes, Matthew felt the boxy van slow. He swayed and braced himself. It was making a right turn, he figured. It rolled to a stop, but the engine continued running. A muted conversation in another language ensued, a door slammed, and then the door slammed again. The van began to roll, slowly at first, but then he leaned forward against the gathering momentum. The truck made two more turns, both to the left and then it bumped along, jolting him this way and that. Finally, it slowed to a stop.

"OK, now we get out. Slowly," Reptilian instructed. "You try anything, you get shot. Simple, right?"

As Matthew vigorously nodded his agreement, the door to the panel van slid open.

30 ~ PROOF OF LIFE

"Not trying anything," confirmed Matthew, sliding across the gritty metal floor of the van and trying to stand outside it on wobbly legs. Looking around, he saw that they were on a rutted dirt road flanked by ditches on either side and woods beyond the ditches. Tall pine trees—that looked to have been planted in neat rows after others had been removed—swayed in a light breeze. The gathering dusk had a decided chill, and he shivered. Two other men stood at a distance beyond the front of the van.

"Now what?" he asked, hands out by his sides.

"Now you go over there and do your business," said Reptilian. "We have a job for you when you get back."

"OK," said Matthew, moving slowly into the edge of the brush by the ditch line and experiencing sweet relief.

What day is it, Matthew wondered. If it's nearly night now, is it only Sunday? Or have I been out for longer? It was Saturday and getting dark when I was snatched, he thought, so it's at least Sunday. His curiosity was soon sated. When he turned to go back to the van, Justin stepped forward.

"Stop there," he said in the thick dialect. "And hold this." He thrust a wad of paper at Matthew.

"Hold it up in front of you, but below your face," added Reptilian, looking at Justin in disdain, as if his English were far superior and he was needed to translate the instructions. "Put your finger here." He moved Matthew's forefinger to a specific spot atop the edge of the paper.

"OK," agreed Matthew as he held the newspaper out in front of his chest. He had a mere moment when the flash from the cell phone camera went off to see the back of the folded page he held and to read it upside down. It was dated Sunday, February second. The newspaper was from someplace in South Carolina that he'd never heard of before.

Long since, Matthew had known that his own cell phone wasn't in the left front pocket of his pants where he normally carried it. He had been relieved of it somewhere along the way. As he had of his Glock 19 and the holster it had been in. But at least he now suspected that a mere day had passed since he'd lost his freedom. If the newspaper was proof of life, then it should also be from the same day. His finger being moved on the page was likely to cover something they didn't want to be seen—like the location, he reasoned. But wasn't the newspaper thing an antiquated practice? Apparently not.

"Now get back in," directed Reptilian, following closely behind Matthew as if a cattle prod might be imminent.

They must be headed north, Matthew reasoned, if they were in South Carolina. Or at least they had been. If the first stop was to obtain the newspaper to have it for the second stop, then they likely still were because there was little time between the two stops to have gone far.

As he climbed in the back of the van, Reptilian, Justin, and the guy with halitosis who'd been on the left of Justin in the warehouse conferred briefly. Like during most of his incarceration, they spoke in another language that Matthew couldn't understand.

It didn't take a brain surgeon, he thought, to determine that it was Russian. He'd heard them say *da* a couple of times. Given his limited knowledge of the language, the information gleaned from Professor Stevenson, and the fact that they'd been in the most heavily Russian-populated area outside of Russia, he was pretty sure he was right about that.

Then there was the fact that he'd figured out who the guy in the dream was and which pastor had been lying. Which was the pastor spy—though he still had difficulty accepting that concept—he was now certain that he knew.

At one point, the conversation sounded heated. He saw Justin throw up his hands—apparently in surrender—as Reptilian seemed to win the argument. Matthew's companion in the back of the van continued to be Reptilian as they all took their places again. Maybe that was what the argument had been about, he thought.

The guy wasn't great company—even if the situation had been amicable—he wasn't an expert conversationalist. He didn't sleep, but his eyes were focused on the wall above Matthew's head as if there were something deeply intriguing there. It gave Matthew time to sift through the ideas that were floating around in his brain without interruption, though, trying to put them in some semblance of order that made sense.

If Fisher were the planted pastor spy, then had he called and given the order to pick Matthew up? No, that couldn't be it because he didn't know they were coming until they arrived, and they were with him the whole time they were at the church. Unless the guy at the dock tipped him off. That could be. Or, maybe he contacted the thugs and Justin between the time he answered the intercom and came to meet them at the door of the church. If he had, he'd done it quickly. That was a possibility.

A van had been in the parking lot when they left the church, Matthew remembered, but he'd thought it was vacant. The hooded figure took their attention from the van, but maybe that was intentional? Was the hooded figure a decoy? Had Danbury caught the guy this time? Where was Danbury, and where did he think Matthew was?

Maybe, thought Matthew—as he weighed the feasibility of each possibility in his mind—Fisher hadn't called anyone. Maybe he and Danbury had been followed all along. If he weren't held captive in a van going literally God knew where that might have caused a shiver, but he was well beyond that now. Where was he headed, and to do what? That's what he most wanted to know.

As had come to be the norm on this trip, there were always lots of questions and—at least until now—very few answers. He had answered the question about which pastor was which. But what did it mean? What was Fisher involved in that he didn't want them to know about, and why had he tried to point the finger at Father Grossman? Matthew couldn't come up with a logical reason why Fisher would do that, so he moved on.

Justin being involved made him realize that this was not only about missing and murdered missionaries and two women and one professor being killed. This was bigger than that. It had to be or Justin wouldn't be anywhere near it. He must be undercover investigating something of far more consequence than what Matthew knew about.

*****

"Hey, we're here," said Reptilian as he punched Matthew in the arm with his fist.

Matthew hadn't realized that he'd dozed off, but he must have. There was no motion, and the stillness was eerie as he slid into an upright sitting position on the makeshift cushion.

"OK," said Matthew, remembering that he'd been warned by Justin not to ask where he was going. He figured the less he said, the better, unless it was to be generally cooperative.

"What's going to happen is this," said Reptilian. "The door will open." As he said it, the door slid open quietly. Justin and the guy with the bad breath who had become "Halitosis" in Matthew's mind appeared at the back. The night was dark, but a distant streetlight showed the back corner of a parking lot that he knew well.

It was across a back street from his church. A shiver of excitement ran through him as he realized that he was in one of the parking lots of his own church. He was home in Raleigh, North Carolina. Well, almost, he thought as he looked up at the three faces staring back at him.

"You will step out," instructed Reptilian. "We will walk across the street. Enter your church building. You will retrieve the leather book, and we will bring it back. You know this book, right?"

"You mean something that Grygoriy Starkovich left behind?"

"That is it, yes."

"I can't get it here," began Matthew, and Justin blinked hard twice. "I mean, Greg left a box here, yes. The book you want was in the box, but I don't have a key to the building. Or a badge to get into the office area," protested Matthew instead. Technically, he thought, he'd never had a badge to the office area because he'd never been on staff here.

"We fixed that," said Justin with the dialect. "The locks are restrained."

"We go," said Reptilian. "Do not try to make any calls, and do not run. Otherwise, we will kill you, and you will exchange yourself for your niece. The one you love. We took you easily, and we will do the same to her. And worse. She is not expecting it. You should have been," said Reptilian, far too matter-of-factly for Matthew's liking.

Matthew felt his stomach flip and he visibly shuddered as he thought of his sister's little daughter—who he did indeed adore— being taken by these brutes. He wondered why their information about him was so accurately detailed in ways that he wished it weren't and so completely wrong in others.

"OK, OK, I'll go in, find the box you're looking for, and then come right back," he looked over Reptilian's head at Justin in a state of panic. He knew that the leather-bound book wasn't in the church but at the police precinct. Did Justin know that? Justin blinked hard once.

"Good, we go now, together, to be sure you return. And that you do nothing stupid while you are there."

"No, I will go," said Justin.

"We do this again?" asked Reptilian. "What is this pastor to you? Why do you care who goes?"

"We'll go together," amended Justin in guttural English.

"I do not need you," threatened Reptilian. "If this does not work, we go to my plan."

Justin's face showed the merest flash of concern, but he nodded his agreement.

"You prepare that plan while we're inside, just in case," said Reptilian.

Justin answered by spewing a rapid-paced string of words at Reptilian, who glared at him before escorting Matthew across the street to the church building. Where was he going? Nobody had called him by name. Did they think he was Mark Kushner? Or did they know his name but think he was a pastor on staff at the church? He wished he'd found a way to get Justin to tell him that.

Deciding to play it safe, he said, "The box with the book was in the senior pastor's office when I saw it last. Before I flew to Miami."

"Then that is where we go," said Reptilian as Halitosis held one of the glass outer doors open for them. He shoved Matthew through it. "You lead."

"OK," said Matthew, going through the big atrium and past the coffee bar that was dimly lit in the middle of the night. "It's through the outer office here." He was surprised that the glass door that led into the staff area opened easily when he pulled.

"It's the second office on the right," he said, stepping aside for Reptilian to pull something from his pocket and approach the door. In less than three seconds, that door, too, swung open.

Matthew stepped in and looked around. "It was in this office that I saw it last. There! That's the box that Greg left." he said, pointing to the taped box on the credenza behind Mark's desk.

That was a true statement, thought Matthew. The book had been in the box, but that was before Mark had handed it over to Danbury to take to the police precinct.

"Good," said Reptilian, keeping a watchful eye on Matthew as Halitosis guarded him from behind, blocking his exit from Mark's office. Reptilian stepped behind the desk and moved the box in front of him, pulling the flaps open. He pulled out four small T-shirts, shook them out, examined each one, and tossed them aside on the floor. The papers came out next, and then he looked up at Matthew in surprised annoyance. "It is not here."

Matthew shrugged. "That was Monday a week ago before I left for Miami."

Reptilian put his hand into his pocket, and Matthew froze in fear that what he'd pull out would be a gun. Instead, the guy pulled out his cell phone and poked it angrily. A barrage of guttural words poured forth from him. A few pauses and some more conversation later, and he said, "You go back to the van. Straight back. While I search the office."

Nodding hesitantly, Matthew turned. He couldn't imagine what Mark's office would look like afterward. If this guy was the one on the surveillance footage going into the hotel, he'd been the one to ransack Matthew's room—he was not a pro. But that was the least of his worries, he thought, as he walked out of the office in front of Reptilian—fearful of being shot in the back—with Halitosis behind him. Out through the atrium he went and into the cold night air. He was still clad in thin slacks, a short-sleeved quick-dry shirt, and a light jacket. At that moment, he was both incredibly thankful for the jacket and entirely fearful that his uselessness had been discovered.

When he got outside the church, Halitosis motioned him toward the van with his hand in a jacket pocket. When they arrived in the parking lot behind the van, the guy pulled a semi-automatic handgun—exactly what Matthew had known was in the pocket—and motioned him into the van with it. Compliantly, Matthew climbed in, and the door closed behind him. Justin had been nowhere in sight. What was Reptilian's plan that he was preparing for?

Matthew's curiosity, he soon learned, would have been better left unsatisfied. After what felt like hours but was probably only about twenty minutes, he heard voices behind the truck. They were arguing about something—he could tell by the cadence and tone—but in the foreign language. He had no idea what they were saying.

After a few minutes, the door to the van opened. Reptilian and Halitosis stared stonily at him. Justin reached in and handed Matthew a vest. "Put this on," he said.

Being shot at was unnerving. Matthew had tasted fear like the metallic iron in blood when a gun was pointed at him and more so when one had been fired at him. But neither of those things compared to the abject terror that coursed through his body in this moment.

Matthew hesitated, and two guns from Reptilian and Halitosis were immediately pointed at him.

"You didn't find the book?" he asked, stalling for time.

"No. We know it is in one of two places. It isn't here. Next plan," said Reptilian, taking the vest from Justin and pushing it to Matthew's chest. "Put this on. Or we'll shoot you now and go pick up your little niece."

Over Reptilian's head, Matthew saw Justin blink hard once.

"OK, OK, I'm putting it on," said Matthew—his voice and his hand shaking as he turned the vest around—trying to avoid touching the wires that ran every which way.

"Sit," commanded Reptilian.

When he and Reptilian were situated in the back, the door closed, and the van bounced its way out of the church parking lot and off to an unknown destination. When it stopped at last, Matthew knew he must be in Raleigh still because they'd made lots of turns but never gained much speed. They must have avoided the 440 Beltline and the 540 outer loop around Raleigh. Vacillating between wanting the van to stop somewhere familiar and not wanting it to stop at all because of whatever was coming next, all he could do was pray. And that he did continuously.

"We're here," said Reptilian.

Matthew looked up as Reptilian stood, and the door opened partway. As soon as he saw it, he knew where he was. From the half-open door of the back of the van, he could catch glimpses of the shimmering massive oak tree through the trees along the other side of the street. On the side of the Raleigh Convention Center, a spreading oak was depicted with thousands of light and dark aluminum squares that flapped with the wind, giving the tree's leaves the appearance of fluttering gracefully in the breeze. Normally, it was an engineering and artistic feat that Matthew paused to appreciate.

Now, however, his mind was whirring to process it all. He was in a parking deck across Cabarrus Street from the downtown amphitheater. From inside the panel van, he had no view of it, but he knew that he was also in a parking deck beside and slightly behind the downtown Raleigh police station. It was where Grygoriy Starkovich's leather-bound notebook had been taken and locked in Danbury's desk.

They could be neither this desperate nor this brazen, thought Matthew. This was a suicide mission. And he was the human bomb wearing the vest.

31 ~ EXPLOSIVE SITUATION

"Now stand up," commanded Reptilian.

On shaky legs, Matthew tried to stand.

"Stand up!" yelled Reptilian.

As the door to the van opened wide, Matthew saw that it was dark in the parking garage. They must have disabled the lights and probably the cameras too. Wouldn't a police department with parking so close to the building have it under constant surveillance? And wouldn't they notice if it suddenly wasn't? Matthew hoped so.

Justin said something in Russian quietly and forcefully to Reptilian as Halitosis joined him behind the van. Reptilian nodded. More quietly, Reptilian demanded that Matthew hold his arms out and stand still. Then he attached metal cable ties and clamps to hold the vest securely on his body while allowing flaps on the front to open and display the explosives.

"Here's what you're going to do," said Reptilian. "You're going to walk in there and demand to be given the notebook from your detective friend's desk."

Matthew's jaw dropped slightly, stupefied that they knew exactly where the notebook was. How could they possibly know that? Somebody inside the police department had to have told them, he reasoned. Either that, or they'd gotten to Mark Kushner or Evelyn Rawlins. Nobody else but those two, Danbury, himself, and maybe a few police officers knew the book was there. He shuddered at the thought that these guys had harmed either Mark or Evelyn.

They had started looking for the book at the church, though, Matthew remembered. So maybe both were still blissfully and safely unaware of the intrusion.

"OK," agreed Matthew as calmly as he could. "And then what?"

"You'll open the vest and show them that you're wired with the explosives," answered Reptilian. "Tell them to hurry the hell up if they hesitate. When you have the book, tell them that there are more explosives in place all over town. If they pursue you, all will be detonated, and downtown Raleigh will be a heap of rubble. Got it?"

"I've got it," said Matthew, feeling any remaining blood drain entirely from his face. Were there other explosives? He had no idea, but he also had no desire to find out.

"If you try to run, kaboom!" said Reptilian. "Sky high. We'll find another way. But the pile of ash you'll become won't know about it."

"I'm not running. I'm cooperating. When I bring the book back, you'll release me then?"

"Perhaps," said Reptilian. "Or maybe you'll need to accompany us a little further. Until we're cleanly away. It depends on how well they listen in there." He motioned in the general direction of the police station. "You're also wired for sound. We can hear you. So don't say anything other than what we've told you to say. It won't go well for you if you tell them anything else."

"Got it," murmured Matthew quietly. Looking past Reptilian, Matthew saw Justin blink hard once.

"OK." Matthew gulped the bile that was rising in the back of his throat. "Anything else?"

"Stay in our sight line as you approach the building. That's all you need to know," said Reptilian as Matthew slid out of the van and turned to walk down the ramp from the parking deck. The stairwell, he reasoned, was a no-go because it would put him out of their line of sight.

Fighting the very real possibility that his knees would buckle beneath him, Matthew walked slowly down the ramp to the sidewalk and turned right to approach the police station. Entering, he shut his eyes tightly momentarily and prayed. His prayers were for himself as well as everyone in the police station, Mark, Evelyn, his niece and family, Danbury, and Cici. Cici. An image of her—the beauty of her smile and the spun golden glow of her hair—everything about her burst through his mind at once. Fervently, he wanted to live to build a life with her and never get anywhere near police investigations again.

"Good evening!" he shouted in a commanding voice. Opening the flaps of the vest to reveal the wires, lights, and explosives, he said, "I've been tasked with collecting a leather-bound notebook."

Two officers turned and drew their weapons on him. They seemed surprised to see him. If that were the case, then who had received the proof of life picture from earlier, he wondered.

"Don't do that," said Matthew with more command of his voice than he felt. "If you do, this bomb will be detonated along with others in this area. I was instructed to tell you that downtown Raleigh will be reduced to a pile of rubble if you don't bring me the leather-bound notebook quickly. It was locked in the desk drawer of one of your detectives. Homicide detective Warren Danbury."

As he said it, Danbury himself swooshed through the double doors that led into the annals of the station.

"Doc," Danbury said, motioning for the two officers to lower their weapons. He hesitated, only momentarily, assessing the situation. He didn't seem surprised as he said, "I see you don't have a choice."

"I don't," agreed Matthew, shaking his head and holding his hands out and away from the vest.

"We need to comply," answered Danbury. "I'll get the book."

"And nobody can follow me," croaked Matthew, the control over his voice waning, his knees wobbling. "Or this and the other explosives in the area will be detonated."

"OK, we understand," said Danbury. "I'll be right back with the book."

Matthew wished he could follow Danbury or run until he was too exhausted to run anymore. Anything but to stand here holding a whole police precinct hostage and risking his own life as well as countless others. Instead, he struggled with everything he had to remain standing there.

It seemed like an eternity later, but Danbury finally returned, holding the leather-bound book in a plastic bag. "Here, Doc," he said, handing it over. "This will be OK."

Matthew wasn't entirely sure who it was that Danbury had been trying to reassure—him or the big detective himself—but it wasn't working. He didn't feel at all reassured. Taking the book, he held it aloft as he held both hands up and away from his body. Turning, he made his way out of the police station. It felt like a death march as he returned to the van.

"Here," he said, holding out the book and handing it to Reptilian. "Release me now, please?" he asked, not concerned if it sounded like he was begging. He would happily beg if they would remove the vest and allow him to walk away—or run if his legs would enable him to. Adrenaline was a wonderful thing, he thought to himself. He'd run as fast and as far as he could as soon as they removed the vest.

"Not yet," said Reptilian. "Get in."

That was the last thing Matthew wanted to hear, but he complied, scrambling into the back of the van and then holding his hands out away from the vest.

"Sit."

Matthew wasn't sure if he sat or slid down the wall of the van, but somehow, he managed to land on the cushion he'd ridden on from Florida. His hope waned as the door of the van closed behind him, and he was left, alone this time, in the back of the van. Were they planning to blow him up in it? Was he a human car bomb now?

He shut his eyes tightly and went back to praying for his family, for his closest friends, and for Cici. Cici. He had tried not to think about the woman he loved and how devastated she'd be at his death. They were finally figuring out a way forward. How would any of his loved ones reconcile his loss?

Unsure if he should be relieved or worried, he hunkered down as the van began to move again.

Bumped and jostled, he felt the van stop and start multiple times. Were they stopping for the red lights in Raleigh? They must be. After more stops, starts, and multiple turns, the van gained speed and rollicked along without stopping again. Matthew tried to gauge the time that he was on the road, but he couldn't get his mind to cooperate. It seemed like hours but probably less than an hour when the van slowed again and began making turns.

The ride got bumpy, and Matthew worried that the bomb in the vest might detonate itself with the jolting. Finally, he felt the vehicle slow and then stop. Then angry voices emanated from behind the van. When the door opened, Justin stood on a gravel road with a pair of bolt cutters. He and Reptilian were arguing over them.

"Get out!" commanded Justin with authority.

Matthew scrambled out and to the ground.

"You're taking this off and letting me go?" asked Matthew.

"No!" commanded Reptilian. "We need you a little longer."

To that, Justin spieled something off angrily in Russian. Reptilian spat back, getting in Justin's face and trying to wrench the bolt cutters from his hand.

Gripping the cutters tightly without backing down from Reptilian, Justin turned his face to Matthew. Inclining his head forcefully, indicating the road behind the van, he blinked once and said, "Run! And don't look back."

Matthew's mind was whirring with questions about what would happen to the explosives that were still strapped to him. Things were moving in surreal slow motion for the next seconds as he saw Reptilian staring Justin down, but he said nothing. The adrenal glands that Matthew had been counting on kicked in, and he began to run, full force, back down the gravel road behind the van.

There were no lights, and the gravel was uneven, but he didn't slow as he half stumbled and sprinted along. Hearing a loud whirring coming up behind, he darted off the side of the road and ran along the edge of a tiny outcropping of trees. On the other side of the trees, fields ran farther than he could see in the dark.

A helicopter, he realized, had dropped down over the field as he darted in and out of the cover of the young trees along the edge of the road. Were its passengers coming for him? If they were, they'd have a harder time locating him in the dark under the trees, he thought, propelled by the rush of adrenaline. Suddenly, there was light, and he could see where he was going.

Before he'd pondered the source of the light or made it much more than a quarter mile away from the van, he felt a crushing weight plow into him and shove him to the ground, knocking the wind out of him in the process. First, one explosion and then another rocked the earth and electrified the air around him. For a moment, he thought the explosives strapped to him had detonated.

In the seconds that followed, he wasn't sure if he was dead or alive. Had he been murdered by the explosives? Had he been taken out by the weight that had thrown him to the ground or protected by it? Rolling over into the ditch line, he saw Justin by his side. They were both alive, so far. At least, he thought so, but confusion clouded his mind.

"You OK?" Justin yelled. Matthew could barely hear him.

"I think so," Matthew yelled back. He paused then and thanked God for that. There had been so many times over the past day—which felt more like a week—when he thought he'd never be so again. Before he could begin to brush himself off and evaluate the situation, he noticed lights blazing from multiple directions around himself and the field.

"What the?" asked Matthew, shielding his eyes and hoping the lights were from their side and not the other one.

It was with a huge sense of relief that he heard the voice from a hulking figure behind the bright beam of a flashlight shout as Danbury ran up the gravel road to them, "Doc, are you OK?"

"I've had better days," Matthew muttered, sitting upright and checking his extremities for injuries. "But I'm happy to be here. Instead of there." He pointed to the fireball where the panel van had been. "What happened?"

"They detonated the explosives," yelled Justin back. "The explosives that everybody thought were in your vest. They were still in the van."

"They detonated them thinking they were blowing me up?" demanded Matthew.

"Yeah, they thought they were blowing us both up when I ran after you," said Justin.

"Then the bomb in this vest is a fake?" demanded Matthew.

"In your belt? Yes," answered Justin. "Hey, Danbury, would you look for the bolt cutters? Viper threw them at me when I started to run. They should be behind the van somewhere."

"Sure," said Danbury, turning the powerful flashlight away, jogging back up the road.

"I wish I'd known that!" yelled Matthew. "I can't get back the ten years that experience shaved off my life!"

"I know. I'm sorry, man. I couldn't get you alone without Viper long enough to tell you anything. I tried multiple times, but I couldn't risk being suspected myself. That would have meant instant death for you. The stakes were high, and we were close. I'd infiltrated too deeply and taken too long to do it to blow my own cover and risk both our lives."

"Viper?" asked Matthew.

"The guy with the snake tattoo," said Justin, and then looked confused when Matthew burst out laughing. He released the tension of the past week in a guffaw that left Justin and Danbury—who was running back with the bolt cutters—staring at him as if he'd suddenly gone mad.

"That's funny?" asked Justin.

"It is. Because I'd been calling him Reptilian in my own mind. I'd made him out as some epic villain, the arch nemesis of a comic book superhero."

"You're not far wrong," said Justin.

"You put fake explosives in this vest? How? When?" began Matthew, befuddled, as Danbury handed over the bolt cutters. Justin crouched in front of him and set about releasing Matthew from the vest.

"While Viper was searching the church. It's why I had them go there first. I needed time to at least rewire your belt. Turns out, I had time to completely switch the packets, not just the wires. The shrapnel that made it heavy was real enough, but the packets of explosives are bogus."

"That was Russian you were speaking to them?"

"Russian with a Ukrainian dialect," Justin clarified.

Matthew paused to consider that statement. It was oddly specific. He'd never thought about speaking a foreign language with a recognizable dialect, though why that thought had never occurred to him, he now wondered. There were multiple dialects of American English, and it was usually easy to determine where, within the country, people were from by listening to them for a moment. He was often able to make a decent guess at what their first language was when he heard people speaking English as a second language with an accent.

"Are there other bombs around the city of Raleigh?" Matthew asked.

"Yes and no," said Justin. "There are packages planted, but the explosives are bogus. Like this one," he said, tossing the vest aside.

Before Matthew could ply Justin with any more questions, two paramedics—who had jogged up the gravel road behind Danbury—began assessing both Matthew and Justin. "You might have a concussion," Matthew thought he heard one of them say.

"What?" yelled Matthew.

"A concussion. You might have a concussion. You hit your head," answered one of the rescue workers, pointing, as they checked him over.

Raising his hand to his head, Matthew realized that he was bleeding.

"Sorry, Matthew," yelled Justin. "I didn't have much time to get you down in the ditch. I had to duck out fast. I couldn't give them a chance to start shooting at me."

"And the chopper? That was a helicopter I heard, right?" asked Matthew, ignoring the paramedic who was looking him over and checking his eyes with a penlight.

"It was," said Danbury with a smug smile. "Until it wasn't."

"That had explosives on it too?"

"No, it was shot down," answered Danbury.

"It was coming in to pick us up," said Justin. "They were expecting all four of us to get on it, which wasn't the deal to begin with. It's what I was arguing with Viper about. I told them taking you was a bigger risk that wasn't worth it."

"Our guys were in place in the field," said Danbury. "They had the chopper in their crosshairs. From multiple directions. And hit it with the lights as it was landing. It lifted off again. Somebody on board opened fire. One ground missile took it out. That was it. No more shots were fired."

"How did I miss all of that?" asked Matthew.

"The second blast was right after the first one," answered Danbury. "It all happened fast."

"That first blast was deafening," yelled Matthew. "I was a little busy being knocked into a ditch, and I wasn't sure by whom. Who told them I was a pastor?"

"I did, inadvertently," admitted Justin. "And I've got some work to do to switch you back."

"Switch me back from what?" asked Matthew.

"Online. If you google yourself right now, you'll find that you have a master of divinity degree from Duke University. As of three days ago."

"Oh," said Matthew, confused.

"I blocked all searches for you going to your medical practice and set up the phony profile showing you as a pastor at your church. But I didn't have time to do a thorough job setting it all up, so they found out about Angel. I'm sorry they dragged your niece into this. That was never supposed to have happened."

Matthew stared in stunned disbelief, not sure what to ask next. It was Angel, his little niece, that had been the final blow. He'd have done literally anything to protect her, and apparently, they knew it.

"I know it makes no sense," said Justin. "But clergy is the one thing they seem to revere. I thought it would protect you. They had pieces of information about you, but they hadn't seen you as enough of a threat to bother to dig deeper—until they decided to use you instead."

"They knew my name but not my profession?"

"Right," said Justin. "And that you were looking for Greg and Darya. That was obvious enough. I was afraid you wouldn't give that up and come home, but I couldn't risk blowing my cover by trying to tell you to. So, I did my best to stay with them when they were on you."

"Are you done here?" Danbury asked the paramedics.

"We can be. If they're able to stand up and move around," answered a woman clad in the uniform of a local fire rescue crew.

32 ~ WHAT JUST HAPPENED?

"OK," said Matthew, moving into a squatting position and then standing to his full height, rolling his shoulders to release the stress that had been stored there for way too long.

Justin stood beside him, reached over, and gave him a big brotherly bear hug. Matthew returned it, thankful that whichever agency Justin worked for already had their sites on whatever was going on before he got involved. But what was that? And who was and wasn't involved?

"Are Mark Kusner and Evelyn Rawlins OK?" he asked.

"They're fine. And not aware of most of this," answered Justin. Matthew felt a huge weight lift from his shoulders with that knowledge.

"And Greg? Did you find him?" he asked.

"Yeah, abandoned in a warehouse. It was inland from Buchanan Island," Danbury replied. "He's not in great shape. He was life-flighted up here this morning. At your pastor's request. He's expected to recover. But it'll be a long road. Darya is with him."

What about the hooded figure?" asked Matthew, turning to Danbury. "Did you catch him? How was he involved in all of this?"

"Her," said Danbury ruefully. "Darya. She'd been following us."

"That was Darya?"

"She ran track in college," said Danbury defensively. "And could have gone to the Olympics. She chose ministry instead."

"I talked them into releasing Darya when I found out that they'd killed Ross and Ivan," explained Justin. "I told them she'd lead them to the book if we told her they would spare Greg's life if she got it for them. She initially led them back up to the church. Then she thought you had the book, and she started following you."

"That was Darya in the church in the black hoodie that night when Mark and I got the box out of the old storage room," Matthew said slowly.

"It was," said Justin. "While the Russian thugs were following Darya, we had a team following them. So, we knew what she knew and what they thought they knew from her."

Matthew shook his head to clear the cobweb complexity of that explanation.

"I'm not sure why, but she was convinced that you had that notebook. So, she stayed with you," added Justin. "You wouldn't believe some of the ways she managed to do that. Smart woman."

"But we never had the book. It was here in Raleigh the whole time."

"I knew that," said Justin. "But they didn't. It's why you were supposed to be safe through all of that. If you didn't find what they were looking for—and I knew you couldn't because it was never down there—then they'd have no reason to bother you."

"And yet," said Matthew. "They shot at us and then abducted me to try to force me to get the book for them."

"Yeah," said Justin, looking momentarily like the little boy who Matthew remembered getting in trouble in their childhood. "It wasn't supposed to work like that. When it did, I made sure I was with them. Viper was told to install that explosive belt on you and send you to get the book. I couldn't let that happen."

"How did they know to go to the church or the police station?"

"They figured out that you didn't have the notebook after they'd searched the Tahoe and your room," began Justin.

"They searched the Tahoe?" interjected Danbury.

"They did."

"When? How?"

"When it was parked outside the Orthodox church on Thursday."

"The same day they ransacked my room," said Matthew.

"Right, before they tossed your room. When they didn't see you with it, they searched the SUV. When they didn't find it there, they went to the hotel and waited for the right opportunity to search your room."

"But not Danbury's," said Matthew.

"Yeah, they never thought he had it for some reason," said Justin.

"You'd have thought they'd search his room too, to be thorough," said Matthew. He considered this for a moment. "What happened to Mike Fisher? He was the pastor spy—probably planted in Florida for some nefarious reason—right?"

"You mean Mikhail Fisherovich? You're right, he was," said Justin. "He was heading up a Russian sleeper cell that was recently activated. His parents emigrated here when he was a child. They claimed that they were seeking political asylum, but they were the hunters, not the hunted. He was trained from birth."

"Where is he?"

Justin shielded his eyes from the lights of myriad vehicles making the field they were on the edge of look like daylight. "About there, and probably there, there, and there," he pointed out into various parts of the field.

"In the field?" asked Matthew.

"In the ash on the field," answered Justin. "He was on the helo."

"Oh! What time is it? And what day is it?" Matthew asked, realizing that he'd neglected the most basic questions.

"Nearly four," said Danbury. "Monday morning. Anybody up for breakfast?"

"Yeah, sure," said Matthew, amused that the big detective was thinking about food.

"I've got a few loose ends to tie up, and then I can join you," said Justin. "Oh, and"—he looked at Matthew—"NSA owes you a cell phone and a Glock."

"What?" asked Matthew.

"Your cell phone was in the truck," yelled Justin. "And Androv had your Glock."

"Androv?" asked Matthew.

"The guy who wasn't Viper."

"Oh, you mean Halitosis," said Matthew, and at that, Justin laughed aloud.

"You're not wrong about that!" said Justin. "Bunking with that guy was rank."

"You work for the National Security Agency?" asked Matthew, not having missed that point. It was a question that all of Justin's friends had ceased to ask because they knew they'd never get a straight answer about which governmental agency it was that he worked for.

In typical Justin style, he answered noncommittally, "It was their op. NSA and CSS. They picked up on some chatter a little over six months back that worried them. They were right to be worried. Anyway, tell me where you're going, and I can meet you for breakfast in about an hour. I'll know what I can tell you by then. Danbury was read in on a lot of it yesterday, most of what I just told you."

"What about my wallet?" asked Matthew ruefully. "I guess I'll have to replace that too, and everything in it. My driver's license, credit cards," and he tapered off, overwhelmed at the thought.

"I've got that. You left it in the Tahoe. And your computer bag," answered Danbury. "I've got your luggage too."

Matthew breathed a huge sigh of relief. Getting a new cell phone set up should be easy enough since everything on the old one was backed up in the cloud, but replacing the contents of his wallet would have taken far longer.

"How about Goodnight's?" asked Danbury, mentioning a downtown iconic restaurant that Matthew remembered as the prom night hot spot for all the Raleigh high schools. "It's open all night. And has great food."

"Sounds good," said Justin. "I'll see you there." With that, he took off at a jog across the field toward the scene of the helicopter explosion.

"And you have a call to make," said Danbury to Matthew, checking his watch. "You can use my phone." He led the way back down the gravel road to where a large black SUV waited—still running—with the lights on.

"A call?" asked Matthew, knowing that he was beyond exhausted and easily confused.

"Cici," said Danbury. "She called Penn yesterday. When she couldn't get you. She tried to FaceTime you yesterday morning. You didn't pick up. And you weren't answering your phone. Penn called me. I told her you were undercover."

"Undercover?"

"Well, weren't you?"

"I went to find four missing missionaries," said Matthew with a shrug. "That's it."

"If that's your story," began Danbury with a grin. "Stick to it."

When Matthew and Danbury arrived at Goodnight's—the all-night breakfast joint—Danbury offered to give Matthew some privacy to call Cici. He unlocked his cell phone, handed it to Matthew, and went in to get them a table. Matthew figured that was code for ordering a huge amount of something to eat and calling it an appetizer before he and Justin got there.

He was thankful to be sitting here getting ready to call Cici, incredibly so. Again, he thanked God for his safety and then tapped the phone.

"Matthew! Where are you? Are you OK?" Cici demanded, skipping all pleasantries.

"I'm OK," he said, trying to reassure her. "It's been a rough week without much sleep, but I'll be good after I get some food and lots of rest."

"You're shouting," she said. "I can hear you fine."

"Oh, sorry," he said, unwilling to tell her that his ears were still ringing and he couldn't hear her very well at all. He figured if he hadn't damaged his eardrums beyond repair playing in a classic rock garage band in high school and undergrad, a couple of explosions probably wouldn't do it either. They'd heal, and the ringing would eventually stop. It was something he wished he didn't know from previous experience.

"Where have you been?" She sounded concerned, but it was like a soothing balm for Matthew. Earlier, he'd been afraid that he'd never see her again. Now, he was finally relaxing into the relief of hearing her voice.

"That's a long story. Turns out looking for missing people in Miami is a dangerous business and one that I never want to get involved in again." He knew his voice was ragged and belied his harrowing experience, but he wasn't going to tell her about it explicitly and scare her. At that moment, he was capturing the sound of her voice in his mind and holding it close.

"I'm happy to hear you say that," she said, and the honeyed warmth of her voice made him ache for her. "I'll be home in a couple of months, and I want to be with you, Matthew. I want you in one piece for us to have a life together—one that we've talked about building for so long. It's time, don't you think, to start that when I get back?"

That, Matthew smiled as he thought, was typical Cici. It was one of the things he'd always loved about her. She was guileless in her forthright manner, but you never had to wonder what she was thinking or where you stood with her—not for long, anyway. If she was thinking it, she told you about it.

"I couldn't agree more," he finally said, choking on the words as he remembered how he'd felt when—a few hours previously—he'd thought he might never see her again. "I wish you were here right now."

"Me too," she said so softly that he almost didn't hear her. "But it's enough for now that you're safe. Promise me, Matthew. I need you to promise me that you'll do your best to stay that way."

"I promise, Cees. I'm resigning as a medical consultant with the police department, effective immediately," he said.

"Good! Because that was never what you were anyway. Danbury has treated you like a police partner, not a consultant at all," she added indignantly.

"Cees, I did drag him into this one," said Matthew. "Or, I guess Mark Kushner pulled us both in. In Mark's defense, the guy naively thought this would be a simple search, find, and return job. He had no idea what we'd be getting into."

"What did you get into?"

Matthew laughed. "Honestly, I'm not even sure I know yet. Justin is meeting Danbury and me for breakfast shortly. I hope he can enlighten me. I've had more questions than answers for over a week now."

"Justin? He was involved in all of this?"

"He was."

"But how?"

"We were chasing some of the same people, I think," said Matthew. "But for different reasons. Or maybe for some of the same reasons, but I didn't know it. I'll explain what I can after I figure it all out."

"OK, you should go get breakfast," she said. "And FaceTime me later?"

"When I get home," Matthew agreed. "I lost my phone, but I'll FaceTime from my tablet to let you know when I get there."

"Please do," she more admonished than agreed.

After they said their goodbyes, Matthew looked around and found his satchel with his computer in the back seat and dug through it. Danbury had put his wallet in an inside zippered pocket. Matthew pulled it out with relief, locked the SUV, and trudged wearily into the all-night restaurant. He needed food, but he probably needed rest equally as much, he thought.

Spotting Danbury on the far side of a booth in the back corner facing out—which was usual for both Danbury and Justin—Matthew walked over and dropped into the booth opposite him.

"I officially resign as a medical consultant for the Raleigh Police Department. Effective immediately."

"But Doc," said Danbury, drinking coffee to clear whatever massive amount of food he'd stuffed into his mouth. "This wasn't official police business."

"I know," said Matthew. "This was probably worse. But to work alongside you, I need to be armed. To carry a weapon in these situations means to be prepared to use it. I'm in the business of saving lives, not taking them. No matter how horribly those lives have been lived."

Danbury looked crestfallen, the expression on his face readable for once.

"I'll still see you all the time," said Matthew. "And Penn."

"I know," said Danbury, regaining his composure and squaring his shoulders.

"You were really worried about me, weren't you?" asked Matthew, understanding dawning.

"I was," Danbury said simply.

Happily accepting the cup of coffee a passing waitress poured him, Matthew dumped in three packets of sugar and lots of cream, stirred, and took a sip before he responded. "We'll get back on our workout routine later this week. I need to start jogging again too. I know you're proposing to Penn soon, and I'm planning to do the same as soon as Cici gets back. I can't be out of shape for that," he grinned. "And I'll be in your wedding. And I hope you'll be in mine."

Danbury grinned too, as Justin walked in behind Matthew. "Here comes your best man," said Danbury and slid over as Justin pulled a chair up to the end of the table.

After ordering nearly everything on the menu between the three of them, Matthew began plying Justin with questions. Initially, he wasn't sure where to begin. Once he got started, though, he was so intrigued that he forgot about being tired.

33 ~ MAKING SENSE

"Did the Broward County police officer who was shot survive?"

"So far, but he might regret it."

"His condition is that bad?" asked Matthew.

"I don't think he's critical anymore," said Justin. "Just a suspect."

"Suspected of what?"

"Taking a payoff to look the other way on a few things. From what we can tell, it was nothing serious to begin with. He thought it was innocent enough and had no idea what he was into until it was too late. When he blocked both you and his partner from the incoming shots, he says it was because he had finally realized the severity of his earlier decisions, and he didn't want them to impact anyone else."

Thanking the waitress and sipping the steaming black cup of coffee she'd poured him, Justin waited for her to walk away and then continued, "He knew the bullets were likely meant for him because he'd gotten cold feet on further involvement with the Russians. After he knew he was dealing with Russians. But you don't walk away from them that easily. Kind of like the Russian Mafia. They wanted to be sure everybody knew that."

"If it was to warn the police away from the warehouse area, that backfired," said Matthew.

"More likely, it was to take out the officer before he turned himself in and pointed to them. And maybe to warn any others working with them of the consequences of deciding not to if anybody else wanted to take a pass. And he'd be dead if you hadn't been there."

Matthew paused to take that in before he said, "What about the Hummer? Was it in the warehouse? And what was the warehouse used for?"

"It was," said Justin. "Androv had gone for one last look around to be certain that everything had been cleared out of the warehouse. Either you arrived earlier than he'd thought, or he took longer than he'd thought."

"Either way, the place was surrounded," said Matthew. "But then he was with you on the way up here. He didn't get caught in the warehouse."

"Right. He was gone when the police went in. There are tunnels under the warehouse—with water-locked chambers for high tide—that go down to the water on the side of that steep bulkhead on the canal. It's one reason Fisherovich wanted that property so badly. They could ship things in and out easily, mostly unseen. Androv got out by water, but he had to leave the Hummer behind."

"And the purple car that fired the shots at us—well, at the officer. Those were Russians too?"

"No, those were local thugs for hire. The shooter was already wanted for armed robbery. He was apprehended, so he's going away. What idiot chooses to shoot a police officer from a purple car and thinks he'll never be found?" said Justin between sips of coffee.

"I have so many more questions," said Matthew.

"We'll be piecing it all together for a while still," said Justin. "But I can tell you what we know so far and what we suspect to be true. You already know more of the answers than you probably think from what I've already told you—and what Professor Stevenson put together. He shared that with you, didn't he?"

"He told us what he thought about the Russian spies and their objectives, yes. Did you know who Mike Fisher was—I mean, what did you call him?" asked Matthew.

"Mikhail Fisherovich," supplied Justin.

"Did you know who he was from the beginning?"

"We suspected him of running a Russian spy ring, yes. But we couldn't prove it."

"I wish we'd known that!" said Matthew. "It would have saved us a lot of trouble."

"He also set up a shell corporation and a host of subsidiaries, which you already knew about."

"We knew it existed, but not who owned it or what its purpose was," said Matthew.

"The sole purpose of the subsidiaries was importing relics here and exporting munitions and funds to Russia. They'd figured out how to get around import and export scrutiny by shipping smaller packages directly below the de minimis threshold. Smaller packages, those below $800 in value, are less heavily scrutinized. Instead of shipping containers, they were shipping exponentially more smaller packages. Their strategy was still being perfected. But they had grand plans for it."

"And the picture you took of me with the newspaper? That was supposed to be for proof of life, right? What was its purpose?"

"It was twofold. I was trying to tell you where you were and what day it was."

"I appreciated that," said Matthew, trying for sincerity and not sarcasm.

"I was also advocating that we send it to the church staff and have them hand over the box," said Justin. "I knew the book wasn't in it, but I was trying to buy time so I didn't have to strap a bomb on you. It was Androv who didn't go for that strategy. I think Viper was willing to do whatever it took to get his hands on that book. It was scary what he was willing to do."

"How did they know the book was either at the church or the police precinct?" asked Matthew.

"After Viper searched the Tahoe and your hotel room on Thursday, they concluded that you didn't have it. But they were sure you knew where it was."

"That was Viper and Androv?"

"No, Viper and another guy whose name you won't be able to pronounce," said Justin. "Androv was driving the Hummer."

"You mean when the passenger was shooting at us," clarified Matthew.

Justin cringed as he answered, "Right." He changed the subject abruptly. "You saw how easily they entered your church."

Matthew nodded. "Yeah, I guess I should talk to Mark about additional security."

"It wouldn't have mattered. Fisherovich's team could have breached almost anything. They're all well trained with their specialties."

"You mean like Androv at driving and Viper at breaking and entering."

"Exactly. That was the second time Fisherovich's guys had been in your church building uninvited. The first was last Friday night when two others bugged your pastor's offices. From those devices, they overheard Mark and Evelyn. A church function was going on, so it was hard to make out what they said. They were talking quietly and discussing the notebook and your progress in Florida."

"OK," prodded Matthew when Justin hesitated.

"Fisherovich's team wasn't sure if Pastor Mark said he'd already handed over the book and it was at the downtown Raleigh police station locked in Danbury's desk drawer or that he was going to hand it over to be locked up there. Either way, they knew the book had been at the church and might still be. Who had it at that point was unknown, but it told them definitively that you and Darya didn't. They knew to look either in the church offices or at the downtown Raleigh police precinct for it."

After a moment to consider all of this, Matthew asked, "What about Greg's schedule conflict? Was he originally planning to meet with Professor Stevenson on Saturday morning?"

"Darya said he was," responded Danbury, looking a bit sheepish. "She planned to drive back Saturday. With Ross and Ivan. But without Greg. He was going to meet Stevenson. Then fly in to the RDU airport. Darya was picking him up. On the way in. Before going back to your church."

"I knew there was a logical explanation," said Matthew with satisfaction. "What about Father Grossman at St. Athanasius Orthodox

Church? Is he innocent?"

"Of everything except bad judgment in choosing his parish council members."

"Victor Pavlov is guilty? I believed him," said Matthew, thinking he'd second guess his instincts forever after if he'd been wrong about that. "I thought he genuinely loved and mourned his wife and family. I believed that he had nothing more to do with Greg's team coming to speak there than offering to pay their additional expenses."

"Not Pavlov. He was as much a victim as Stevenson—and both their wives."

"They only wanted the warehouses from Pavlov?"

"Right. To test their import and export strategy. They wanted that particular location—near an airport and the canal, the direct waterway to the ocean."

"If it wasn't Pavlov, then which parish council member was it?" asked Matthew.

"Strausbaum was the person of interest in Father Grossman's church. He's smart, incredibly dangerous, and, unfortunately, his whereabouts are still unknown. We don't think he was on the helo."

"Stanley Strausbaum?" asked Matthew, incredulous.

"He's a Russian intelligence agent," said Justin. "Some of his transactions were not as secure as he thought. That's what tipped off the Central Security Service."

"He was planted? At the Orthodox church?" asked Danbury.

"Right. About the same time, Mikhail Fisherovich became Pastor Mike Fisher in Aurora Springs. Working together, they were trying to locate the invaluable relic that they suspected belonged to the Greek Orthodox Church. That—and throwing suspicion on Grossman—is why Strausbaum was planted there. The church on Sunny Isles had several benefits. It was in the middle of a huge Russian-born population. Part of Strausbaum's objective was to find all who might be sympathetic to the plight of Mother Russia and convince them to help. There was also a convenient tie between the saint the church was named for and the relic they were searching for. If it all went south, as was happening when you got there, they were planning to set the

Orthodox church up to take the blame."

"They wanted to convince church members to help spy?" asked Matthew.

"Their object was not to gain spies but to gain support, allies, not adversaries. But to the Russians, coerce or convince—sometimes it's one and the same. They made some enemies who were happy to cooperate with us."

"Stevenson and Pavlov?" asked Matthew.

"Neither of them, directly, but there were others like them who had been threatened, and they were willing to point us in the right directions."

"What did they want from Stevenson?"

The answer to the question was interrupted as the waitress brought their orders and quietly slipped away. After Matthew blessed their meal, pouring out his thanks aloud, Justin munched as he answered. "Stevenson had a group of students working on what they thought were minor artifacts from an excavation on Greek peninsulas a couple of summers ago."

"That, we knew about," said Danbury between huge bites of omelet. "They stole the professor's badge. Didn't they? To access the artifacts."

"Right," said Justin. "They were searching for a particular item. It was a piece that Stevenson had validated and translated the text on two years ago. Fisherovich doubted Stevenson's translation and wanted to see it for himself."

"What was the object?"

"Stevenson believed a flat square stone with an inscription chiseled on it had been the base of a gold statue. Maybe statue isn't the right word. It was a gold cross rumored to be a replica, or tiny scaled model, of a huge one made of solid gold. Obtaining the full-size cross was their objective. Some Russians hold the Orthodox church—and any of its relics that are forbidden to be accessed by any but the most sacred priests—in the highest regard. Most revere the priests and pastors by extension. Others hold the sanctity of Russia itself in higher regard than anything else. Funding the country's return to greatness is their objective. They have no regard for any intrinsic religious value."

"A giant gold cross?" Matthew asked, swallowing hard and sliding forward on his seat, remembering his vivid dream.

"Right. It would provide funding for generations to come if Russian officials could get their hands on it. Its weight isn't known. Neither is the amount of gold. If it exists, its value is incalculable. Stevenson refused to hand over the base with the inscription. He insisted that his translation was accurate and that he'd changed nothing. But he wouldn't allow anyone outside the university access to it."

"Seems simple enough," said Danbury. "Why not infiltrate the university?"

"They did. The stone base wasn't on display anywhere. And it wasn't logged with the other artifacts. It was securely locked up, and only the professor knew where."

"That's why they killed him and searched his office," said Matthew. "That's what they were looking for there. It wasn't the notebook."

"They wanted that too," confirmed Justin. "But they didn't think Stevenson had it. When they realized that Grygoriy Starkovich really didn't have it, they thought you did."

"Does anybody know," began Matthew, hesitating and then changing his question. "Do you know if the huge gold cross exists? If it does, where is it?"

"I don't know. There's a map in the back of the book that they thought would lead them to it. But it points to a location that was destroyed by fire back in the eighteen hundreds, and all major artifacts contained there were obliterated. They never knew that, though. They were taking the book to Mikhail Fisherovich and escaping with it and him in the helicopter to a waiting ship offshore. Their identities had been exposed, and getting their hands on that notebook was critical to them before they fled."

"They never saw it?"

"No. They hadn't examined the book. Fisherovich gave strict instructions to bring it directly to him."

"But you saw it?"

"No, I intercepted what Danbury here sent to his buddy to translate."

"You what?" asked Danbury indignantly. "Those were secure servers."

Justin shrugged.

"What if it does exist?" asked Matthew. "And what if it's exactly where the notebook says it is?"

"Do you have reason to believe that?" asked Justin.

Taking a deep breath, Matthew explained the dream he'd had, how vivid and immersive it was, involving all five senses. He told Justin about how the face of the man who'd been turned away as an intruder had plagued him until he realized that it was Mike Fisher's face— AKA Mikhail Fisherovich—that he'd seen. The fleeting expression of hatred there had been foreign until he'd caught a mere glimpse of and finally made the connection—before he'd been snatched and silenced.

Matthew explained how, awakening from the dream, he'd searched for pictures of Mt. Athos—Simon Peter's monastery, specifically. "It's where I was in the dream," he said. "The guy was an impostor of the worst kind. My dream was right about that. What if it's right about the location too?"

"Then that's dangerous information," said Justin, furtively looking around him.

"What are you going to do with that knowledge?" asked Matthew. "What should I do about it?"

"You are never going to mention it again. To anybody," said Justin. "And I'm going to destroy it."

Pulling his phone from his pocket and tapping it, Justin excused himself from the table and said, "I need to make a call. I'll be right back."

"What's he doing?" asked Matthew. "The book was already destroyed. It was in the van when it blew up, right?"

"I think so," said Danbury, rubbing the stubble on his chin with his thumb. "I destroyed our copies of it. Both physical and the thumb drive. But there's Mark's electronic copy. And the record of it on the copier. Justin accessed secure servers, at least once already. My guess? He's going to wipe it. All trace of it. Probably end to end. It won't be in my buddy's inbox anymore. Not when Justin's finished. It'll be like it never existed."

"Makes sense," said Matthew, feeling awake and revitalized after the coffee, sugar, and protein breakfast. "We need to talk to Mark. He, Greg, and probably Darya are the only other ones to have seen that map. Unless Mark told the church leadership about it."

"Let's hope not. Can you get Mark to meet us there? At his office?"

"Yeah," said Matthew, looking around and locating a clock on the wall. "It's only five thirty—not a decent time of morning to be disturbing him, but this is urgent."

"It is," said Danbury and nodded. "Mikhail Fisherovich is out of the picture. But Stanley Strausbaum is still at large."

"And probably others like him, from what Justin said."

Pulling his wallet out when the bill was placed on the table in front of them, Danbury paid for his breakfast. Matthew paid his and Justin's tabs before using Danbury's phone to call Mark, who agreed to meet them at his office. Matthew briefly admonished him not to explain anything about the book to his wife—or anyone else. Ever.

Justin returned to the table and confirmed Danbury's assumption about having all traces of the documents—that the three men agreed never to speak of again—removed as if they'd never existed.

"That leaves," began Justin.

"Mark's copy, and wiping the electronic record of it from the copier and his computer," Matthew finished the thought. "I called him. He's meeting us at his office."

"Nice work," said Justin. "I'll meet you there."

"Thank Danbury. It was his idea," said Matthew as the bell above the door jingled, and they were back out in the chilly moist predawn air.

On the way to the church, Matthew questioned Danbury about what Mark knew and what he would be told. Mark knew that Mike Fisher was a spy, and he'd been told to contact Danbury immediately if he heard from him. What he didn't yet know was that Fisher was dead—but he needed to know that too. And, argued Matthew, he should also know about Stanley Strausbaum and that the guy was still at large. Surely, he wouldn't show up here, Matthew thought, but he wanted to protect Mark, in case he was wrong about that.

When they arrived at the church, predictably, Mark was already there.

"Come on in," he said. "I've shredded my printed copy of the book, as you requested. And deleted the copy on my computer."

"That's a start," said Justin after Matthew reintroduced them. Justin had been to the church many times over the years with Matthew, but mostly as a boy. He explained how deleted documents could be reconstructed from hard drives and other devices.

After confirming that Evelyn hadn't seen the contents of the book and that Mark had shared that with no one else, Justin went to work on both Mark's computer and the copier. Danbury was looking over Justin's shoulder while Matthew and Mark both slumped into the guest chairs in Mark's office.

"You look exhausted," Matthew's lifelong pastor said to him in genuine concern. "And troubled."

"I am. Both," responded Matthew. He was feeling the temporary boost from the sugar and caffeine waning as he asked the question that had been bothering him most. "How do you reconcile something like this? A Russian spy posing as a pastor and doing it so well that he was believed. He was 'leading'—and I use that term loosely—a whole congregation of several thousand people."

"First of all, I want to apologize for dragging you into this," said Mark. "I'm thankful to you for finding Greg alive and getting him medical help so quickly, but it's taken its toll on you, hasn't it?"

"Danbury did that," said Matthew, realizing that Mark hadn't been told even half of the story. "And you had no idea what we were up against. Neither did we. You should know that Mike Fisher is dead. He won't be deceiving anyone again, churches or otherwise."

"Oh," said Mark, stiffening in his chair. "Still, I feel responsible, and I am truly sorry. As for reconciling this situation, of course, it has troubled me. Churches are under enough duress these days without something like this. I don't have a ready answer for you, you know. Just my own thoughts in dealing with it personally."

"That's a start," said Matthew. "Whatever you're willing to share."

"We do have an adversary," began Mark. "Jesus himself said we'd be like sheep among wolves. He called us to be as shrewd as snakes and as innocent as doves. I've been thinking about that a lot."

"That's in my book," said Matthew, smiling in reminiscence of a childhood joke between him and Mark—that both had names of contiguous books in the Bible.

"It is." Mark grinned back at him. "It's found in Matthew 10, along with lots of other admonitions that are very applicable here. Jesus told us we'd have trouble in this world because there is an evil one roaming around looking for people to devour. Also in Matthew, he said there would be false prophets appearing to deceive even the elect, if that were possible."

"So, what you're saying is this isn't as surprising as we think it should be," summarized Matthew.

"That's right," said Mark. "That's exactly what I'm saying. Jesus prayed for us to be protected from the evil one. I plan to follow his example. I am praying for the church on Buchanan Island. For restoration, to find a truly godly pastor to lead them, and that they are no longer deceived."

"Makes sense," said Matthew, dropping his chin into his hand on the arm of the chair.

"The church members of Aurora Springs won't be told that Mike Fisher was Mikhail Fisherovich and a Russian cell leader," said Justin. "That information doesn't leave this room."

Matthew nodded as Mark answered, "I understand."

"They'll be told that he died tragically," said Justin. "There's something else we need to do today." Justin explained to Mark that the offices were bugged. Though the receiving apparatus had been destroyed, a team would need to sweep through and remove the listening devices.

"OK, tell me when they're coming," agreed Mark. "Every time I begin to think that nothing else can surprise me, something else does.”

“I’m finished with the computer,” said Justin. “I’m shutting it down now.”

“And what happens to Ross and Ivan?” Matthew asked. “Their remains, I mean.”

“A couple of members of this church,” Mark began, looking meaningfully at Matthew. “Have stepped forward and covered the expenses to ship their remains back to Ukraine so that they can be interred by their families in their homeland. The pastors and staff will have a service here as soon as Greg gets out of the hospital. It’ll be last minute as soon as he’s released. Both he and Darya are anxious to get back home.”

“I can completely understand that,” said Matthew, who could only imagine how hard it would be to be away from their small children that long.

“I can let you know when that celebration of their lives happens if you’d like to attend,” said Mark.

“I would. A celebration,” Matthew echoed Mark’s words. “We all need something positive now.”

“Well, we can also start talking about some weddings,” said Mark, grinning at Danbury and Matthew.

“That sounds great,” said Danbury, and Matthew nodded.

“Am I missing something?” asked Justin.

“I thought you already knew everything,” said Matthew, teasing his lifelong friend. “Danbury is proposing to Penn, and Mark has agreed to marry them. I’m going to start shopping for rings too, to propose to Cici when she gets back from London. I haven’t officially asked Mark if he’d marry us yet.”

“It was understood,” Mark nodded.

“Congratulations to both of you!” Justin said, and Matthew noted the faraway look in his eye.

“You might want to wait. They haven’t said yes yet,” joked Danbury.

"But they will," said Mark. "I'm sure they will."

"I hope so," said Matthew. "But right now, I'm toast. Would one of you take me to the airport?"

"The airport?" asked Danbury.

"Yeah, I left my Honda Element there in long-term parking when I flew out for Fort Lauderdale. That seems like an eternity ago now."

"Oh! Right. Sure, Doc. I'll take you," said Danbury.

"I'll stick around long enough to fully debrief your pastor," said Justin, nodding to Mark. "There are a few things you still need to know, Sir."

"Including Stanley Strausbaum?" asked Matthew.

"Especially, Stanley Strausbaum," said Justin. "And I'll meet with Greg and Darya Starkovich later today. They'll be fully debriefed too."

"On second thought," said Matthew, rising wearily from the chair before his pastor could ask who Stanley Strausbaum was, "Take me home. I'll replace my phone and get my car tomorrow. Or maybe the day after. I'm calling my office and Cici, then I'm going to sleep for a week."

"You can use my phone," said Danbury, following Matthew to the door.

"Thanks, Danbury. And I'm never getting anywhere near police or detective work again," Matthew declared.

"Famous last words, Doc," said Danbury.

*****

Want more Matthew Paine?

Matthew has resigned—again—as a medical consultant with the Raleigh police department, but since when did that stop him from helping homicide detective Warren Danbury? More importantly, when would that ever stop him from helping a friend?

Join them in *Killer Convergence*—next in the Matthew Paine Classic Mystery series—and finally learn Danbury's backstory. Will

Danbury's quest for answers to a deeply personal twenty-year-old murder investigation that was never solved to his satisfaction put both him and Matthew in a killer's crosshairs? *Killer Convergence* – coming soon!

AFTERWORD

You'll no doubt have noticed that *Forbidden Relics* takes place in 2020 at the beginning of the COVID outbreak but before Russia invaded Ukraine. Tensions between the two countries were, as Matthew notes in the story, running high at that time. Though the book is completely a fictional work, the truth in the story is that there absolutely are missionaries who served in Ukraine then and who continue to faithfully serve now.

The week that Ukraine was attacked, nobody was expecting it at exactly that moment, and neither were they anticipating the full-scale assault on the whole country. I know this because my own church, much like Matthew's, though not located in Raleigh, supports missionaries in Ukraine. One of the missionaries from Ukraine was here—in the United States, visiting my church—when he got the text that the war had broken out.

I suppose I should begin by introducing the Smolin family. First, I want to make it completely clear that they are NOT the characters in the book, nor is the backstory of the characters even remotely similar. The dedication and faith of the Smolin family in the face of war, death, and desperation go far above and well beyond what I attribute to the characters in the *Forbidden Relics* story. In 2009, Vitaliy and Natalia Smolin left California with one-way tickets to Ukraine and created Smolin Ministries and the Open Door Foundation. They partnered with organizations in the US in support, prayer, and service to Ukraine. That ministry was already established well before the war began.

On February 28, 2022, Vitaliy Smolin was visiting the US. He was having dinner with our pastor at the home of one of our neighbors when he got a text from his wife, Natalia, who was in Ukraine. She said that an attack had begun and was wreaking havoc and devastating Ukraine quickly. He told her to get out of the country and to text or call as soon as she was across the border and into Poland. If they could get out of Ukraine, then they could get back here, to the US, and to safety. Prayer began immediately for Natalia and their daughters to escape safely. What followed is one of the most amazing stories I've ever heard, and it is my privilege and honor to share it.

Vitaliy, with our church leadership, fervently prayed and waited—knowing that hundreds of thousands of refugees crowded the border and that cell towers were overwhelmed as chaos reigned. Twenty hours later, the call finally came from Natalia but the message she conveyed wasn't at all what Vitaliy, or any of us, expected. What mere mortals thought and what God had planned were apparently at opposite ends of the spectrum.

Natalia described what she had been through to get out of the country, helping several people along the way, and the desperate need of the hundreds of thousands of others who were not able to do so. She told Vitaliy that she wasn't coming to the United States, but that she was going back into Ukraine to do what she could to help with the suffering—to try to help meet the basic human needs for food, clothing, and shelter. He was to remain in the US to seek funding and support. I met Vitaliy the following Sunday morning.

I showed him pictures on my phone of the most famous buildings and structures around the world being lit and draped in the blue and yellow of the Ukrainian flag. There were tears in both of our eyes as he saw the global support. A couple of days later, Vitaliy flew back and reentered Ukraine. He didn't sleep for the next ten days. Rallying support, his ministry provided shelter and food, blankets, and coats. They took in the orphans and homeless to every building his ministry occupied and any others they could get access to. As a chaplain, he also helped care for the dying.

Over the next few months, we all prayed for the Ukraine, for the war to end quickly and decisively. That was not to be. The Smolins continue to need our prayers and support, as do the myriad mission teams who are continuing to provide for the needs in that area.

If you'd like to learn more about the Smolin's ministry in Ukraine or contribute to Open Door Foundation to help support them financially, do visit their website:

smolinministries.org

Want to start at the beginning?

- Get the prequel short story, *Pre Kill*, for free!

  https://dl.bookfunnel.com/k3xwi6l5f4

- Get Dead Spots, first in the series, from your local bookstore or all major online retailers:

  https://buy.bookfunnel.com/bgb7d97qo9

Be in the know!

Join the author group to get all the latest updates on new releases, events, giveaways, and more!

  https://cypressrivermedia.com/connect-with-us

Acknowledgments

As the Dedication indicated, I am thankful for my life-long friendship with Tera McWhorter. I am also appreciative that she took the time to review the section where Matthew is treating the police officer and travels with him to the emergency department. Her insight as an ED nurse is also reflected briefly there.

As always, I'm thankful for the editors who provide their expertise to put these books through multiple levels of review and critique prior to making them available to readers. Very special thanks to Genie Clark, my most trusted content editor.

Thanks also to Ginny Glass of <u>AZ Editing</u>.

About the Author

Lee Clark is a coffeeholic and dark chocoholic who resides in North Carolina with spouse, two mostly grown children who are in and out, and a dwindling petting zoo of geriatric dogs and cats.

A North Carolina native, Clark is originally from Raleigh, with family roots in Virginia. Clark attended Campbell University, obtained a degree in journalism from East Carolina University, and then obtained a master's in technical communication from North Carolina State University.

After working in the software technology industry for over twenty years, creating and building highly technical user information for software developers, Clark decided it was time to pursue a true passion: fiction writing.

Matthew Paine is a fictional character, though inspired by two very important men in the author's life, brother Sean and son Will. Both will see characteristics of themselves in the character and identify with some of Matthew's struggles.